I0524509

The Viking's Heartwish

Heartwishes, Volume 1

Daisy Dexter Dobbs

Published by Department of Daydreams, LLC, 2022.

THE VIKING'S HEARTWISH

First edition. May 10, 2022.

Copyright © 2022 Daisy Dexter Dobbs.

ISBN: 978-1587850837

Written by Daisy Dexter Dobbs.

Dedication

This book is wholeheartedly dedicated to my paternal grandmother, Daisy Hogan. Grandma Bekka, a beloved character in my Heartwishes series, was inspired by Grandma Daisy. At an early age, listening to Grandma's oft-repeated, larger than life tales, told in her rich, singsong Irish brogue, greatly influenced my decision to become a writer. How I loved the magical tales her vivacious imagination conjured, including her assurances that one day I'd find, fall in love with, marry, and have a storybook happily ever after of my very own. My dear grandma was right on all counts and, happily, lived long enough to meet my prince charming, as well as her great granddaughter. I'm convinced the spirited, loving woman who helped me survive a fearful and dysfunctional childhood is now my guardian angel. Thanks to Grandma, years later, my writing goal remains the same: to weave tales as captivating as hers, infusing my stories with smiles and abundant laughter to help brighten the days of readers the same way Grandma's tales brightened my days.

ABOUT THIS BOOK

~< >~

A half-naked Viking, with horned Brunhilda-helmet, sword and shield, is the last thing Delaney Kullerton expects to find on her doorstep.

Introducing himself in broken English, he claims he's Varik the Bold and he's come to play. Stunned to hear the name of her lifelong secret fantasy Viking, Delaney knows Varik is sent by heaven. Well, more accurately, by her dearly departed grandma's estate, via a male escort service.

One year ago to the day, Delaney's professor husband dumped her for one of his grad students. The timely arrival of the rugged Norwegian confirms Grandma must have instructed her attorney to ensure Delaney isn't alone and grieving again on her birthday.

Not about to belittle her grandmother's final parting gift by rejecting this sinfully sexy man chosen to provide her with a prepaid night of bliss, Delaney invites him in. Varik, and their time together, is glorious. Sensational. Perfect. Until a horrendous series of misunderstandings leaves Delaney utterly mortified.

Protecting her heart, she packs her bags and moves across the country to her grandmother's enchanting cottage on the Oregon coast, tucking her precious memories of Varik the Bold away, consigning them to her innermost fantasies.

Varik, however, has entirely different ideas, implementing them with a helpful touch of magic from Norse god Odin's heartwish ring.

Heartwishes, Book 1: Straitlaced trusting heroine, hot endearing hero, loveable troublemaking dog, heart-melting misunderstandings, abundant humor, a pair of angels, and a magical sigh-worthy wish. This guaranteed HEA romcom can be read as a standalone.

~<>~

Chapter 1

LIKE A BOLD, GLORIOUS WARRIOR, the golden-haired stranger was garbed in reindeer hides and a horned helmet, brandishing a gleaming sword and shield. He was tall, with an impressive physique. Breathtaking. It didn't matter that his impassioned words were in a language she didn't understand. Her heart knew they shared the same soul-deep secret.

"Is it you?" she whispered. "My Viking? My Varik the Bold?"

With the hint of a smile, he nodded. Pursing his lips, the Viking blew the merest whisper of breath down the length of the sword he'd aimed at her heart. Watching the polished blade glint, she had no fear he'd come to slay her. On the contrary, his mission was to ensure her consummate pleasure.

Mesmerized, every fiber of her being tingled with longing as his blue-eyed gaze lovingly appraised her body. Reaching out to him, she silently beckoned. Upon sheathing his sword, his fingers extended toward her and she anticipated the thrill of feeling them exploring her flesh.

A sigh escaped her lips as she realized their physical union was imminent and she was about to be blissfully seized by her beloved Viking.

Lust, or perhaps it was love, danced in his eyes as his lips drew close and he whispered...

"I've got an early staff meeting. Can you put on a pot of green tea while I jump in the shower?"

~ ~ ~

"Hmmpf?"

No...oh please, no. The last thing Delaney Kullerton wanted was to be roused from her delicious dream, especially right before her Viking was about to—

"I need you to get up, Del. I'm running late."

Cracking one eye open, Delaney spied the alarm clock on her nightstand, groaned and pulled the covers over her head. Four-thirty. An hour earlier than her usual wake up time. How cruel. She could have spent that hour wrapped in the arms of—

"Del! Come on, get up." This time she was being poked and prodded, effectively eradicating the last delicious vestiges of her dream. If that weren't enough, at the sound of his master's voice, her husband's gargantuan dog galloped into the bedroom, barking his fool head off.

Clapping her hands over her ears, Delaney admonished the creature—the dog, not her husband—with a firm, "Knock it off!" She threw back the covers and sat up. "Okay. Okay, Roger. Green tea."

Late winter's chill permeated the bedroom, invading her bones through the thick flannel of her nightshirt. Being a cheapskate as well as a health nut, Roger kept the thermostat set low to save money, and because he believed cold air was healthier.

Still foggy, she cocked her head in wonder. "Roger...I thought you said you didn't have any classes today." In the next instant, Ruff jumped up, bracing his front paws on the bed and giving her a big sloppy lick. Uttering an audible gasp, Delaney grabbed a handful of tissues from the box on her nightstand and wiped her face.

"Down, boy." She pushed the beast off the bed. He sat there looking dejected but she refused to feel guilty. It was too damn early in the morning to be baptized with dog spit.

"They called a special faculty meeting," Roger said.

"But I was hoping we could—"

"Could what? You're working today, aren't you?"

"Just until noon, remember? Maybe this afternoon we can—"

"It's most likely an all-day meeting."

"Oh."

Ruff angled his head, whimpering as he looked at her, almost seeming to sense her disappointment. But that was ridiculous. He was nothing but a dumb, destructive, trouble-making canine.

Delaney didn't know why she bothered to hope she and Roger might spend the afternoon together. Even if he remembered it was her birthday...and Valentine's Day, which he never had in the past, he wouldn't make any effort to celebrate it. Roger lumped birthdays and holidays, like Christmas and Valentine's Day, into the same category. They were nothing but crass commercialism, just another excuse for retailers to line their pockets with his hard-earned money.

She remembered feeling cheated as a kid on her birthday once she was old enough to realize all the fuss was about some saint named Valentine, instead of celebrating the day she was born. With all the Valentine exchanging, and heart-shaped boxes of chocolate being given and received, people generally forgot about her birthday. She eventually grew used to it, not minding too terribly much because she told herself that one day when she grew up and got married, she'd have a wonderful, considerate husband who adored her enough to make her feel special on her birthday.

After marrying Roger, Delaney decided that on a list of husbandly qualities, the trait of ignoring birthdays and holidays probably wasn't such an awful thing. Mature adults were supposed to overlook such minor disappointments. It was childish for her to expect to be the center of attention just because it happened to be the anniversary of her birth.

She eyed the toasty spot on the bed she'd just vacated, longing to return. Maybe if Roger hadn't finished with his morning rituals she could squeeze in another fifteen minutes of cozy warmth. "Have you done your yoga and meditation yet?" she asked.

"Done," he said. "I'm getting in the shower now."

Delaney stifled a groan. "You want your smoothie for here or to go?" Giving in to a mighty yawn, she stretched and stepped into her fleece-lined slippers. Ruff was right at her side, acting all chummy because he knew she'd be feeding him and letting him outside once they got to the kitchen. Somehow Ruff's care had mostly fallen on her shoulders.

"I'll take it with me," Roger said, entering the bathroom. "There won't be anything to eat at the meeting except for donuts, bagels and muffins, and you know what I always say..."

Nodding, Delaney answered with the expected response, which was easy enough because she'd only heard the mantra a million times for each year they'd been married. "The devil's in the white sugar and flour."

"Remember that." Roger pointed a cautionary finger.

"Always," she replied. As if she could ever forget.

"Don't forget to add the mustard greens leftover from last night's salad."

"I won't."

"And make sure to add the powdered wheatgrass and brewer's yeast. You forgot them yesterday."

"Okay. Sorry." She stifled a shudder at his treasured combination of superfood ingredients.

"Remember to add the ground flaxseed *after* the yogurt and molasses so you don't overheat the flax in the blender."

"I'll remember." She nibbled her bottom lip. "I, um, don't suppose you'll be letting Ruff outside or filling his water or food dish before you leave."

"No time. You'll have to do it. While you've got the cutting board out, chop some fresh raw beet greens along with some of the turnip peels I told you to save. Add them to Ruff's food dish along with a sprinkle of the brewer's yeast and a clove of raw garlic. He loves it and it keeps him healthy."

"Will do," Delaney acknowledged to the closing door, nixing the juvenile urge to salute him with a crisp "Yes sir, Professor Kullerton, sir!" If Roger ever greeted her one morning with a sunny disposition or an affectionate peck on the cheek, she'd know without a doubt he'd been taken over by aliens...which wouldn't necessarily be a bad thing. The wicked thought had her chuckling.

She headed to the kitchen, following the merrily prancing Ruff. No way in hell would she add beets, turnips, brewer's yeast or garlic to the dog's food, not when she was the one stuck cleaning up after the animal. She'd learned the hard way that colorful-veggie-spiked dog food made for a disgusting elimination nightmare, nearly impossible to scoop up outside, much less clean off the deep pile carpet. Then there was the most godawful *Caution: Gasmask Mandatory* issue as a result of Ruff's unbearably odoriferous gas wafting through the house.

About to open the patio door, she looked down at Ruff and sneered. "So you have a discriminating palate, do you? You love stinky colorful veggies and brewer's yeast because they keep you healthy, hmm?" she scoffed. "Yeah, right. You're nothing but a living, breathing four legged trash can." The simple minded dog responded with a tongue-lolling smile.

After letting the dog out and seeing to his rations, Delaney plugged in her phone's earpiece, tuning to one of her favorite playlists, a combo of jazz and rock selections. The earpiece was necessary to hide her listening choice from Roger, lest she get another tongue lashing about her mind-rotting music versus brain enriching classical music. It's not that she didn't appreciate classical, but Delaney preferred starting her day with something lively.

Stepping and swaying to the music as she quietly sang along, she opened a kitchen cabinet, smiling when she spotted the six-inch tall crocheted teddy bear greeting her.

The lopsided stuffed animal sat on the shelf between the canisters of green tea and coffee beans, a bar of premium milk chocolate nestled in its lap. The heart-shaped Valentine resting against its belly read, "Happy 35th birthday, Delaney! And Happy Valentine's Day, sweetheart! Enjoy your special day. Have fun and celebrate! Love, hugs and kisses always..."

"Aw Roger..." she whispered as her fingertip traveled across the card embellished with hearts, flowers and a smiley face drawn in marker. "How sweet and thoughtful of you." She closed her eyes and hugged herself, luxuriating in the loving feel of the message. It was the perfect visual to start her Valentine birthday morning.

It would have been even better if the note had actually been from Roger.

It wasn't.

She only pretended it was.

She'd written it herself last night, setting it in on the tummy of the teddy bear she'd lovingly crocheted. Roger rarely opened kitchen cabinets, so Delaney wasn't concerned he'd find her fanciful self-congratulatory display. Just as she'd planned, seeing the greeting first thing in the morning made a positive difference in her special day.

As far as Delaney was concerned, reality was overrated. Embroidering a touch of harmless fantasy atop reality made her happy...and happiness was every bit as healthy as greenish-gray drinks brimming with wheat grass juice. If that meant occasionally resorting to squirrelly behavior, like creating sweet notes and handmade teddy bears for herself and pretending they were from her unimaginative, unromantic husband, then so be it.

Mindlessly listening to the music, Delaney prepared Roger's tea, allowing her thoughts to linger on the hunky nocturnal Viking. She'd had similar dreams multiple times over the years, frustrated and disappointed that they always ended at the same spot. Something inevitably interrupted before she and the gorgeous specimen of masculinity had an opportunity to become intimate.

She'd never be unfaithful to Roger in real life. He might be peculiar, persnickety, and sorely lacking when it came to romance, but he had plenty of positive qualities. She chose to focus on those. He was smart, well read, logical, ethical, organized, and a dedicated, caring educator. He was also passionate about his health and hers, tirelessly researching the latest scientific findings to ensure their hale and hearty longevity.

However, if living to a hundred and ten meant weak green tea and blended vegetable drinks each morning instead of indulging in an occasional donut and cup of coffee, she'd rather check out of life at a happy, well-fed ninety-five.

"My Viking wouldn't ask for a soy yogurt molasses wheatgrass drink," she muttered. "Varik the Bold would prefer a mug of strong brewed coffee, some eggs, bacon, sausage and a crusty chunk of bread slathered with real butter instead of soy margarine. No, scratch the coffee. He'd demand a tankard of ale." She hoisted an invisible stein.

The thought of coffee made her sigh. She was dying for a cup but after ten years of marriage she knew better than to start the coffeepot before Roger left for the university. He refused to have his morning *polluted* with the odors of unhealthy food or drink.

She wished she could be as steady, rational and controlled as Roger. He couldn't understand her habit of operating from emotion rather than logic, and failed to comprehend why she was so stubbornly optimistic, even in the face of opposing facts. He made no attempt to hide his disappointment at her lack of self-discipline when it came to her unhealthy addiction to chocolate either.

He was right, of course. Roger was always right.

Fortunately, he loved her enough to be remarkably patient and persistent. Although clearly frustrated by her frequent failings, Roger refused to give up on her.

"From now on I'm going to act more responsibly, more mature," she vowed, measuring ingredients into the blender.

She'd start tonight by cooking *Roasted Beet and Turnip Loaf*, a recipe she'd found in Roger's collection of health food cookbooks. Along with that, she'd serve *Pureed Kale-Soy Gravy* and a side of *Rutabaga Tofu Puffs*.

"And I'll cook and serve it all without even gagging once." She lifted one shoulder in a shrug. "I might even try to eat it." Delaney smiled at the satisfying thought of serving a celebratory dinner on her special night...even if she couldn't eat it.

"Roger will be ecstatic, absolutely transfixed by my new acumen in the kitchen."

The tapping of dog nails on the patio door reminded her to let Ruff inside. She groaned when she saw he was caked with snow. He must have rolled around in it and now the stupid mutt would get it all over the house.

God forgive her but she was half-tempted to leave him outside. Maybe he'd get the hint and run away.

Ruff tapped the glass with his paw again, offering Delaney a sad-eyed pleading look. He wasn't an ugly dog. She had to admit he was kind of cute with his short black fur and tan eyebrows and trim that made him look like he was sporting a goatee. He appeared to be part German Shepherd and part...donkey. His rambunctious personality kept him from being truly appealing.

He looked at her again with those huge dark eyes and Delaney's heart thawed a little. "Dammit, I couldn't live with myself if I was responsible for turning the poor dumb animal into a dogsicle."

She cracked the door open just enough to reach out and clean off the snow clumps, but Ruff took advantage of the opportunity, muscling his way inside. He jumped up to greet her, bestowing another face lick, before running off to wreak havoc throughout the house.

It wasn't even six in the morning and already she been baptized twice with a profusion of dog spit. Now she was sopping wet with snow too. Shivering, she disconnected the music and put her earpiece in a kitchen drawer before heading back to the bedroom to change, vowing yet again that one day they'd leave Chicago, moving someplace without frigid winter temperatures, ice and snow.

Her grandma's adopted town of Glassfloat Bay, Oregon sounded ideal. Rebekka Eriksen waxed poetic about the small coastal town's charm and its warm, friendly residents. There were no glacial temperatures in the winter or hot, sticky days in summer. Pacific Northwest winters were overcast and rainy, but as Grandma Bekka liked to say, "You don't have to shovel rain." The abundant rainfall provided lush foliage the rest of the year, along with plenty of sunshine.

Once Delaney's sisters, Laila and Reen, and her brothers, Gard and Nevan, had visited Bekka they fell in love with the Pacific Northwest, moving there one by one. When their youngest sister, Kady, finished her overseas backpacking trip, she planned to settle there too. They kept urging Delaney to visit, certain she and Roger would love Oregon.

She had no doubt they were right. She'd been trying to talk Roger into a trip to Glassfloat Bay since Bekka moved there nearly ten years ago. He argued the cost of airline tickets was too great, and traveling across the country by car would eat up too much of his vacation.

So Delaney satisfied herself with the plentiful photos her grandmother and siblings had texted and posted online, along with their stories about the little town. She'd love to live in a picturesque spot like that one day...maybe when she and Roger retired.

"Wearing your good khakis, I see," she noted as Roger dressed. "I hope the dean is impressed." She offered a playful wink.

Stepping into his slacks, Roger gave her a distasteful appraisal. "Look at you. You're all wet."

Delaney couldn't help laughing at her husband's astute observation. "That's because your beloved fur-bag decided to frolic in the snow. We got several inches overnight." She caught a glimpse of her raccoon-ish reflection in the mirror, groaning at her wet, messy black hair and the smudges of makeup beneath her eyes.

Roger chuckled. "Dogs will be dogs." Ruff chose that moment to prance to his master's side and glance up adoringly. He mussed the dog's fur. "I'll bet you had a good time out there in the snow, didn't you, boy?" Ruff responded with a cheerful bark. "Animals innately know the brisk, cold air is healthy for them," Roger informed Delaney.

She paused briefly, biting her tongue to avoid saying *bullshit*. Wives of English professors didn't resort to such crude verbalization.

"If you say so, dear," she responded instead. It boggled her mind that her overly health conscious husband apparently saw nothing wrong with having a big, hairy, four-legged beast run amok in their house, spreading dog germs over every surface, even peeing and depositing disgusting piles of poop on occasion.

If Roger would ever clean up one of Ruff's messes, rather than leave them for her, he'd probably change his tune pronto.

A few months ago Roger found the big shivering mutt huddled next to the trashcans outside their suburban one-story townhouse and brought him inside. Delaney's first memory of the sizeable creature was watching him lift his leg and pee on the side of the sofa she'd just had reupholstered. "Do you have any idea what dog pee does to wool tweed?" she'd asked the dog. Not getting an answer, she posed the question to Roger who didn't reply either.

The found-dog announcements they posted went unanswered. When no one came forth to claim the lively fiend, which was no surprise to Delaney, Roger decided to keep him. She only tolerated the animal because Roger claimed Ruff reminded him of the dog he'd had as a boy and lost to a car accident. Well hell. How could she throw the beast out—Ruff, not Roger—after a heartbreaking story like that?

Delaney ran the hairbrush through her damp hair. A moment later she reached for a tissue, wiping at her smudged eye makeup.

"Are you sure you have time for all that personal grooming? I've got to be out of here no later than—"

"Your tea has steeped. It's ready and waiting," Delaney assured. "And your smoothie will be ready when you are. Just like always." Jiggling in place, she made an O-face. "But right now I've really got to run to the bathroom to pee."

Roger's pained expression, accompanied by a distinct shudder, couldn't be missed. She knew what was coming before he even opened his mouth.

"Why must you insist on using such crude, rudimentary terminology?"

Fighting back a giant tsk, Delaney smiled at her proper-grammar-obsessed English teacher husband. "What I meant to say, of course, is..." pretending to hold a monocle to her eye, she affected an upper crust accent, "I must abscond to the lavatory so that I may urinate before my bladder ruptures." She couldn't help tacking on a giggle. "Better?"

"I find nothing amusing about this, Delaney. We are judged by our speech."

Her shoulders slumped. It was too early in the morning for this. "I know, I know...but Roger, it's not even dawn and I'm still half asleep. Give me a break, huh?"

"Once proper English is ingrained it flows naturally regardless of circumstances or time of day."

Her mouth popped open to object but she snapped it shut. Since he'd only find a way to condemn her protests, she figured she may as well play it safe. "You're right, Roger. Sorry. I'll make more of an effort." Before returning to the kitchen she glimpsed her husband's attire. Determined to maintain a chipper attitude despite his usual morning crankiness, she noted, "Must be an important meeting. You look very professor-ish today."

Roger stood statue-still for an instant. "Professor-ish?" Gazing at his reflection in the dresser's mirror, he gathered his thinning auburn hair into a ponytail at the nape of his neck. "Is that bad?"

"No." She gave him a kiss on the cheek. "You look very debonair. See you in the kitchen."

He'd become self-conscious about his thinning hair and his appearance in general lately, which was certainly understandable. For Delaney, losing weight had become more difficult after turning thirty, but at least she'd be thinner after a diet. Poor Roger, however, couldn't do anything to restore his hair, except for resorting to hair plugs or a hairpiece.

She'd tried to tell him in the kindest way possible that, rather than make him look younger, the ponytailed style only drew attention to his hair loss. Roger disagreed.

By the time she'd chopped all the veggies for his smoothie, Roger was at the table sipping his unsweetened matcha green tea.

Nudging the folded Lifestyle section of *Northwest Suburban Gazette*, their local newspaper, closer to him, Delaney cleared her throat to get his attention. It didn't work.

"Did you see the paper, Roger?"

He was totally absorbed in a *Happy Peaceful Planet* magazine article extolling the overwhelming virtues of veganism. She only knew the nature of the article because he'd instructed her to read it the day before. Calling the tedious article mind-numbing was being kind.

Without looking up he said, "No."

"Take a look," Delaney encouraged, tapping the newspaper with her fingertip. "There's something *very* special you might want to read. A brand new column that just debuted today." She was so excited she could barely contain her delight but knew better than to do anything as silly as a happy dance in front of her husband. He'd think she was nuts.

Glancing at the paper, he glowered. "I have no interest in the Lifestyle section. You know that. I don't read that sort of tripe."

A monumental sigh escaped her lips. "Roger, it's my new weekly column, "Delaney's Diary." I told you about it, remember? Complete with my own byline. There's even a little headshot." She smiled as she glanced at the tiny photo. Damn, if she didn't look just like a writer! Oh God how she wanted to squeal with joy.

"It begins with *Dear Diary*." Her fingertip traced beneath the type. "It's the same way I start my blog posts and newsletters, to make it feel more personal. Good idea, hmm?"

She'd had a few articles published online and in women's magazines but nothing important had ever come of it. After years of submitting her work to publishers, she'd collected enough rejection slips to paper a small bathroom. Getting her own column was monumental, and having the first column debut on her birthday was the icing on the cake.

Roger looked at her as if she'd just suggested they jump out of a plane without a parachute.

"Good idea?" He spat the words as if they were venomous. "It's immature. Juvenile."

Delaney flinched.

"I thought we talked about this," a weary looking Roger reminded her. "I'm not enamored of my wife writing a humor column for our local paper, much less having it plastered all over the internet for any simpleton to read. It isn't dignified. This latest whim of yours is ridiculous."

Oh what Delaney wouldn't do for a good, strong cup of coffee right now. Maybe with a good, strong shot of Kahlua on the side. Okay, Kahlua wasn't strong by any means, but it might help soothe her wounded ego.

Resisting a tsk, she countered, "There's nothing undignified about it. Some people might even think it's quite an accomplishment." Roger shot her another disbelieving look. "I just muse about daily life with a humorous slant. Kind of like Erma Bombeck, Dave Barry, or even Nora Ephron."

His features soured. "Who?"

Delaney forgot. She couldn't expect a man born without a humor gene to know anything about humor writers.

"Erma and Dave had syndicated newspaper columns, which grew into books, TV shows and movies."

Crickets...

"I'm sure you're familiar with Nora. She wrote *When Harry Met Sally*, *Sleepless in Seattle*, *You've Got Mail*, ooh, and she wrote *Julie and Julia* too. You know, the movie with Meryl Streep and Amy Adams about Julia Child and the blogger?"

Still silent, Roger gave her that same blank, vacant look.

Sucking in a breath, Delaney continued. "My editor thinks "Delaney's Diary" has great potential for syndication." Tossing her arms up with enthusiasm, she said, "Can you imagine? Who knows what that could lead to, Roger? Isn't that exciting?"

Roger's attention was solely focused on his stupid vegetable article.

"I'm using my maiden name, see?" She pointed, trying again to drum up a smidgen of interest in her accomplishment. "Delaney Malone. That way you won't have to worry about your coworkers disapproving."

She'd finally succeeded in snagging Roger's attention.

"And just how many Delaneys do you think there are writing silly, mindless fluff for our local paper, Del? Everyone will know it's my wife. That's humiliating."

"Aw, Roger, just read it, please. It's short. It won't take you long. I-I thought maybe you'd be proud of me. It's not easy getting a newspaper column. It's a big step for a fledgling writer."

"My time is valuable." Roger breathed an extended sigh of frustration. "I don't choose to waste it reading an inane article you wrote for an addlebrained female audience. You want to make me proud? Use your brain to actually learn something of importance, like how to speak proper English for instance. I can imagine how you can expect me to take you seriously as writer when you can't even speak the language properly."

Ouch.

"Or you could take a class in how to prepare healthy vegan meals. Or..." she detected a semi-sneer as he gave her a head to toe appraisal, "perhaps you could learn how to curb your gluttonous chocolate habit."

Delaney swallowed a sharp retort. She knew arguing wouldn't get her anywhere and would only antagonize him even more.

Maintaining her calm, she said, "I try, Roger. I really do. And I promise to do better. Just wait until you see the wonderful vegan dinner I'm making for you tonight. You'll be so impressed!"

"If you insist on writing for the newspaper," Roger continued his harangue, "then for the love of God, write something intellectual...meaningful. Articles like this one." He gave a backhanded slap to the magazine with the godawful boring vegan article.

Tears bristled behind Delaney's eyes but she refused to cry. She wouldn't allow Roger to ruin her special day.

"I hope you're making a smoothie for yourself too this morning." Roger cracked a half-hearted smile. His change of subject and demeanor indicated he was finished discussing her newspaper column...or her writing career. "It's important to begin each day with food-derived antioxidants, chlorophyll and phytonutrients."

"Absolutely," she lied, waving a handful of parsley and attempting an enthusiastic smile. "I'll make a fresh one to take to the office just before I leave."

"Don't add too much apple, beet or carrot. You don't want to start your day with too much fructose."

Heaven forbid. "Right."

She'd never been a big meat eater, but oh what she wouldn't give for a few strips of bacon, a burger, or a slab of baby back ribs now and then, without the guilt of feeling like a wayward child.

But Delaney's idea of a satisfying meal was at direct odds with Roger's vegan dogma. He had a nose like a drug detection dog, except he used it to sniff out meat. Those rare times she'd transgressed, eating an offending food during the day, he'd sniff the air, wince and declare she stank of dead animal flesh. Then came one of his dry lectures about the evils of consuming anything that once had a face or a mother.

The man excelled at taking the joy out of appreciating a good cheeseburger.

It wasn't like Roger didn't have any positive traits. He was honest, loyal and patient...well, semi-patient. And he was highly respected in his field—all exemplary qualities in a husband. Just because he had no idea what the split end of a hammer was for, didn't know what a socket wrench was, and was clueless about needle nosed pliers, didn't mean he wasn't a real man. After all, just because she was handy with tools and could fix whatever needed fixing around the townhouse didn't mean she wasn't a real woman.

Roger groaned. "I feel a tension headache coming on." Looking pained, he massaged his temples. "I could use some extra protein. Better add some tofu to my smoothie."

"Sure." Delaney stifled a smile as she drew the tub of tasteless white slabs from the refrigerator.

Varik the Bold would curl his lip in disgust at the thought of ingesting tofu.

"I'll be leaving in precisely six minutes," Roger informed her, glancing at the display on the perfectly synchronized watch he trusted more than his phone's digital readout. Without looking in his wife's direction, he held out his hand, wiggling his fingers.

After plucking Roger's earplugs from her gadget drawer, Delaney placed them in his outstretched hand, waited for him to put them in, then turned on the blender. He was convinced the noise, as well as high decibels generated by any loud appliance, including the vacuum cleaner, wreaked havoc with his inner ears, thereby creating all manner of health problems Delaney didn't really understand or care about.

To her, it simply meant Roger's inner ears were far too delicate to allow him to turn on the damn vacuum to clean up after his damn dirty dog.

Six minutes later, a stainless steel thermos of goopy gray-green liquid in hand, Roger was out the door. There was no "Have a nice day, honey," or "Thanks for getting up an hour early for me, sweetie." And most certainly no "Happy birthday" or "Happy Valentine's Day" or a thumbs up for the coup of getting a weekly column.

But that was Roger.

Tossing his earplugs back in the drawer she sighed. "He's a little lackluster and opinionated but at least he's faithful."

She thought about her mom as her mind wandered while she put away jars, bottles, tubs and cut produce before cleaning up vegetable peelings and the rest of the mess from making Roger's smoothie.

Astrid Malone managed to hold down a fulltime job and still be the world's best mom, the one who was always there when one of her six kids needed her, and never missed an important school function. As the oldest child, Delaney would never forget the hardships her mom endured maintaining a relatively sane, stable household while raising the children on her own.

Their dad was a fallen firefighter who heroically lost his life in the line of duty saving children, including her brother, Gard, from a grade school fire. The survivor death benefits weren't very substantial, so her mom's income was limited. All the Malone kids pitched in, doing their best to help with chores and, later, when they got after school jobs, sharing their earnings with her without Astrid ever asking.

It's one of the reasons Delaney rarely dated while in high school and college. There was little time for that as she helped with cooking, cleaning, and taking take care of the younger kids. Astrid felt guilty for Delaney missing out on so much before she married Roger, but it was the least Delaney could do for her amazing mom.

"If anyone missed out, it was you, Mom," Delaney muttered as she worked. Astrid devoted herself to her lively brood of six. She gave up so much, yet never complained about what she'd missed. Even now, her mom was still sacrificing, passing up the chance to move away from the harsh Chicago winters just so Delaney wouldn't feel abandoned.

More than anything, Delaney and her brothers and sisters worried about Astrid growing old alone. If anyone deserved a happily ever after with a good man, it was their mom. Delaney's eyebrows furrowed as she realized there was little chance of that happening.

"I never want to find myself in a similar position." Delaney scrubbed the counter with more vigor than was needed. "Which is why I'd rather bite my tongue and put up with Roger's intolerant, antiquated mindset than risk getting a divorce."

The big mutt sidled up against her leg, gazing at Delaney as she spoke. It seemed like he was really listening and cared about what she had to say. If only Roger would do the same.

"I'm not sure if I'm more afraid of being alone or of getting into the whole stressful dating scene," she admitted to Ruff. "At thirty-five the last thing I want to think about is online dating." The thought made her shudder. "The lies and exaggeration, the nervousness and anxiety and, maybe worst of all, the rejection." A lengthy sigh escaped her lips.

After she'd finished washing the knives, cutting board and prep tools, she paused, glancing down at her captive audience. "What do you think, Ruff? Do I really want to subject myself to all that stress and difficulty?" She didn't have to think about it long. "Hell no. It's far better to find ways to placate myself, even if that means planting teddy bears and chocolate in a kitchen cabinet on my birthday." Ruff offered a companionable woof in response, which Delaney interpreted as his agreement.

As long as she had her Viking dreams to fantasize about, she could put up with Roger's idiosyncrasies and dictatorial ways.

"It's not like my Viking dream boy's about to ride up on a white charger, or row up in a longboat, and whisk me away from my humdrum existence. Nope, I need to be practical and make the best of what I have," Delaney muttered absently. "Roger's a great catch. Plenty of women would love to be in my shoes."

Thinking about all of this was depressing, and that's the last thing she wanted on her birthday.

She turned on her phone's music app, sans the earpiece, filling the kitchen with the melodic sounds of jazz as she put on a pot of strong, earthy coffee to brew.

"Here I come, Teddy." She returned to the cabinet with the teddy bear and plucked the chocolate from its chubby lap.

Chapter 2

~<>~

WITH THE REVERENCE a fine piece of Belgian chocolate deserved, Delaney unwrapped it slowly, sniffing deeply as the rich, milky fragrance infused the space. Next, she rescued a croissant from the depths of her refrigerator, from behind a can of vegan protein powder and the tub of tofu. She'd purchased it from the bakery, praying Roger wouldn't sniff it out and confront her.

Removing the flaky, buttery bit of flaked-almond-covered goodness from its bag, Delaney was tempted to caress it. She salivated while it crisped in the toaster oven, just enough to warm the almond paste inside. As it toasted, she imagined biting into the pastry, then nibbling some chocolate. The combination would be sheer bliss.

The kitchen came to life, redolent with mouthwatering fragrance. This didn't go unnoticed by Ruff, but Delaney had wisely prepared in advance for this moment.

"I have a very special treat for you, you miserable fleabag," she told Ruff, using baby talk as she opened another cabinet and drew out a giant rawhide bone. She smiled at the brainless creature and maintained a kind tone. "Now go away, monster dog, and leave me be so I can enjoy my birthday breakfast in peace." As if he understood, Ruff clamped his jaws on the bone and scampered off.

"Score one for the human brain and zero for the tiny canine brain." She marked a line in the air with her finger.

Soon her perfectly warmed croissant was centered on the dessert plate, acquainting itself with the Belgian chocolate. Delaney didn't bother suppressing an anticipatory giggle. She held the plate beneath her nose, closed her eyes and breathed in. Her celebratory indulgence smelled luscious.

"Happy Valentine birthday to me!" she cooed, doing an impromptu little dance around the kitchen.

She realized it might be somewhat extreme for a grown woman to get this excited over a piece of chocolate and a croissant, but she supposed there were other diet-policed spouses who became just as enthusiastic about secretly rendezvousing with a sporadic sinful indulgence too. All she cared about right now was sinking her teeth into her treats and sipping her rich, bold coffee spiked with real sugar and the honest to goodness dairy cream that she'd hid in an empty tub of soy margarine.

Delaney set her retro turquoise dessert plate on the table next to a matching cup and saucer. After posing Teddy, with his tan body and turquoise bowtie, against the sugar bowl, she paused a moment to admire the inviting still life she'd created.

She took a photo with her camera, smiling at the result. "Just like Rembrandt." When she got to the office she'd text it to Grandma Bekka and the rest of the family in Glassfloat Bay.

She kept her colorful kitchenware hidden in the pantry and kitchen cabinets because Roger claimed her choice of turquoise accessories caused an imbalance in his chakras.

Tranquil smile still in place, Delaney gave the culinary setting a final appreciative glance before turning and heading for the coffeepot.

What happened next was so rapid and ghastly it seemed more like something out of a horror movie than real life.

The hound from hell swooped into the kitchen while her back was turned, stole her treasured birthday delights from their plate and sped from the room, absconding to the safety of a corner beneath one of the end tables in the living room.

A scream gurgled up from Delaney's throat as she watched the grisly event unfold. Her shrill cry of outrage sounded inhuman, even to her own ears.

Unwilling to surrender her birthday breakfast without a fight, Delaney followed the dog, getting to her hands and knees and crawling under the table, ready to snatch the remaining uneaten half of the croissant and the small piece of chocolate from the beast's grubby paws. Closely guarding his bounty, Ruff gave a toothy warning growl, which Delaney returned with a growl of her own.

"Goddammit, it's mine, you croissant-thieving sonuvabitch. Mine! Besides, you fur-covered moron, chocolate is poisonous for dogs."

She extended her hand and the devil dog's nostrils flared. His maniacal glare suggested he was fully prepared to snap off her fingers with his fangs should she dare encroach on his prize.

"I'm trying to save your worthless life, you idiot," Delaney reasoned. "Now hand over the chocolate before it kills you or, I swear to God, I'll kill you myself!"

The damned dog not only ignored her plea, it sneered at her in dogly triumph as it wolfed down more of its treasure.

Whipped, beaten and cruelly betrayed by the creature she'd gone out of her way to purchase a behemoth-sized rawhide bone for, Delaney begrudgingly renounced her claim on the remaining food and trudged back to the kitchen.

A few crispy flakes of dough, a smattering of sliced almonds, and microscopic bits of chocolate dotted her wet-from-dog-spit plate. Crazed beyond reason, Delaney gathered every last speck with her fingertips, depositing the tiny treasure on her tongue. If she died later that day from a strain of deadly antibiotic resistant dog saliva bacteria, then so be it.

At least she still had her coffee. As she was about to sip from her cup, Ruff's bizarre, hacking noise caught Delaney's attention. He looked terrible and sounded even worse.

In between horrific sound blasts, which Delaney feared must be a canine death rattle, the blameworthy croissant stealer gave Delaney a sorrowful, beseeching look that clutched at her heart.

She was fairly certain if he could speak he'd be saying, "I am *so* sorry I thoughtlessly stole your Valentine birthday breakfast and ruined your morning, Delaney, but I can't help being a dumb dog who acts on sheer impulse, and now I'm paying for my unforgiveable transgression by dying, so please, oh please won't you take pity on me and save my worthless life?"

"Oh God, oh God...how will I ever explain to Roger that I killed his dog with chocolate?" Delaney bit her nails. "The vet. I have to call the vet!" Racing back to her phone she looked through her contacts, stopping when she heard gagging followed by the unmistakable sound of retching.

She looked up to see Ruff barfing chocolate all over the rug.

"No!" It was more a stunned gasp of disbelief than a command.

And then came the pooping.

"Oh Ruff," Delaney's face contorted, "no...nooo!"

Within ten minutes, clearly no longer in the throes of death, Ruff was spry and chipper, joyfully galloping around the house while Delaney gathered a bucket, pine-scented disinfectant cleaner and plenty of hot water to deal with his mess.

"Happy effing birthday to me," she spat as she scrubbed, eradicating German Shepherd donkey vomit and all other evidence of the birthday breakfast that never was, all the while contemplating the assassination of the loathsome dog.

Glancing at the wall clock when she'd finally finished, Delaney's shoulders slumped. Because of the rotten, conniving animal, she didn't even have enough time to sit down and enjoy a cup of birthday coffee before leaving. She poked her finger in the cup she'd poured. It was cold now anyway. Emitting a sigh that sounded more like a wounded moose call, she cleaned up and eliminated all evidence that she'd made coffee, sprayed the kitchen with room deodorizer, and headed for the bedroom to get ready for work.

"Don't think I'm going to forget this, you four-legged bully," she promised the gleeful dog. "Ever." With a narrow-eyed gaze, she added, "And wipe that smug look off your satisfied muzzle, or I'll do it for you."

Clearly terrified, Ruff wagged his tail in response, slanting his head this way and that while doing his best to look adorable.

~<>~

Arriving at her receptionist job at the local newspaper Delaney found a card and a vanilla-frosted yellow cupcake with a candle centered on her desk. A department store gift card was tucked inside the envelope, along with hand-scrawled notes from Paul Richardson, her boss and editor-in-chief, and all the staff congratulating her on the debut of her column.

She especially appreciated their kind thoughtfulness after the morning she'd had.

Over the next hour she enjoyed short, pleasant conversations with her mom, sisters and brothers who'd called to wish her happy birthday. Her boss didn't mind her taking occasional personal calls as long as it didn't interfere with her work, and Delaney never abused the privilege.

"Good morning, Northwest Suburban Gazette," she said, answering another call. An instant later she grinned as a chorus of cheery voices boomed, "*Gratulerer med dagen*, Delaney!" It was Norwegian for happy birthday. A boisterous round of Happy Birthday, sung in English, followed.

"Thank you, Grandma Bekka. Happy Valentine's Day to you and your friends!" None of Bekka's friends or neighbors were Norwegian or spoke the language but she'd taught them this birthday phrase well.

"We're all here at Griffin's Café," Bekka told her, "toasting you with steamy cups of cocoa and a big platter of your sister's almond cherry scones." Delaney's spirits brightened. This call was exactly what she needed after her stressful morning.

"Oh what I wouldn't give for one of Laila's delicious scones! I miss those, and I miss you *so* much, Grandma."

"I miss you too, *min kjære*." It meant *my dear*.

"I really love the beautiful hat and scarf you knitted for me. Thank you."

"Good! I was hoping they'd arrive in time for your birthday."

"The lavender yarn is so soft and pretty. What kind is it?"

"Mohair. I got it from String Me Along, the yarn shop in town. I think your sister, Reen, spends more time there than the owner." Bekka's laughter was like a tinkling bell. "You wouldn't believe how professional Reen's knitting and crochet projects have become."

"Unlike me, Reen's a natural when it comes to all things yarn related," Delaney said, withdrawing the crocheted teddy bear from her purse. It was the one she'd placed in her kitchen cabinet with the chocolate bar in its lap.

Setting it next to the other handmade critters on her desk, she said, "I used the crochet pattern you sent me for the teddy bear. It turned out really cute." She angled her head, eyeing the slightly lopsided stuffed animal, deciding her favorable appraisal might be a teensy exaggeration.

"Hold on a second and I'll send you a picture of Teddy."

A moment after she'd sent the text, Grandma Bekka oohed and aahed. "So cute! Oh what a wonderful job you did, Delaney."

Chuckling, Delaney knew the bear could have looked like a blindfolded five-year-old made it and Bekka would still praise it like it was museum-worthy.

"I made the bowtie a little too big," Delaney fingered the floppy tie, "and one ear's bigger than the other, but I think it suits him. I still have a long way to go to be as good as you, Mom, or Reen. Once I'm better at crochet I want to learn how to knit too."

"I've been teaching knitting classes at String Me Along. You can take one when you come to visit me. We'll have so much fun."

"I'd love that. Nothing like learning from the best." Delaney wished she could fly to Oregon to visit Bekka but there was no way she could afford it, and no way Roger would agree to foot the bill. As they chatted, she bent to pick up the envelope that had slipped out of her purse when she'd pulled out the bear.

Bekka traveled to Illinois every couple of years to visit but as she grew older, Delaney worried each visit might be her last. Thankfully, her grandmother sounded as lively and healthy as ever.

In between answering company calls, Delaney and her grandmother caught up on what had happened since their last conversation. Delaney studied the sealed envelope as they spoke. Her name was scrawled on it in Roger's handwriting.

A birthday card? A Valentine? It would be the first of either in ten years, so she doubted it. But then, she had noticed changes in him lately.

She used to wish he might suddenly have an Ebenezer Scrooge-like epiphany, embracing birthdays and holidays, especially Christmas and all the merriment of the season. Not only didn't Roger celebrate the holiday, he also frowned on Delaney making what he considered a garish spectacle by putting up a tree or any decorations.

Maybe he'd seen the light. Maybe he'd been purposely tough on her this morning so she wouldn't suspect he had a birthday surprise in store for her.

The envelope had Delaney imagining her husband seated at his desk, writing his first ever love letter to her. Or perhaps it was a poem...an ode to his wife on her Valentine birthday. How befitting for an English professor.

She wondered if it could be tickets for theater and dinner. The tingle of excitement she felt was brand new. Roger had never been one for surprises.

She told Bekka about the envelope, listening as her grandmother excitedly told "the girls" that it seemed her granddaughter had received her first ever love letter from her husband.

"Haven't I always told you to have faith in your dreams?" Bekka asked. "And to believe that one day you'd find the happiness you desire and deserve?"

Turning the envelope back and forth, extending the delicious sense of anticipation, Delaney nodded. "You did indeed, Grandma. It seems Roger tucked the envelope into my purse as a surprise so I'd find it when I got to work. I'm amazed. And to think...it's only taken ten years." She laughed and Bekka followed suit. "Hold on. I'll open it and tell you what's inside."

The envelope held a folded sheet of paper, Roger's official university stationery.

"Ooh, it's a handwritten birthday letter, Grandma!" Giddy, she read aloud. "Dear Del, I've orchestrated it so that you'll open and read this letter once you get to work. It's best that way since you tend to be overly emotional..."

A lump formed in her throat and she swallowed hard. She doubted Roger was talking about her becoming overcome with joy. "...and will, hopefully, be less prone to making an embarrassing scene in public."

Oh God...

A distinctly disagreeable warmth flushed through her. Delaney steadied her shaking hand before continuing. "I regret to inform you that I am leaving you." Struck with disbelief, she sucked in a sharp breath.

"Oh no...my poor little Delaney," Bekka said.

"It's...it's okay, Grandma. Really, I'm okay," she lied, brushing a fat tear from her cheek before answered a business call. "Good morning, Northwest Suburban Gazette," she said, doing her best to sound like her usual cheery self. A moment later she returned to Bekka's call.

"Tell me what else Roger had to say," Bekka said, all traces of levity now absent from her voice. "I want to hear everything."

Thankful the business calls were few this morning, Delaney was relieved to be able to talk to her grandmother. She continued reading aloud from the letter.

"Our lack of compatibility or common interests has long been apparent. More importantly, my patience with your apparent dearth of interest or initiative to improve yourself, even though I've offered you my guidance repeatedly, has been exhausted."

She paused, staring at the letter, meticulously examining what she'd just read, certain she'd misunderstood it. Roger simply wouldn't do something like this. He wouldn't.

After a lingering silence, Bekka said, "Delaney? Honey? Are you okay?"

Shaking off her initial shock, Delaney replied, "Yes...I'm here, Grandma. I'm okay. Here's the rest of the letter." She took a fortifying breath and continued. "I have found a more compatible mate with whom to spend my life. A graduate student of English at the university, this young woman is still impressionable enough to be molded to my ideology."

Her hand flying to her chest, Delaney gasped.

"It is my earnest desire that you too will find a suitable companion in time. I recommend that you focus on the self-improvement necessary to become a woman of worth for a future partner."

Delaney's teary eyes bugged. "A woman of worth?" His heartless words were like a knife to her heart.

Her grandmother muttered something in Norwegian.

"By the time you get home from work," Delaney continued to read, "you'll find I've cleared out all my personal belongings, including the blender and library of nutrition books since they'd only gather dust in your care. My attorney will be in touch with you shortly. As soon as I am able, I'll return for my dog, Ruff."

Seized by the overwhelming desire to laugh and cry at the same time, Delaney succumbed to both, doing her utmost to hold it together, lest she live down to Roger's expectations and create a scene at work.

"Lucky me," Delaney said to Bekka. "I get to be caretaker for my husband's monster dog. What a prince Roger is. He woke me an hour earlier than usual this morning, obviously lying about going in for a meeting on his day off. I can't believe I actually spent my birthday morning catering to his whiny breakfast requirements so he and his compatible new grammatically correct girlfriend could ride off into the sunset together."

She bit her lip to keep from swearing, but Grandma Bekka had a few choice words of her own to share.

"That son of a bitch!"

The words, complete with her heavy Norwegian accent, sounded so strange coming from the elderly woman that Delaney couldn't help laughing. It was the first time she'd ever heard her grandmother say anything off color.

They spoke a short while longer, with Delaney ensuring her there was no need to worry. The last thing she wanted was for her grandma to be upset on her account, especially since she was so far away.

"You've always taught me there's a silver lining for every cloud." Delaney did her best to sound lighthearted as her heart shattered. "I believe that with all my heart, Grandma. Don't worry...I really, truly do."

Her grandma didn't need to know that Delaney no longer believed in silver linings.

She wanted to end their conversation with a cheerful quip, saying something silly, but any glib comment stuck in her throat.

She ended the call on a calm note, exceedingly thankful she had to tend to the suddenly busy phones, which allowed her little time to think...and no opportunity to give in to bawling like a baby.

Dear Diary: The bad news is that my husband cruelly left me on my Valentine birthday for a graduate student who seems an ideal match for Roger. The good news is that I'll be stopping by a barbecue joint so I can pig out on baby back ribs for dinner tonight.

Delaney picked up the crooked little teddy bear, hugging it to her chest.

Chapter 3

One Year Later

~<>~

MY DEAREST DELANEY,

Although it's been many years since you were little and we spoke of hopes and dreams and the future over mugs of hot chocolate, I'm certain you'll remember the magic heartwish ring enclosed here.

When you were a child, I promised one day, when the time was right, it would be yours. It is the most precious possession I own. More valuable than any amount of money. This ring, with its mystic stone, has been passed down through our family for generations. It must be held against the heart when making a sincere heartwish. Place it on your finger. It will remain there until it is time to pass it on. You will know the right time...and who should receive it.

Each owner of the ring may use it only once. Though your mind may be cluttered and uncertain, your heart will know the right wish to make. Always trust your heart, my dear.

You've suffered great heartache, but I trust you haven't lost your faith in the power of love and magic, for it is indeed real. Believe me, Delaney, I know. You must believe that one day your true love, Varik the Bold, will come to you. He will. I guarantee it.

As you'll see in the enclosed copy of my will, I have divided my estate between you, your sisters and brothers, and your mother, my dear daughter. This box also includes some of my favorite possessions—things I know you will treasure and pass down to your children one day.

It saddens me that the arrival of my letter and package will make you cry. Please do not mourn, for though I am gone from you in body, my spirit lives on. Know that it makes my heart glad to be reunited with my darling husband, Jamie. I promise you, my sweet little Delaney, we shall all meet again one day in the great majestic halls of Valhalla.

Jeg elsker deg, now and forever,
Grandma Bekka

~ ~ ~

Delaney read the letter aloud for the third time, erupting in a new wave of thunderous sobs. Sent from Glassfloat Bay, the letter arrived with a large package a few days before her birthday—the second birthday in a row she'd spend alone and grieving.

"*Jeg elsker deg*," she repeated, tracing the words with her finger. "I love you too, Grandma. Now and forever." She kissed her fingertip, touching it to the paper.

The loving words she'd just read stood in direct contrast to the coldness of Roger's self-serving exodus letter a year earlier. His words had jolted her with the swiftness and potency of a stomach punch. Delaney heard he and his perky young graduate student were married right after the divorce was final.

As terrible and startling as being blindsided by her cheating rat bastard husband had been, the blow was minor, truly insignificant, compared to losing her beloved grandmother.

Delaney's hurt and heartache a year ago were greatly soothed by the unanticipated arrival of sweet Grandma Bekka only a week after the phone conversation when she'd learned Roger had dumped her. The aging woman had flown in from Oregon, alone, just for Delaney. Bekka said there was no way she'd let her granddaughter go through such a difficult time without her.

The two weeks they spent together were filled with love, joy and laughter. Delaney gave Bekka her bedroom and Delaney slept on the small sofa bed in the spare bedroom. She'd converted the sterile study, once Roger's domain, into an inviting writing space for herself.

Living less than twenty minutes from Delaney, Astrid stopped by after work each day so the three of them could share dinner together. Not one to sit idle, Bekka made herself busy each day making delicious meals and scrumptious desserts like her delicious *pepperkaker*.

Delaney couldn't remember feeling so spoiled.

Innumerable calories aside, she loved having her small kitchen redolent with tantalizing aromas and abundant laughter, something sorely missing during *The Roger Years*, as she now thought of her marriage.

Lovingly fingering her grandmother's handwritten letter, Delaney gave a weepy smile. "You didn't die because you were old," she said, "you died because you missed Grandpa Jamie and wanted to join him...in Valhalla." Delaney had never met her grandfather. And Astrid had never met her father. Jamie Eriksen died before Astrid was born. Bekka remained devoted to him the rest of her life, certain they'd be reunited one day.

One thing that gave Delaney comfort about her grandma's passing is that it happened while Astrid was in Oregon visiting. It was almost as if Bekka knew, and waited for Astrid, her only child, to be there with her.

Delaney's mom and grandma called her while enjoying scones and cocoa at Griffin's Café. She enjoyed listening to Astrid wax poetic about Glassfloat Bay, and to Bekka's continued urgings for them both to move out there. It sounded like a perfect final visit for mother and daughter to share—which is exactly how Astrid said she felt about it.

The package from the executor of Rebekka Eriksen's estate arrived addressed to Ms. Delaney Malone, which made Delaney smile. She was happy she'd followed her grandmother's suggestion to drop the Kullerton name during the divorce and return to her maiden name. Best decision ever.

The executor's document advised Delaney that she, her siblings and their mother had inherited Bekka's house in the coastal town of Glassfloat Bay, Oregon, as well as Bekka's log home in Lillehammer, Norway.

Tucked in the box were two softball-sized glass balls, one in turquoise and the other cobalt blue. The attached note explained the clear, hollow balls were glass fishing floats from Norway that Bekka discovered while strolling along the coastline. Most of her collection was from Japan's deep sea fishing industry. Some still had fishnet secured around them. The number of floats found in the area gave the town of Glassfloat Bay its name.

"These are just a few of the special treasures you'll find in your new Oregon home," another handwritten note from Bekka explained.

Delaney lifted a small box from the package, opening it to find the heartwish ring. She absently traced the band's metal scrollwork as she studied it. The sturdy jewelry was slightly more masculine than feminine in design. In the center sat a lustrous, dark-hued opalescent stone. How she'd adored that ring as a little girl. Bekka told her she'd love to let Delaney try it on but the ring wouldn't budge from her finger until it was time for Delaney to own it.

"I'll never forget, Grandma," she whispered. "I'll always remember you and your grand, romantic accounts of love and fairytale-like happily-ever-afters."

Delaney recalled listening to her grandmother with rapt attention. The woman was a born storyteller, enjoying the way Delaney gobbled up legends of enchantment and tales of strong, handsome Vikings. Delaney loved when Bekka held up her fingers, wiggling them so the stone shone as she spoke of Norse folklore. Family legend said the magical heartwish ring had been given to the matriarch of a Viking king by Odin, the most powerful of Norse gods.

The stone's asymmetrical shape made it appear as if it had once been a larger stone that had broken in half. Though still visible and slightly rough to the touch, the stone's uneven edge had smoothed with time.

Spellbound as her grandmother turned her hand to and fro, Delaney listened to Bekka's conspirator's whisper, "Odin broke the enchanted stone in half, dividing it between two deserving families. There is just one other heartwish stone ring in existence, Delaney...the matching half to this one."

As she held the ring now, Delaney's smile was wistful. "Oh how I loved hearing your fanciful tales, Grandma. Little did I know they were make-believe." She couldn't help the ruminating sigh that escaped. "My dear, whimsical grandma, you may have been naïve enough to believe in myths, magic rings, Norse gods and the rest of that paranormal gibberish, but I know better."

A single fat tear coursed down her cheek.

"I know firsthand that life is hard and fairytales, just like Santa Claus and the Easter Bunny, are meant for wide-eyed children."

Brushing away the tear, she turned her attention to an envelope in the package. It held a long braided lock of hair along with her grandma's photograph. Delaney fondly recalled the ever-present plaited coil of white-blonde hair affixed to the top of Bekka's head. As a child she'd wished she could have flaxen locks like her mother and grandmother instead of her stark black hair.

While Delaney had the tall, large-boned, full-bodied physique of her mother's Scandinavian side of the family, she got the black hair and midnight-blue eyes from her father's side. The Black Irish, her dad called it. Both sides shared the pale, easily sunburned skin.

Her fingertip lightly outlined her grandmother's features. The photograph so perfectly captured Bekka's kind, pale blue eyes...eyes that seemed to hold the secrets and wisdom of the ages. Bekka would instruct Delaney to look deep into her eyes, promising that if she gazed hard enough, she would see her true love.

Focusing all her concentration on Bekka's eyes, Delaney would squint, convinced she saw a Viking.

"What does he look like? Is it Erik the Red?" Grandma Bekka asked. "Or perhaps his son, Leif Eriksson? Maybe Harald Hardrada, or Olaf Tryggvason?"

"He's tall and handsome, Grandma, with long, golden hair, lots of muscles and a sword and shield."

Smiling, Bekka squeezed her granddaughter's hands. "It sounds like Varik the Bold," she offered, evoking the name from one of her stirring Viking tales. "The one who looks like Thor."

"Varik." Delaney gave an affirmative nod. "He's my favorite. The Viking who feared no man or beast."

"Now take another look in my eyes. Concentrate. Think of nothing but Varik, your Viking."

Delaney focused with as much intensity as she could muster, fidgeting with impatience until the image of Varik the Bold appeared.

Bekka covered her ring with Delaney's small hand. The stone glowed as it grew warm—clearly an impossibility drummed up by Delaney's childish imaginings. "Memorize every detail," Grandma Bekka instructed, "his face, his eyes, his hair, his smile, his bold warrior's body."

As if gazing at a photograph, Delaney concentrated, committing everything about Varik the Bold to memory.

"Keep his picture in your mind and heart always. Think of him often, dream of him at night. He will come to claim you as his own one day."

"Will he, Grandma? Really?"

A reassuring smile lit Bekka's eyes. "*Ja, ja*...he will for sure. I know it."

It was the grandest, most romantic dream a little girl could savor. Gullible little Delaney Malone had convinced herself that she'd spied her true love in her grandmother's eyes. Bekka's suggestions were powerful because Delaney dreamed of her Viking often while growing up. As an adult, the dreams took on a more sensual nature. While she loved dreaming of Varik the Bold, it was frustrating because the dreams always fizzled out before they reached an ending.

It didn't matter though—the handsome Viking was nothing but a figment of her overactive imagination anyway.

Perhaps if she'd envisioned someone more realistic than a strapping golden-haired hunk wrapped in reindeer hides, wearing a horned helmet and brandishing a sword and shield, she might have had better success realizing her dreams.

Perhaps if she'd pictured a brainy, lackluster guy in baggy slacks, his thinning hair gathered in a ponytail, carrying a leather briefcase, and pushing slipping spectacles up the bridge of his nose...

Oh wait...that was Roger...who turned out to be more of a nightmare than a dreamboat.

Delaney imagined there must be a happy medium between the two diverse image choices, but it was irrelevant because she'd given up any expectation of finding the right man.

Real life intruded on Delaney's childish hopes when she met Roger Kullerton in the grocery store's produce section, where he stood wearing khakis instead of reindeer hides, contemplating the selection of curly kale versus dinosaur kale. He'd asked Delaney's opinion and her clueless expression must have struck him as amusing because Roger laughed. As she came to learn later, it wasn't a sound she'd hear often.

After a brief engagement, she married the bland, stuffy educator with the lifeless brown eyes and nary a muscle on his less than six-foot frame. There was a logical reason she'd married a no-nonsense man so contrary to her childhood Viking vision—she'd finally accepted reality.

Delaney was close to twenty when she begrudgingly admitted to herself that Varik the Bold would never show up on her doorstep. As a big-boned woman who stood nearly six feet tall, she was lucky to have any man knocking at her door, much less a gorgeous Viking. During school and later, not many guys were interested in going out with a girl who dwarfed them.

Roger was the only man who'd been interested enough in a slightly chunky Norwegian-Irish Amazon to propose marriage. When he did, she didn't have to think twice, figuring it would be her only chance to be married and have a family of her own.

"Roger seems like perfect husband material, honey," Astrid had told her. "You don't want a man who's too handsome or charming. He'll be a good provider and he'll be far too busy with academics to ever think about straying."

Ha!

But Delaney knew what her mother meant. When they were little, Delaney and her brother Gard overheard their parents arguing late one night. Mom had discovered their dad, a charming, handsome Irishman, had cheated on her and she was devastated. As far as they could tell, their parents had patched things up before their father, Sean, died rescuing kids during the school fire. Delaney and Gard made a pact never to let on to their mom, their siblings, or anyone else about what they'd heard. All these years later they'd kept that promise...and would forever.

The only one who cautioned Delaney against marrying the dreary English professor was Grandma Bekka. "Wait," she urged, "have patience. Your Viking will come for you."

"But I'm almost twenty-five," Delaney argued then. "If I don't get married soon I'll end up an old maid, all alone."

"My darling granddaughter, you're still so young. Just a baby," Bekka had said, chuckling while finger-combing Delaney's hair.

"Not according to the romance novels I've read," Delaney argued. "The heroines are between eighteen and twenty. And they're all itty-bitty things, not Amazons like me."

"Nonsense. You, my dear, are a beautiful young woman with plenty of time, *years* before you need to worry about being an old maid. Decades." Bekka chuckled again. "Don't be so eager to tie yourself to a man just for the sake of being married."

But no matter how hard her grandmother tried, she couldn't convince Delaney to wait.

Delaney sighed now at the bittersweet memory. If only she'd listened to her grandmother's sage advice.

About to stash the box from Bekka in the closet, she hesitated. It was almost as if she heard, or was it felt, the heartwish ring calling to her. That, of course, was beyond ridiculous. Pure wishful thinking. The lure of recapturing the innocence of her childhood.

And yet...

After all, her beloved grandmother had made a special effort to send her magic ring to her granddaughter, complete with a loving letter written in her own arthritic hand. Not wearing the ring would be like a slap in the face to Grandma Bekka, and Delaney couldn't do that.

She took the ring out of the box, holding the gleaming, weighty piece of jewelry in the palm of her hand. The ring's detailed craftsmanship was amazing and the stone was just as mesmerizing as she remembered.

Since Bekka loved extolling the virtues of magic to everyone she knew, Delaney wouldn't be too surprised if this ring was one of several the old woman kept tucked away in a drawer. She'd probably left instructions for her executor to dole out heartwish rings to all her relatives and friends, complete with her mystical tale of supernatural powers and one-time use. Delaney smiled. Everyone in Glassfloat Bay probably wore one of her grandmother's *magic* rings.

She slipped the ring on her finger. It fit perfectly, which was interesting because Bekka's fingers were at least a size larger than Delaney's.

~<>~

Delaney drove to work on her birthday in the midst of a fierce February blizzard that subsided only after she'd been blanketed in white while trudging across the parking lot to the office. Her hat, scarf, gloves and boots provided little protection against Chicago's near gale-force winds. By the time she got inside the building, she was caked with ice crystals and chilled to the bone.

While married to Roger she'd insisted on working, against his wishes. He was old school in his thinking that a woman's place was in the home, plus he feared his colleagues might think he wasn't a good provider.

They'd be right. He wasn't. Roger was a damn cheapskate.

She used her income to pay for her clothing, phone, internet access, cable TV, books, magazine subscriptions, and anything else that didn't come under his list of absolute necessities. She also treated herself to the pricey coffee she preferred, and to occasional real food instead of subsisting on Roger's rigid health nut diet twenty-four seven.

Since the divorce she was responsible for the townhouse's mortgage payment, which ate up the major portion of her earnings.

Happily, after Paul learned of Delaney's predicament, he promoted her from receptionist to executive secretary, which brought a substantial raise. While on pregnancy leave, his former secretary decided to quit and be a stay-at-home mom. The extra money Delaney made from her weekly column added enough to keep her living in the townhouse and affording the monthly bills.

One thing she loved about her new position was having her own office. This morning she sat at her desk, gazing out the window as she sipped her favorite coffee while enjoying her birthday breakfast, one of Laila's almond cherry scones from Griffin's Café in Glassfloat Bay. The package from Oregon had arrived at the office early this morning. It was a breakfast fit to make Roger gasp in horror, which is one of the reasons she enjoyed it so much.

The box also included several whimsical hand knit and crocheted animals created by Delaney's sister, Reen, to add to her collection. Café owner Annalise Griffin had written a lovely letter and tucked it into a large Valentine's Day card which was signed by many of the townspeople.

"Bekka told me how much you miss your sister's scones," Annalise wrote, "so Laila baked a birthday batch just for you. She said to tell you these are new. They're lower in calories, fat and sugar than her original ones and she wants your feedback on the new recipe. Personally, I can't tell the difference and think they're scrumptious!"

"Mmmm..." Delaney's eyes fluttered shut as she took another bite. "She's right."

Annalise told Delaney of their sadness at losing Bekka, and offered some favorite memories of their times together. They hoped Delaney would visit soon, and maybe even decide to move into Bekka's vacant house.

Delaney held the letter close to her heart and cried. They were happy tears because, as difficult as it was losing her grandmother, Delaney felt certain the years Grandma Bekka lived in Oregon had been happy ones.

Her office window presented Delaney with a clear, sunny day after she'd braved the morning blizzard. Moments before she left work, the heavens opened again. Scraping ice and snow from her car's windshield, she muttered a string of curses when the plastic ice scraper snapped in half.

"As soon as I save enough money for a cross country move," she promised herself, grunting as she used a portion of the broken scraper to clear away enough ice so she could see well enough to drive, "I'm moving to Glassfloat Bay." The scraper remnant broke into an even smaller piece, which had Delaney swearing like a sailor. "God, I'm sick to death of this winter weather!"

Finally behind the wheel, she reached for the glove compartment, eager to sink her teeth into a chocolate truffle, knowing the sensation of rich velvet creaminess melting on her tongue would soothe her ice-savaged psyche.

"Mmm...birthday chocolate..." She salivated with expectation as she reached inside, only to suffer icy terror at the realization the cupboard was bare. She'd forgotten to replenish her emergency stash after eating the last piece of chocolate.

"No. No! Nooooooo!"

Leaning forward, banging the heel of her hand against the steering wheel, she felt the heartwish ring's band dig into her finger.

"Lot of good you've done me, you cheap chunk of costume jewelry." Removing her glove, she blew on her frozen fingers before trying once again to yank the ring off, but the darn thing wouldn't budge since she'd first placed it on her finger.

The melancholy of birthday chocolate deprivation eased when she thought about her other emergency chocolate reserve tucked in her nightstand drawer. She smiled...no, grinned, confident she could hang on to her sanity until she got home and ripped into her chocolate stockpile.

After crawling through bumper to bumper traffic, snarled by throngs of rush hour drivers, Delaney finally pulled into her driveway. She smiled when she heard her best buddy, Thursday, whimpering as she closed the garage door and entered the house through the kitchen. At least her faithful dog would be with her for her Valentine birthday.

Her ex-husband found the dog on a Thursday, the day of the week named after the Norse god, Thor, son of Odin. With all the imagination and creativity of a thumbtack, he named the dog Ruff. Delaney changed the dog's name the day after Roger walked out.

He'd demanded custody of Ruff when they divorced, which was fine with Delaney, saying he'd return for the dog once he was settled. That was twelve months ago. She and Thursday hadn't seen Roger since.

And then a funny thing happened.

Delaney and the monster dog got to know each other. They got to be friends. Really bonded.

"Do you know why I love you so much, Thursday?" she'd asked him. "Because you listen to me when I need to talk. You watch my favorite movies without making fun of them and don't glare at me like I'm a moron when I cry at the happy parts. You eat whatever I've prepared without grumbling. You don't leave clothes strewn all over the house for me to pick up. You don't insist I drink muddy shakes with brewer's yeast, desiccated liver, and beet tops. You don't shudder when I make a grammar faux pas. And you don't love me any less because I wear a double-digit size."

Then she'd massage the back of his ears, getting a juicy face lick in return.

Yes, she'd even come to tolerate dog spit.

"I swear," Delaney said now as she entered the kitchen, lovingly and enthusiastically greeted by Thursday, "if I'd known at twenty-five what I know now, I would have opted for a dog instead of a husband."

Squatting on her heels, she mussed his fur and gave him a hug. Thursday was her sweetie pie, her loving, adorable, attentive pal. "I missed you today, Thursday, did you miss me?" He gave her a big sloppy lick in reply.

Stepping through the kitchen and into the living room, Delaney's heart stuttered. Her eyeballs popped out of her head, dangling on springs as she viewed the catastrophe before her. She zeroed in on the remnants of the bag of Oreos that trailed from the living room to her bedroom. And then she saw the Snickers, Hershey's, and Reese's Peanut Butter Cups wrappers. It was every bit of chocolate from her nightstand drawer.

Clutching her hand to her chest, she surveyed the room and screeched, "Thursday!"

A quick scan of the floor revealed he'd christened the shag carpeting with dog vomit. Dark, crisp, scattered patches of mustard yellow with black cookie crumbs and chunks of regurgitated chocolate embedded in the midst of it all. It was a gruesome reminder of what the monster dog had done to her a year ago when he'd pilfered her birthday breakfast.

The idiot dog, who was probably on a sugar high, had toppled the silver aluminum Christmas tree, leaving her treasured family heirloom ornaments resting in splotches of dog puke. Granted, the artificial tree and its multi-color rotating light wheel shouldn't still be up in the middle of February, but she'd been deprived of any holiday trappings all during *The Roger Years*.

This was the first tree she'd had in ten years and Delaney hated to box it away just yet. Each day she contemplated taking it down but decided she wanted to look at it a little while longer. It made her smile. She found the tarnished vintage aluminum treasure at the curbside on a garbage pickup day last spring. It reminded her of the one Grandma Bekka had when Delaney was little, so she dragged it home. Some of the branches were bent and the tree leaned slightly to one side but once she'd cleaned it up and made some repairs it was almost good as new.

After hearing Delaney's anguished cry and glimpsing her crazed expression, Thursday hastily skulked off, tail between his legs, to some hidden corner.

"Yeah, you'd better hide, you fiend, because at this very moment I'm planning your grisly demise."

As if navigating through a minefield, Delaney gingerly sidestepped the barf and padded into the bedroom. Her shoulders slumped and she groaned. Not only had Thursday vomited on the granny square afghan she'd recently crocheted, but he'd deposited a nasty clump of poop on the carpet. And there wasn't a single uneaten cookie or piece of chocolate left anywhere in sight.

"Damn it, Thursday! Damn it, damn it, damn it!"

How in the world he'd managed to open the drawer of her nightstand was beyond her. And how he could so selfishly devour her precious stash without leaving anything for her made her see red. Like a cat with nine lives, once again her dumbass dog had miraculously managed to avoid death by chocolate. She supposed she should be relieved that he barfed it all out, but at the moment...

As Delaney stood slump-shouldered in the midst of the mess, grieving the loss of her chocolate and bemoaning the fact that she'd be stuck on her hands and knees with her face mere inches from dog puke for hours as she scrubbed, there was a knock at the front door.

"Hell," she grumbled. "Now what?"

She wasn't going to answer...but what if it was some kid selling chocolate bars for scouts or a school event? They were always coming to her door hawking their oversized bars of chocolate, laced with her choice of plain, crisped rice or nuts. She usually turned them away. As every chocolate connoisseur knows, resorting to cheap, waxy fundraiser chocolate meant you'd hit rock bottom. Delaney had never stooped that low.

There was more knocking, then the doorbell rang. Desperately in need of chocolate, she dragged her frazzled nerves across the room.

Reasoning that stooping to a new low was justifiable under the circumstances, Delaney opened the door.

Uttering a gasp of astonishment, she clapped her hand to her chest, the metal band around her finger suddenly growing warm.

Standing across her threshold was a living, breathing golden-haired, half-naked hunk of a man in full Viking regalia.

And she was pretty damn sure he wasn't selling fundraiser chocolate.

Chapter 4

~<>~

"HALLO. I SORRY to bothering you," the tall, astoundingly handsome man said in broken English. His deep, accented voice was sexy as hell. "Need to play. You help?"

Gawking at the towering presence filling her doorway, it took Delaney a long moment before she was capable of speech. His flowing mane of sandy hair fell just beneath his shoulders, glistening in the winter sunlight. A well-manicured mustache and beard highlighted his strong jaw.

Like a Viking warrior of long ago, the muscular man looked fierce, rugged and boldly masculine. Powerfully built arms, broad pecs, robust thighs, sun-bronzed skin, striking ice-blue eyes...

Oh my God...it was Varik the Bold, her childhood fantasy come to life!

"What?" she eked out breathlessly, doing her best to dismiss the alarm clanging inside her head—the one telling her she was in the throes of a complete mental collapse.

"English not so good, my pardon I beg. I be lock. Need to play." He gestured to his skimpy Viking getup. "You help play?"

Delaney twisted the ring around her finger, unable to focus on his words because she was too busy worrying she'd end up in a straitjacket before morning.

The tall stranger had a sword sheathed across his back and carried a round shield. He was breathtaking and she was mesmerized.

Good God...she was actually salivating.

If she had to go crazy, this awesome hallucination wasn't a bad way to do it.

Her fingers reached out, feathering a touch across the animal hides he wore. They weren't fake, they were real. She glanced up to catch one of his eyebrows hiking at her familiarity.

Logic told her it was ludicrous to verbalize her inner thoughts because he wasn't really there. He couldn't be. He was just a fabrication of her sudden insanity...a magnificent illusion brought on by a second straight year of birthday chocolate deprivation. But Delaney couldn't help herself.

"Is it you?" she whispered, just as she had each time she'd dreamed of her Viking. "My Viking? My Varik the Bold?"

The Viking cocked his head. "You knowing my name?"

She blinked hard. The guy's name was Varik the Bold?

No. Uh-uh. Totally, completely, one-hundred-percent impossible...unless... The verdict was in. Delaney Malone had finally graduated from being a little squirrelly to full-blown nut case.

"There's no other explanation," she muttered. Unable to tear her gaze from his chiseled features, she said, "I don't suppose you're here to sell fundraiser chocolate?"

He gave her a clueless look.

"I didn't think so."

This wouldn't do at all. She had to get a grip. Whether she was loony or not, drooling like a hormonal teenager over a perfect stranger could lead to...well, the guy could be an ax murderer for all she knew. Her gaze fell on his weapon. Or a sword murderer.

Maybe she wasn't crazy. Maybe she'd died and gone to heaven without realizing it. The shock of chocolate withdrawal combined with the loss of her grandmother had been too much for her heart.

Or maybe it was Nordic magic and her dead grandmother had sent Delaney her promised Viking, straight from the great halls of Valhalla.

Grandma Bekka. Of course...that was it! Delaney wasn't insane after all. Relief washing over her, she felt her dazed, dubious expression morph into a grin.

"I get it. My grandmother set this up, didn't she?" The guy gazed at her with the same oblivious expression Thursday had when she spoke to him.

"No inner stand."

Delaney's features twisted. "What?"

"Eh...not inner stand."

"You mean *understand*?"

Looking relieved, he smiled. "*Ja, ja*, not understand." He clapped his hand against his chest. "Need to play."

Delaney looked him up and down, uttering a throaty chuckle. "Oh, I just bet you do, big guy, but not with me you don't." She started to close the door, but the Viking's hand caught it.

"Please. Help Varik play."

His mouth was sensitive, his jaw sturdy. Lust, pure and potent, coiled deep in Delaney's belly. She hadn't felt anything like this since...well, ever. Unable to drag her gaze from his mesmerizing eyes, she was so turned on by this walking, talking embodiment of her fantasies she could barely breathe.

"Yes," she said, trying to maintain her composure, "this would fit perfectly with Grandma Bekka's romantic mindset. So my grandmother arranged for the executor of her estate to send a Viking to poor lonely Delaney for her Valentine birthday. Is that it? Well look, buster, I'm not *that* lonely. So—"

"*Gratulerer med dagen!*" The Viking's smile was radiant as he wished her happy birthday. It was one of the few Norwegian phrases she knew.

She felt her cheeks heat.

"*Glad Valentinsdag bursdag!*" the Viking amended.

"You-you just wished me happy Valentine's birthday...in Norwegian."

"*Ja.* Happy Valentine birthday." The Viking's head bobbed and Delaney could have sworn she saw his ocean-blue eyes sparkle, just like in a Saturday morning cartoon.

Along with a sigh, the words "Thank you" escaped her lips. She was unused to a man who actually recognized the holiday, much less her birthday. His words and engaging expression warmed her heart. How sweet. How endearing. How utterly...

And then reality dawned.

Well of course the big pretend Viking knew how to wish her happy Valentine's birthday in Norwegian—just the way her grandmother had taught her friends at the café. After all, he'd been paid to say just the right words upon delivery, hadn't he? The muscled, near-naked idol of her girlish dreams stood there smiling across her threshold, having the audacity to look abnormally perfect.

Model perfect.

Movie star perfect.

Paid uptown gigolo perfect.

Her eyebrows knitted. The impossibly perfect guy was schmoozing her, doing his damnedest to charm the pants off her with fake Norwegian charm. All because her misguided grandma thought her lonely granddaughter needed a fantasy roll in the hay on her birthday.

Delaney drew in a breath to stave off impending tears.

Presenting what she hoped was an aloof, confident air, she told the man in no uncertain terms, "As I was saying, I'm not that lonely. So you can take your phony accent and your animal pelts and your horned helmet and your big sword..."

For some ungodly reason Delaney chose that particular moment to drop her gaze to the man's crotch. She sucked in a deep breath.

"And, and, and...and you can just get out of here," she finally managed, making a shooing gesture with her hand. "The last thing I need in my life now is some big, overgrown muscled—"

Varik touched her cheek and Delaney gasped. He cupped her chin. And, like an idiot, she just stood there letting him.

"Why lonely?" he asked. "You so beauty."

He looked so caring, so hot and gorgeous as he spoke, that she wanted to rip those pelts off him with her teeth and feast on him. Her hand flew to her forehead, where she expected to feel evidence of a raging fever. What other explanation could there be for her excessively lusty reaction to a total stranger? She should slam the door in his face. She should call the cops. She should...

His thumb stroked her cheek.

Everything inside Delaney went melty and gooey. She yearned to rush into his arms, wailing like a baby against his broad chest about how unfair life had been and how it sucked to be without someone to love and how she was thankful for her four-speed vibrator but felt sure it couldn't compare to a flesh and blood Viking. And she wanted Varik the Bold to respond by uttering a manly grunt before mercilessly ravaging her.

She swallowed hard. Dear God it was true...she really *had* lost her marbles.

"Help Varik to play, please."

"Oh that's really good." Delaney eyed him. "You sound so sincere. Plus you've mastered the look of a pleading puppy dog."

Locking gazes with her, he shook his head from side to side. "Not inner...eh, *under*stand."

Absently fingering the ring, her thoughts raced. Nothing about the guy in the authentic-looking Viking costume gave the impression of being cheap or sleazy. His appearance, manner and accent were impeccable. The man on her doorstep was clearly a high-class male escort—which was a nice name for prostitute—hired by her late grandmother's executor.

Apparently, Varik the Bold here was Bekka's final parting gift to her granddaughter, to keep her from feeling alone and abandoned on her birthday.

Delaney appraised the hunk of prime beef, amazed at his accurate portrayal. It was as if Rebekka Eriksen had the power to see what was in her granddaughter's mind and then custom ordered a perfect replica. Her heart skipped a beat as she took in the Viking's sensuous lips, the glimmer in his eyes.

Lord, she was so tired of being good, of being proper. She'd been a good girl her entire life, always doing the right thing, always putting others first. She'd been a good daughter, a good sister, and a good loyal wife, who'd never considered cheating on her husband. And what did all that goodness get her? Not even a lousy bar of fundraiser chocolate—just a great big bagful of heartache and grief.

Now here he was, standing half-naked on her doorstep. Her chance to finally shed her good girl image...to do something bad, something frivolous and naughty and exciting in real life instead of just in her private fantasies.

"Why not?" Delaney said just above a whisper, shrugging one shoulder as he smiled down at her. "What could it hurt? Who would know?"

"So...yes? You help? Play?"

He was the perfect incarnation of her lifelong Viking dreams. How many people got a chance to experience, to actually physically touch, their dreams in the flesh? How could she consider passing up this once in a lifetime opportunity, especially after her beloved grandma had made a point to sanction this sexy rendezvous as one of her last acts before leaving the earth?

Delaney's belly churned with excitement and uncertainty. No decent woman would ever conceive of doing what she wanted to do.

Oh hell, decency be damned!

She could be bold, brazen and devil-may-care just this once in her lousy goody-two-shoes life. Lots of women did this sort of thing every day without turning into pillars of salt. Tomorrow, after tasting life as a shameless hussy, she'd gladly go back to her lonely, monotonous existence.

"Men do it all the time," Delaney reasoned absently, her gaze locked on his broad chest. "Satisfy themselves with prostitutes." Her gaze shifted to his handsome Nordic features. "I'm all for equal opportunity."

The Viking angled his head, looking clueless again. On him it looked cute. Hot. Sexy.

"You prostitute?" His naïve expression curved into a curious smile.

Delaney laughed. "Oh that's rich. Very funny. I like a man with a sense of humor. Roger didn't have one." Her gaze hardened at the unsavory memory.

"All right, *Varik the Bold*," she gave an exaggerated wink while hooking invisible quotes around his preposterous title, "I suppose we can play. My grandma would never engage anyone for the job who hadn't been thoroughly vetted beforehand. If an elderly woman put her stamp of approval on her granddaughter doing the horizontal mambo with a one-time lover, who am I to argue? I should graciously accept her generosity and indulge, right?"

"*Jeg forstar ikke*...eh, sorry, mean not understand. Much talk so fast." His fingers moved, mimicking chatter.

"Oops, sorry." Delaney giggled. "I tend to babble when I'm nervous." She also tended to giggle. "But I'm sure you can understand why I'm edgy since I've never done anything like this before." She appraised him yet again, deciding that having sex with a Viking would be much more satisfying than chomping on a few measly pieces of chocolate.

Taking in a deep breath, she exhaled with a whoosh, imagining her next "Delaney's Diary" column...*Dear Diary: Today I rabidly jumped the bones of a too sexy to believe Viking prostitute lovingly sent to me by my deceased grandmother...*

She blinked. Perhaps some things in her life should remain private.

"Okay, Varik the Bold, how—"

"Okay?" he cut in, gifting her with another smile. She'd be lying if she said his eagerness wasn't flattering.

"Right...how much did my grandmother's estate pay you?"

"Pay?"

"You know, money?" She rubbed her thumb against her fingers.

"Ah, *penger.*"

Delaney shrugged. "Whatever. And how long do I get to keep you?"

The Viking angled his head again and stared. She couldn't tell if he was truly dumbfounded or just trying to stay in character.

"Well?" Folding her arms across her chest, she tapped her toe against the floor, doing her best to look perturbed. She wasn't really impatient, she just didn't want him thinking she was too easy, which was probably stupid because, honestly, why should she care what a male prostitute thought of her?

He shook his head, as if to clear it. "How long you keep me?" He thumped his chest.

She nodded. "Yeah. How many hours? One, two?" She held up her fingers and he gave her that strange look again, which should have made her irritated as hell by this time but it didn't because he was so adorable she was tempted to lick him. All over.

"This would be a lot easier if they sent a guy who could speak English."

"Sorry bad English." He nodded.

"You know," she narrowed her gaze at him, "you should stop pretending you can't speak or understand English. Most Norwegians speak it fluently."

"*Ja*," he offered an apologetic shrug. "Fault of *bestefar*...eh, grandpa."

"So it's your grandfather's fault that you can't speak English?" He nodded again. Delaney didn't have a clue what the hell he was talking about. "Look, if the accent is phony you can drop it now, otherwise this will take too much time."

"Time?"

Growling in frustration, Delaney tapped her bare wrist to indicate a watch. "Yes, time."

"Time be play fast."

Apparently the accent was legit.

"So it's one hour?" She pointed to her wrist again, then held up her index finger.

"No. Play two hour."

Two hours? Delaney couldn't imagine what they could possibly do for that long. It only took Roger three minutes, tops. Since the Viking had been paid to satisfy her, maybe they could spend the other hour and fifty-seven minutes cuddling and talking, something Roger never did.

"I guess we'd better get down to business. I need to jump in the shower first. And I insist on you using a..." she felt her cheeks flush and she swallowed, "a, um...condom," she finally managed. It certainly wasn't the usual conversation she had with a man. "A prophylactic," she explained because he had that bewildered look again. "You know, a rubber. No matter how clean you are, understand?"

Without waiting for an answer, Delaney snagged his arm. "You'll catch your death of cold standing out there half naked." She pulled him through the doorway then pushed the door shut. "Besides, just because I'm about to do the deed," she rolled her eyes at the thought, "the whole neighborhood doesn't need to know about it."

Chapter 5

~<>~

SHE AND VARIK glanced around the room. With his appearance at her door, she'd completely forgotten about the disgusting disaster Thursday had created.

"I'm sorry about the mess...and the smell, but my dog got into the chocolate and," she made a sweeping gesture, "this is the result." She uttered a sigh. What a pity her shameless trollop opportunity had to be tainted with dog puke.

At that moment the big mutt, head hung low and limbs shaking, braved a tentative path into the living room.

"This is Thursday, the wretched hound responsible for all of this," Delaney explained.

The Viking held out a hand and Thursday sniffed it. After sniffing the stranger's crotch and butt, the dog seemed satisfied. With nary a growl, he planted himself next to the Viking's long leg.

Delaney hadn't expected that. "He took to you right away. Thursday isn't usually that cordial with strangers."

"Ahh, Thor's Day," Varik the Bold said, petting the dog. Lapping up the attention, Thursday lavishly swiped his tongue across the Viking's thigh. A similar gesture to what Delaney had in mind. "Good Viking name." Varik's smile stole her breath away while whipping her hormones into a frenzy of sexual longing.

"Yes." Delaney returned the smile, just standing there ogling the eye candy while trying to convince herself this was all really happening. "Uh, anyway, my bedroom's in worse shape than the living room, so we can't do, um...*it* in there. The room I use for my writing. It's got a small sofa bed that I recently slipcovered in the cutest pink and yellow flower material that I found at a church rummage sale for next to nothing, so we can use that instead."

When he didn't respond she became edgier. "I made matching throw pillows too. They turned out so cute." She could feel her smile grow ridiculously wide. "I added a strip of cornflower blue braided trim to the pillow edges, then I took little white pearls and—"

Varik's vacant stare finally prompted her to shut her big fat motor mouth.

His expression came as no surprise to Delaney. After listening to the veritable bucket of mindless verbosity spilling from her lips, no wonder the poor man's eyes glazed over. Wringing her hands, she blamed her babbling on her whopping case of nerves...along with her inexperience at being a wanton woman.

She watched the Viking as he scanned the catastrophe her living room had become. The man certainly was substantial—tall, ripped and solid. "I hope the sofa bed's big enough to fit us both," she said absently.

"Fault of Thor's Day?" He pointed to the mess. Closing her eyes, Delaney nodded. When she opened them again, the Viking was waving a chastising finger at her dog. "Not nice, Thor's Day. *Skam deg.*" The dog dropped on his back, baring his belly in submission, again mirroring an action at the forefront of Delaney's thoughts.

Oh good grief, she'd become a sex-crazed slut in less than thirty minutes.

"I say shame on you," Varik translated.

Nodding, Delaney felt sure she'd be busy reprimanding herself with a round of *skam deg* as soon as the Viking left. But now wasn't the time to think of that.

"Not that you even care," she licked her lips fretfully, "but I feel the need to tell you that I've never done anything like this before. Have sex with a paid male escort, I mean. Or any stranger, for that matter. In fact..." she felt her cheeks burn, "to be quite honest, I'm sort of rusty. I haven't had sex in more than a year, since my ex left me for one of his college students."

"Sex?"

Nodding, Delaney rambled on, "I'm not experienced in anything, um...advanced. Roger, that's my ex, wasn't open to trying anything imaginative in the bedroom. It was pretty much straight missionary style sex, if you know what I mean." She gestured with one hand flat on top of the other.

Varik gaped at her, repeating the word. "Sex?"

Delaney's shoulder hiked in a shrug. "Naturally I wouldn't be telling you all this personal stuff about my sex life if you weren't a professional. I just thought it might help if you knew the whole situation before we get to the sex part."

Varik the Bold frowned. "To understand..." He straightened, elevating one eyebrow and clapping a hand to his chest as he eyed her. "You want me sex?"

Delaney gulped. Well hell. He was going to make her say it...ask for it. He looked so fierce, so imposing when he frowned. His size and deliberate manner were intimidating...and exceptionally sexy.

His question was straightforward, but not easy to answer. Of course she wanted him. What woman in her right mind wouldn't? But voicing her desire was easier said than done. Delaney had never been particularly bold when it came to discussing sex. Any such talk made Roger squirm, and not in a good way.

"Yeah, sure, why not?" She attempted to sound nonchalant. "As long as you made the trip and got all costumed up in your Viking gear, we may as well do it, right?"

"Do it? Sex?"

"Oh for heaven's sake, yes. Yes! I want to have sex with you." Her hands flew into the air, then crashed at her sides. "There, I said it. Are you satisfied?"

The Viking grinned and nodded. He was all flashing blue eyes, white teeth and irresistible charm.

"Understand." He scooped Delaney up into his arms as if she weighed no more than a bar of fundraiser chocolate. Before she could blink, he kissed her, plundering her mouth with his tongue. Lord, the man knew how to kiss!

"Wow…" Delaney whispered once their lips parted. "They must teach you guys all sorts of amazing carnal techniques at male escort school." She couldn't wait to find out what else he'd learned.

Still cradling her in his arms, Varik strode across the room, sidestepping the putrid blotches of dog barf. Delaney pointed to her office.

"In there," she said, surprised at how husky her voice had become. "I'll get the sofa bed ready and jump in the shower." In the room, his smoldering expression had every muscle in her body liquefying. He kissed her again. It seemed he had no intention of setting her on her feet.

"Varik, you have to put me down," she said on a satisfied sigh after the spellbinding kiss. "It's okay if I call you Varik, isn't it?" Her finger twirled circles on the bare area of his chest. "I mean, your real name doesn't matter since this is my birthday fantasy, right? It's probably better if I just think of you as Varik the Bold because I'll never see you again after today."

He just smiled again, without making a move to release her. She'd never had a man gaze at her like he wanted to devour her before. It was unsettling…in the best possible way.

"Down, Varik." She pointed to the floor. "Me, down."

"Yes, down." After setting Delaney on her feet, Varik gently eased her to the carpet, straddling her.

"No!" She gasped as her hand flew against his chest. "I meant—" Varik's mouth opened over hers in ravenous demand. His taste was so appetizing it scattered her senses. "Wait, wait…*wait a minute*!" she said as soon as they came up for air. It was getting awfully hard to think straight because those professional kisses of his had a drugging effect. "Me dirty. Understand?"

"Dirty sex?" Varik's eyebrows jiggled playfully.

Desire radiated deep in her belly as she imagined all sorts of deliciously naughty scenarios. "No! Oh for heaven's sake, Varik. I feel like we're playing me Tarzan, you Jane. How am I supposed to make you understand?" She grumbled in frustration.

"Not understand." Varik glowered. "You not Tarzan. Me not Jane. I be Varik. You be who?"

She touched her chest. "I be...I mean, I am Delaney."

"Delaney?"

"Mmm-hmm. I know, it's an unusual name. I like it better as an adult than I did as a kid. Kids at school called me Del, which I hated because of all *The Farmer in the Dell* jokes. My full name is Delaney Malone. It used to be Kullerton but I took back my maiden name after the divorce...from Roger. Roger always called me Del, even though I'd asked him not to because I dislike it but he did it anyway." She gazed up at him in wonder. "Didn't they include my name in your work order, or whatever the escort service calls it?"

Damn. She'd been babbling again. Varik's slack-jawed expression told her his brain had probably short circuited due to extreme verbal overload.

She had one chance to create a perfect memory and she was blowing it. Why couldn't she handle this tryst with grace and sophistication instead of like a bumbling fool?

Her gaze slipped from his face to his chest. A whimper escaped as Delaney's mouth went dry. When her gaze journeyed further south to the Viking's nether regions, she found herself wondering if that particular area was as bold and impressive as the rest of him.

As if in response to her lustful musings, he pressed against her.

If she'd known a Viking song of joy, she would have belted it out just then.

Oh good grief. What had happened to her? She used to be a proper, conventional wife who never thought about strange men's nether regions...or exploring their broad chests with her tongue. She'd been a chaste wife during the entire time she and the unfaithful Professor Ratfink were married.

That was then.

Now her lascivious desire for the Viking obliterated everything else. Her clothes scratched against her hot skin. There was amazing stuff going on inside her she couldn't even define. If she felt this good now, she could hardly imagine what she'd feel like once she and her paid escort with the substantial family jewels got down to the business of—

"Delaney." His voice was as deep and seductive as the look in his eyes. "Good name. I like."

Spilling from Varik's lips, *Delaney* sounded like poetry. She'd never think of her name the same way again.

"You have to let me up, Varik."

"Up?"

She nodded. "You, me, up."

"Dirty sex up?"

Delaney dissolved into laughter. "I have absolutely no clue what you mean but—" She stopped herself from adding, *frankly, it sounds good and I have a feeling I'd probably like it.*

Scooting out from under him, she scrambled to her feet as images of raw, sweaty vertical sex danced across her mind. She'd never done it that way, didn't even know if it was possible or just something they did in those romance novels she read. But one look at the tall, muscled Viking told her if it were at all feasible, he'd definitely be able to pull it off.

"Just so you know, I was this close," she held her thumb and forefinger an inch apart, "to being a virgin when I got married so...I'm not really very experienced."

"Virgin?" His eyebrow elevated.

"Well no, not anymore...but I used to be." She rolled her eyes at her idiotic response. "Well of course everyone was once. I just meant that..."

Good God, she needed to just shut the hell up.

Reclining on his side, Varik levered himself up on one elbow, propping his head on his fist. He gazed at her as if she were a three-scoop banana split draped with hot fudge. Even if he'd been trained to do that at escort school, it still made her feel like a sexy Viking queen.

"Not worry. I be tenderly with Delaney, *ja*?"

"*Ja*," she repeated with what she feared was a dopey grin.

She glanced at the decades-old Kodak Instamatic camera her mother forgot to take home with her after she'd stopped by for dinner the other night. Disregarding the teasing she got from Delaney and the rest of her kids, Astrid refused to give up the camera she and her late husband had used to take all the family photos as the kids were growing up.

Delaney practically knew her mother's refrain by heart: "I don't know, maybe it's silly but I think there's something special about this old camera, and holding an actual photograph in your hands, then keeping it in an album. So you young people can keep taking photos with your phone cameras. I'm sticking with my trusty vintage model."

The old camera gave Delaney a deliciously naughty idea. Kodak in hand, she asked, "Um...do you mind if I take your picture? As long as it's not prohibited by the escort service. It would be a wonderful memento. Plus," she shrugged, "I doubt I'll ever have the opportunity to snap a photo of Varik the Bold, my very own personal Viking, again."

"*Fotografi?*" He touched his chest in question. "*Ja* sure." He got to his feet. "Like this?" Drawing his sword and positioning his shield, he posed.

He looked so tantalizing every nerve ending in her body quivered. Expelling a dreamy sigh, she nodded. "Yeah...exactly like that. Just let me pop in one of the flashcubes and..." She snapped the first photo.

After she'd taken half a dozen, he held out his hand. "Now together." Embracing Delaney with one arm, he held the camera in his other hand pointing the lens toward them. The film counter showed two shots left. She made a mental note to take another couple photos to use the film up as soon as he left, then take it in to get it developed. Immediately.

"I guess this is how they took selfies in the old days," she quipped, met by Varik's quizzical expression. She couldn't help smiling, certain this would be the best selfie ever.

These photos wouldn't end up in a coffee table album. She'd keep them in her nightstand drawer to gaze at longingly at...special times. Imagining the raised eyebrows of the film developers upon seeing her gorgeous Viking made her cheeks grow warm.

"*Rosa kinn,*" Varik said, touching her cheeks. She didn't need a translation to figure out he'd noticed her blush.

Gesturing to the wall clock, he added, "Must sex now so I play." An engaging smile lit his face.

"Ah yes...the clock is ticking." After draping a fresh sheet over the sofa bed, Delaney stood in the doorway, raising a finger. "I'll be right back after my shower. I'll be fast." She walked out of the room, then popped her head back in. "Don't go anywhere."

"I stay." Pointing to her phone, Varik asked, "I *telefon?* Need for lock."

Not sure what he meant, she said, "You need to make a phone call?" He nodded. "Sure, go ahead." She scurried out of the room. Her desire for the Viking had escalated from smoldering to an aching, aggressive heat. It was murder to walk away from him at that moment, especially since her time with him was counting down, but after the rotten day she'd had, she felt grimy.

Besides, she certainly couldn't have Varik the Bold peel off her clothes to find sturdy white cotton underwear. No, if Grandma Bekka went to the trouble to send her a sexy bought and paid for Viking stud, the least Delaney could do was sex herself up a little.

Everything had to be as perfect as possible. The memory she'd lock away must be remarkable enough to sustain her for a lifetime. That meant she had to be clean and wearing... What? She didn't own anything even remotely sexy.

Roger had never shown any interest in embellishing their sex life with seductive garments, candles or champagne. It was nothing but practical basics for him. Delaney hadn't bothered buying sexy nighties since Roger didn't care, and because he kept their bedroom only moderately warmer than their refrigerator. So it was flannel nightgowns and pajamas for the cold months and oversized T-shirts for summer nights.

About to give up hope, Delaney remembered she owned one alluring Christmas outfit. She'd purchased it online during their first year of marriage, before she'd learned Roger was an unimaginative stick in the mud who loathed anything holiday-related. She'd only worn it once, taking it off when he frowned, expressing his displeasure at what he called her cheap, tawdry, streetwalker getup.

Other than prancing back into the room buck naked after her shower—and she definitely didn't have the confidence for that—the holiday outfit was her only choice. At least it was sexy. She hoped. She also hoped the decade-old getup still fit.

She gave a dismissive wave, reminding herself that it didn't really make a damn bit of difference how good she did or didn't look in the outfit, or out of it for that matter. She'd never see the Viking again. The guy was probably paid to tell her she looked great even if she wore a burlap sack.

She padded into her bedroom, dug the outfit out of the deepest recess of her closet and headed for the shower. She'd almost tossed the outfit in the trash after Roger's less than enthusiastic response, but she held on to it, hoping one day he'd become more playful in the bedroom.

Once she was clean and fixed up as pretty as she could make herself, Delaney took a deep breath and walked down the hallway. Varik must have located her music app, tuning in to classical selections, because she heard the inviting melody of Debussy's "Clair de Lune" playing softly in the background. Yes...*this* was the time for classical music.

Before reaching the room she spotted the golden flicker of candlelight. She had one large pedestal candle in the room that he must have spotted. She was amazed the man had taken the time to set the stage with mood music and lighting, making this one time experience even more memorable for her.

Then she reminded herself that these were probably exactly the sort of extras he was paid to think of.

Crossing her fingers, praying she looked alluring, Delaney turned the corner, entering the room.

As soon as he saw her, Varik's eyes popped.

And as soon as she saw him, her eyes popped.

"Delaney!" He leapt to his feet, naked except for his helmet and the round shield strategically positioned in front of his Viking family jewels. "You be Mrs. *Julenissen.*" His grin, wide and genuine, lit his eyes, forming little crinkle lines at the outside corners.

The name tickled Delaney's memory. "Right, Mrs. Claus," she confirmed, recalling Grandma Bekka's stories about Norway's version of Santa. "Boy, the escort service sure didn't skimp at filling you in on background information, did they?"

She patted the white-fur-trimmed red velvet panties and matching pushup bra. The elastic in her panties was dried out and crackly, which, she supposed, is what happens to ten-year-old elastic. She hoped the panties stayed put until it was time to remove them.

"I'm sorry," she shrugged, "it's the only semi-provocative thing I own." The panties started a slow glide down her hips and she tugged them up.

"No be sorry." He shook his head slowly. In a low, sexy rumble, Varik told her, "You so beauty. Much sexy." He held up one finger. "Delaney stay." He moved toward the camera, holding it as he squatted with his shield still covering his dangly Viking bits. "These *fotografi* for Varik after develop."

Drumming up her confidence, Delaney posed as beguilingly as she could for the hired Viking while Varik snapped the last two shots left in the camera. Apparently he wanted to add her picture to his wall of...what was it they called a male prostitute's female clients? Not Johns. Jills maybe? In any case, he'd never see the shots because they'd never see each other again.

He gave her a slow appraisal. His smile was different now. Hot. Hungry. Expectant. So steamy it made Delaney's toes curl, which wasn't evident because of the matching fur-trimmed red velvet stiletto-heeled ankle boots she teetered on—the ones with the turned-up elfin toes with jingle bells attached at the ends.

She didn't even want to think about the single silver bells centered on each breast or the jingly cluster sewn into the white ball of fur on her butt.

Until Varik flicked the bells on her bra.

One lousy little jingle had her moaning. God she was easy.

She watched as his smile turned almost feral.

Snapping one of the bells, he informed her, "Make happy sex." His grin was slow, suggestive, wicked. "Then we go play." He advanced until his legs were on either side of hers. His Viking shield pushed snug against her belly while one of his big hands cupped her butt, kneading and stroking her cheeks. His touch had her squirming against him in response.

"Whatever you say, Varik. You're the expert. Or should I say sexpert?" She laughed at her silly quip, then let her head drop back so she could look up at him. It was weird and wonderful being with a man she didn't tower over. He was so tall, probably a good six-six, she felt like a sprite next to him. There was nothing more delicious for a towering, amply-padded woman than to feel positively diminutive next to a brawny man.

She smiled, tracing the outline of his jaw with her thumb. "Just how big are you, anyway?"

"Big." He tossed his shield aside and ground against her.

Holy Moses... The escort service obviously employed only the cream of the crop.

Unable to resist, Delaney backed up enough to look down. "Oh my word! You're..."

"*Ja.* Big," he finished for her.

She clutched his chest with one hand while the other hand curled over his biceps. Before she knew what she was doing, her hands happily, shamelessly, traveled down his back and grabbed his butt. Those Viking buns were of mythic quality.

Dear Diary: Grandma Bekka may have been old, but she clearly knew how to choose a stud.

A smile tickled at Delaney's lips when she pictured the old woman scrutinizing a stack of male escort photos and selecting the perfect Viking for her granddaughter.

"Be sex with Delaney now." Varik looked stern and mighty as he nudged her toward the sofa bed. "Inside you." He nudged harder. "Make you melt under my flaming eyes."

It was amazing how much the man could convey in so few nonsensical words.

At a rare loss for words, Delaney stood mesmerized. When the back of her knees hit the edge of the sofa bed, her panties conveniently slid down until the jingle-belled backside met the mattress.

Giving a gentle shove, Varik straddled her, devouring her with his gaze as he tugged the bell-trimmed cups of her bra down, exposing her breasts. The look in his eyes and the raw groan rumbling deep in his chest delighted Delaney to no end.

"Plenty." Varik's hands closed over her breasts. "Big beauty." He slipped his hands beneath her, unhooked her bra and snatched it from her chest, tossing it aside with a jingle.

Delaney felt hot, flushed and completely exposed under his unwavering stare. His mishmash mixture of accented words, as strange as they sounded, were the most beautiful any man had ever spoken to her.

He took his time playing with her, showing such loving appreciation of her that Delaney almost cried. He seemed to enjoy all the preliminaries, the foreplay Roger could never be bothered with. The difference in technique between her ex and her Viking was incalculable.

"Oh Varik," she sighed absently, "this is my dream come true. You just can't imagine..."

Releasing her for a moment, he reached up to grasp his great horned helmet. "Sorry. Forget take off."

"Oh...no." She stilled his arm. "I'd...I'd rather you left it on." She felt certain her cheeks blushed crimson. "Part of the Viking fantasy, you know?"

"Viking fantasy sex?" She nodded. "Understand. Viking make fantasy sex to beauty Delaney now." His gaze was intent, taunting, sensual.

Lost in the sensuality of the moment and charming cadence of his admiring words, she was only vaguely aware when Varik opened a condom packet with his teeth and sat back on his heels to roll it on. After her earlier demands that he use a prophylactic, she'd forgotten all about it. No doubt men of his trade were schooled to ensure both his safety and hers.

He made love to her. That's the only way she could describe their union. *Sex* would be too pedestrian a word for the way he pleasured her in ways she'd only read about. Varik treated her as if she were a cherished treasure, worthy of adoration. His warm, admiring smile and growling sounds of enjoyment boosted Delaney's joy quotient to a new level.

She relished the feel of her Viking's idyllic masculine body. He was every bit as magnificent as her dreams and fantasies. Everything about their joining was perfect, so much so that she feared he might suddenly disappear and she'd discover he'd been nothing but a divine hallucination.

Her hands roamed his muscles. She'd never had the pleasure of being skin to skin with anyone like Varik before. Roger's physique was thin and soft...like a squishy pillow with bones. Varik was hard and firm in all the right places and supple where it counted.

Sex with Roger would have been over long ago and she'd be up making him a pot of green tea by now. As her time and pleasure with Varik progressed, Delaney no longer had any trouble imagining how to spend two blissful hours in bed with a man.

Sensing her initial timidity and apprehension, Varik was patient, considerate, whispering beautiful foreign words in her ear and gently massaging her tense muscles. Once her nervousness subsided,

Delaney found herself responding to her Viking in bold ways that surprised her, and seemed to delight Varik.

"Such goodness you be. Excellent happiness you sex make me."

She feathered a kiss across his lips. "I guess when you have sexual relations with a skilled professional, reacting appropriately just comes naturally." Saying nice things to her was probably part of the services her grandma had paid for—no doubt Bekka had opted for their premium package. But for now, Delaney pretended he really meant them.

Her mind wandered as they enjoyed each other. The Viking must have passed Sex 101 with flying colors at escort school, because he knew exactly how to satisfy a woman. She wondered if he had a specialized degree...something like Bachelor of Orgasm. She was confident Varik, or whatever his real name was, had been at the head of all his sex classes.

Just when she thought she'd experienced the ultimate in ecstasy, he did this amazing twisty thing that had her writhing and caught up in a lingering moan.

"Good?" Varik asked.

"Incredible." He must have hit some internal erogenous zone of hers, just like he had GPS. Until that moment, she figured they'd neglected to equip her with one of those spots when she was created. Of course, that's before she'd encountered a man who lettered in sex.

She sighed, succumbing to the sweet sensation of a man's strong but gentle hands cherishing her. He slowed his rhythm, folding his body over hers until his lips were a mere breath away.

"Delaney beauty make my heart melt," he whispered, capturing her mouth in a drugging kiss. Varik's words and gestures seemed so heartfelt, so sincere, they brought tears to her eyes. It was increasingly difficult to remember he was nothing more than a paid escort, superbly trained in the art of satisfying a woman.

But she didn't want to dwell on that during one of the most perfect, glorious moments of her life.

"You're my very own Varik the Bold." Her voice was low and throaty. "All mine. Every delicious, scintillating, magnificent inch of you. Just for tonight." She slid her hands over his torso, exploring the unyielding muscle beneath her fingertips. "Just for these two, magical, beautiful hours," she whispered, vowing to imprint the moment on her mind forever.

Varik's smile left her breathless. "Not just tonight. I always be Varik the Bold for Delaney. Love make sex to you many time, many night."

"God help me," Delaney said through a husky chuckle, "if I could afford it I'd take you up on it. Every Saturday night, at least." Something akin to a tornado whirled inside her as he worked his sensual magic. Whatever was coming had such power and intensity it almost frightened her. Gasping, she clutched at his biceps, digging her fingers in hard.

"Relax. Be happy." He kissed her. Not just her mouth, but her nose, her eyes, her chin, her cheeks. "I take you visit Valhalla," he vowed. "We go Viking heaven together."

An instant later, Varik the Bold kept his promise.

Chapter 6

~<>~

UNACCUSTOMED TO HEARING his mistress in the throes of rapture, Thursday valiantly galloped into the room, barking and doing a fine impression of a vicious attack dog. Unfazed by Thursday's ominous warning, Varik rolled over to the edge of the sofa bed and sat up.

Extending his hand, he smiled, speaking calmly in Norwegian, inviting Thursday closer. He praised the dog, clapped Thursday's flanks and scratched him behind the ears. Soon Thursday was on his back, tongue lolling and belly exposed. A moment later, the dog happily nestled himself in a corner with a rawhide bone.

Varik had succeeded in winning him over for all time, just like he'd done with Delaney.

She smiled at her chocolate-stealing canine protector and then at the man who'd just turned her world upside down in the most remarkable way. Reclining next to her again, he tucked Delaney close, spooning her from behind. She heard herself sigh for the umpteenth time since they'd been together. She couldn't help it. He was just so perfect, so right, so made to order.

Life would never be the same after Varik. It couldn't be. She may as well become a nun after this. Why bother having sex with any other man? Once you've been made love to by a well-schooled Viking, what could possibly compare?

The memory of tonight's scintillating lovemaking would last her a lifetime. On cold, frosty nights, when she was ninety and her old bones creaked, good old Thursday would huddle at her feet and Delaney would sip hot cocoa. Opening her special, private photo album, she'd recall this one magical interlude with her fantasy Viking come to life.

Another sigh.

"Thank you, Varik." He stroked her skin and nibbled her ear in response and she melted against him. "It was a beautiful, sexy fantasy. You made it so romantic too. You're worth every cent they pay you." Delaney entwined her fingers with his, pretending Varik had enjoyed their time together even a tenth as much as she had.

"No. Thank *you*," he insisted. He turned her on her back, kissing her deeply, tenderly. "For make Varik great happy."

The next kiss was even better, embellishing her memories with richly woven fantasy that she'd lock away in a secret part of her heart forever.

He knew exactly what to say to set her heart aflutter, to build her self-esteem. His kisses were extraordinary, far too incredible not to be the product of superior kissing education. She envisioned a large room with a banner emblazoned across the front reading Acme Escort School: Kissing 101. There'd be sizeable pull-down maps of the anatomy, flowcharts depicting the correct placement of the tongue within the mouth and how to move it in such a way that it drives the kiss recipient mad.

A roomful of hunky men would take notes as they watched instructional videos, then they'd practice their techniques on anatomically correct blowup dolls. For their final exam, they'd demonstrate what they'd learned on a human subject. Delaney shook away the image of a sexy chick outfitted in a leather bustier, fishnet stockings and stiletto heels floating across her mind.

"Something is wrong?" Varik stroked her arm from shoulder to fingertips. He was on his side, head braced on his hand, gazing at Delaney with thoughtful attention.

"No, nothing at all." She caressed his face, studying every inch of it and committing it to memory. "I was just thinking how sad and lonely it will be tomorrow when you're not here."

His hands cupped her face and he gazed into her eyes. "No sad. No lonely. Varik here now."

Delaney wrapped her arms around the back of his neck, drawing him close. "I know," she whispered, kissing him, thinking how unfair it was to burden a stranger with her insecurities. He might get paid to pacify sad, lonely women, but she really didn't want to taint their time together by being too needy. It was important to focus on the moment instead of what she'd be feeling after he left.

"This Delaney?" Varik picked up the Lifestyle section of the Northwest Suburban Gazette from the edge of the sofa bed, tapping her photo. Delaney had folded the paper to the page with her "Delaney's Diary" column earlier.

"Yup. That's me."

"I read when Delaney putting Mrs. *Julenissen*."

"You read my column while I was getting ready?" Utter astonishment was evident in her voice. Her own husband couldn't be bothered to even glimpse at her writing and here a complete stranger had taken the time to look at her column, even though the man could barely speak English.

"Could you understand it?"

"Some." Varik held his thumb and forefinger an inch apart. He crinkled his brow as he asked, "What watching submarine races mean?"

Delaney's fingers flew to her lips and she laughed. "Oh that...well, it's from a story my mom told me about a date she'd gone on back in high school. The boy drove them down to the lake, telling her they were going to watch the submarine races. And my naïve mom believed him."

"Ahhh," Varik's head bobbed and he grinned. "*Han lurte henne*...eh, he fooling her, *ja?*" Delaney gave a confirming nod. "Good writing. Funny."

Her eyes welled with tears. Cupping his face, she smiled. "Not only are you the sexiest Viking ever, you're also a truly sweet soul. Thank you, Varik." She gave him a chaste kiss. What a gem Grandma Bekka chose for her.

"Now I read *hver dag.*" Catching Delaney's confused expression, he amended, "Every day."

She knew there was no way Varik would ever bother reading her newly syndicated column again but just the fact that he'd say something so kind and thoughtful touched her heart.

A glint from his finger caught her attention. Awestruck, she lifted Varik's hand toward the light.

"I can't believe I didn't notice this before. Where did you get this?"

Turning his hand left and right, Varik wiggled his ring finger. "*Hjerte onske* ring." He appeared to be concentrating as his eyes closed in a long blink. "Heartwish," he translated a moment later, opening his eyes and smiling. "From *bestefar*...grandpa."

She heard Varik's intake of breath when she held up her hand, wiggling her fingers.

"I have one too, from my grandmother." The rings were nearly identical. It was clear that her ring and Varik's shared the same stone, halved, which validated her grandmother's story about Odin splitting the stone in two.

Good grief, what in the world was she thinking? There was no such thing as magic and certainly no such entity as Odin.

"Great magic inside," Varik claimed. His grandfather must have touted one of those magical tales about the ring's supernatural history too. Tracing along the broken edges of her stone and his, Varik pointed out, "You half, me half, see? Same stone. Odin break."

"Uh-huh," Delaney replied, not wanting to be the one to burst the guy's bubble. So he'd been told the same mystical story. She changed the subject to avoid further conversation about their doubtless dime a dozen rings.

Varik made the wondrous evening even more special by remaining with her long enough to snuggle and talk. The extra time in her Viking's arms made the experience flawless. The head honchos behind the escort service were no dummies. They'd obviously made it their business to study the female psyche, learning how to create the most satisfying and romantic experience from beginning to end. She'd have to find out the name of the business and send them a letter praising her Viking's thoughtful, considerate performance.

"Do you have a business card with your name and the name of the escort service? I want to let them know how pleased and satisfied I am with your...um...your level of professionalism and expertise."

"Business card?" Varik thought for a moment. "For job?" Delaney nodded. "No. Card come later."

"Are you going to tell me your real name? It's okay, I promise I won't tell." She winked and her fingertip trailed a path across his chest. She couldn't help touching him. They had so little time left together.

"Name Varik, I tell you before." He flexed, treating her to a bold pop of muscles. "And I bold." His beautiful smile followed.

She threaded her fingers through his long, sun-streaked hair. The Brunhilde helmet must have slipped off during some point in their escapades. It was a miracle neither of them was impaled by those sharp horns.

"Apparently they instruct you to keep up the pretense so the fantasy remains as genuine as possible for the customer."

"Sorry," he frowned, "not understand."

"It doesn't really matter. They must have someone on staff who can translate for you and the other foreign employees. Maybe an

English teacher? Otherwise it would be awfully difficult for you to understand all the particulars for each assignment." She smiled at Varik's clueless expression. "Translator? English teacher?"

"Learn English, *ja*. Varik cousin teach."

"Your cousin?" Delaney's eyes widened. "So this is a family enterprise, hmm?"

"*Ja*, family."

He pointed to the wall clock. "Sorry to go. I must be play." Feathering a kiss across Delaney's lips, Varik got up and gathered his Viking outfit, slipping into it as she watched in fascination.

So he was off to play with someone else. Well, at least she'd had him all to herself for this brief, enchanting interval. She'd miss his skilled, sensuous mouth, the exquisitely satisfying sex. Varik was every orgasmic fantasy she'd ever had, rolled into one perfect package.

The only minor flaw being that he was a male prostitute.

He clasped her arms, bringing Delaney to her feet. After embracing her, he said, "Put clothes now. Take Varik play, *ja*?"

Delaney's perfect little fantasy bubble burst at his insensitive request. "What?" she was surprised how much her voice sounded like a whimpering child. "You expect me to deliver you to your next play date?"

"Thank you." He put on his horned helmet. "We go now."

She jumped when her phone rang.

"You want who?" she said after answering. "Mr. Jenssen?" She looked at Varik who smiled and thumbed his chest. She held the phone out and he took it, speaking to the man on the other end, probably the dispatcher from his escort service telling Mr. Jenssen he was running overtime. Her sigh was louder than she'd intended as she padded into her bedroom and threw on a pair of jeans and a T-shirt.

"Lock man call, tell when coming," Varik told her when she returned. She followed him into the living room.

"Who?" She cocked her head, trying to decipher what the heck he was talking about.

Varik shook his head in seeming frustration. "Smith lock." He made a twisting motion with his hand. "Eh...locksmith," he corrected as he opened the front door and motioned to the townhouse unit a few doors down—the one that had been for sale for the past few months.

Delaney peeked around the hulk of male flesh, noting the for sale sign now read SOLD.

"Varik house." He proudly slapped his hand against his chest.

A jiggle of panic zigzagged up Delaney's spine.

"Your house?" He nodded and she broke out in goose bumps that had nothing to do with the frigid temperature outside. "You live there?"

"*Ja.*"

"Wait...you're my new neighbor? I have a Viking for a neighbor?"

She must be hallucinating. The stress of Thursday defiling her chocolate cache, followed by sizzling hot, mind-boggling sex with Varik the Bold had been too much for her. Maybe she'd fainted and was dreaming all this and didn't realize it. A quick pinch to her arm dissolved that theory.

Varik nodded. "Neighbor."

Her heart, brain and all internal organs imploded, oozing out of her toes to mingle with the putrid mess Thursday had left on the floor.

Still in possession of her vocal cords, she asked, ever so slowly to make sure he understood, "Are you telling me you're not a male prostitute? You're not a paid escort hired by Rebekka Eriksen's estate?"

Varik frowned. "You prostitute?"

"No! You are..." she bit her bottom lip, "aren't you?"

"Varik, prostitute?" He roared with laughter. "Delaney make funny joke."

Finding it difficult to breathe, Delaney heard a strangled sort of gack sound sputter up from her throat.

Oh God.

Oh God, oh God, oh God...

"Be happy. We neighbor now. Make much sex all the time." He cupped her face, sweeping a gentle kiss across her lips. "I be last Viking in play for childrens. Lock out. No key drive auto to play. Need go house of play. Go Delaney auto now, *ja*?"

That was the most he'd said at one time since the Viking first appeared on her doorstep.

"The community theater," a dazed Delaney muttered beneath her breath.

"*Ja*! Theater. Help Varik to play, please."

Excruciating realization emerged with an icy chill. "The annual winter play at the community theater," she said, recalling the ad in the paper and the posted flyers. "The Last Viking. You came to my house because you're locked out and need a lift to the theater?" Suddenly feeling crowded by his proximity, she took an involuntary step backward.

An enlightened grin spread across Varik's features. "Yes. Need a lift. Keys inside house. Sorry. Never be so stupid to do lock out before." Then he grabbed Delaney and kissed her, holding her tight against his chest. "But so happy we be sex together."

"Happy? *Happy*!" The unspoken rage of all her Norwegian and Irish ancestors combined swelled up inside her. "Well of course you're happy, you imposter! After you pretend to be my Valentine birthday Viking and drag me off for a cavalier roll in the hay. Of all the audacity!" She shoved him hard enough to elicit an ooph and catch Varik off balance so that he slipped off the icy front door stoop and fell backwards onto the frosty grass next to the walkway.

Delaney gasped as Varik's head clunked against the ground and his Brunhilde helmet skidded across the frozen lawn while he lay spread-eagle.

In her righteous state of ancestral rage she'd killed him!

"Oh my God! Varik, I'm so sorry. I didn't mean for that to happen. Are you all—" Rushing to his side, she slipped on the same patch of ice he had and went sailing, landing face to face on top of Varik with enough force to knock the wind out of them both.

Varik bellowed a groan. Not a sexy kind of groan, but more of a 'you crushed my balls and I'm dying' kind of groan. And because of that, Delaney was relatively certain the thunderous foreign chatter that followed meant something other than 'Don't worry, Delaney, I'm all right.'

The good news was that he was still alive.

For the moment.

As soon as she could move, Delaney rolled off Varik and knelt next to him. "I am *so* sorry, Varik." The only sign he was alive was the pained grimace etched across his handsome features. "Should I call a doctor?"

Opening his beautiful blue eyes, Varik did his best to crack a smile. "No. I strong. Not cry, Delaney." With obvious discomfort, he reached up and wiped the tears from her cheek with his thumb. She hadn't even realized she'd been crying. "I okay. Must be play now. Help Varik play?"

"Yes. Yes, of course." Once she got to her feet, she extended her hand, tugging Varik into a sitting position. He struggled not to show pain. The sour brine of humiliation and embarrassment spurting through her cells all but pickled Delaney's insides. Varik finally stood on his feet and gave her a half-hearted thumbs-up.

"Okay, don't move. Just stay right there." She patted the air. "I'll be right back." Carefully maneuvering on the ice, she reached her front door. "I'm going to open the garage." Talking to herself out loud like she was a crazy woman, Delaney grabbed her purse and keys, heading through the kitchen to the garage. When she opened it she saw the injured Viking straighten, standing tall, as if to show he felt no pain.

One glimpse at her Volkswagen Beetle had Varik's jaw dropping. "This Delaney auto?"

Eyeing Varik's considerable height, she knew what he must be thinking. "I got it used. It's all I could afford," she said with a shrug. Although she had her doubts he'd be able to fold himself into the diminutive car, since it was barely big enough for her own tall frame, she added, "It's a lot bigger inside than it looks." Varik didn't look convinced. She wasn't either.

"If Varik fit, maybe Varik never get out," he astutely noted.

"Well this is your only option. Come on. Be careful not to slip."

Conveying a leery expression, Varik followed her to her car, doing his best to make baby steps resemble a manly stride. She felt terrible about accidentally on purpose knocking him down.

"Are you sure you shouldn't see a doctor? I don't think you're in any condition to act in a play."

Full of bravado, he insisted, "Varik fine."

As the Viking struggled to fold his impressive bulk into the passenger seat of the small car, Delaney watched his muscles bunch and cord. It would have been a challenging enough task on its own, but to tackle it after she'd almost killed him made it more demanding.

"You must be freezing," she said, eying the pelts of wet fur covering just a portion of his gorgeous body once he'd managed to fit inside and close the door. "It has to be twenty-something outside."

Varik gave a nonchalant shake of his head, stopping when it connected with the roof of the car. "I be used to cold. I come from—"

"No, don't tell me. Let me guess." Delaney raised her hand. "You really are from Norway, right?"

"Oslo." He beamed a perfect white-toothed smile.

Her sigh of acceptance filled the car. "What about your real name. It can't possibly be Varik."

"*Ja*, Varik Jenssen."

"No." She shook her head. "That's not possible. Varik is just a made up name from a Viking storybook I read as a kid. Do you have any idea how incredible the odds are of your name actually being Varik? I mean, it would be too weird...like something right out of a science fiction movie."

"Too much words. Not understand." He pointed to her chest, revealing a knowing grin. "You be cold."

Delaney looked down at the telltale signs of coldness beading through her T-shirt. In all the commotion she'd forgotten a coat...or a bra.

"Keep your eyes on the road," she instructed, although she was the one doing the driving. "Just forget anything sexual happened between us because, trust me Mr. Jenssen, it is never, *ever*, going to happen again. Got that?"

"Angry Delaney pretty. Want Varik make pretty teats warm again?"

Delaney's jaw dropped. She socked him in the arm, determined to ignore the sudden crackle of desire. "I am not a cow. I don't have teats. You mean tits." As soon as the offensive word slipped past her lips, Delaney couldn't believe her own ears. She hated that crude term. "What I meant to say was—"

"Big tits," Varik said, clapping a hand on her breast.

So angry...or was it aroused...? So angrily aroused she could barely drive, Delaney slapped his hand away. "The word is breasts." And, God, how she wanted his attention on them again. "Don't talk to me while I'm driving. And don't touch me. Anywhere. Ever again."

Indifferent to her angst, he chuckled. "You love Varik *mannlig kjonnsorgan*." He grabbed his crotch. "Make Delaney happy."

Sucking in an audible gasp, Delaney nearly ran the car off the snowy road. "What!? Oh my God, I can't believe you just said that."

"In English is...cock, *ja?*"

"For heaven's sake...the correct term is penis, not—" She grumbled aloud. "Why am I even having this conversation? Never mind. Just forget it."

"Varik love you *skjede* too." Now his hand covered her crotch. "Mean posse in English."

"It's pussy. I'm not a sheriff," Delaney corrected, lifting his hand from between her thighs. Uttering a groan, she thumped the heel of her hand against her forehead. "Dear God, what the hell am I saying? I sound like a porn star..." She let out a gargantuan sigh. "Look, just knock it off, Varik. You're not funny or amusing or charming in the least," she lied. "Whether it's in Norwegian or English, I absolutely do not want to hear about tits, cocks, pussies, or any other body parts. Understand? That's just plain crude."

"Crude?"

"Yes. C-R-U-D-E, crude. Derogatory. Disrespectful. Insulting. Offensive. In America those terms you used are considered dirty and improper language in mixed company. Understand?"

"Varik *nedsettende...stotende*." His eyebrows knitted. "Very sorry for dirt words. But we make excellent sex, *ja?*" His concerned expression transformed into a self-satisfied smile.

"I especially do not want to talk about sex! Oh, good grief. Look, Mr. Jenssen, I am not that kind of woman."

His eyebrow lifted. "What kind?"

"The kind who...look, I don't even know you. We're total strangers. For Pete's sake, don't you understand? I thought you were a—"

He grasped Delaney's hand and pumped. "How you do? I Varik Jenssen. You neighbor. Now you know me." His endearing smile was hopeful.

Delaney hated that she laughed just then. "Varik, you are positively incorrigible."

His pleasant expression morphed into a frown. "Not know this word. Mean handsome? Big *mannlig kjonnsorgan*?" He jiggled his jewels. "Sexy man?" His eyebrows bounced devilishly.

In the blink of an eye she was back to fuming. "Stop. Just stop right there. This conversation is finished. Over. The end. I'm not kidding. I mean it."

Sure, it was flattering to have someone resembling a Norse god coming on to her, especially when he wasn't being paid to. But Varik wasn't flirting because he thought she was beautiful or nice or smart. It was because she was an easy lay. A lonely woman who'd dragged him in off the street and jumped his bones. The guy probably figured she was the neighborhood slut or a cheap hooker who just happened to live down the block. She couldn't blame him a bit.

"Why angry?" He rubbed her thigh, trailing his fingers up until they rested atop her perfectly satisfied posse. "I not make you excellent sex? Make happy travel to Valhalla?"

Excellent? The word didn't begin to do justice to what she'd experienced. There was no word, no phrase, no definition sufficient to describe the magic of being in his arms.

Lifting his hand from her crotch, she plopped it in his lap. After opening and closing her mouth a few times without uttering a word, she snapped it shut and looked straight ahead as she drove.

Pulling up to the community theater, she turned to him. "I'm not angry with you. Not really. What happened isn't your fault, it's mine. Try to understand, Varik. I am mortified, ashamed, embarrassed beyond words. I doubt I'll ever be able to look at you again without being reminded of my stupidity and how I threw myself at you."

"Eyes so sad." Varik brushed away the tear trickling down her cheek. "Not understand why sad be in Delaney eyes."

Having him be so sweet and endearing was almost more than she could bear. The big Viking just didn't get it and she was at a loss as to how to make him understand her abject humiliation. Maybe he'd figure it out when she was nowhere to be found tomorrow morning.

Dear Diary: Of course it was a chore gathering up all my worldly possessions and sneaking out of town before dawn, but I managed...

"You'd better get inside the theater," Delaney told him. "You don't want to be late for your play."

"*Takk*...eh...thank you."

She was glad she got to see his knockout smile once more. It was something she'd never forget. When Roger smiled, his lips quirked momentarily. When Varik smiled, it reached his eyes and his whole face lit up.

Unable to return his smile, Delaney said, "You're welcome." She wanted to add that it was her pleasure, but thought better of it. "Goodbye, Varik."

"Before goodbye," he said, his gaze intense as he clasped her hands, "need ask Delaney."

"Yes?" She did her best not to succumb to a dejected sigh.

The killer smile again. "You eat me tonight, *ja*?"

For the fortieth time that night, her eyes bugged and she gasped in outrage. "Oh my God! I will do no such thing! That does it, Varik. Get out of this car." He didn't move. He had the nerve to just sit there smiling at her. "You can just wipe that smartass grin right off your face, mister Viking imposter, and get out of my car. How dare you suggest that I—"

"*Kveldsmat.*" Varik gestured as if shoveling food into his mouth with a fork. "Supper, after play," he said. "You eat, me eat. Food."

"Oh." Delaney's tiny voice warbled like a baby chipmunk. Could she possibly be any more of a moron?

His lips quirked into a smile, soon followed by full-blown laughter. It was a beautiful sound and he was a beautiful man and, Lord help her, she did want to eat him.

"Understand now. Delaney so funny." He caressed her cheek. "Make me smile many time."

She touched his hand as he cupped her face. "Are you asking me to have dinner with you? Like...like a date?" She was pretty sure she batted her eyelashes just then. If she were a game show contestant, this is when a neon sign with EASY spelled in big block letters would flash overhead.

"*Ja.*" He nodded. "Dinner date." He gestured to her and to himself.

Delaney couldn't help smiling.

Dear Diary: This is no ordinary man. Varik is something special. He can make me swoon one moment, get my hackles up the next, and somehow manage to leave me laughing an instant later. Maybe I was wrong and he doesn't think I'm a tramp. Maybe he just thinks his new American neighbor is exceedingly hospitable...

Her hopeful smile grew. Maybe she wouldn't have to skip town after all. Maybe they could start over, begin anew, forget they'd ever—

"Then after dinner date, we be no clothes and make more excellent sex. *Ja?*"

"Get out of the car, Varik. Now."

Chapter 7

~<>~

CLUTCHING THE RING around her finger, Delaney woke up smiling Saturday morning. Varik had starred in her dreams. It was basically the same dream she'd had throughout the years but it seemed more tangible this time—so much so that she was sure the dream wouldn't end before the good part. She was frustrated when, once again, it stopped abruptly, before reaching a satisfying conclusion.

Aside from no ending, the only other thing spoiling her dream was waking up in an empty bed when she'd much rather be cozying up to the arrogant Viking. That, of course, was impossible now. She could never face the man again.

While it wasn't feasible for her to disappear into the night as she'd originally intended, she'd definitely have to put her townhouse up for sale as soon as possible and move. Far away. All the way to Oregon.

She smiled at the thought as she put on a pot of coffee. She could actually do it—move to Glassfloat Bay. Grandma Bekka had left her house and all of its contents for the family to share. Delaney's siblings, who already had places to stay, encouraged her to move into the house.

The Pacific Northwest weather was mild compared to Chicago, and she'd be living in a house close to the ocean. *The ocean*!

"I could have the Pacific Ocean as my backyard," she said with an easy smile. "Grandma's seaside cottage is sitting there waiting for me, already furnished and filled with her keepsakes."

Nope, she didn't need Chicago...and she didn't need her life cluttered up with any Vikings either.

Aside from what her family had told her and what she'd seen in movies, Delaney knew very little about Oregon. She'd have to Google it to prepare for her move.

"It'll be fun hiking along the Oregon Trail searching for Sasquatch. I can follow in the footsteps of Lewis and Clark as they searched for the Northwest Passage. Maybe I'll meet a handsome fur trapper wearing buckskins and a Davy Crockett coonskin cap who'll teach me how to catch salmon with a sharp twig, fall madly in love with me, and make me his frontier bride." The image triggered a dreamy sigh.

A moment later, her Wild West daydream was spoiled when the handsome trapper morphed into Varik. Delaney blinked away the intrusive image of her sexy new neighbor, momentarily reliving her humiliation.

After receiving Grandma Bekka's letter, Delaney had planned to move to Oregon as soon as she could scrounge up enough money. Under the circumstances, it would have to be sooner rather than later. If she were smart she'd just leave all her possessions behind, get on a plane and never come back.

Her gaze fell on the soiled carpet. Sucking in a deep breath, she mentally prepared herself for the nasty task ahead. "Coffee first," she muttered, pouring herself a mug.

Once she got down to the dirty business of scrubbing, Thursday was smart enough to steer clear. Everything would have cleaned up a lot easier if she'd taken care of it immediately after finding the mess last night, but unexpected hot Viking sex got in the way.

She winced as she scoured, hating to be reminded of how lamebrained she'd been. One big, sexy, bought and paid for Viking, courtesy of Grandma Bekka, indeed. The poor woman was probably rolling in her grave at the deplorable notion of her sending her granddaughter a male prostitute for her birthday. How could Delaney possibly allow herself to believe anything so preposterous?

"You big naive dope," she reprimanded herself, working furiously to brush out an ochre stain. "It's one thing to be lonely, but quite another to be lonely and pathetic."

Still lost in thought when the doorbell rang, Delaney ignored it. "Ha! Fool me once..." she said, recalling how she'd gleefully yanked the half-naked stranger on her doorstep into her spare room and—

The doorbell rang again.

Nope. No way. She wasn't in the mood for witty repartee with the Viking two doors down, no matter how irresistible or charming he was. It would be a long time before she could comfortably face him again, if ever.

Thoughts of a quick cross-country relocation were looking better and better.

Delaney listened as footsteps crunched on the icy walk leading away from her door. With visions of poor Varik slipping on the ice after she'd accidentally deliberately knocked him down, she vowed to remember to salt the sidewalk since the townhouse homeowners association kept neglecting to do it.

She peeked out the living room window in time to catch a glimpse of Varik, sans the sexy Viking getup and fully clothed, getting into his car and driving away. Once he was out of sight, she opened the door to find a box tied with red ribbon resting against it. A card with her name was taped to the box.

Her heart skipped a beat. She couldn't remember the last time a man had given her a gift... except for the set of do-it-yourself handyman books Roger gave her once for no particular occasion other than their compact townhouse was falling apart.

He was thoughtful that way.

Peeling off her rubber gloves and tossing them aside, Delaney carried the box inside, setting it on the kitchen table. She poured another cup of coffee and studied the package for a while, savoring the moment, drawing out the anticipation. The length of the box seemed too short for flowers. But what else would a man be sending after an evening of...

Sipping her coffee she smiled, feeling all toasty inside.

By all rights, she should return the box and card unopened—on her way to the airport for her long distance move. The last thing she wanted to do was encourage a man who thought she was the neighborhood hooker.

She nibbled her knuckle while studying the box. "Oh hell, I've got to open it." She felt like a kid at Christmas as she slid the ribbon down the box and removed the lid. Beneath the tissue, two ornate little figurines were huddled next to a handwritten letter.

"Ohhhh..." All it took was one glimpse of the letter's three-word greeting for her to surrender to a breathy sigh. Before getting to the meat of the letter, her eyes brimmed with tears...

~ ~ ~

Dear Beauty Delaney,

I writing this with translate book of Norwegian-English phrase. Please to be patience. I do my best for you to understand my terrifying English.

I think about you and me and sharing of intimate. Was very nice. I fright you feel shame and you worry I not respecting you after we intimate. Not so. Never thinking you be prostitute, Delaney. I thinking you smart, pretty woman with heart of kindness. Woman who maybe need kindness of good man.

We not knowing each another so much. I like to changing this fact. Liking for us soon be good, friendly neighbors. Sex is big happiness. But thinking you not ready for more happy sex until you know me more greatly. Yes? I understanding this. Is okay.

I make mistake to put intimate hands on you in auto, and saying nature of dirty toilet words. I try making joke to make you feel joy and laughing after we sexing together. But this not happen. I see sad in your eyes. Not good. So sorry.

Start over. Okay? All new. Important word is "gentleman" that I promise to being. Yes? So I like you come my house eat supper tonight, after I be play. 9:00 is good? I make Norwegian food. Bring Thor's Day. He good dog. I give meat bone for him.

In box is Mr. and Mrs. *Julenissen* ornaments I bring from Norway. For you fallen Christmas tree. You look at this and you think of Varik and you be smile again. Yes I hope?

You sincerely good friendship neighbor with much respecting you,

"Varik the Bold"

~ ~ ~

Delaney clutched Varik's letter to her breast and cried. Buckets. It was her first love letter. Ever. Even if it wasn't technically a love letter, it was close enough. She couldn't help compare Varik's heartfelt words to the cold, dry letter of intent she'd received from Roger a year ago. How lost and devastated she'd been then, wondering what her future held, worried she'd be alone and lonely for the rest of her life because she wasn't "a woman of worth."

Even through Varik's broken English, Delaney felt the kind sincerity in his words. She imagined it must have taken the man a small eternity to write, striving to ensure she'd understand what he meant. The adorable ornaments were such a thoughtful addition. She'd seen similar Norwegian characters on Grandma Bekka's Christmas tree.

The big, bold, masculine Viking wanted to cook her dinner? Wow...the only thing Roger ever made in the kitchen was a mess with his paperwork and dirty dishes.

"He says I should bring you," she told Thursday. "He'll have a bone for you." The dog looked up at Delaney, licking his chops. "What do you think, Thursday? Should I tell him I'll come for dinner?" He'd written his phone number at the bottom of the letter, asking her to text him.

"Will he think I'm too anxious, Thursday? Too forward? Do you think he really meant what he said about wanting to be good friends and neighbors?" Thursday angled his head and moaned.

"You're right," Delaney agreed with a resolute nod. "I should go. But no matter what happens, no matter how hot or sexy he is, I need to remain aloof. Well, not *too* aloof. I want him to think I'm a lady but not totally indifferent...or frigid, you know what I mean?"

Thursday rested his head in Delaney's lap, looking up at her. She sensed he was telling her to send Varik a text accepting his invitation. So she did.

~<>~

Delaney's closet housed a sparse collection of matronly clothing befitting the wife of a stuffy English professor. Until now, there hadn't been much reason to upgrade her drab wardrobe, plus she didn't want to spend money frivolously since she was living on a shoestring after refusing alimony from Roger during their divorce settlement. Her mother told her she was foolish to turn down alimony but Delaney wanted absolutely nothing from the cheating louse, except her freedom.

The time had come to dip into the small savings she'd built for needed house improvements before she put her townhouse on the market. Delaney decided she deserved treating herself to that small luxury.

While she looked forward to shopping for clothes, the idea was intimidating. Dressed in baggy jeans, a bulky sweater, and a clunky pair of clogs, she picked up the bag of sadly outdated clothing she'd gathered for donation and headed for her car.

Living with the hypercritical Roger had chipped away at her self-esteem to such a degree that Delaney had all the self-confidence of a slab of tofu. She felt she had little to offer a man. She was too tall, neither fit nor slender enough, too clumsy, overly sentimental, she lacked polish and poise, preferred reading genre books over literary fiction, and she turned her nose up at nutritional gray-green smoothies.

Somewhere deep inside, the heart and soul of a graceful, confident, and probably even attractive, woman existed. But trying to excavate those attributes wasn't easy. Growing up, she held her head high and felt good about herself, confident she was smart, artistic, had a good sense of humor and a big heart.

This was the happy, gregarious, optimistic package of traits she brought to her marriage. This was the Delaney Malone she offered to her new husband. She'd loved Roger Kullerton, accepting him for who and what he was, flaws and all. Guilelessly, she believed he felt the same about her. It was only after they said *I do* that she discovered Roger was resolved to transform her...just like in *My Fair Lady*.

The last thing Delaney ever expected was to become Eliza Doolittle to Roger's Henry Higgins.

Outside the university, Roger preferred spending time alone, reading and doing research. He viewed other people, including Delaney, as intrusions upon his prized private time. He loathed eating in restaurants, going to movies, or anything involving social interaction, so their social life was a big black hole.

Sorely out of practice when it came to socializing, Delaney needed to get her mix-and-mingle mojo back.

As she'd expected, clothes shopping was murderous. After trying on dozens of outfits that didn't work, she was about to give up when she found The Dress. It was a wrap dress in figure-slimming black that accentuated her curves without drawing negative attention to them. But with its low-cut vee neckline, the dress smacked of being too sexy for a casual dinner date with a friendly neighbor. She looked so good in it that she bought it anyway...just in case there was a second or third not-so-neighborly date in her future.

Another dress caught her attention. The long-sleeved tomato red jersey knit was simple yet stunning. It was so different from Delaney's bland, wheat-colored wardrobe she barely recognized herself.

She was about to shrug out of it, worried the color might be too showy, when she looked at herself—*really* looked at herself—pausing long enough to study her reflection from all sides in the three-way mirror.

Hands planted at her hips, she smiled at her transformation. Her pale skin and black hair came alive against the red. She hadn't worn a fashionable dress in so long she'd forgotten how attractive and feminine she could look and feel.

"Well what do you know?" she whispered with genuine amazement, a fresh injection of self-esteem coursing through her veins. "Delaney Malone, you're one foxy lady."

After shopping, she did some baking before spending time on her hair and makeup. Once she was all primped, she felt...*hoped*...she'd achieved just the right air of glamour and sophistication.

Even though there'd be no repeat of last night's erotic activities, it made her feel pretty and feminine to wear her new black silk undies. It was nice to have something sexy on without fearing the ancient elastic might have her panties falling around her ankles.

~<>~

Varik came to call for her at nine. Replying to her text, he'd told her a gentleman always picks up a lady, even if she lives just two doors away. She loved that he was a curious mix of old world values and modern day hunk.

"This is?" he asked, noting the foil-covered platter she carried as they walked.

"Dessert." She offered a proud smile as she hefted the plate of homemade ginger cookies.

"No need. I cook tonight."

Stopping in her tracks, she gave him a reproachful look. "I told you in my text that I'd come for dinner only if I could bring dessert, remember?"

"Okay *ja*, I forget." Giving her one of his captivating smiles, he lifted the foil for a peek and sniffed. "Smell is like my favorite, *pepperkaker*. Is very good."

She hoped he was right. Not much of a cook or baker unless she painstakingly followed recipes to a T, Delaney used Grandma Bekka's treasured recipe for *pepperkaker*. Happily, they seemed to turn out perfect.

"That's right. You're very astute."

His eyebrow hiked. "This means?"

"Perceptive."

The expression he gave her was born of frustration.

"Wise," she clarified. "You know, smart."

"Ahhh, *ja*," his head bobbed, "I very much wise. Very smart."

"Mmm-hmm, and humble too," Delaney teased, failing to elucidate when he gave her another of his befuddled looks.

"Still some boxes," Varik apologized as he ushered Delaney and Thursday into his home. "Take time to settling new house."

Delaney was impressed. By the same builder, the subdivision tract townhouse was a larger model than hers. Varik's home was neat, clean and showed few signs of disarray from his recent move. He even had pictures on the walls already.

It was clear the previous owners had kept the house in excellent condition, while her place was a classic handyman special. Although she'd worked diligently on repairs over the years, fixing broken cabinets and drawers, replacing peeling floor tile, stripping atrocious wallpaper that defied removal, rewiring improperly installed lighting fixtures, and more, she didn't have the time or finances to do all that was necessary.

After setting the platter of cookies on the kitchen counter, high enough to be out of Thursday's greedy range, her gaze fell on the blond wood acoustic guitar leaning against a chair's hassock.

"What a beautiful guitar."

"Gift from *bestefar*...grandpa," Varik said.

"You play?"

"*Ja*. Grandfather teach me. After salmon and potatoes I guitar for you." He looked hesitant. "You liking music?"

"Very much. I'd love to hear you play." She'd always had a thing for guitar players. And Vikings. This promised to be a most interesting evening.

She'd worried about bringing Thursday, considering his propensity for wreaking havoc, but Varik assured her the dog was welcome. He said he'd simply tell Thor's Day to be good and behave.

Ha!

He did just that. In Norwegian. Amazingly, Thursday sat in rapt attention while Varik spoke, shifting his head from side to side as Varik alternated between patting the dog's head and punctuating his words with a warning finger. She found it fascinating to watch her dog react as if he fully understood Varik's firm but soft spoken instruction. If only she could get Thursday to listen half as well when she trained him in English.

As promised, Varik presented Thursday with a sizeable beef soup bone, setting it in a corner of the kitchen. Taking his appointed spot, the newly obedient dog's eyes practically rolled up in his head as he gnawed on the treat.

"I take coat," he motioned to her, holding an arm out.

"Thank you." Delaney slipped out of her coat, growing nervous at the peculiar way he stared at her once she'd removed it and draped it over his waiting arm. He stood there for a full minute with that odd expression, not saying a damn word. It made her itchy all over, wondering what the heck was wrong. Had she forgotten to remove a tag? Was the hem hanging? Maybe there was a split in one of the seams.

Oh dear Lord, let it be something like that rather than Varik thinking she just looked plain awful in her nice new red dress.

"Is...um...is something wrong?" she finally got up the courage to ask when the man continued to stand statue-still, gawking at her, making her want to search his house for a full length mirror.

"Eh...no...no." He averted his gaze and cleared his throat. "I put coat closet."

"Well," she said beneath her breath when he left the room, "that went well." She rolled her eyes, hoping the rest of the evening wouldn't be as awkward. He was gone just long enough for her to do a quick self-check. Failing to find any tags or other problems with the dress, she wasn't sure if she should be relieved or concerned.

Returning to the living room, Varik gestured to the sofa for Delaney to take a seat. She couldn't help feeling disappointed when he sat in an adjacent chair, which she realized was an absurd reaction. If their initial meeting had been normal and ordinary, without her surprising the hell out of her new neighbor by jumping his bones, she certainly wouldn't expect him to cozy up to her on his couch.

It was strange and awkward to have your first official date with someone after you've already shared an orgasmic journey to Valhalla and back the night before.

Now as they sat, exchanging polite smiles, Delaney was painfully aware they knew next to nothing about each other. Suddenly panicked over that fact, as well as his weird reaction to her dress, she wished she hadn't accepted his invitation. If she were smart, she would have gotten on that damn plane for Oregon.

On the positive side, Varik apparently found her to be a pleasing partner in bed, but as her romantic-as-a-rutabaga ex-husband was fond of saying, "Men aren't particular. Put a paper bag over their heads and women are all the same." She *really* wished she hadn't thought of that just now.

Before Varik came to pick her up this evening, her confidence level was decent. Now it steadily declined, doing a slow glide the way her red velvet jingle bell panties with the ancient elastic did yesterday.

Folding her hands in her lap, she slumped down a little. As far as she knew the only thing they had in common was their shared Norwegian heritage. While Varik's broken English was charming, it presented frequent opportunities for misunderstanding. It was difficult enough for her to come across as interesting and likeable without the additional challenge of a language barrier.

If only she'd paid more attention when her mother and grandmother tried teaching her Norwegian. Their attempts to convince her being bilingual was advantageous fell on deaf ears. She'd picked up a smidgen of the language, enough to understand some fundamental words, but not enough to hold a basic conversation.

"I liked your letter very much." She wished she could aptly express how much she appreciated the kind sentiments in the sweet note he'd written. But nothing she'd say could adequately explain how he'd touched her heart. "And the ornaments are adorable. Perfect for my tree. Thank you, Varik."

"Mine pleasure." He leaned forward as he sat on the edge of his seat, resting his arms on his knees and twiddling his thumbs. Apparently she wasn't the only one feeling uncomfortable.

"Understand words okay?"

"Yes, you did a fine job translating."

"Good, good..." He nodded at her.

She nodded back.

He smiled.

She smiled back.

It was the epitome of awkward.

Doing her best to appear relaxed and casual, Delaney glanced around the room, studying anything and everything to avoid having to make eye contact or inane small talk. The more she looked, the less she saw as her nerves took over.

She'd read somewhere that asking people questions about themselves made them think you were a brilliant conversationalist. Sitting straighter in her seat, she cleared her throat. "Did you just move here from Norway? Or have you been in America for a while?"

"Just move but visit Tore, cousin, here many time."

Though Varik seemed more at ease now with their silence broken, Delaney winced at the mention of his cousin, recalling how she thought the guy was tied to a family-run escort service.

"Tore teach me English so I speaking excellent like him. Good teacher. Learn much already."

"Well you certainly know much more English than I do Norwegian. I think you're doing a great job." Feeling restored by their give and take conversation, Delaney let out the breath she was unaware she'd been holding.

"Delaney Norwegian?"

"Half. I'm Irish on my father's side."

"Speak Norwegian?" he looked hopeful.

"That would certainly make things a lot easier, wouldn't it?" She screwed her expression. "I only know a few words and phrases." She thought for a moment. "*Jeg liker a hekle.* Did I say that right? It means I like to crochet." She made the motion with her fingers.

"*Ja.*" Varik nodded. "Excellent."

"Aside from *hekling*, which means crocheting, *strikking*, which means knitting, and *garn*, which means yarn, I'm afraid most of the other Norwegian words I know have to do with food." She gave an apologetic shrug. "What can I say? The women in my family like to bake a lot."

"Is okay. Food is good. Tell me Norwegian words you know."

By all the questions he asked, it seemed Varik already knew the secret of being a brilliant conversationalist.

"Let's see...there's *julekake*, the fruit studded bread Grandma Bekka made each Christmas." Thinking of the yeast-raised holiday bread drizzled with icing made her miss the fun she and her grandmother had together in the kitchen. "And I loved Grandma's *pepperkaker*." She gestured toward the kitchen counter. "I used her recipe to make those."

"Both be Varik favorite. I cook but no bake. Miss good *pepperkaker*."

It was a plus that he appreciated baked goods. Roger hadn't allowed treats into their home, even during the holidays, believing their sugar and white flour content made them the equivalent of rat poison. Each time Bekka sent Delaney a home baked food gift, she hid the tins behind the cleaning supplies in the linen closet where Roger would never find them. Munching on them when he was out of the house was a great guilty pleasure.

"Now that my grandma's gone, my sister, Laila, is the star baker in the family."

"Sister here?"

"No, she moved to Oregon several years ago. The rest of my family is there too, except for my mom. She still lives nearby. I really miss Laila," her smile grew wide, "and all her baking."

"You visit there?"

"Not yet but I...I'm thinking about moving there soon."

Varik frowned. "Not happy news for Varik, new neighbor friend."

Though they barely knew each other, other than carnally, she liked hearing that, whether he was sincere or not.

"As for the other Norwegian words I know," she hurried along, changing the subject, "sometimes my grandma made *pikekyss*, which are meringue cook—"

"Kiss," Varik said, throwing her off guard.

She blinked. "What?"

He puckered his lips and kissed the air between them. She felt her temperature rise.

"*Pikekyss*. Means girl's kiss." He sat back, crossing his ankle over his knee and spreading an arm across the back of his chair. It was the relaxed, open gesture of a confident man who felt at ease. She guessed it was because their conversation was proceeding easily, which helped her feel calmer too.

"I didn't know that. I just knew they were meringue cookies."

"Kiss nice. Like very much." He had a certain look in his eye causing her to wonder if his comment was about the cookies or kissing her.

The cookies. Of course he was talking about the cookies. She had to stop reading something extra into his every little word or nuance.

Varik got up and left the room, gesturing with his finger that he'd be right back.

She heard him whistling in the kitchen and wondered how she should interpret that.

For God's sake, stop over-thinking everything and get a grip!

"*Gratulerer med dagen* and *Valentinsdag* toast to Delaney," he said, snapping her out of her reverie and handing her a mug of warm red liquid. Appreciating his thoughtful birthday Valentine toast, she was pretty sure his fingers lingered on hers a moment longer than necessary. His smile warmed her heart as the mug warmed her hand.

The spiced fragrance emanating from the mug was warm, welcoming and familiar. Sniffing the mug, she closed her eyes and smiled. "This smells heavenly."

"Wassail," he said.

"Grandma made hot mulled wine every Christmas. I felt very grown up as a kid when she'd give me my own small portion." She took a sip. "Mmm, delicious. Sweet and spicy. Perfect for a cold February evening."

"Good." After sipping, Varik licked his lips. "Taste like Christmas. What more Norwegian you know? I like hear you say my language."

The names of Norwegian foods flooded her brain. Even if she was somewhat obsessed with food, she didn't have to advertise it. There must be something non-food related she could recall...

"Let's see...of course! Grandma Bekka always signed each letter and ended each phone call with *jeg elsker deg*. It means—"

"I love you," Varik said. He wasn't smiling. He just said the words, gazing at her intently.

Delaney felt her cheeks flush under the force of his scrutiny. If he didn't stop looking at her that way she'd melt into a puddle of goo and ruin his nice carpet.

After a small eternity, he lifted his mug in salute. "*Jeg elsker deg*...I love you. Good words in Norwegian and English, *ja*?"

Raising her mug, Delaney agreed, "*Ja*," trying to affect a cheery, blasé expression while ignoring the carnal itch she longed for him to scratch. "Good words in any language."

The night before, when Varik was garbed in reindeer pelts, she tried picturing him in street clothes without much luck. She couldn't imagine him wearing anything but his Viking costume. Or nothing. It was amazing how delicious a modern day Viking could look wearing a crewneck sweater and butt-hugging jeans. He had an air of casual elegance, making him look as if he'd just stepped out of the pages of GQ, while his wild, glorious mane was more apropos for the cover of a pirate or barbarian-themed romance novel.

Varik's sandy sun-streaked hair perfectly enhanced his chiseled features. His blue eyes were so mesmerizing Delaney had a difficult time not fixing on them.

"*Kveldsmat* ready soon. Hope you liking salmon?"

His question snapped her out of her delectable daydreaming.

"I'm sorry, what did you say?"

"Supper soon. Delaney like salmon?"

"Mmm...love it," she cooed, realizing her voice sounded far more sensual than your standard cooked fish commentary. Appalled, she wished she could blame her passionate response on a hearty enthusiasm for salmon but...

His lips curling into a half-smile, Varik's spellbinding gaze grew heated.

"I mean salmon's good," Delaney backpedaled. "I like it. It's a very likeable fish. And it's full of omega-3 fatty acids, which makes it really healthy...and, you know, likeable."

Clamping her jaw tight to keep from any further babbling, she vowed to avoid any variation of the word *love* for the rest of the evening. The absolute last thing she wanted Varik to think was that she was trying to come on to him the way she had last night.

His attentive expression grew curious. "Why are you smiling at me like that?" she asked, expecting a suggestive reply.

"Because, like salmon, you be very likeable."

"Oh." Delaney's face fell. She'd never been compared to a fish before. "Well...thank you."

His gaze swept her. "Nice eyes. Nice hair. Nice lips. Nice all over."

She doubted he was still talking about salmon.

"Red," he gestured to her dress, "excellent color for Delaney." His tender smile becoming a grimace, he shook his head from side to side. "Sorry. Not neighbor friend talk, but cannot help say how very beauty you appearing tonight. When you take off coat, I breathe hard. But I worry to say how very excellent Delaney look in red dress."

Wow...that was all *way* better than the fish analogy. Now she knew why he gave her that curious look when he took her coat. Whew!

"Thank you, Varik, but you don't have to apologize for giving me such a lovely compliment. In fact, I was just thinking you look quite handsome in clothes."

He blinked.

She blinked.

"That came out wrong. I mean—"

His robust laughter filled the room. "Not to make explain. *Forsta*...I understand. Mostly I wearing clothes." He motioned to his sweater and jeans. "Only be Viking in plays."

And in my dreams.

Striving to shift her dangerous train of thought, Delaney noticed his home was decorated with sleek, contemporary furniture and accessories, shades of black, gray, mushroom-brown and white being predominant. It was the same color scheme Roger preferred, although their tastes were worlds apart. Roger had zero aptitude for design while Varik had a propensity for style and ornamentation, with smart bold pops of color placement bringing life to what could otherwise be a monotonous room.

Making a few safe comments about his décor, Delaney asked about the grouping of striking black and white photos. He told her he'd taken them himself, in Norway. It was pleasant conversation. Thankfully, she avoided making a fool of herself for a good fifteen minutes.

When he led her into the dining room, she was captivated by his obvious effort to set a romantic table for the two of them. Four tall ivory candles sat in crystal cube holders placed around a bottle of red wine on a sleek stainless steel serving tray at the center of the table. White dinner plates, silverware, and wine and water glasses sat on sleek black placemats with paper towels for napkins. He apologized for not having unpacked the linen napkins and tablecloth yet.

His apology had her swallowing an inappropriate burst of laughter.

The only time Roger set the table for her was the day after Delaney had all four of her wisdom teeth pulled. She looked like a gluttonous squirrel with its cheeks full of nuts and felt like death warmed over. He'd set out a bowl, fork, can opener and a can of green beans, telling her they'd help her heal faster eaten without heating. She took a pass, making herself a cup of tea instead.

When she tried to help Varik, he insisted she stay put as he zipped back and forth between the kitchen and dining room, serving their dinner. Unaccustomed to having a man wait on her, she was filled with a curious mixture of guilt and pampered pleasure. He lit the candles, poured the wine and turned on soft music.

Wow...she could really get used to this.

The delicious meal began with *agurksalat*, a salad of thinly sliced cucumbers with vinegar, sugar, salt, pepper and onions. Wine-poached salmon was accompanied by Varik's homemade potato dumplings sautéed in bacon fat. The dumplings were so damn good Delaney fought the urge to grab the serving dish, licking up every last remnant.

As they ate, Varik's questions surprised her, making Delaney realize that some men do actually pay attention.

"Many time you say Bekka. Who this? And Roger...you face angry," he demonstrated with a distinct frown, "when say his name. Be heartbreak man make Delaney lonely?"

She remembered mentioning Roger last night but didn't realize she'd brought him up again. She hoped to hell she hadn't been absently rattling on about her ex.

"My goodness." She couldn't help smiling. "It's downright astonishing how perceptive your observations are."

Looking mystified, he held his hands a foot apart, then brought them closer together. "Please smaller words or must look phrase book many time." He punctuated his request with a wink.

"Sorry." Delaney could only imagine how difficult deciphering conversation must be for someone learning to speak English. "I'll try to remember. Just ask if there's something you don't understand, okay?"

"Okay." He poured them another glass of *rodvin*, Norwegian red wine, and they clinked glasses. "Tell Varik about you life."

This was virgin territory for Delaney. She wasn't used to being catered to by a man, much less having him invite her to talk about herself.

"Nope, sorry, there's no way I'm going to monopolize our conversation by blabbing all about me, myself and I. Let's talk about you for a change."

"Monopolize?" Varik enunciated slowly.

"Oops, small words...I forgot. Monopolize means to take over. Dominate. You've been a gracious host, asking me about myself but I don't want to just talk about me. I want to hear about you too. Understand?"

"Except gracious host. Is good thing?"

"Very." She offered a reassuring smile. "It means you're a nice gentleman."

"*Ja*. See?" He rapped the edge of the table with his fingers. "I promise Delaney I be good gentleman." He lifted his wine glass. "We make toast to Varik be good gentleman, *ja*?"

He looked so endearing she was tempted to hop into his lap and hug him. Instead, she said, "Definitely." Raising her glass, she clinked it against his and they sipped. "Tell me, Varik, why did you move to Chicago?"

"To go school like Tore. University. First Tore come Chicago. Now I come."

"I think it's wonderful that you and your cousin want to continue your education here."

"Education good. For me," he spread his fingers on his chest, "is very important."

"I feel the same way. I've got a liberal arts degree that I haven't put to much use. One day I'd like to go back and take a few writing courses. Maybe journalism." Spotting his clueless expression resurfacing at the word, she continued, "That means writing for news media like newspapers, magazines or other news-related things."

"All good," he agreed.

She realized she'd fallen into the trap of chatting about herself again. "When did Tore move here from Norway?"

"Long time. Almost *tjue ar*." Varik tsked. "Sorry. Forget. Twenty."

"Years? That *is* a long time. So he's been here since he was a child?"

"No, Tore older. Now he *omtrent femti*. Eh...about fifty," he corrected. "Translate make talk much hard."

"It does, doesn't it?" she agreed through laughter. Whether they fully understood each other or not, it was still the most stimulating conversation she'd ever had with a man.

Chapter 8

~<>~

"NOW WE TALK about Bekka. See much love in Delaney eyes when talk about grandma. Tell me."

"Rebekka Eriksen..." Just saying the name brought a warming sense of love coursing through her. Although the subject had shifted back to her, Delaney never minded talking about her late grandmother. She told Varik about how supportive Bekka had been, and how she made the trip alone from Oregon to stay with Delaney after Roger walked out.

Varik was wonderfully attentive as she spoke about Bekka's fanciful Vikings stories, and why Delaney mistakenly assumed her grandma had been responsible for Varik appearing at her door dressed as a Viking. She wasn't sure how much Varik understood, but he smiled and nodded as she related her story.

As she prattled on she felt better. It was as if Varik knew chatting would be therapeutic. She watched for signs of impatience or boredom but they never materialized. He seemed genuinely interested.

She teared up when she got to the part about Bekka dying. The pain of losing her was still too fresh.

"Sorry, I didn't mean to cry. My grandma was very special to me. I miss her so much."

Varik patted her hand. "Sometimes cry is good." Rising from the table, he headed for the kitchen, returning with a handful of paper towels. "Sorry for great sorrow." He covered his heart with his hands. His kind words and sympathetic expression were so unlike anything Roger ever offered.

Her tears didn't make Varik squirm or roll his eyes with annoyance. She had to stop the mental comparisons to her ex, but Roger's idiosyncrasies were all she'd known for ten years. Delaney had no clue two men could be so vastly different.

Returning to his seat, Varik reached across the table, clasping Delaney's hand. "One day you see Bekka in Valhalla, great Viking hall." He smoothed his thumb over her wrist. "Happy feast with Odin for eternal time."

Dabbing her tears with a paper towel, she smiled at the pleasing thought of her grandmother still existing on some plane, happy and free of earthly cares or illness. "Grandma promised we'd meet again there."

"Delaney grandpa Valhalla too?"

"Yes." She truly wanted to believe they'd reunited. "Grandpa Jamie died long before I was born. He was the love of Bekka's life."

"Sadness be for Roger too?" Varik asked. "Missing him?"

That snapped Delaney back to the present. "Miss him?" A strangled laugh caught in her throat. "No. Oh *hell* no." She said it with such vehemence that Varik's eyes flashed wide. His stunned expression quickly had laughter replacing her tears.

"Good. Delaney pretty when laugh. So Roger not good man? Make big angry?"

"He did. But it's not polite for me to share negative thoughts about my ex-husband." While Varik may be understanding, Delaney had enough brains to realize whining about her ex would top the list of things not to do on a first date. "He's out of my life now." She gave an indifferent flit of her hand. "Believe me, I'd much rather be lonely than miserable."

"How long Roger go?"

Delaney huffed a humorless laugh. "Yesterday was one year."

"No." Varik frowned. "On Delaney *Valentinsdag* birthday?"

She nodded.

"What kind of man do this?"

Lifting her shoulders in the tiniest of shrugs, she lowered her eyes and stroked the handle of her fork. She had some choice answers to his question. None, however, would have been suitable dinner conversation.

"It doesn't matter anymore," she said with a smile. "I've moved on and I'm doing fine now." Delaney kept herself from spilling her guts about Roger's unexpected betrayal. The only comments she could possibly drum up would be ugly and unkind, making her sound like a bitter spurned ex.

"Other woman?"

Delaney ignored the question.

"Tell Varik." Those liquid blue eyes of his were as encouraging as his words.

"I appreciate you being interested, Varik, but I really don't think I should talk about—"

"*Ja*...good for Delaney tell Varik." His warm, sincere smile reached his eyes. "Varik listen."

Silent for a while, she gazed at her plate, unsure about how much to say.

"My husband left me for one of his graduate students." She couldn't help the escaping sigh. "Several years younger than me. Roger told me in a letter. He said I wasn't a woman of worth." She blinked back the tears that still welled whenever she recalled the hurtful admonishment. "I-I don't even know what that means."

"What? No!" Varik shot her a look of astonishment. "This Roger bad, stupid man, not appreciate good woman...excellent woman of worth. Woman of beauty and kindness heart."

Delaney lifted her gaze at his touching words, and watched as Varik's features knitted into an angry scowl.

"Sun is on the beach." He pounded the table. "Rotten buzzard."

She slanted him a questioning look.

"Bad translation?" His eyebrows quirked in question. Drumming his fingers on the tabletop he thought for a moment. "English hard to learn," he said, clearly frustrated. "Spanish and German easy."

"You speak Spanish and German?"

Varik gave a confirming nod. "Also French, Russian and," he held his finger and thumb an inch apart, "little Japanese. English most hard."

"You're multilingual. That's impressive. You put me to shame." The guy was amazing. Getting to know him was like peeling an orange, finding all that sweet, juicy goodness just beneath the rind. She was eager to keep right on peeling, wondering what other surprises she might find.

"I try again..." Varik closed his eyes in a long blink before speaking again. "Roger be sun in the bleach, rotten buster?" His hopeful expression crumpled when Delaney's lips curved into an amused smile. "Blister? Busted? Base..." he shook his head and frowned, "no, not baseball..."

Covering her mouth with her fingers Delaney made a valiant effort not to laugh.

"Help correct words," he said, obviously discouraged and thirsty for knowledge.

"Well..." an easy grin spread across her face, "I think you're trying to say son of a bitch and rotten bastard. But, you know, Varik, I think I like your broken English even better. What's more...I wholeheartedly agree with your opinion."

"*Ja!*" Varik's expression brightened. "Roger son of a bitch, rotten bastard." An instant later his enthusiasm dimmed and his expression pinched. "Ooh...sorry...forget self. Excuse dirt words with lady here."

"No apologies necessary." Threading her fingers with his, she squeezed his hand. "Thank you, Varik."

"For dirt words?" He eyed her strangely.

"For making me laugh. I needed it."

He looked genuinely pleased. "Excellent."

If things were different and she had an amicable relationship with Roger, she'd suggest Varik contact him for private tutoring. Her ex might be a rotten buzzard, but he was an excellent teacher.

"Did they teach English in school when you were a child?" she asked.

"Not go school."

Nearly doing a double take, she asked, "Ever?"

"Until university in Oslo, and university here."

He couldn't have said anything more surprising. She had so many questions but the last thing she wanted was to make him feel uncomfortable after he'd been so kind.

"You like Varik tell story of why no school?"

Delaney responded with an encouraging smile. Listening would provide the perfect opportunity for her to sit and gaze at him.

She learned Varik's parents died in a skiing accident when he was four. He barely remembered them. He was raised by his paternal grandfather, Anders Jenssen, a stern, good-hearted mountain man who kept to himself.

"This sounds suspiciously like Heidi," Delaney teased.

"Much same," he agreed.

She gave him a skeptical look. "Are you sure you're not pulling my leg?"

"You like me pull you leg?" Straight-faced, he slipped down in his chair as if to peek under the table. His ready sense of humor was an uncommon delight.

Automatically scooting her legs back, she was determined not to let on how tempting she found his offer. "Never mind that," Delaney warned with a playful smile. "Just go on with your cute, Heidi-like story."

"Come." Reaching for her hand, Varik had a twinkle in his eye. "I show you Anders *fotgrafi*." Still holding hands, Delaney followed him to a room down the hall. Along with a variety of books, the walls were lined with dozens of framed photos similar to the ones she'd noticed when she'd first arrived. Most were black and white and looked good enough to be in a gallery.

"You took these too?"

"*Ja*, enjoy make *fotografi* for hobby." He pointed to a series of photos all featuring the same older man. There was one framed and matted color photo at the center, surrounded by four smaller black and white shots. "*Bestefar*...eh, Grandpa Anders." His fingers lovingly traced the outside of the center frame.

"Wow, the hair, the mustache and beard..." The grouping couldn't have surprised her more. "These look just like..." Delaney turned to look up at Varik who stood behind her now with his hand at the small of her back.

Smiling, he gave an understanding nod. "*Ja*, I know...Heidi grandpa."

"He's even wearing those fancy suspender shorts." She pointed to show Varik what she meant.

"Lederhosen. Not wear all the time. Only for *München, Tyskland* eh..." he snapped his fingers a couple times, "Munich, Germany, for Oktoberfest." With a faraway look in his eyes, Varik broke into a grin. "Good school."

"You mean he took you to the Oktoberfest as part of your education?"

"Sure. Drink plenty beer too." He laughed. "Fun time."

"Better than any classes I ever had." Delaney joined him in laughter. Looking at the comfortable, masculine décor, she asked. "This room is your library?"

"*Ja, bibliotek*." He patted a neat row of hardcover books. Delaney browsed his shelves, spotting books in various languages with a fairly even split between fiction and nonfiction, at least for the titles in English. "It looks like you're an avid reader."

"Love books." He gestured around the nicely arranged room. A small table topped with a reading lamp sat next to a comfortable looking brown leather chair and ottoman, finished with decorative upholstery tacks. "Many good books here too." His hand skimmed over a Kindle on the table. "Favorite room."

She could definitely see that by the care he'd taken in ensuring the library was an inviting sanctuary.

"Sit." He patted the seat of the leather chair. "I get Anders favorite brandy."

She sank into the butter-soft leather while Varik headed for the glass doors of the corner bookcase. He set a half-full bottle of brandy and two glasses on the table. After pouring each of them a small amount, he sat on the ottoman and raised his glass.

"To Anders and Bekka. *Skal!*" He took a sip following his toast and Delaney followed suit.

As they relaxed and chatted she learned he'd been homeschooled by his grandfather. They traveled to Oslo annually to have Varik tested on his scholastic progress. By the time he was twelve, he was testing at college level and had been called a boy genius.

English was the one subject Anders neglected to teach his grandson. Most Norwegians were taught English all through grade school, learning to speak it fluently. Anders, however, was a proud old-school Norwegian who believed it was important to preserve their native language and not let English take over. He told Varik that one day, when he traveled to America, he'd be able to learn English if it was still of interest. That's what Varik meant yesterday when he'd said it was his grandfather's fault that he didn't speak English.

"*Bestefar* not *usosial eremitt* like Heidi's grandfather." Noticing Delaney's befuddled expression, Varik added, "Must to think..."

Cradling his head, he massaged his temples. "*Ett* moment." He went to the desk at one corner of the room, returning with his Norwegian-English dictionary. After looking up the words, he smiled. "Grandfather not unsociable hermit." With an apologetic shrug, he said, "Sorry. Hard sometimes." He stuffed the slim paperback into one of his back pockets.

"Don't apologize. You're doing great."

"We live in small village. Grandpa excellent teacher...excellent friend." There was a distant look in his gaze as he continued. "Good man. Much love." Varik knocked his fist against his chest. "Next time I see him in Valhalla." His smile was wistful.

"How long ago did you lose him?" Delaney was touched by the obvious love he had for his grandfather. It sounded like they'd shared a close bond similar to hers and Bekka's.

"Two year. Still missing him like you missing grandma." He reached into his back pocket, drawing out a little maroon colored drawstring bag. Inside was a foil packet. He opened it, holding it beneath Delaney's nose. The aroma was a pleasant aromatic mix of fruit and tobacco. "Grandpa *pipetobakk*." The word was easy enough for her to interpret without his help. "Keep close. Favorite memory."

"Mmm, smells good. Like cherries. Are you a pipe smoker too?"

Wrapping it again, he stuffed the pouch of tobacco back into his pocket. "No. Maybe someday, when I am grandpa." His eyes lit up with a smile. "Come now." He stood, holding out his hand. "Time for play."

Delaney stiffened.

"Guitar," Varik added, with a mischievous smile.

"Shame on you. You did that on purpose," she laughingly accused.

"Maybe. Love see Delaney laugh." Taking her by the hand, he drew her up from the cushy chair. Once they reached the dining room, she started bringing plates to the kitchen but he stopped her.

"Guest no clean." He clapped his chest. "I clean later. Time now for relax."

This was an entirely new occurrence for Delaney.

Draping his arm over her shoulder, he led her to the loveseat in the living room. Back in the kitchen, he uncovered the platter of pepperkaker she'd baked, popping a cookie into his mouth and giving her a thumbs up sign.

"Mmm, very excellent delicious." He put on a pot of coffee, bringing each of them a mug when it finished brewing, along with the cookies.

After turning the lights low, Varik started a fire in the fireplace. Flickering flames soon gave the room a warm, golden glow along with gentle heat. Perfect ambience for her date with the Viking.

"I'm not used to being pampered like this." She sipped the good strong coffee, thoroughly charmed by his gallant behavior.

"No? Very sad." He sat next to her, studying her for a long moment. "Varik change that. Delaney deserve feel special."

He was so loveable, so caring and considerate. What an exceptional time she was having. It was almost as if she'd stepped into a fairytale.

Delaney cozied back into her seat, watching as he set down his mug and brought the guitar strap over his head. Half expecting to hear a guitar version of chopsticks, she was stunned when his fingers danced across the strings, playing a familiar classical piece.

"I know that. It's "In the Hall of the Mountain King" by Edvard Grieg."

"*Ja.*" He looked particularly pleased as he strummed. "From Henrik Ibsen's play, Peer Gynt. You like song?"

"Very much. It was my grandmother's favorite musical piece and Grieg was her favorite composer. When I was little she'd sing it to me in Norwegian. It brings back very fond memories."

"Good." Varik patted the guitar like it was an old friend. "You like I sing Norwegian words for you?"

"I'd love that." This dinner date just kept getting better.

He patted the cushion next to him. Slipping off her heels, Delaney sat facing him, curling her legs beneath her.

Watching his fingers expertly working the guitar strings as he began the song's introduction was almost hypnotic.

"*Slagt ham! Kristenmands son har daret...*"

His voice rang out in a bold, clear tone somewhere between tenor and baritone. The man could really sing! The swell of the music had tears brimming in her eyes. Live music moved her that way.

"I understand," Varik said, momentarily breaking from the song. "Feel music here." He touched his chest and then hers.

Watching his features change was fascinating. His eyes blazed and his lively, emotion-filled lyrics held her captivated. Hearing him sing and speak in his native tongue, without the frequent hesitation he had when speaking English, presented him in an entirely new light.

With the Viking at her side, so close she felt the warmth radiating from his body, she was in serious danger of swooning.

Once he finished, Delaney clapped with enthusiasm. "Bravo! Bravo, Varik!"

Rising, he performed a sweeping, theatrical bow.

"That was incredible."

"*Takk.*" He beamed a smile. "Means thank you." With a quizzical glance, he asked Delaney, "You know what song story about?"

She shook her head. "Not really."

"Try my best to tell you English." He rested his hand on her arm, further igniting the slow burn she felt inside. "Tore teach me English words to song."

They sat silent for a long moment, gazing into each other's eyes. Finally, Varik returned his attention to the guitar.

Continuing to play the song's tune, he half spoke, half sang the words, playing the notes more slowly as he explained the tale to Delaney. It was clear he gave each line much thought so it came out correctly in English.

"Peer Gynt have dream," he told her. "Enters hall of mountain king. Many trolls, gnomes and goblins there. King on throne. Crown on head, and holding—" He gave Delaney a questioning look.

"A scepter?" she said, acting as if she were holding one.

"*Ja*, scepter." Varik nodded. "King's children and family near. Peer Gynt come close to king. Mighty yelling begin in hall. Trolls of king say, 'Slay him! The Christian's son bewitched mountain king's fairest daughter! Slay him!'"

"Ah, so that's what the song is about," Delaney said. "I've always wondered."

Nodding as he continued to strum, he resumed the story. "Other trolls ask, 'May I hack him on the fingers? May I tug him by the hair?' Woman troll say, 'Let me bite his haunches!' Witch troll say, 'Boil him into broth for me.' Troll with big knife ask, 'Shall he roast on spit or brown in stewpan?'"

Delaney laughed. "Good grief, what a bloodthirsty lot." Varik's explanation gave her a better understanding of the gusto her sweet grandmother used when singing the fierce lyrics.

"*Ja*. At end of song, mountain king say, 'Ice to your blood, friends!'"

"Wonderful." Delaney clapped again. "You did an excellent job translating. I understood everything perfectly."

"Good. Hope so." He looked quite pleased. "Soon I speaking perfectly English."

"How long has Tore been tutoring you?"

"*To uker*. Eh…" Varik took another quick glimpse at the book in his back pocket and held up two fingers. "Two weeks."

"I think you probably mean two months, not weeks."

"*Nei*...no. Mean weeks, for sure."

Incredulous, Delaney said, "Wait, you're telling me you just started learning English two weeks ago?"

"*Ja*...yes. Never speaking English before that."

Her jaw went slack. "That's incredible. You really *must* be a genius."

Offering a nonchalant shrug, Varik confirmed, "*Ja*, I told you."

"And you're extremely modest too."

"Not know modest." He looked confused.

"Yes, that's obvious," she teased, although she agreed he had every reason to feel proud and confident.

"Like song better in Norwegian or English?"

"Norwegian. It's much the same as hearing an English translation of Italian opera. It never sounds right to me."

"Maybe one day I teach you Norwegian. And you help me English."

"That would be fun." In her enthusiasm, Delaney absently touched his knee. As soon as her hand landed, she retrieved it. "If I had paid better attention as a child I'd probably be able to speak Norwegian fluently by now." Her gaze fell on his hair, studying the way the long, thick sandy strands so perfectly framed his face.

"I see you look Varik hair many time." He brushed a lock of dark blond from his eyes.

Oops...caught.

She'd never been a fan of long hair on a man but it suited Varik perfectly. "Long hair looks good on you." She felt the telltale warmth of a blush across her cheeks.

"Long because live in mountains. I cut and shave," he stroked his mustache and beard, "after finish being in Viking play. Better not to wear *parykk*." He patted the top of his head. "Wig. Not to worry. Cutting soon to look American."

"I wasn't worried at all. I think it's very—" She stopped herself from saying *sexy*. "Attractive. You're the spitting image of a Viking warrior." She tried unsuccessfully to picture him clean shaven with corporate-length hair.

"Varik the Bold," he told her with a conspirator's wink.

For the longest time after that, he didn't speak. He didn't smile. He just sat there watching her. At first she thought it was just wishful thinking, but soon Delaney realized his face was drawing near. He was leaning in for a kiss! A superb squiggly feeling zigzagged up and down her spine. Her heart thumped like crazy. Her breathing stopped.

Varik's sensuous lips were kissably close. It was taking an eternity for him to reach her lips, which wasn't really a bad thing because the anticipation itself was delicious. A million thoughts raced through her mind. Should she lean in or stay put? Should she whisper his name or keep her mouth shut? Should she—

"Delaney..." Varik whispered, his hands on her shoulders, his lips an inch from hers. His hot breath on her mouth had her liquefying. "Delaney..." he said once more, looking into her eyes, gazing into her soul.

"Yes, Varik?" she whispered back, her eyes half-lidded as she absently licked her lips.

"You go now," he said, still within kissing range.

Her mouth formed an O.

An instant later he pulled back from her, abandoned the loveseat, and went to the kitchen, returning shortly with Thursday in tow. The dog had been so quiet and well-behaved, she'd forgotten he was even there.

"Time for end of date," he told her with what Delaney decided, or hoped, was a look of sincere regret.

"Oh...?" What the hell had just happened? His was a mere breath away when he retreated. Maybe her breath smelled like salmon...or cucumber-onion salad.

"Must be gentleman. Delaney make hard to keep friendly neighbor promise."

Her mouth opened, then snapped shut. She wasn't sure what to say. The jumbled thoughts whirring inside her brain left her clueless.

She wanted to stay but if she disregarded his request to leave and did what she longed to do—shrug out of her dress, letting it pool at her feet in front of him so she'd be standing in nothing but her new black silk undies—Varik might think she was from Tramps-R-Us and all this nice platonic time they'd spent getting to know each other would go right down the toilet.

"It's been a lovely night, Varik." Her voice was barely audible. "The dinner was delicious." *And so are you.* "And I loved your rousing version of the song." *And I feel like I love you but that's impossible because we're still strangers and nobody in their right mind falls in love that fast.* "And I really enjoyed getting to know you better."

"*Ja*, happy night." He reached out, almost touching her, but let his hand drop, shoving both hands in his pockets instead. "Uh...loving Delaney excellent pepperkaker. Bekka's recipe good." His head bobbed.

"Thanks, I'm glad they turned out well." Her nodding head mirrored his. She took Thursday's leash and tugged. "Come on, boy, time to go home." The dog didn't budge. "Thursday." Nothing. The dumb dog just grinned up at her. Glancing at Varik she noted, "I guess you've got a friend forever since you spoiled him with that soup bone."

"Maybe Thor's Day sleep Varik house tonight?"

"Oh I couldn't possibly impose on you like that."

"Is okay. He good dog." He bent to scratch Thursday behind the ears. "We be friends, *ja*, Thor's Day?" He got a big lick from his new buddy.

So that's how the night would end...with her persuasive dog finagling his way into having a sleepover at Varik's house when the pajama party should by all rights include her.

"Well...if you're sure you don't mind," the green with envy Delaney said. "I can stop by and pick him up in the morning."

"I bring him to you in afternoon. I take him to English lesson. Tore love *hunders*...dogs. Return Thor's Day before I go Viking play, okay?"

"Okay." Delaney took a step toward his door and smiled. "Goodnight. Thanks again."

At a loss, she waved.

Varik waved back.

"Bye."

"I walk Delaney home," he suggested.

"That's not necessary. I'm just two doors down." She gestured. "Goodnight."

"*Godnatt*...goodnight," Varik corrected, waving again.

"Bye, Thursday." Before she'd even had the words out, the disinterested dog had trotted back to the kitchen and his bone.

Delaney sighed.

In less than two minutes she was home, unwrapping the chocolate bar she'd purchased while clothes shopping earlier. She closed her eyes and sank her teeth into the creamy candy.

It wasn't nearly as delicious or satisfying as Varik.

Chapter 9

~<>~

LEANING AGAINST THE kitchen counter, phone in hand, Delaney made an exasperated face as she listened to her mother shoot question after question. She was thoroughly disgusted with herself this morning, greeted by the dirty living room carpet she was supposed to finish cleaning two days ago.

First, she'd let the mess sit overnight while she...dallied with the sexy Viking. Then yesterday, after getting Varik's invitation to dinner, she merrily abandoned the rest of the task so she could shop for a new outfit.

The room still smelled like dog barf. She doubted she'd ever manage to get all the stains out. It wasn't at all like her to be so lax.

Her thoughts raced as her mom droned on.

Dear Diary: Here I am, wearing my grubbiest jeans and rattiest sweatshirt the morning after being spurned by Varik the Bold, hauling a scrub brush and a sudsy bucket of pine-scented cleaner from one crusted splotch to another. I guess this is what happens when you turn into a sex-crazed thirty-something.

If she hadn't answered the phone when her mom called she'd be much further along with her grubby task. But she had a feeling her mom needed to talk about their joint loss of Bekka, which they did at length. Looking around as she spoke to Astrid, she winced. She had to get this cleaned up before Varik brought Thursday home. She couldn't have him thinking she was a slob, especially after seeing how immaculate he kept his house.

"What? No, I'm listening, Mom," she lied. "Yes, really, everything's fine. I'm doing great," Delaney assured. "No, I'm not feeling blue because I'm thirty-six, divorced and alone. No, I'm not just saying that." She laughed, wondering if her mother would ever stop worrying about her.

"Yes, I have special plans for tonight. I have a date with a pint of butter pecan ice cream, a jar of caramel sauce, fudge brownie chunks, and a can of whipped cream, which I'll thoroughly enjoy all mixed together while sprawled on the couch watching Hallmark romance movies. See, Mom? The ideal post birthday celebration."

Although Delaney thought her reply was rather amusing, it only served to fuel her mother's concerns. "I was only joking, Mom." Slapping the heel of her palm against her forehead in frustration, Delaney added, "No, Mom, my plans do not make me sound like a sad, lonely, depressed woman who's in denial about being middle aged and alone. And, come on, since when is thirty-six middle aged?"

At the sound of the next "but" that came out of Astrid's mouth, Delaney growled. "Mom! Stop. To tell you the truth, I'm feeling terrific. I...I've met someone."

The expected third-degree followed. She hadn't intended on telling her mother anything about Varik because she knew she'd have to endure an interrogation, but it was better than having Astrid worry that her oldest daughter was depressed a year after she'd been unceremoniously dumped on her birthday.

"Yes, he's very handsome," Delaney answered, "and much taller than me, even when I wear heels, believe it or not. He's Norwegian, just moved here from Norway."

Delaney left out the part about him showing up on her doorstep half-naked and how she essentially forced herself on him because she thought he was a male prostitute sent by Grandma Bekka.

"I'm not sure if he has a job, the subject didn't come up." Delaney tsked. "It just didn't, Mom. I wasn't going to give him the third degree on our first date." Listening to the barrage of questions, she smiled, remembering the night before. "His name is Varik Jenssen," she replied. "He cooked dinner for me, which is something Roger never did even once in ten years. Salmon and potato dumplings," she answered. "Just like Grandma's. And he plays the guitar and sings and he acts, and he—"

Delaney sighed as her mother rambled on about how she should be careful of men who were too charming because of how easily distracted they could be by other women. She'd heard her mother's cautionary speeches dozens of times.

"Mom, listen...I don't want to make you feel bad or angry, but if you remember, the last time I took your advice about men I ended up marrying Roger, a man completely devoid of charm, and look what happened. He dumped me for a kindergartener."

Cleaning invisible spots on the counter with a paper towel, she listened. "No, I don't think every man in the world is a scumbag because of Roger," she told her mom. "It just means that sometimes life is unfair."

The doorbell rang. Delaney's eyes bugged. She glanced at her vintage black cat wall clock with its moving eyes and swinging tail. It was just past noon, too early for Varik to arrive...unless Thursday had reverted to his disobedient persona and Varik decided to drop him off early. Panicked at the thought of him seeing her looking like a scrubwoman, Delaney dropped to her hands and knees, crawling behind the kitchen counter, hiding so she couldn't be seen from the living room window or the door's glass side panels.

"I've got to go, Mom, someone's at the door," Delaney whispered. "I'm whispering," she explained, "because I'm in the middle of housecleaning, look like crap, and don't want anyone to see me."

There was pounding at the door followed by a familiar voice...one she hadn't heard for twelve months. She sat back on her heels, dumfounded.

"Holy sh—" She stopped herself from swearing in her mother's ear. "It's Roger! No, I have no idea why he's here." He was knocking and ringing now. "I'd better answer it. I'll call you later. Yes, don't worry, I'll be okay." Delaney wasn't so sure about that last part. She couldn't imagine what in the hell would bring her ex back a year after walking out.

"Shit," she allowed herself to mutter after ending the call.

She worked to compose herself, not about to give Roger the satisfaction of seeing her emotionally distraught.

"Just a minute," she called in a singsong voice from the kitchen as she got to her feet. Fussing with her wet, grubby scrub clothes, she suddenly stilled her hands, deciding it didn't matter if she looked like hell because she didn't give a damn what Roger thought about her anymore.

With a fortifying breath, she headed for the door and answered it.

One glimpse of the charmless man standing opposite her, looking like an aging imitation of a college kid, almost had Delaney laughing at the irony of it all. The only thing worse than Thursday's dog barf mess, or Delaney mistaking Varik for a prostitute, was standing on the other side of her threshold.

"Hello, Del." Roger gave her a sneering onceover as he spoke.

"Roger," she said through clenched teeth, glaring at her louse of an ex-husband.

He'd changed in the last year. His hair was gathered in back into what Delaney suspected was a man bun beneath a brown suede cap worn with a tilt to the side. He had a mustache and longish squared-off beard. He'd swapped his standard wire-rimmed eyeglasses for a pair of black horn-rims. Roger's tight, low-slung black jeans had holes at the knees and were rolled up at the ankles. He wore brown oxfords with no socks. A white shirt, suspenders and bowtie were topped with a short, fitted black leather jacket full of zippers and rivets.

He was either costumed as a reject from a bad high school movie, or striving to come across as his idea of a super cool hipster. On a hunk like Varik the getup might look hip. On the marshmallowy Roger Kullerton, it was downright hilarious.

"Cool threads, Roger." Delaney's voice was tinged with sarcasm as she eyed him from head to toe. Roger was an ever bigger dork now than when he left her.

"Thanks." With the affirmative nod of a man brimming with confidence, he said, "I was tired of looking older than my years."

She thought it was so cute that he actually thought she'd given him a genuine compliment.

"So do you dress like this," her gazed roamed over him again, "when you teach at the university?"

"Yeah, the students are pretty jazzed about my new style."

"I have no doubt." *Jazzed*, hmm? Interesting...Roger the fussy grammarian had never used words like that. Having trouble ungluing her gaze from her transformed ex, she imagined his new look was the talk of the campus. Roger Kullerton was quite obviously in the throes of a midlife crisis, a clear and cringeworthy descent into second childhood, which was pretty sad, considering he wasn't even forty yet. She almost felt sorry for him.

Almost.

As he looked past Delaney into the living room, his mustached lip curled into a sneer.

"Looking for your bouncy but compatible teenybopper?" Delaney asked. "Sorry, I'm afraid she's not here. She must have sensed I'd run out of milk and cookies." She couldn't help smirking.

"Let's be adult about this," Roger suggested.

"About what?" She gave him an incredulous look. "You're the one who showed up on my doorstep. What do you want, Roger?"

Before he answered, Delaney heard a woman's voice coming from the direction of her bushes.

"I need to use the lavatory," came the whisper, using Roger's favorite synonym for the bathroom. Yup, the new Mrs. Kullerton was an English major all right.

"Do I hear the alluring voice of your child bride?" Delaney asked through a saccharine smile. "Oh dear, has she gone through her last diaper?"

"Come on, Del," Roger's jaw muscle twitched, "Karen needs to use the lavatory."

So her name was Karen...

"Be my guest." She stepped aside, gesturing for them to enter.

Roger turned, beckoning toward the bushes. "Come on, Karen. She won't bite."

"Don't count on it," Delaney muttered, anchoring her arms across her chest.

A hugely pregnant young woman waddled up the salted walk, sidling next to Roger. Delaney made a conscious effort not to let her jaw drop. She had no idea the nearly adolescent home wrecker was expecting.

Karen's sleek brown hair flowed to her shoulders in a blunt cut. She wore oversized black horn-rim glasses similar to Roger's, and a simple navy blue maternity dress under a camel-colored wool trench coat. A pair of no-nonsense shoes completed the ensemble.

Resembling a stern, straight-laced school teacher, the homewrecker was far more attractive than Delaney had imagined...or hoped.

"It's a pleasure to meet you, Delaney." Karen presented one hand to shake while her other hand traced the enormous bulge in her middle.

Surrendering the fight not to slip into sarcasm, Delaney said, "So are you two here to ask me to be the godmother of little Roger, or whatever his or her name is, in there?" She gave a humorless laugh as she gestured to Karen's sizeable protrusion.

Uttering one of those little cough-laughs, Karen lifted an eyebrow as she gave Delaney a scathing head-to-toe appraisal. "That's hardly something you need to worry about, Delaney."

Yes indeed...Karen was an ideal match for Roger. "I'll try to get over my disappointment," Delaney replied with her most insincere smile.

"Where's Ruff?" Roger blurted. Delaney had been so embroiled in the icy give and take with Karen she'd nearly forgotten Roger was there.

"Thursday," she corrected.

"What are you talking about? It's Sunday."

"The dog. I changed his name to Thursday."

Roger screwed his features. "That's a preposterous name for a dog. Why in God's name would you name Ruff after a day of the week?"

"He's named for Thor, the Norse god of thunder."

"Then why not just name him Thor?" Roger continued.

With a roll of her eyes, Delaney explained. "Because you brought him home on a Thursday, the day of the week named after Thor. Thor's day."

His beady-eyed expression reminded Delaney of a horn-rimmed-eyeglass-wearing rodent.

"I can see that reasoning." Karen offered a curt nod. "It's a logical conclusion."

"On the contrary," Roger looked as though he'd swallowed curdled milk, "it's the most asinine, ridiculous thing I've ever heard."

She looked at the watermelon in Karen's belly, than back at her ex-husband's getup and smiled. "Not as ridiculous as some things, Roger."

In truth, seeing his young wife pregnant stung. Delaney longed to have children, but Roger put his foot down on the matter from the beginning, insisting he had neither the time nor inclination to be a father. Naively trusting in her husband's judgment and the advice of the doctor he'd taken her to see, a university colleague of Roger's, Delaney allowed herself to be coerced into having a tubal ligation, ending any possibility that she might accidentally get pregnant.

She'd had the surgery only a year before Roger walked out. If only she'd known...

"Look, Del, I don't have time for games. I'm here for Ruff."

"You're what?" That threw her. Granted, Thursday may have violated her emergency chocolate stash and ruined her carpet, but Delaney loved him fiercely and wasn't about to give him up to the jerk who couldn't be bothered to visit the poor dog even once in the past twelve months.

As Delaney opened her mouth to respond, a jiggling Karen spoke up, "I truly do need to use your facilities, Delaney." Her colossal belly bounced as she cradled it. "I have an urgent need to urinate."

Alarmed all that rattling might shake the baby out onto the living room floor, Delaney said, "Oh, please don't bounce like that. Through there, down the hall, first door on the left."

Delaney's attention returned to her ex as she pinned him with a steely glare.

It had been awful watching the dog waiting eagerly by the front door every day for his master. She'd see that stubby tail of his wag as he glimpsed every passerby from the living room window, clearly hoping it was Roger. He'd make a low, moaning whimper that sounded like a dejected cry. Then he'd slant his head and look to Delaney as if she had the answer. It just about broke her heart.

It was two solid months before Thursday finally stopped waiting for Roger's return. After that, he began waiting for Delaney to come home from work, greeting her with the same love and enthusiasm he'd previously reserved for Roger.

The big mutt had wheedled his way into Delaney's heart, taking up a treasured place of residence. Now he was all she had left. And she was all Thursday had. He was her buddy, her pal, her friend. They were family! She couldn't give him up now. She wouldn't!

Roger fell into the all too familiar stance of exasperation he did so well. A dimpled smirk, thumbs looped in his jeans pockets, and weight resting on one leg. She used to think that expression was endearing. Now she wanted to rip it right off his dorky hipster face.

"I've come for my dog. Where is he?"

"Gone. He ran away."

"I can always tell when you're lying, Del." He scanned the room with an expression of disbelief, uttering a growl of revulsion. "What the hell happened in here?"

Delaney had almost forgotten about the spattered carpet. "Oh, that." She shrugged. "It's the aftermath of a wild party. I was just cleaning it up."

Karen came back into the room. Breathing in an audible exclamation, she stepped over the messy patches on the carpet, wincing as if they were land mines.

"Wild party? Hardly," Roger jibed. "This is Ruff's mess."

"Oh good grief. All this..." Little Miss Preggers noted, gesturing around the room, "is making me queasy." Turning her attention to her husband, her eyebrows knitted. "I thought you said he was a well-behaved dog, Roger."

"It's exactly what I would expect with Ruff living under Del's lackadaisical influence," he replied as if Delaney wasn't even in the room. "My ex has never been a proponent of hygiene."

Delaney's jaw dropped. "I beg your pardon?"

"Where's Ruff?"

"He's skulking." Delaney was unable to expunge the sneer from her expression.

"Chocolate?" He pointed to the mess that used to be her stylish living room. She nodded. It wasn't a question as much as an accusation as he glanced at the shredded packaging. "What the hell's wrong with you, Del? You know dogs aren't supposed to eat chocolate."

"Well of course I know that, Roger. I'm the one who warned *you* about chocolate being toxic for dogs, remember? I also informed you garlic can be poisonous for dogs, which is one of the reasons I never added it to his meals even though you kept insisting that I do just that. You don't think I purposely fed chocolate to Thursday, do you?"

"You? Share chocolate?" Roger snickered as he gave his ex-wife a onceover. "That'll be the day." His gaze landed on the toppled Christmas tree. "What, pray tell, is that?"

"Exactly what it looks like," Delaney answered.

"It's February."

"Yes, and it's my townhouse. I can do whatever I want, whenever I want. It's none of your business."

"A decades-old aluminum Christmas tree..." Karen studied the fallen tree as though it were a purposeful art installation. "How terribly...quaint."

"I'm so glad you approve," Delaney said.

"I'm afraid you misunderstood my reaction," Karen said with a passing smile.

Shifting his weight from one leg to the other, Roger emitted an impatient sigh followed by a yawn.

"Nap time for you youngsters? Good idea. It's time for you and your playmate to leave, Roger." Delaney gestured to the door.

"Let's not have a scene. Just give me my dog and I'm out of here."

"You call *that* a scene?" Delaney said incredulously. "Just wait until you see what I'm capable of if you try to take my dog."

"My dog," Roger snarled.

"Look, Roger, you can't just waltz in here and take Thursday away from me."

"I most certainly can. According to the court, Ruff is mine, remember?"

"You haven't even bothered to see him since you walked out last year...on my birthday." The memory of Roger's heartless departure iced Delaney's spine and she stiffened.

Shifting her attention to Karen, Delaney said, "Did you hear that, Karen? My ex-husband, left me on my birthday...Valentine's Day." She elevated her chin. "*That* is the kind of man you married."

One of Karen's shoulders lifted in an elegant shrug. "While I sympathize with your obvious sense of resentment mixed with bereavement at losing Roger, Delaney, I don't see what possible difference the day of the year makes."

"Wow..." Delaney gave the woman a long, hard look. "You really mean that, don't you?"

"Indubitably." Karen's condescending titter was something a pompous stick in the mud might give. "But then, unlike the masses, I've never been a slave to mawkish sentimentality."

"Forget it, Karen," Roger piped up. "It's like speaking Greek to her. Del is an immature, over-emotional woman who has no real concept of the crass commercialism of days expressly designed for celebration by greeting card companies and florists."

"That's a pity." Karen said it like Delaney was a dull-witted moron and it was the saddest thing she'd ever heard.

"No doubt you now you have a better understanding of what I tried to convey to you about her," Roger said.

"Incontrovertibly," Karen responded.

Determined to remember the ten-dollar word so she could look it up later, Delaney folded her arms across her chest, reminding them, "I'm standing right here, you know."

Any anger she'd initially felt at their arrogant comments fizzled. She couldn't possibly dream up a more suitable partner for her ex. No doubt Karen's fondness for sophisticated verbiage made Roger horny. Yes indeed, theirs was a match made in grammar heaven. It gave Delaney a sense of perverse joy to realize they'd live miserably-ever-after together.

As for the pity Karen mentioned...Delaney gazed at the woman's swollen belly, sorry for the joyless existence their baby faced.

Barging ahead, Roger asked, "Since when did you become such a big fan of Ruff's anyway? I thought you didn't want anything to do with him?"

"Thursday. And that was before."

"Before what?"

"Before you abandoned him and I had to watch him cry every day for two months until the poor pining dog finally realized you weren't coming back."

"Leave it to you to become incongruous and irrational." Roger stared at her with unveiled loathing. "Dogs don't cry, Del. They're senseless, stupid animals."

"Oh really? Then how did he figure out how to open my nightstand drawer and find my chocolate stash, hmm?" Proudly jutting her jaw, she braced her fists against her hips in defiance.

"Why am I not surprised you're still hoarding chocolate?" Roger's contemptuous onceover made Delaney painfully aware of every extra pound on her frame. "I knew you'd never lose the weight."

She pinned Roger with a frigid glare. "I could come back with a crack about knowing your hair would never grow back either..." Her lip curled into a half-smile. "But that was before I spotted the hair plugs." She eyed the dotted areas of his scalp, visible at the edge of his cap and smirked. "It'll take more than a hair transplant to fight off impending middle age, Roger."

Tugging his cap snug, he snarled, "Hair plugs is an antiquated term. The procedure now used is called follicular unit transplantation, or FUT."

"FU...does the T stand for *too*? As in, FU too, Roger?" Granted, it was childish, but Delaney couldn't help snickering.

"Try to abstain from your juvenile antics, Del. And I'd advise you not to make this ugly or you'll force me to file a lawsuit." His cold gaze chilled her to the bone. "Karen's brother is an attorney. He's agreed to take my case if you become obstinate."

Oh God!

Delaney squelched the hot rush of tears threatening to surface. The last thing she wanted was for her heartless, hair-plugged ex to see her crumple into a sniveling heap.

"Let me elucidate the state of affairs for your edification," Roger said in professor-speak. "I wasn't fully prepared to take the dog until now."

It was impossible for Delaney to miss the fact that he spoke to her as if she were a two-year-old. Some things never change. She didn't miss Roger's condescending attitude one single iota.

"The child's arrival is imminent." His hand rested on Karen's bulge for emphasis...in case poor addlebrained Delaney didn't know what child he was talking about. "I want Ruff to be there so he and the baby can bond. He'll be good company for Karen and the infant while I'm teaching classes."

"As long as the animal is sufficiently trained before allowing him free reign in our new house," Karen added.

"New house?" Delaney's gaze shot to Roger in time to catch him swallowing hard, looking self-conscious, as he damn well should. She'd spent the last decade fixing up the ill-kempt handyman special he chose to purchase for them. The cheap son of a bitch claimed they couldn't afford repairs, much less a house in better condition. He reasoned that since Delaney was mechanically inclined, she could devote her time to getting the fixer-upper into functional condition.

Arching an eyebrow, Delaney turned her attention to Karen. "My, isn't that thoughtful of Roger to ensure you'll be living the American dream."

"Thoughtful as well as level-headed," Karen agreed. "We're living on the North Shore in a neighborhood and dwelling more befitting a professor of Roger's stature."

"Karen..." Roger started, looking more uncomfortable by the second. And with good reason. The North Shore was one of the most affluent, elite areas of Chicago.

"You chose a fine property, Roger." Patting his arm, Karen went on, "I'm sure the dog and the child will enjoy having the scenic brook just beyond the backyard."

"Does it babble?" Delaney asked.

"I'm sorry?" Karen was clearly confused.

"Karen, it's not necessary to share our personal details with my ex-wife."

"Tell me, Karen, wouldn't you prefer to have a brand new dog to go with your brand new house, your brand new baby, and your brand new husband?"

"Frankly, I've never been a dog or cat person—or a baby person for that matter." Karen absently smoothed her hand over the sizeable protrusion again. "However, this is a matter of importance to my husband and I support his affection for the creature."

"You mean the dog or the baby?" Delaney asked with an innocent batting of her eyelashes.

Delaney saw Roger flinch out of the corner of her eye as Karen eyes flashed with annoyance.

"It's time to get back to the purpose of our visit," Roger said. "The dog. *My* dog, Ruff. I don't have all day, Del. Where is he?"

It was as if a thousand hot needles pricked at Delaney's heart and soul.

"Please, Roger...don't take him away from me." This time she couldn't stop the sob that escaped.

"You're making this far more difficult than it has to be." Roger's already beady eyes tapered to slits.

"But, Roger, you don't understand. I need—"

"Come on, Ruff," Roger called out. "Time to go, boy." He followed that with a shrill whistle. "Ruff! Here, boy. Let's go."

Delaney's eyelids closed and she steadied herself against an end table, worried she might pass out from the stress. She'd never fainted in her life but she'd never faced this magnitude of tension either. The thought of losing her beloved canine companion was a million times worse than losing Roger.

Opening her eyes, she turned a pleading gaze toward her ex-husband, fairly certain it wouldn't do her any good, but she didn't know what else to do. Maybe somewhere under that cold unfeeling exterior of his, buried deep inside, Roger had a heart.

"Roger, please," she began, chilled by the steeliness of his scowl. "Can we talk about this? There must be something we can do to come to a compromise."

There wasn't even a flicker of change in his expression. Perhaps if she appealed to Roger's propensity for penny pinching...

"I'd be happy to buy you and Karen another dog. I'll pay for its training." She turned to Karen. "It'll be fully trained. No worries about spoiling your nice new house like this." Delaney motioned to the mess across her rug. "You'd like that, wouldn't you, Karen?" She got a blank, bored stare in return. "For heaven's sake, Roger, I'll even pay for its food and grooming for the first year." It didn't matter that she'd have to get a second job to keep her promise. Keeping Thursday was worth any amount of time or money.

Emitting a lengthy sigh, Karen took her phone from her purse, glancing at the time. "If we don't conclude this unfortunate episode quickly, Roger, we'll be late for our Lamaze class. Either get your dog or forget about it. Either way, we're leaving in ten minutes."

Clearly, Roger's wife was just as callous as he was.

"I'm willing to do anything, Roger, if only you'll agree to let me keep Thursday. I just can't bear to let him go." Tears rolled down Delaney's cheeks. "You have Karen and a newborn on the way. I only have Thursday. He's all I have left. Please, Roger...*please.*"

Delaney's heartfelt pleading didn't matter. The look Roger gave her was akin to a knife in her heart.

"After being married a decade, you should know I've never been moved by histrionics." His tone was perfect practiced calm. "Legally the dog belongs to me. You've merely been the animal's caretaker this past year, nothing more." Looking around the room in disgust, he added, "And you've obviously failed at that." Fishing a folded paper from his pocket, he waved it. "This is the court document giving me ownership. I'm not leaving here without my property."

With that declaration, Delaney's heart shattered and her entire world came to a screeching halt.

Chapter 10

~<>~

"NO! THOR'S DAY stay with Delaney!"

Gasping at the sound of Varik's booming voice, Delaney whipped her head around. She almost peed in her pants when, in full Viking regalia, he strode into the living room from the kitchen, Thursday trotting at his side. She fought the urge to run to the mirror before she remembered that a little primping couldn't change the sad fact that she looked like a scummy dishrag.

"Who the hell is *that*?" Roger squawked through a drop-jawed, bug-eyed expression.

Karen's wide-eyed, arched eyebrow look telegraphed her unconcealed interest as well, as the three of them watched the glorious half-naked Viking strut his stuff.

Delaney was speechless. It took her a minute to realize Varik must have come in through the back door, which she'd left open because of her repeated trips to the trashcan while cleaning Thursday's mess.

Varik kept his eyes on Delaney, issuing a warm, reassuring smile. "I be..." he cleared his throat and started again, "I *am* Varik the Bold," he corrected himself, flexing his impressive muscles and clapping the shield against his chest. Boldly seizing Delaney into his arms and bending her backwards, he swooped over her and took her mouth in a passionate kiss.

"Happy Sunday to you, my beauty Delaney," Varik whispered, his lips a hairsbreadth from hers.

"Oh...Varik," Delaney whispered back. He smiled down at her and winked. Even in the midst of all this turmoil, she felt a warm rush of desire course through her.

"Delaney is my woman," Varik fiercely announced. "I am Delaney's man...her lover." He stood tall and defiant, tugging Delaney close to his side and wrapping a protective arm around her.

Roger's jaw fell. For once, the pompous English professor was blessedly speechless.

"I am here for beautiful Delaney, so she is never lonely again."

It had to be the most beautiful, exquisite, romantic moment in Delaney's entire life. And, oh dear God, how she wished to hell she wasn't dressed like a grungy scrubwoman and didn't reek of dog puke.

"Varik the Bold...holy—" the clearly astonished Karen began in a momentary lapse of her usual propriety.

"Karen!" Roger chastised, yanking her arm. "I expect you to act with at least a modicum of decorum."

After a few rapid blinks, Karen regained her composure. "Of course. My apologies, Roger. I blame my fleeting break from respectability on pregnancy hormones. Fear not, love, I only have eyes for you." Looking up at him, she made an air kiss.

Glowering, Roger grumbled something unintelligible.

"This," Varik whispered to Delaney, "is heartbreak man? And this is girl bride?" Surprise was evident in his voice.

"Yes," she whispered back. "He wasn't a hipster the last time I saw him though."

Varik laughed quietly. "Very funny." As if part of their furtive conversation, Thursday offered a subdued bark.

"He really is quite charming." Noticing Roger's indignant glare, Karen patted her husband's chest. "I'm talking about the dog, not the Viking."

Turning her attention to Thursday, Karen uttered a round of baby talk that Delaney doubted she'd learned in her graduate English classes. "Come on, Ruffy. Good little doggie woggie."

"Thursday doesn't respond to baby talk," Delaney pointed out, amused by the woman's abrupt change in character. Pregnancy hormones indeed. "He hates it."

When Karen smooched the air, Delaney was about to tell her again that Thursday didn't react to such actions. Unfortunately, Thursday chose that moment to make a complete fool of Delaney by doing his *look how positively adorable I can be* routine in answer to Karen's continuing prattle of baby babble.

While Thursday performed in response to Karen's attention, Varik leaned down to whisper again in Delaney's ear. "Delaney all right? Not look so good."

"Oh..." she yanked the bandana from her head, fluffing her flattened hair. "I'm sorry," she whispered back. "I've been scrubbing the floor and—"

"No." Varik tsked. "You always beautiful to me. I mean you look bad emotion."

Delaney noticed his English had already improved since she saw him last night. Even though she stood there looking vile and revolting, the kindhearted Viking knew exactly the right words to soothe her soul.

"Thank you." Looping her arm with his, she leaned against his shoulder. "I just don't know what I'll do if I lose Thursday, Varik. That silly dog has been my whole world this last year."

"Do not worry." He kissed her temple. "You not lose Thor's Day."

They returned their attention to Thursday as Roger got into the act, roughhousing with the dog. Although Thursday should have been filled with righteous indignation at being abandoned by Professor Hipster, the fickle hound basked in Roger's attention.

After the bond they'd built over the last year, watching old movies and eating popcorn together, going for morning walks, playing in the backyard, it seemed Thursday was ready to trot off into the sunset with Roger and Karen. After she'd let him take over Roger's side of the bed, and after he bulldozed his way into her secret emergency chocolate cache and devoured every melt-in-your-mouth morsel, Thursday was going to abandon her...just like Roger had.

"Thursday," Delaney whimpered, flinching at how pathetic she sounded. "You want to stay here with me, don't you, boy?" If her heart wasn't crushed she would have laughed at the pitiful, sniveling crybaby she'd become.

After flashing Delaney a gleeful canine grin, Thursday returned his attention to Roger, jumping up on him and baptizing his face with a series of slurpy licks.

That was it. Delaney had lost him. She knew it.

Because of her ex she couldn't have any children...and now he wanted to take away the closest thing to a child she'd ever had.

Cold, heartless, unfeeling bastard.

The dog looked for all the world like he was smiling as he pranced back and forth between Roger and Karen, relishing their lavish attention.

Tsking, Varik stepped forward, yanking on Thursday's collar. "Thor's Day be good. Act like a man," he admonished with gentle firmness. Thursday licked his chops, then, to Delaney's amazement, he sat obediently at Varik's knee.

"You not be a good man, Roger." Varik jabbed a menacing finger toward him. "Make pain in heart for Delaney." He thumped his chest. "You go now."

"Are you threatening me?" Roger spat. "Is he threatening me?" he repeated to Delaney. "Because I'll sue Mr. Fancy Pants here in the blink of an eye if he so much as lays a finger on me."

"No." Placing one hand against Varik's chest, Delaney held the other out to Roger, stop-sign fashion. "He's just trying to protect me, Roger." She turned to Varik and smiled. "Thank you, my wonderful, gallant Viking, but I have to let Thursday go." A fat tear trickled down her cheek. "Legally he belongs to Roger, even though Roger is a—"

"Rotten buzzard," Varik offered through an arresting sneer that could send the bravest of men running for cover.

"Bastard," Delaney corrected. Nodding in agreement, Varik repeated the word.

"So the guy playing Viking dress up is your lover, huh?" Roger's tone was skeptical as he gave Varik a onceover. "That's really rich. Muscleheads like him don't take overweight matrons, especially ones who smell like they just rolled through vomit, as lovers. Unless they're paid to." Roger snickered. "So what did you do, Del, order yourself a rent-a-stud for a little birthday whoopee?"

Roger's cruel words hit too close to home. Every shred of Delaney's self-esteem evaporated. Feeling fat and ancient, she didn't even have enough energy left to sigh.

"Ignore hate words," Varik advised Delaney, wrapping his arm around her waist and holding her close, possessively, while glowering at Roger.

"Roger!" Breathing an audible gasp, Karen's expression was etched with shock. "I don't expect that sort of hostile behavior from you. That was exceedingly harsh." Turning a surprisingly compassionate expression toward Delaney, she said, "Just ignore him. He's obviously overwrought and taking his ire out on you."

"And doing a great job of it." Delaney finally found enough energy to sigh after taking a moment to regain her composure following Roger's exacting tirade. "Thank you, Karen."

"I'm betting your gigolo," Roger went on, oblivious to anything other than the towering Viking before him, "is gay. Those beefed up male model types usually are."

"What in God's name is wrong with you, Roger?" Dropping her head into her hand, Karen said, "Please tell that's not how you act in front of your students."

Varik closed the distance between himself and Roger with a long stride. Everyone inhaled sharply as he grabbed the smaller man by the shirt, lifting him off the floor. "You listen, squeaking pipe..." He turned to Delaney with a quizzical expression. "Is that right?"

Glancing from Varik to the dangling Roger and back again, Delaney offered, "I think you mean pipsqueak."

"Pipsqueak," Varik bellowed into Roger's ashen face.

"Put me down this instant, you crude behemoth," Roger blustered.

Varik held tight. "Delaney is full of beauty. She not old. Not fat. Not need to pay money for sex. Understand? *Ja*, maybe she smell of retching, but she still fine beauty to me. She true woman of worth but you too stupid to see."

Delaney dissolved into a girlish sigh.

"Put. Me. Down," Roger repeated more vehemently. Varik set him on his feet and Roger took a few steps back. "Acting like a big man to impress the ladies, huh?" Jutting his chin, Roger repositioned his slipping cap. "All the machismo in the world doesn't change the fact that you're gay," he snarled, brushing his shirt sleeves and straightening his collar.

"Roger, do you hear yourself?" Karen looked aghast. "Please stop embarrassing yourself...and me."

"What? I don't see a problem," Roger protested. "I'm simply stating the facts as I see them. I mean, all you have to do is look at him." He gestured from Varik's head to feet.

"Yeah..." Karen said dreamily. "Look at him."

Roger's beady eyes got beadier. "Shut up, Karen."

Varik looked at Delaney. "What is meaning of gay?"

"Homosexual. Roger means you like to have sex with men," Delaney explained.

"What?" Clearly stunned, Varik returned his attention to Roger. "No! How you would think this misunderstanding?" Drawing Delaney into his arms again, he kissed her tenderly. "I have strong heart attraction for Delaney, who is woman. *My* woman," he said, gazing into her eyes. "We make best, most happy sex together. Not for money."

"Oh Varik..." Delaney whispered, feeling her heart expand in her chest.

"Understand now?" Varik finished, directing the question to Roger.

Delaney's cheeks hurt from smiling so wide. She took one look at Roger's dazed expression and her grin grew even broader. "Oh, I think he understands perfectly now, Varik."

Zipping past Delaney and Varik, Roger headed for the safety of the kitchen, putting the island counter as a barrier between himself and Varik. He grabbed his phone from his pocket, waving it at them. "Well here's something for *you* to understand. I'm calling the police to have you arrested for assault and battery, you ignorant ox. Got that? Or do you need your woman to translate for you?"

"I'm stunned...and so disappointed," Karen admitted, looking increasingly uncomfortable, her gaze slipping between her husband and Delaney. It seemed she was getting a crash course in *The Real Roger* and was disillusioned with her realization.

Having been there herself, Delaney understood Karen's chagrin completely.

"Roger, please...let's not involve the police," Karen pleaded. Her eyes closed in a long blink and she shook her head back and forth. "I can't believe how quickly this has escalated. I feel a migraine coming on. Let's just leave before this becomes any uglier. *Please*."

"No worry, Karen," Varik said, striding over to Roger. "He will not make call." He snatched the phone from the startled Roger's hand before he'd finished punching in the numbers.

"I can't believe you just did that. Give that back to me...and don't you dare touch me again," Roger warned, backing into a corner of the kitchen as Varik neared him.

Varik set the phone on the counter. "I know you teach at university," he said, standing arms akimbo. "I teach at university too."

Roger, Karen and Delaney all slanted Varik bewildered looks. Even Thursday cocked his head.

His features scrunching with skepticism, Roger said, "What are you talking about?"

"You are English professor, yes?" Roger nodded and Varik grinned. "I, Varik Jenssen, am Scandinavian Studies professor."

"You're what?" the three chorused in disbelief.

"That's preposterous." Roger perched a fist on one hip. "How can you possibly teach college-level courses when you can't even speak English? If you were a professor at the university, believe me, I'd know about it." He issued Varik another caustic onceover. "Honestly, the audacity of some people. A professor indeed."

"I have best university professor to teach me English," Varik said proudly. "I begin teaching for new term in fall," he explained. "I speak excellent English by then. Better English than you, I bet."

"That's ridiculous...absolutely outrageous." Roger huffed a humorless chortle. "I'm the foremost English professor at the university."

"No. Tore Thorkelson best."

"Professor Thorkelson?" Varik had Roger's full attention now. "The Chair of the university's English department?" Roger said incredulously.

"I be...I am Tore's cousin." Varik arched an eyebrow, clearly enjoying Roger's dismay.

"Well, I'll be damned," Delaney said as Roger went ashen again.

"Tore my best friend for long time. Like brothers. Maybe I tell Tore about you be so mean. So cruel. You go now, take pregnant child bride home. Thor's Day stay with Delaney. Then maybe Varik not tell Tore you are buzzard—bastard," he immediately corrected.

"That's blackmail," Roger spat.

"Not know this blackmail word yet. But sound good." Varik nailed him with a seething gaze. "Go." He pointed to the door.

With a nervous swipe of his tongue across his lips, Roger stood stock still, evidently deep in thought. "Maybe Ruff would rather be with me," he said to Delaney. "Have you considered that? If you really love the dog, you want him to be happy and well cared for, right?"

Roger sure as hell knew the right buttons to push to make Delaney feel selfish and guilty.

"Remember...regardless of your lover's threats, I'm still the dog's legal owner. I'll make you a deal if you promise to keep your caveman off my back."

Delaney blanched. Maybe Roger was right. What if Thursday really would be happier with Roger, Karen, and their baby? He wouldn't have to spend the days alone while Delaney was at the office. "What are you suggesting, Roger?"

"Simple. Let the dog choose. Leave the decision entirely up to Ruff. We'll both call him and whoever he comes to keeps him. That's fair and equitable." Roger glanced up at Varik, who transmitted a heated glare. "But remember, if I win you see to it that lover boy keeps his mouth shut about me to my department head."

"Not good to deal with devil," Varik cautioned, shaking his head as he braced his arms over his chest.

"It's a deal," Delaney agreed quickly.

"Delaney..." Varik said through a frown.

"It's only fair to Thursday." Delaney touched Varik's chest, smiling up at him. "I love my dog that much, Varik."

Delaney and Roger positioned themselves at the far end of the living room while Varik held Thursday by the collar.

Removing his hand from his pants pocket, Roger stroked his beard, then took off his hat and raked his fingers through his thinning *FU Too* hair before squatting and patting his knee. "Come on, Ruff. Come on, boy," he called.

"No cheat! You wait for Varik to count!" Varik admonished. Taking Thursday, he headed out of the room.

"Where are you taking my dog?" Roger complained.

"Kitchen. I talk to dog first."

"Well of all the most idiotic..." Roger muttered, trailing off with a roll of his eyes.

Though Varik was partially hidden from view, Delaney's position allowed her to see him get down on one knee. Placing his hand against his heart, he whispered something in Thursday's ear while stroking the dog. Thursday responded by licking his face.

In the blink of an eye, the entire kitchen lit up with a bluish glow that bled into the living room.

"What on earth...?" Karen uttered.

"Holy...what *was* that?!" Delaney cried. "Are you okay, Varik?"

"*Ja*, okay," he called from the kitchen as the light receded.

"What's going on?" Roger asked, belligerence coloring his tone. "What's he doing in there, hypnotizing my dog?"

At a complete loss to explain the brief glow of blue light that had disappeared as fast as it came, Delaney answered, "Right, Roger. Varik is hypnotizing the dog." She rolled her eyes at him. "Get serious, will you?"

"Thor's Day ready now," Varik announced, leading the dog back into the living room where he quietly sat alongside the Viking. "I count to three. Get ready." Delaney and Roger did exactly that, positioning themselves at the opposite end of the room. "*En. To. Tre.* Go!" Varik counted in Norwegian before releasing the dog and giving him a pat on the rump.

Delaney bent low and clapped her hands. "Thursday, you want to stay with me, don't you, boy? Come on, sweetie." She patted her knees. "Come to mama."

Roger whistled. "Ruff! Here, boy."

Tail wagging and tongue lolling, Thursday looked from Delaney to Roger and back again before padding forward and making a beeline for Delaney. Her heart leapt with joy until...when Thursday was a foot away from her, Roger extended his hand, snapping his fingers.

Thursday angled his head, sniffed, and flashed Delaney a gleeful canine grin before licking her ex-husband's hand, jumping up on him and baptizing Roger's face and head with lavish licks.

"Good boy," Roger said triumphantly as he played with the dog.

Delaney wheezed a tortured gasp. "Oh Thursday," she whimpered, sounding like someone who'd just lost her best friend...because she had. The dog turned, slanting her a questioning look.

Karen's intake of breath was barely perceptible but the sympathetic look in her eyes as she glanced at Delaney said it all.

Rising to his feet, Roger wrapped two fingers under Thursday's collar, yanking hard. Thursday looked at Delaney a moment longer before turning to follow Roger.

"I won fair and square." Roger jabbed an accusatory finger toward Delaney as he stood near the front door and reached for the doorknob. "Fair and square," he boasted again to Varik. "You'd better live up to your part of the bargain, Del. Make sure Jenssen here keeps his mouth shut." He opened the door and Thursday merrily pranced alongside Roger as he and Karen left the house.

"I'm sorry, Delaney," Karen muttered before the door slammed.

Delaney's heart splintered into a million shards. "I've lost him. I've lost my Thursday forever."

Wrapping his arm around Delaney, Varik squeezed her close, whispering soothing Norwegian words in her ear as she stared out the window. "No...Delaney not fear. Thor's Day come back to you. I know. I promise."

Delaney noticed for the first time that it was already dusk. She'd spent the entire afternoon embroiled in a fighting match with her ex-husband.

"Roger wasn't always so cruel," she said absently, watching the Kullerton family get in their car. "At least I don't think he was. Maybe I just bring out the worst in him. I find it hard to believe that one man can be so single-minded and unreasonable."

"He is man who cares only about self. Man with no heart," Varik concurred. "Much like woman I know."

His admission caught Delaney by surprise. She'd never heard Varik talk about any of the women in his life. She'd have to remember to ask him about it later, when she wasn't on the verge of sobbing her heart out.

When Roger's car pulled away from the curb, she released the drape, letting it fall back into place. The contorting muscles started at her chin, making their way to her eyes and Delaney collapsed into tears.

"I wasn't anywhere close to being this upset when Roger walked out a year ago."

"Sad for you. I know. Very bad day." Bringing her head to rest on his chest, Varik continued to soothe her, smoothing his fingers through her hair. "But Delaney see, Thor's Day return. I know for sure."

"Thank you so much for trying to help me, Varik," she managed through another round of tears. "I don't know what I would have done if you hadn't been here supporting me. I'll never forget it." She took in a wavering breath.

Less than a minute later, a ruckus outside had Delaney and Varik exchanging baffled glances. Peering out the window, she saw Roger's car stopped in the middle of the street half a block from the house. It was the first time she noticed he was driving a new Lexus.

"Thor's Day make much barking," Varik noted.

That was followed by the raised voices of Karen and Roger. The car's back seat window slid down and Thursday sprang out. Barking like a rabid animal, he headed for the house. Roger sprinted after him through the snow with Karen waddling behind them both.

Thursday leapt at the door, scratching and howling. Delaney hauled the door open and Thursday jumped at her so hard she fell to the floor—right in the midst of the caked-on dog barf. Thursday licked her face and wagged his tail so fast it seemed to be electrified. She started to laugh and cry at the same time and then she heard Karen shouting something down the street.

"It's not acceptable, Roger. What you did is wrong."

"You screeching at me isn't helping matters, Karen," Roger, the man who hated scenes, shouted at her loud enough for all the neighbors to hear. "Keep quiet and get back in the car. I'm going to get Ruff's leash so I can secure him in the back seat."

"You were dishonest, Roger. That's inexcusable."

"You're really irritating me, Karen. Stay out of it."

"Something happen," Varik said to Delaney as he stood looking down the street. "Big fighting. Roger in hurry to get back here."

A moment later Roger arrived back at the townhouse. Sidestepping Varik's bulk, he stood looking at Thursday and Delaney sprawled on the soiled carpet before he advanced toward the dog.

"I've had just about enough out of you, Ruff. Let's go." He reached for Thursday's collar and Thursday let out a low, menacing growl.

Delaney pulled herself to a sitting position before getting to her feet. About to brush off her clothes, she remembered what she'd been rolling around in and thought better of it.

Roger took a step toward her. "This is your fault, Del," he yelled. "You brainwashed my dog somehow."

"Brainwashed?" Delaney gave an incredulous laugh. "So I brainwashed him and Varik hypnotized him? Do you know how ridiculous that sounds...especially coming from a persnickety English professor? All I did was give Thursday the love and attention he needed and deserved."

"Maybe you should have invested in behavioral training instead of mollycoddling him," Roger spat. "That damned dog went nuts trying to get out of my car. He..." Clearly bewildered, Roger shook his head before continuing. "I still don't believe it...but he somehow figured out how to push the button to lower the window, clawing up the leather interior in the process."

"Of your shiny brand-spanking-new Lexus?" Delaney tsked before smirking at him. "Aw gee, that's most unfortunate, Roger."

"He deceived you!" Karen blurted when she reached the house, leaning against the doorjamb, fighting to catch her breath and supporting her belly bulge with the other arm. "Roger cheated. The contest was fraudulent."

"That's quite enough, Karen!" Roger jerked her arm, making Karen wince. "I told you to get back in the car."

"You're hurting me." Glaring at her husband, Karen yanked her arm free.

"Hands off wife," Varik growled, stepping between them. "Or I make puny professor very sorry." He scowled down at Roger.

"This is none of your business, you hulking costumed behemoth. She's my wife!"

"I make it my business." His face inches from Roger's, Varik warned, "You treat wife with respect."

"Varik's right, Roger," Delaney agreed. "God help your baby if this is any indication of your parenting style."

"When the dog realized we were leaving without you," the still huffing Karen told Delaney, "he started howling and struggling to get out of the vehicle and back here to you."

Delaney gazed down at Thursday with a big teary smile. "I knew you loved me." She mussed his fur and got a gleeful lick in response.

"I was horrified to discover that Roger has a chocolate bar in his pocket. He—"

"Damn it, Karen, keep quiet and stop acting infantile!" Roger pounded the doorjamb.

The abrupt transformation of Karen's neutral expression into a mask of fury was fearsome. "Infantile? How dare you speak to me that way."

"You're making a scene," Roger informed her in the most condescending tone imaginable.

"Is that so?" Karen responded through a wicked smile. "Well, if you think *that* was a scene, trust me, you're in for one hell of a humdinger if you don't confess to Delaney about what you've done." She pinned him with a mighty glare. "You know...you've given me food for thought here, Roger...perhaps you're not suitable husband or father material after all. Perhaps I'd be better off returning to my family."

Delaney and Varik silently exchanged stunned glances. Even Thursday had gone mute. It took every bit of Delaney's restraint not to yell out a rousing *Bravo!* and applaud like mad. Instead, she sent Karen a smile along with an admiring nod.

A wealth of emotion played across Roger's face. Delaney suspected his reaction could very possibly make or break their marriage. Looking again at Karen's distended belly and her determined expression, Delaney prayed he'd have the sense to man up and do the right thing to keep his family together.

"Okay, okay." Pulling a resistant Karen into a hug, Roger soothed her. "You're right. Absolutely right. I profusely apologize for my uncharacteristic behavior. I don't know what came over me. Forgive me? Please, I don't want to lose you or our baby. I love you, Karen."

Delaney blinked back tears as she watched them embrace. If she'd been savvy enough years ago to handle Roger like Karen just did, things likely would have been far different in their marriage. She glanced up at Varik to see him offer a brief nod of approval. He may not have understood much of what Karen said, but Delaney was sure he comprehended the essence of her words as well as Roger's.

"I love you too," Karen told her husband. "Which is why it's important for you to tell Delaney what you did...before I tell her for you. I know—I *trust*—you'll do the right thing."

Closing his eyes in a long blink, Roger sighed. He remained that way so long Delaney wondered if he was zoning out in some sort of weird meditation. When he finally opened his eyes, he gave his wife a contrite smile.

"I'm sorry," he said to Delaney. Roger's words were so foreign she almost asked him to repeat them. "I was...somewhat less than honest. I rubbed the chocolate on my fingers, beard and hair before calling the dog over." His surprising admission obviously pained him.

Giving him an incredulous look, Delaney muttered, "You didn't..."

"He did," Karen confirmed. "That's why Thursday came to him instead of you, Delaney. Once I realized, I simply couldn't allow that kind of subterfuge."

Instinctively, Delaney went to Karen, embracing the woman as close as the beach ball in her belly would allow. "Thank you from the bottom of my heart, Karen." She looked at Roger and, while she wasn't able to offer a smile, and certainly not a hug, Delaney told him, "I appreciate your honesty, Roger." He nodded in response.

"Cheating son of a jackass," Varik barked at Roger. "Very bad man. No honor."

"I will admit I had a momentary lapse in judgment." Roger raised his hands in defense. "However," he directed his comment to Delaney, "this doesn't change the fact that the animal legally belongs to me."

Delaney's shoulders slumped. So much for Roger turning over a new leaf.

Her ex reached for the dog's collar and Thursday did something Delaney had never seen him do before. He bared his teeth, looking for all the world like a devil-dog from hell. His growl was so ominous it sent chills up Delaney's spine. It must have had a similar effect on Roger, because he leapt back.

"You really do love me, don't you, Thursday?" Delaney gave him a hug and he slobbered a lick across her face.

"Time for you to go." Varik gave Roger a light shove. "Before I forget I am gentleman."

"Oh...oh...*ohhhhhhhhh*! Oh...my...God!" Karen wailed before Roger had a chance to respond to Varik's thinly veiled threat.

Including Thursday, four heads whipped in Karen's direction.

"Karen?" Roger's face blanched.

"It's the baby!" Karen clutched her enormous belly. "My water just broke."

All eyes were on the floor where a small puddle formed.

"You need to get me to the hospital, Roger. This is it."

"The baby's coming?" Delaney nearly shrieked.

After a loud, guttural grunt, Karen nodded. "Oh yeah. Definitely."

"Now? You have to do it now?" Roger asked. "The timing is inopportune to say the least."

"God damn it, Roger!" Karen growled in a voice so threatening it would strike fear into any man. "This is no time to be an asshole. Stop your whining and get me to the damn hospital. Now!"

Delaney had to bite the inside of her cheek to keep from laughing. Varik took Delaney's hand and squeezed. She looked up and saw the corner of his mouth twitch.

"Okay, Karen, okay." He put his arm around his wife. Turning to Delaney, he said, "Fine. Go ahead and keep the damn dog. He's more trouble than he's worth." He turned to Thursday. "You had your chance, Ruff. I'm getting a puppy to replace you. A pedigreed puppy."

"Looks like I'm not the only one being replaced by a younger model, Thursday." Delaney winked at her furry, four-legged pal.

"Rogerrrrrr!" Karen howled in between the weird puffing breaths she was making. "Stop! Just stop yapping! I'm...*uuuggghhhhh*...having contractions!"

"Yes, okay, we're going," Roger said, turning to leave.

"Hey," Delaney called as her ex reached the door.

"What?" he answered without turning back to look at her.

"I want that court document, the one giving you ownership of the dog."

"Fine." He took the folded document from the pocket of his slacks and tossed it at Delaney. "Here."

Catching it, she held it out to him. "Sign it."

"As you can see, I'm in kind of a hurry, Del." He spun around on his heel. "Come on, I already said you can have the animal. Don't you trust me?"

"Ha!" Karen commented.

"Ditto." Delaney acknowledged.

"Sign the damn paper so we can go," Karen ordered through gritted teeth. "Do it...*now*!" An ungodly growl followed...not from Thursday—from Karen.

"If you try anything funny," Delaney warned, "you'll find yourself back in court facing a formal request of alimony from me. I doubt I'll have any trouble, seeing as how you just bought a fancy new house on the North Shore, and a big new luxury car. Got it?"

Before Roger could respond, Karen commenced with a series of grunts, wails and more peculiar breathing noises she must have learned from her Lamaze classes. The feral look in her eyes could have turned a man to stone.

Looking white as a sheet, and probably fearing he just might be turned to stone if he wasn't careful, Roger snatched a pen from his pocket, scrawled his signature on the paper and slapped it into Delaney's waiting hand. "Okay, done. I've legally relinquished ownership. Ruff's all yours now. Satisfied?" He patted Varik's arm. "No hard feelings, okay, buddy?"

Varik glared at him, energetic fury sizzling in the depths of his eyes. "Never call me buddy. I be watching you." He made a V-sign with his fingers, pointing at his own eyes first, then Roger's. "Be good, honorable man or I tell Tore you are very bad devil. Okay, *buddy*?"

Roger gave a cursory nod and Karen screeched again. She must have hit some hidden octave because Thursday's head gyrated just before he started bellowing.

Amidst the cacophony, Roger scratched his head, put his cap on and looked at Delaney in a way he hadn't done in years, almost as if he were seeing her for the first time. There was a time she would have done anything to have Roger gaze at her like that. Funny...now it just left her cold.

"Time for you go away, now," Varik instructed. Delaney assumed he must have seen Roger's longing expression. "Leave Delaney for me to love her and take good care of her always like woman of worth deserve."

Weak-kneed at Varik's loving words, Delaney turned to her ex. "Varik's right, Roger," she said kindly. "Your future awaits. You'd better get Karen to the hospital before she spits the newest Kullerton out on the soiled carpet."

Eyeing them both, Roger remained silent.

"One more thing," Delaney said. Roger responded with a questioning arch of his eyebrow. "Take care of Karen and the baby. Treat them right, Roger. They deserve much better than what you gave me." With a quick nod to acknowledge Delaney's words, Roger turned away.

One hand clutching her belly, Karen waddled over to Delaney, drawing her into a somewhat awkward hug. "Thank you, Delaney. Goodbye." Karen's smile quickly morphed into an expression of agony as she growled through another contraction. A moment later, she and Roger were gone.

"See?" Varik got to one knee, clapping the dog's flanks. "I promise you Thor's Day come back."

"You did..." She gave him a curious look. "What made you so certain?"

Shrugging his broad shoulders, Varik said, "I told Thor's Day I make him big steak and potato and give him beer. I tell him in Norwegian so he understand."

"But he doesn't understand Norwegian."

Nodding confidently, he told Delaney, "His name is from Norse god. He understand plenty."

Taking in his confident expression, Delaney offered a heartfelt smile.

"I also make wish for Thor's Day return to you." He clapped his chest. "Special wish from heart." He tapped two fingers over his heart. "One day I tell you about it."

Opening her mouth to thank him, a whopping yawn came out instead. Delaney's fingers flew to her lips. "Oh, I'm sorry!"

Tracing her face from temple to jawline with his knuckle, Varik laughed quietly. "Poor Delaney tired after much emotion."

To her horror, she yawned again, mortified she'd actually yawned twice in the presence of her wonderful Viking. "How embarrassing."

"Is okay. I understand." She could tell he meant it. "You have much bad, eh...stress today. Need plenty rest tonight. Must go to work tomorrow, yes?"

"Bright and early." Delaney nodded, mentally preparing herself for the long night ahead. There was no way she was about to go to sleep before she finished cleaning the rest of Thursday's chocolate disaster from the rugs. She feared some of the stains might already be permanent, and new carpeting definitely wasn't in her budget.

Glancing at the clock, Varik said, "Time for me leave soon for play. Tomorrow we eat supper together, *ja*?"

"That sounds lovely," Delaney said.

"Good. We *feire*...eh...celebrate, for you have Thursday back. Go restaurant and make happy time together. Forget sadness of today. Sound nice?"

"Sounds perfect." Delaney smiled up at him, her heart full of gratitude that this man had come into her life. "I'm mighty glad you showed up on my doorstep, even if you weren't selling fundraiser chocolate."

"Best of accidents." Leaning close, he kissed the tip of her nose. "I think of excellent plan for us. You like to hear?"

"Sure." She couldn't imagine what he meant but hoped it included lots of hugs, kisses and cuddling.

"For two week we do friendly neighbor planet dating. Is good amount of time."

"Planet dating?" He had her stumped this time.

Varik's eyebrow curved. "Mean no sex."

"Ah...platonic," Delaney said.

"Platonic," he repeated. "Be hard to not make sex with beautiful Delaney," smiling down at her, he caressed her face, his thumb lingering on her bottom lip, "but Delaney feel more safe to us know each other better first, *ja?*"

Although she felt she already knew everything about him that really mattered, she nodded, knowing he was right, regardless of what her libido screamed. His plan was clearly designed for her benefit, which, as far as she was concerned, propelled Varik into the same league as all her favorite romance heroes.

"It's a wise plan," she agreed.

"At end of two week..." his eyebrows danced with a devilish jiggle, "we make special celebration night. All night. You in Varik's arms."

"Perfect." She wrapped her arms around his neck, stroking the back of his hair. "Your English may be broken but you still have a wonderful way with words, Varik."

His kiss was far better than a verbal response. A dreamy sigh escaped her lips after his passionate goodnight caress. It was a delicious promise of what was to come.

Chapter 11

~<>~

AMIDST MOUNTING sexual tension, the next two weeks were heavenly. They talked about everything and anything, including topics Delaney and Roger had never discussed in their ten years together. Each day brought improvement in Varik's English, in just two weeks it had vastly improved. She had no trouble believing he'd be speaking perfect English by the time he started teaching in the fall.

They learned each other's preferences in books, movies, music, travel, food and more. Delaney adored his quick wit and sense of humor. It was a rare man, or woman for that matter, who could easily laugh at themselves. Varik had no trouble at all. The man loved to laugh and loved making her laugh.

It was a pleasure to cook for Varik. He lavished her with praise each time she made a new dish for him, making her feel like a master chef while, in truth, she was an average home cook.

"Tomorrow we celebrate," Varik announced on the final evening of their two weeks of platonic dating, with sexual tension at its peak. Nuzzling her neck, he said, "I will cook this time. We start with champagne and liverwurst."

Delaney wrinkled her nose.

"Pickled herring?" Varik asked, then laughed at Delaney's "O" face. He was the more adventurous one when it came to sampling unusual foods. Delaney was determined to change that, little by little...with liverwurst and pickled herring at the bottom of her *must try* list.

"Cheese and crackers?" he suggested.

Relieved, she offered a thumbs up. "Now that sounds appetizing."

"Then we will have baby back ribs. I remember you say they are your favorite."

"I can't believe you remembered."

Taking her hands in his, Varik studied her face. "I find everything about you unforgettable, my beautiful Delaney." His kiss was sweet and tender, as if he cherished her.

"Tomorrow evening will be magical," he promised. "How can it not be when I hold you in my arms all night, skin to skin, heart to heart?"

Delaney surrendered to a dreamy sigh in response.

It all seemed too good to be true. Varik Jenssen had a body to die for, movie star looks, rock star talent, and a great sense of humor. He was kind and considerate, yet a fierce protector. He was a genius, and the man's cooking rivaled Julia Child's.

And he was incredible in bed too.

Dear Diary: I must have done something very good in my life to end up with the ideal man. I've definitely hit the jackpot. I can't help looking heavenward and smiling. If you had anything to do with sending Varik into my life, Grandma Bekka, thank you from the bottom of my heart. Maybe fairytales really do come true after all...

All the planets had aligned perfectly, the universe was in perfect harmony, and Delaney Malone's life was synchronized with the heavens. At least that's the way she felt Sunday morning.

Tomorrow morning, Monday, the first day she and Varik would wake up together, needed to be special. One culinary aspect Delaney had mastered fairly well was making breakfast. She'd whip up a couple cheddar-chive omelets, fry some crisp bacon, toast and butter

English muffins, and serve them breakfast in bed with apricot jam, mimosas and strong coffee.

She wasn't sure if Varik had everything she needed at his place, so she'd head to the grocery store to pick up the necessary ingredients and take them to his house when he came to pick her up this evening.

Imagining their special date tonight was enough to make her swoon...or maybe it was giggle. Probably a little of both. Delaney felt like a schoolgirl anticipating prom night with the popular captain of the football team.

She'd asked her boss, Paul, for Monday off, sidestepping any explanation of how magical it would be waking up in Varik's arms after spending the night with him. Since Delaney was a veritable fixture at the office, never calling in sick or taking a day off, Paul was glad to see her finally taking some time for herself, assuring her the newspaper wouldn't collapse and fold without her there for one day.

On his way to the airport tonight, Paul was stopping by at six-forty-five to drop off and explain the files she'd need during his absence next week. The timing was perfect, since Varik wasn't picking her up until seven-thirty. Delaney would just get ready a little earlier than she'd planned.

She spent the afternoon organizing and tidying her townhouse, which was in far better shape than when it was purchased. After being up most of the night two weeks ago, scrubbing, she'd managed to clean and sanitize all the carpeting until there were no more traces of Thursday's mess. Then she got the bug to clean everything else. Though she should have been exhausted after the stressful visit from her ex, plus getting so little sleep, she felt oddly refreshed and revitalized the next morning.

Daydreaming about the platonic two week courting period Varik had personally planned gave Delaney all the vitality she needed.

On the way to the grocery store she noticed the weather was picture perfect. Bright, sunny and mild with a light sprinkling of fresh snow sparkling in the sunlight, concealing the shoveled piles of dirty gray snow on the roadside as if they'd been sifted with powdered sugar. It was one of those beautiful days that almost had her loving Chicago in the winter.

Everything had neatly fallen into place. It was as if all her ancestors conspired to grant her the happiness she longed for.

It wasn't until Delaney was on her way home from the store that it hit her.

She'd fallen in love.

"But how is that possible?" she asked herself while driving. "I've known Varik less than a month." Doing her best to be logical and rational, she wondered if this was only a case of lust. She'd be an idiot to deny her libido had been working overtime since they'd met. God knows she'd never experienced anything remotely close to the passion she and Varik had shared that first day. But then...maybe she'd simply been carried away by having amazing sex with a gorgeous guy in costume.

Then she remembered all of Varik's endearing qualities, all the wonderful traits that had nothing to do with his prowess as a lover. He was unlike any man she'd ever known. It was almost as if he'd been created just for her. As if they were true soul mates, destined to be together.

"And that all adds up to love," Delaney said, pulling in to her driveway. "There's no other explanation."

As the garage door rose, she expelled a wistful sigh and glanced down the street to Varik's townhouse, daydreaming about the perfect romantic night she had in store.

She was just in time to see a shapely blonde wrapping herself around Varik when he opened the door. A moment later, after sharing a passionate kiss, they'd disappeared into his house.

And Delaney Malone's entire world imploded.

~<>~

At a loss as to what to do, Delaney paced, muttering aloud with Thursday pacing at her side, moaning in commiseration.

"Maybe she's his sister," she mused, frowning when the image of the statuesque woman draping herself over Varik came into view. "Perhaps Norwegian brothers and sisters are more...demonstrative than their American counterparts," she reasoned, aware her pseudo logic was ridiculous. If they were siblings that greeting would have bordered on incestual.

Thursday chose that moment to whimper. "You're right, Thursday. There has to be a reasonable explanation. Varik's a good man. He wouldn't do this to me. He just wouldn't..." Thursday responded with a soft bark.

Her mother's frequent warnings about too-charming men soared to the forefront of her mind. It was the last thing Delaney wanted to think about now. Nonetheless, the memory stuck, followed by disagreeable recollections of her decidedly anti-charming ex-husband.

Varik oozed charm, while Roger was devoid of it. Maybe Delaney was meant to find someone in the middle. A man of mediocre charm.

"Varik's not like Roger," she told the dog. Thursday gave her a doubtful look. "He's not," she insisted. Recalling all the sweet things Varik had said to her, all the kind, loving words he'd spoken in adorable broken English, had her succumbing to a wistful sigh.

"What if I only think I'm so smart and it turns out I was just fooled by a charming guy the way my mother always warned me?" Only a fool, a complete idiot, would brazenly drag an unknown man dressed like a Viking in off the street, telling herself he was a paid prostitute parting gift sent from her departed grandmother.

Tears sprang to her eyes.

"He was a stranger. I had hot naked sex with a total stranger, Thursday. Sex that I initiated."

Standing in place, she felt a rush of heat. Not a pleasurable, passionate rush, but the sick, mortifying burn of humiliation.

"Well of course the man's going to bend over backwards being charming and cordial after I welcomed him to the neighborhood with a rousing roll in the hay. Why wouldn't he? After all," her hands flew into the air and came crashing down at her sides, "he's got to keep the whore two doors down pacified so she'll happily perform the horizontal mambo again when the mood strikes him."

When the mood strikes him...

That would be tonight, Varik's carefully calculated conclusion to the *neighborly* phase of their relationship. She thought of all the deliberate planning he must have put into the past two weeks, working hard to gain her trust, intentionally making himself irresistibly charismatic so she'd have no objections when it came time to switch from friendly neighbors to neighbors with benefits.

The grim thought had her shuddering.

Burying her head in her hands, she moaned. "How could I have been so foolish?" Spreading her fingers, she gazed at the dog, who gave her his rapt attention. "Thursday, what am I going to do?" He rubbed his muzzle on her calf in a clear display of sympathy.

That clandestine move to Oregon was looking better and better.

She had to make a decision. She could turn out all the lights and not answer the door, pretending not to be home when...*if,* Varik came to the door at seven-thirty. Or she could answer the door, coolly, calmly and directly confronting him with what she'd seen...in which case she'd come off like a bitchy, jealous lover, especially if there really was a logical explanation for the amorous blonde she'd spotted.

Glancing at the small box of bakery cookies she'd picked up to take to Varik's for dessert along with all the breakfast fixings, she got an idea. She could walk over there early with just the cookies, before he came to pick her up. He'd answer the door and she'd offer a bright smile, telling him she stopped by early to see if she could be of help in the kitchen and to drop off the dessert.

Then, while Varik's jaw was still dropped in surprise, Delaney would *just happen* to notice the breathtaking blonde draped over his arm and, still smiling, she'd nonchalantly say, "Oh, this must be your sister, Varik."

Yeah. That seemed perfectly normal.

A glimpse at her watch told her it was five-thirty. That gave her ample time to freshen up and change. She'd reserved the sexy black wrap dress she'd bought for tonight's celebration. It was perfect. If she was going to Varik's with the intention of meeting The Other Woman face to face, then she was damn well going to do it looking her best.

While getting ready, Delaney went over a variety of scenarios in her head until she felt confident she'd covered all likelihoods. If this happened, she'd say that. If that happened, she'd say this. Above all, she'd be poised and dignified. A veritable model of sophistication. No sniffling or crying. No nonsensical babbling. No nervous giggles. Whatever happened, she'd leave there with her head held high, proud that she'd maintained her dignity.

At six-fifteen she was dressed and ready to go, mentally as well as physically. It gave her ample time before Paul stopped by with the files that needed her attention. Satisfied she looked as attractive as possible, she slipped into her coat, picked up the box of cookies and headed out the door. Thursday would stay behind this time, since the distraction of a dog might muddle the all-important *aha!* moment of surprise. The new rawhide bone she provided would keep him focused and occupied while she was gone.

Muttering to herself as she walked down the block, Delaney noticed the same sleek, red Porsche parked outside Varik's house that she saw earlier, when she got home from the store. It was the sexy sort of car The Other Woman might drive, which meant it probably belonged to the blonde, in which case, she was still inside. Good. That's exactly what she wanted. Since Varik was supposed to pick Delaney up in about an hour, he'd probably be getting rid of the woman soon.

Delaney needed to see Varik and the woman together, to experience his immediate reaction at seeing Delaney and his blonde plaything in the same room. She wanted to hear the first words out of his mouth, to hear whatever feeble excuse he'd try to foist on her.

Tsking, Delaney reminded herself she shouldn't be so negative, jumping to conclusions without giving Varik the benefit of the doubt.

If she was wrong and the blonde really was his sister or another relative, she'd prostrate herself in remorseful submission before him, wrapping herself around his ankles, holding on for dear life while begging forgiveness for her foolish, unwarranted suspicions.

"Good grief, I'm losing my mind," she told herself as she turned up his walk, her pulse racing at an improbable speed, her stomach turning somersaults, perspiration forming above her lip when it was thirty degrees outside.

"I don't know what the hell I'm doing. I shouldn't be doing this. I need to turn around and go back home," she said, watching helplessly as her finger reached out, pressing the doorbell as if in slow motion.

A small eternity later, the blonde answered the door, throwing Delaney off. It wasn't supposed to happen this way. In each of her practiced scenarios, Varik was supposed to answer the door. A quick glance to the left and right of the blonde confirmed Varik wasn't in the vicinity. Damn.

Her gaze zooming in on the striking woman close-up had Delaney's heart leaping out of her mouth and tumbling to a patch of frozen lawn. It was like coming face to face with some dazzling celebrity.

"Yes, can I help you?" she said in perfect, accented English.

She was gorgeous, every bit as beautiful as Varik was handsome. They could have easily been the prototypes for Barbie and Ken. Eyeing the blonde again, Delaney modified it to Superhero Barbie and Ken. The woman had an hourglass figure, enhanced by the off-white wrap dress she wore with the plunging neckline. It resembled the black wrap dress Delaney had on beneath her coat, except for the cleavage-baring neckline, which Delaney had pinned to a more modest opening.

Eyeing the box in Delaney's hands, the woman lifted an eyebrow. "You are selling something?"

It took a long moment for Delaney to find her voice, suspecting her larynx had likely vacated her body along with her heart at the sight of the towering blonde.

"Oh, um, no." A gush of nervous laughter betrayed Delaney's unease. She hated that she wasn't calm, cool and collected in the presence of this sophisticated beauty. "I..." Delaney cleared her throat. "Is Varik here?" She figured he must be because the aroma of roasting pork ribs was unmistakable.

Giving Delaney a lingering appraisal, the blonde said, "Yes but he is...indisposed at the moment. Was he expecting you?" Her tone was blasé and impassive. Delaney could almost swear the blonde had a visible aura of confidence, which suffocated the miniscule air of self-assurance Delaney had mustered.

"No. Well, yes. Well not until later, that is," Delaney replied.

"Come to think of it, Varik did mention he'd made an appointment for this evening before he learned I'd be arriving from Norway this afternoon. Was it with you? Oh dear, Varik can be so forgetful at times. I hope he didn't forget to cancel."

Cancel...cancel...cancel...

Delaney swallowed hard. "No, no, nothing like that. His appointment must have been with somebody else," she lied, not really knowing why. It just seemed like the right choice.

"Well I'm glad to hear that. He said it was unimportant, just something trivial to pass the time while he was waiting for me."

Her words stung worse than if a thousand army ants had blanketed Delaney from head to toe, eating her alive. So that's all she meant to Varik. She was nothing more than a stand-in, a handy companion to share a neighborly dinner of macaroni and cheese.

Wounded to the core, she thrust out her hand. "I'm Delaney Malone." Her face stretched wide as a hyena-like grin took hold. "I live down the block. Just two doors down." Pointing in the direction of her townhouse she felt like she was back at school trying in vain to relate to one of the cool kids. She'd hated herself back then for her pitiful *like me...please like me* demeanor and she didn't feel any better about herself at this moment.

"Ah, I see. You are, what is it they call it here in the States? The Welcome Wagon, yes?"

"Eh...not exactly." Although she supposed that could have been Varik's impression when she found him on her doorstep and pounced on him with a welcoming bone jump.

Accepting Delaney's hand, the woman shook it with a limp-fish grip. "Pleasure to meet you. I'm Ursula Lovdahl."

The name rang a bell. Delaney took a moment trying to clear her thoughts so she could focus on why the woman and her name seemed familiar. "Lovdahl..." she muttered absently. And then it struck her. "The actress?" She winced, noticing she sounded like a teenage boy whose cracking voice was changing.

"Ah, it's nice to know I'm becoming familiar to American audiences. You've seen one of my movies?"

"Heartbreak on the Slopes," Delaney replied distractedly, shaken by the fact that not only did Varik have another woman, the woman was a stunning, internationally renowned actress.

"Yes, *Sorg I Bakkene*," Ursula said, apparently repeating the title in its original Norwegian. "Such a deep, meaningful role. I was fortunate to get the part."

"Meaningful indeed," Delaney said, not meaning a word of it. "I saw it at a foreign film festival held at the university. My ex-husband is a professor there."

The dark film, full of death, betrayal, loss of love, and insanity reminded Delaney of Swedish director Ingmar Bergman's films. She understood little of it, even with the English subtitles. Ursula's character was an angry, vengeful, depressed woman who murdered her lover...or at least she thought she had. It turned out that, in her confused mental state, she'd actually killed herself instead. Yeah, it was one of those bizarre foreign films which, of course, had Roger singing its praises as a classic five-star masterpiece.

"Wonderful performance, Miss Lovdahl," Delaney said, fully cognizant of why Varik would find the woman alluring, intriguing...beddable. Compared to the impeccable Ursula, Delaney felt like a bumbling dork. "Really super cool," Delaney finished, channeling teen lingo for some ungodly reason while offering a thumbs up, just in case she hadn't already come across as enough of a dweeb.

"Call me Ursula. Lovdahl is my stage name. My real last name is Jenssen."

"Like Varik!" Delaney blurted, thrilled to hear they had the same last name. For the first time since she'd arrived at Varik's house, her world brightened. Feeling infinitely better, her posture relaxed.

"So you must be his sister," Delaney happily presumed, beaming a smile while sending up a silent prayer of thanks. Apparently Norwegian siblings were exceedingly chummy after all. And of course Varik would want to spend time with his sister who'd just arrived from Norway, for heaven's sake. Delaney had gotten all flustered for nothing.

Her expression telegraphing how ludicrous she found Delaney's assumption, Ursula said, "Hardly." Punctuating her reply with a husky chuckle, she clarified, "I'm Varik's wife."

Somehow during all the imagined scenarios that had traipsed across Delaney's brain, the striking blonde being Varik's wife had never been among them, leaving her at an utter loss for words.

"You're Varik's wife," she repeated after an undying eternity, agonizingly aware she sounded like a teeny mouse. No doubt about it, she deserved an Oscar for standing there pretending her world hadn't just caved in around her.

"Yes." Resting one long arm high on the doorjamb Ursula's gaze traveled Delaney's length. Offering an icy smile, she lifted one shoulder in an elegant shrug. "I would invite you in but I was just about to join my husband in the shower...for a pre-dinner rendezvous." She winked. "He's making ribs for me. He knows how much I crave grilled meat when I'm expecting." With a loving glance downward, she cradled her flat belly, smoothing it.

"You-you're having a baby..." It was more a statement than a question.

Ursula nodded. "Varik is so excited."

Dear Diary: Oh God. Oh God, oh God...I slept with another woman's husband. A pregnant woman's husband. My Varik the Bold has a pregnant wife! That makes me a million times worse than a run of the mill neighborly slut...I'm a freakin' adulteress, a homewrecker.

Delaney's stomach lurched. It was hard to breathe. For some absurd reason, the sensuous image of the half-naked Varik, garbed in reindeer pelts and his Brunhilde helmet, chose this instant to take center stage in Delaney's mind. Her hand flew to her forehead as she willed the untimely vision away.

Ursula's expression quirked and she eyed Delaney strangely. Delaney wasn't surprised. She imagined she looked wretchedly pathetic at the moment.

"Is something wrong? You look like you're about to faint. Shall I get you some water?"

"Uh, no...no, that's okay. I'm just tired. And I need to get home. To my dog," she said without a clue as to why that popped out of her mouth. "He doesn't like to be left alone for too long. I gave him a rawhide bone before I left but I'm afraid he might get into something else. You know how dogs can be." A volley of nervous laughter spouted forth.

Good grief, just stop already! What in the world is wrong with you? Stop talking and get the hell out of there while you still have an ounce of self-respect left!

"He got into my chocolate a couple of weeks ago," Delaney helplessly babbled on, making it worse. "He threw up all over." She rolled her eyes, wishing she could duct tape her flapping jaws shut. "Chocolate can be poisonous for dogs, you know. It made a real mess."

"Hmm..." Ursula sort of remarked.

Delaney tried, she really, honestly, sincerely tried, with every bone in her body, to shut the hell up, lift her feet, turn around and just walk away. Really, really fast. The longer she stood there in the presence of Varik's beautiful pregnant wife, the closer she came to succumbing to a classic textbook mental collapse just outside their front door.

"So I'd better be going," she went on like the world's most annoying wind-up doll. "You know, home...to my dog." She grinned, then started bobbing her head up and down.

That did it. She'd succeeded in plummeting to the lowest common denominator on the spectrum of chic refined sophistication and doubted she'd ever find her way back to a state of semi-normalcy.

"Are those a welcome to the neighborhood gift for me and my husband?" Ursula asked, nodding toward the cookies.

Her husband...her husband...her husband...

"I think I feel another craving coming on." She patted her belly.

"These?" Tearing her gaze away from Ursula's belly, Delaney looked at the bakery box in her hand as if she'd never seen it before. She was pretty sure she saw the label on the box flash *Delaney Malone, Adulteress.*

"Those."

"Oh. Yes. Sure. Absolutely." Thrusting the box at Ursula, she felt the sting of tears behind her eyes. "Welcome to the neighborhood." It was time to hightail it out of there before she humiliated herself further by collapsing into a sobbing, whimpering, snotty mess.

"Okie dokie then..." *Okie dokie?* She never said that. Ever.

"My dear," her eyebrows knitting together, Ursula reached out, touching Delaney's elbow, "I do hope you're all right. My appealing husband has a history of...well, let's just say Varik can be overly pleasant and flirtatious with the ladies. You wouldn't be the first woman to come under his spell."

With that liberal dose of salt added to her fresh, gaping wounds, Delaney stood silent for a long moment, staring at Ursula, trying to decide if this was reality or if she was caught in the midst of the worst, most convincing nightmare imaginable. There was so much pain, a deep sense of shame, such incredulity that she could be that laughably gullible.

Her mouth felt dry as sand when she opened it to respond. "Your husband and I are nothing more than casual neighbors," Delaney said, doubting Ursula believed her. "I need to get going now. Home. To the dog. And I have to be there for Paul. He's my boss. He's dropping off some work for me to do." At that moment Delaney would have paid a fortune for a roll of duct tape so she could slap a strip over her motor mouth. "I'm his executive secretary and he's—"

Backing up, she stepped off the threshold, slipped on an icy patch and fell on her backside, landing spread eagle, ideally positioned to make adulterous angels in the snow.

Perfect. Just perfect.

"That's okay, I'm all right," Delaney cheerfully assured, scurrying to her feet. "I've got plenty of padding back there." She clapped her butt and laughed. At the same time she couldn't help notice that amusement rather than concern was evident in Ursula's expression.

"Bye now," Delaney waved, "enjoy the cookies. And congrats on..." her arms rounded the air over her belly, "your upcoming little munchkin."

Ursula looked at her like she was crazy. And why not? Mercifully, after making a complete ass of herself, she made it to the sidewalk without falling on her ass again.

It took Delaney four score and twenty years to reach her front door. At least that's how it seemed.

Chapter 12

~<>~

"URSULA?" Varik frowned, eyeing his ex-wife's backside as she knelt on the sofa, looking out the window toward Delaney's townhouse. "I thought you leave already." He scraped his fingers through his damp hair. Glancing at his watch, he saw it was nearly ten to seven. The last thing he needed was her hanging around, tonight of all nights.

Letting the curtain over the living room window drop and shifting to a seated position, Ursula positioned herself suggestively, as if posing for a magazine spread.

"Why still here? Remember, I tell you, I have dinner guest for seven-thirty." Stuffing his shirttails into his jeans, he headed for the kitchen. A quick check proved the ribs and russet potatoes in the oven were almost finished cooking. It was important that the pork be cooked just the way Delaney liked it. It was important that everything be just the way Delaney liked it tonight.

The last two weeks had been both wonderful and agonizing. Countless times during the pleasant evenings they shared he'd wanted nothing more than to seize her like a lust-driven Viking who hadn't seen a woman in months, and wordlessly demonstrate to Delaney exactly what she meant to him.

"Yes, with the new woman in your life," Ursula oozed. "I remember. Mmm..." she watched him squat at the oven, basting the ribs, "have I told you lately how delicious you look in tight jeans?"

Rising to his feet and facing her, Varik crossed his arms over his chest. "Never mind sweet talk. You must go. Not to make troubles for Varik tonight." If all went as he'd planned, the night would be perfect, marking a passionate progression for his and Delaney's relationship. He'd never been a particularly romantic man but he'd strived to be exactly that these last two weeks. Tonight he planned to pull out all stops, treating Delaney to ample doses of romance before capturing her in his arms, carrying her to his bed, and making love to her until the sun came up.

Gud help him...he'd fallen hard for this woman. Fortunately, he suspected she might feel the same for him.

"You don't need to worry, darling." Ursula cozied up to him, wrapping her arms around his neck and crushing herself against him. He was all too familiar with the way she communicated, using her obvious feminine charms. There was a time when it worked on him but not anymore.

"I always worry when you around," Varik countered, scraping Ursula off him, distancing himself from her. The woman had been a thorn in his side for too long. Clearly even his move across the ocean hadn't dissuaded her from hounding him. Varik wished to hell she'd find herself another man to fawn over...another poor sucker whose life she could ruin.

"I have little time, Ursula, and much to do before I go to pick up my date."

"Picking her up? And when she's just two doors down? Sweet." She smiled. "As always, my Varik is the perfect gentleman."

"Not your Varik. Do as you promise and go now," he told her. Not one to be easily put off, she embraced him again while Varik stood stiff, with his arms at his sides. "Go," he repeated, looking down at her devoid of any feeling other than frustration.

When it finally hit him, Varik stilled, his blood running cold as he nailed Ursula with a purposeful glare. "How you know she live two doors down? I not tell you this."

"I was just about to mention that I met your lady friend," Ursula informed him, tiptoeing her fingers up his sleeve. "There's really no need for you to rush. You see, she stopped by while you were in the shower to say—"

"What?!" The icy blood of a moment ago converted to a tsunami of heat, searing through his veins. "Delaney was here? She saw you?" His head throbbed as he imagined what Delaney must have thought when the oversexed actress answered his door. "What you tell her? Did you—"

"Relax, darling. Your gawky, awkward dinner date came by to tell you she had to cancel your little rendezvous this evening." Her pliant curves undulating against him, Ursula glanced down between them and smiled. "See that? Your body is very happy to see me, even if your brain isn't."

"Never mind." He scowled, fully aware of his traitorous *mannlig kjonnsorgan* pressing against her. He stepped back. "Cancel?" Varik felt sure she must be mistaken. "Why?" The thought of Delaney not coming was enormously disappointing. "She is ill?"

A bubble of laughter spilled from her throat. "On the contrary, she was all pink-cheeked and glowing. She brought these." Ursula lifted the bakery box by its string, letting the box swing from her fingers. "As an apology for having to break your dinner date. She said she felt terrible giving you such short notice, but something more important came up."

More important? Than their long awaited evening together? A crisis perhaps...maybe something happened to her mother.

Perplexed, he muttered, "I don't understand. Delaney have emergency?"

"Oh, I doubt this would fall into that category, darling." Offering another blip of laughter, she explained, "Apparently an old boyfriend, the one she was in love with before she was married to her professor ex-husband, is back in town because he heard about their divorce." Tapping her finger against her cheek, she added,

"Hmm...on the other hand, maybe she *did* consider their reunion an emergency. She looked like she couldn't wait to—"

"Boyfriend..." Varik could barely wrap his mind around Ursula's words. "Boyfriend..." he repeated absently. This couldn't possibly be his Delaney she spoke of...not after what they'd shared together...not after what they'd planned together. No, this was clearly a mistake. But then...how would Ursula know Delaney's ex-husband was a professor?

"George Clooney's double was waiting for her in his car when she came to the door," Ursula went on.

"What? I not believe you." He couldn't...he wouldn't.

Ursula shrugged. "Look for yourself. You can still see his car parked in front of your lady friend's house." She got on her knees on the couch again, spreading the curtain for Varik to take a look. "See the sexy dark blue Mustang? That's his. They must be inside for a quickie before they go to dinner."

Frowning, Varik joined Ursula on the sofa, looking down the street. He saw the car but was sure there had to be another explanation. The news about Delaney with another man had his blood boiling but he knew the conniving Ursula well enough by now not to trust her.

"I was watching as they got out of the car together," she claimed. "It gave me the opportunity to check out your competition. Classic tall, dark and handsome. Maybe blonds aren't her type." Closing the distance between them, Ursula finger-walked up Varik's shirt placket. "Of course, no one is as handsome as my delicious Varik."

"Not your Varik anymore." His gaze narrowed as he leapt off the couch, away from her persistent reach. It was like battling an octopus.

"Are you making more of your old tricks? Tell lies?"

With an audible gasp of indignation, she assured him, "Of course not. I'm your wife, darling. I would never do anything to—"

"Ex-wife," Varik corrected, becoming more exasperated by the moment.

"Oh, that little technicality." Ursula gave a throaty laugh along with a dismissive wave. Stretching her lithe body, making the most of her curves for Varik's benefit, she yawned. "I'm exhausted from that long overseas flight. And terribly hungry."

"Ursula..."

"Dinner smells divine, luv. I've missed your delicious cooking." She gazed up at Varik, batting her eyelashes. "Did I mention your neighbor looked downright smitten with her handsome new beau?"

Varik's jaw clenched. He wasn't sure how much longer he could maintain his cool.

"Anyway," Ursula continued, "after Darlene—"

"Delaney."

"Yes, of course. After she left I thought I may as well stay and share dinner with you before I head back to my hotel. Unless, that is," she sidled up to him toying with his shirt collar, "you'd like for me to stay the night. It could be just like old times." Her fingers raked through his hair. "Remember the fun we used to have? Besides, from the lost look on your face I have a feeling you could use some company tonight. I'm *very* good company."

"Stop!" Gritting his teeth he fought to retain his composure. "No more touching. No more sexy smile. No more sex. We are over, Ursula. For two year now. You forget already how you bed other men when married to Varik?" He clapped his chest. "You maybe forget. Not me. Now you go." He pointed to the door.

Ursula pouted. "You're really going to send me away, out into the cold, without any dinner? Especially when you have a big slab of ribs waiting to be eaten? When did you become so cruel and heartless, Varik?"

"When I learn about witchery of my wife," he spat.

"You know how truly sorry I am, darling. I don't know what more I can say or do to convince you." She sniffed the air. "Mmmm...even with your hearty appetite I doubt you could polish off all that pork by yourself," she noted. "And I know you hate to waste food." Her eyelashes fluttered.

Ursula's behavior swapped from sex kitten to helpless innocent like a light switch being flipped. He couldn't trust a damn thing she said or did. Cynicism running through his veins, Varik scowled at her.

"Why you even here, Ursula? Why you come see Varik?"

She looked struck, wounded as her fingers quivered at her throat, gazing at him as if he'd just slapped her. "Because we have so much to talk about, dear Varik. You were always so good to me. I...I came here to see you to make amends...to give us proper closure." Her voice broke and tears filled her eyes. "You deserve at least that much from me."

His posture stiffened. Damn! He didn't want to be moved...and he certainly didn't want her preying on him again. Between his ex and Delaney's deceit, Varik's thoughts were chaotic. He no longer knew what to think.

"All I'm asking, Varik," her tentative fingers reached out to him, imploring, beseeching, "is for us to sit like civilized exes and have one last polite dinner together. Is that really too much to ask?" The inner edges of Ursula's eyebrows lifted, drawing together, while her bottom lip trembled. "Oh Varik, my sweet golden boy...is it?"

Always the actress, she performed her role to perfection, clearly doing her utmost to appeal to his compassionate side. Much to his chagrin, she was succeeding.

Pushed beyond the point of vexation, Varik's hands flew into the air. "Fine," he said on a reconciled sigh. "Eat food, then go. No Visit Varik again, understand?"

So what if she stayed for dinner? What did it matter now with Delaney off with her lover? The bitter idea churned in his gut like acid. Once again he'd been stupid enough to let a beautiful, conniving woman make a fool of him.

Something still nagged at him. There was still that doubt, that irksome concern that Ursula was, once again, making a fool of him. Before he bought his ex-wife's story, Varik needed to learn the truth for himself. He'd never forgive himself if he believed Ursula only to learn later this was just another one of her lies.

"Before we eat food, I go see Delaney," Varik said. "Need be sure Ursula not making lie." He eyed her with a cynical gaze.

"Do you really think that's a good idea?" Ursula asked. "You'd be acting like a jealous lover. The Varik I know is a proud man who holds his head high...not a lovesick puppy who chases after a woman who has deceived him."

He knew Ursula was probably right, that he was in danger of making himself look like an idiot marching over to Delaney's to confront her. But he had to be sure...he had to see it for himself. What if the car belonged to some guy making a delivery, or asking directions, or maybe it was someone from her office?

"*Ja*, Ursula, is good idea I go now. To be sure." No matter what she said, no matter how convincing, he wasn't about to change his mind.

"Maybe I should come with you."

Varik was about to tell her to stay and wait, but what difference did it make at this point if she was with him or not? If he learned Ursula had been lying, he could lock the conniving witch out in the cold and let her freeze into a block of ice for all he cared. But if she was telling the truth...

His shoulders sagged under the weight of his woman problems.

"Do what you want, Ursula. I not care."

Not bothering to put on a jacket, Varik yanked open the front door, tsking in frustration as he turned to wait for Ursula as she called after him, shrugging into her coat. She grabbed onto him to keep from slipping on the icy walk and continued holding his arm as they made their way down the sidewalk.

With each step she whispered to him, stoking the raging fire in his gut, telling him of Delaney and the other man and, worst of all, offering Varik her sympathy.

This was the one time Varik prayed his deceitful ex-wife was lying.

~<>~

Operating on automatic, Delaney inserted her key into the lock. Like a walking zombie, she felt dead to the world, and the world dead to her.

After greeting Thursday, who loved her enough to take a few seconds away from his new bone to welcome her, she shrugged out of her coat and plucked her phone from her purse. Thankfully, the sense of calm that had so cruelly eluded her while talking to...Mrs. Jenssen, was fully in place now, which was good because she had a lot to do in a short amount of time.

There was no need to call Paul to give him her two week notice because he'd be arriving soon. The first call she made was to Margaret, the woman who'd taken over Delaney's former job as receptionist after Delaney was promoted to her executive secretary position. Fully qualified as a secretary, Margaret would be a perfect replacement for Delaney. An added plus, Margaret's husband was in real estate.

The last call was to her mom, Astrid, who was delighted, though surprised, to hear Delaney would be coming home to stay in her old room for a couple of weeks. Delaney promised to clue her mom in on what had transpired once she arrived.

Following their short conversation, Delaney got busy dismantling the aluminum Christmas tree and boxing up all the ornaments. All the housework and scrubbing she'd completed over the last couple of weeks had paid off. The place looked clean, organized and, thanks to her careful repairs, in far better condition than the handyman special it was when she and Roger had purchased it.

When the doorbell rang, Delaney did a quick mirror check, hoping she didn't look as bad as she felt. Although she hadn't yet shed a tear since learning about Varik's wife, and her eyes weren't puffy and her nose didn't rival Rudolph's, the first words out of her boss's mouth when he saw her were, "Delaney, you look terrible. What's wrong?"

She hadn't planned to cry and she certainly hadn't planned to tell Paul what had happened with Varik. She and her boss had a good, professional working relationship, one that didn't involve much personal sharing. The only time he'd been privy to anything major going on in her personal life was the day he happened to see Roger's "Dear Jill" letter on her desk just over a year ago.

Regrettably, seeing Paul's concerned face and hearing his kind words were all it took now for Delaney's waterworks to kick in.

He led her to the sofa in front of the living room window where they sat together. He asked her a series of questions. Was she ill? Had something happened to a loved one?

Breathing a great sigh, Delaney looked up at him. She knew from the personnel files at work that Paul was forty years old. He was a handsome man, strikingly so, but she'd never been interested in him as anything other than a good, fair employer. And Paul, happily married with four kids, had never made any inappropriate advances.

She could tell he was uncomfortable watching her try to control her tears, but he was also patient and considerate. Careful not to go overboard, whining and complaining about her woes, Delaney briefly explained what had happened. To the man's credit, he didn't squirm, tsk, roll his eyes, or make any of the impatient gestures Roger had the few times Delaney needed to vent. Paul merely listened, allowing Delaney to talk it out.

The only time he became visibly unnerved was when she gave him her two week notice.

He objected, did his best to talk her out of it, but ultimately accepted her decision and offered his thanks for suggesting Margaret as her replacement. Since Margaret was already familiar with the daily operations of the newspaper, and Paul had always been satisfied with her work, the transition would be smooth.

"You've been a great asset to the *Northwest Suburban Gazette*," he told her. "It just won't be the same without you. If there's anything I can do, Delaney, you just let me know. I'll give you a glowing reference, letters of recommendation, whatever you need."

"Thank you, Paul. I really appreciate that."

"Just make me one promise."

She looked up from the tissue she was twisting in her lap. "What's that?"

"Promise you won't forget us little people when your wonderful "Delaney's Diary" column goes viral." He gave her a wink.

He looked as relieved as Delaney felt when his comment made her laugh.

"You going to be okay tonight?" he asked her. "You're welcome to spend the evening with me, Sylvia and the kids...although," he chuckled, "I'm not sure how soothing four boys under the age of ten would be on your nerves."

"You're the best, Paul." They pulled each other into a hug which, while outside the norm, felt entirely natural under the circumstances.

"Thanks, but I'll be fine. "I'll make myself some cocoa, add a shot of brandy, and cry into it." She laughed.

"Sounds like good medicine to me." Chuckling, Paul smoothed Delaney's back. "Okay, you take care of yourself and give me a call if there's anything you need." He gave her a kiss on the cheek before they broke their hug.

~<>~

"There, you see?" Ursula nudged Varik's ribs with her elbow. "What did I tell you? There's your lady friend and her George Clooney making out right there in the window for everyone to see."

The pain searing through him as he watched Delaney locked in an embrace with another man was like nothing Varik had ever experienced. The sensation of his heart being hacked with a cleaver completely eclipsed any grief he'd suffered from his split with Ursula. Along with crushing pain there was an overwhelming sense of anger, which made the usually non-violent Varik want to punch a hole in a wall...or into the Clooney clone's jaw.

He started up the walk to Delaney's townhouse when Ursula grabbed his arm, yanking him hard.

"What are you doing?" She sounded panic-stricken.

"I go see Delaney. Tell her what I think of her."

"No," Ursula insisted. "You can't do that. Varik," she jiggled his arm, "listen to me. Where is your pride? Your self-respect? You can't barge in there like a caveman. Don't give her the satisfaction of seeing you like this. Don't let her know the power she held over you. You'll regret it...believe me." She tried tugging him away again. "Ask yourself, Varik, is she worth it? Worth you humiliating yourself over her?"

She was right. Damn, Ursula was right. A man of Viking stock shouldn't allow an unscrupulous woman to have such a hold over him. The breath Varik had been holding released with a whoosh. Without another word, he backed up, shoving his hands into his pockets as he headed back to his townhouse.

~<>~

Feeling much better and more composed after their talk, Delaney asked Paul to go over the material on the flash drive he'd brought.

"I won't be taking tomorrow off after all," she told him after he explained what was needed. "I'll give the project top priority and have everything completed by the end of the day tomorrow."

"Delaney, that's not necessary. Take the day off with pay and do something relaxing for yourself. Go dress shopping, or to the hairdresser, or whatever it is women do to feel better. Sylvia tells me there's nothing more rejuvenating than spending the day, and my money," he laughed, "at the mall. Seriously, we're running the article in Thursday's edition so I don't need the material completed until Wednesday. Believe it or not, the office can survive if you take a day off." He extended his hand. "Deal?"

Delaney considered what her boss said. She could certainly use a full weekday to herself to get the ball rolling on all the major life changes she was about to make.

"You talked me into it." Smiling, she shook his hand, thanking him once again for his understanding.

Fifteen minutes after Delaney's boss left, Margaret's real estate agent husband arrived and did an inspection of her home. Spreading paperwork, brochures and a contract across her coffee table, he gave Delaney the good news that she could expect a quick sale at a good price, and showed her where to sign on the dotted line.

As soon as he left, Delaney got out her suitcases, packing what she'd need for her last two weeks of work here and for the first couple of weeks in her new location. She knew she could count on her mom to manage the sale of her furniture, decor items, household goods, and whatever else wasn't essential for the move.

The few belongings and keepsakes she wanted to save would be boxed for shipping to her new home, the house Grandma Bekka had left the Malones in Glassfloat Bay, Oregon.

Chapter 13

~<>~

"MY POOR VARIK." Ursula wound her clingy self all over him like the persistent ivy growing in the backyard. There was nothing he hated more than pity, especially from a woman. Especially if that woman was his ex-wife.

"*Hvorfor ikke bare snakke med meg pa norsk, elskling?*" Ursula asked, clearly doing her best to look alluring.

"No, I do not want speak Norwegian to you. I speak English now." He let forth a growl of frustration. "And not anymore to call me *elskling*, eh..." he thought for a moment, "darling," he translated. "You and I not darlings. And Varik not need Ursula's pity, understand?"

"Yes, Varik. There's a great improvement in your English. Tore is teaching you well."

"Tore very good man," he said, recalling a painful time he wanted desperately to forget. "Thank *Gud* Tore know better than to bed with Ursula. So very bad...so wrong you try that with my cousin."

"You're absolutely right," Ursula freely admitted. "What can I say? Men are my weakness."

"*Ja, jeg vet.*" Frustrated he'd slipped back into Norwegian, Varik corrected himself. "Yes, I know." He found it difficult to remember to speak English when he was angry or upset. "Then you should not be a married woman," he told her. "You make great heart pain and *elendighet*...eh...misery for me and many other."

He thought about the vast differences between his ex-wife and Delaney. Ursula probably didn't have an honest bone in her body.

While beautiful, she was devious, self-serving and amoral, while Delaney was sweet, loyal and honorable.

His lip curled into a sneer. At least that's what he thought before he'd heard Ursula's gut-punching news, and had seen the proof of it for himself.

"You're right," she said again. "I've been a very bad girl." Her cherry-red lips pouted and she gazed up at him from beneath long, lacquered lashes.

Undeniably striking, she looked younger each time he saw her. Obviously a hefty percentage of her earnings lined the pockets of plastic surgeons. It was the one thing he pitied Ursula for—her dreaded fear of aging. At forty-seven, she was nearly ten years older than Varik, which he hadn't realized until after they'd married. She'd had her publicity people shave several years off her age for her official biography. It wasn't the age difference he minded, it was her dishonesty about it.

With Ursula's arresting looks she easily could pull off the lie. But one day it would catch up to her, perhaps due to a greedy cosmetic surgeon with loose lips. He feared his ex would suffer a mental collapse should the truth about her age be revealed.

"I never wanted to hurt you, Varik," she said in her most convincing manner, snapping his thoughts back to the present. "You must believe that. You're the only man I've ever truly loved. The only man I still love. I flew all the way here, right after they stopped shooting my scenes, just so I could see you. I want your forgiveness, Varik, and another chance for me to prove I can be a good wife to you."

Eyeing his ex up and down, Varik remembered how taken he was when they'd first met. Already well known throughout Scandinavia, the model and actress was just beginning to achieve international acclaim. Spotting Varik in an Oslo restaurant, Ursula sent a drink to his table. Intrigued at the bold move, Varik, temporarily in the city taking courses at the university, strode to her table. After dismissing the others who sat with her, she invited Varik to sit next to her. He found her beauty, power and obvious confidence addictive.

Having been raised by his grandfather without television, radio or movies, Varik had no idea Ursula was a celebrity. He only knew she was gorgeous and sexy as hell. Fascinated by the only man she'd met who didn't know who she was and who didn't seem to have an agenda to sleep with a famous actress, then sell his story to the papers, she pursued him in earnest.

After a whirlwind courtship, the two married, against the advice of his grandfather who'd warned him about the woman after meeting her. The perceptive old man had been right all along about Ursula's questionable character. But, smitten, Varik didn't want to hear it, deciding Grandpa Anders was simply behind the times.

It wasn't long before Varik grew tired of being known as Mr. Lovdahl. The constant intrusion of photographers, her agent and publicity people, her celebrity friends, and throngs of persistent fans left them little time alone. He wanted to start a family but Ursula had no interest in children, telling him pregnancy would destroy her perfect figure. He soon learned she had no interest in much of anything domestic, or the time-honored tradition of fidelity in marriage.

It was during one of Tore's visits back home to Norway that Varik learned the extent of his wife's adulterous nature. His older cousin took him aside, warning Varik that Ursula had done her best to seduce him. Tore readily admitted he was tempted—what red-blooded man wouldn't be? But Tore assured Varik he loved his wife far too much to cheat on her.

The worst part of Ursula's treachery was that Tore's wife was dying of cancer at the time...and Ursula knew it.

While Varik didn't want to believe the worst about his wife, he had unflinching faith in his cousin, knowing the man had no reason to lie about something so devastating.

So after two less than blissful years of marriage, Varik divorced Ursula, which made headlines all across Scandinavia. It was impossible to go into a supermarket without seeing his name and photo splashed across one of those trashy magazines. That, and his grandfather's death, propelled Varik to move to the States.

Fortunately, Varik made amends with Anders before he died. His grandfather accepted Varik's apology, assuring him that he understood. Sometimes the only way a man can learn a good lesson, especially when it comes to women, Anders told his grandson, is by experience.

Seemingly Varik hadn't learned his lesson well enough the first time.

He moved back to his grandfather's secluded cabin in the mountains of Oslo where he'd remained the past two years, waiting for his divorce to become final. The day it did, he bought his airline tickets and headed for America.

Varik flatly refused Ursula's substantial offer of a financial settlement. Hardworking and self-reliant, he didn't want or need her money to make a life for himself. Ursula told Varik he was the only man she'd known who didn't try to take her for everything she was worth.

The last thing he expected today was to find Ursula on his doorstep. The unwelcome sight of his ex-wife brought back a flood of unpleasant memories.

"No, Ursula," Varik responded now. "I give you no more chances. You need to find a good man and treat him right, treat him with respect. Love him the way you want to be loved. That man is not me. Sorry, my feelings are dead for you now. I can forgive but never forget."

He watched Ursula's eyes spark with what appeared to be veiled rage.

"Well what a shame, especially seeing as how your new little friend, Danielle—"

Expelling a whopping groan, Varik corrected, "I already tell you, it is Delaney."

"Right. Now that she's off overnight with her handsome boyfriend, at the hotel where they'd first met some years ago—"

"Overnight..." The word reverberated through his head.

"Right." With a guiltless expression, Ursula tacked on, "It all sounded very romantic."

A thousand thoughts roared through Varik's head. How could he have been so wrong about Delaney? He could have sworn she'd developed strong feelings for him. She seemed interested in exploring a loving, monogamous relationship. That had Varik huffing humorless laughter.

Anger and disgust swelled inside until he could almost feel his heart being encased in steel. Never again, he promised himself, would he allow any woman close enough to access his heart.

"My poor Varik," Ursula said for the tenth time. "You look mad enough to spit nails." She pulled him into a hug. "I'm sorry to be the bearer of bad news, luv. I had no idea she was important to you. If I had, I wouldn't have said anything. She's a foolish woman to give you up."

Varik shook his head back and forth. "I do not care. Delaney mean nothing to me."

"Good..." Ursula cooed, smoothing her hand along his shirtsleeve. "That's just what I wanted to hear. You're too good for her, Varik. You deserve better."

This was one time he decided his ex-wife was right.

The kitchen timer rang and he headed for the oven.

"I was going to set the table but I see you've already done it," Ursula called from the dining room.

Varik snickered. "You set a table?" he said, pulling the food from the oven. "This thought is too funny." It took him a few minutes to get the ribs, potatoes and the salad he'd made on the table. He didn't bother taking the same care he'd reserved for dinners with Delaney. The candles remained unlit and the wine glasses empty.

"True, I may not be very domestic, but I'm good at pouring wine," Ursula said, settling herself in what was to be Delaney's chair and pouring herself a glass before filling Varik's. "What, no candles?"

"No candles."

"Don't be silly." She rose from the table, returning with her purse a moment later. Retrieving a diamond-encrusted lighter, she lit the candles. "There. That's much better, isn't it?"

"Ursula."

"Yes, darling?"

"Remember. You just eat then go."

"Yes, of course, if that's what you want. It's just that...well, everything is so nice and cozy. I thought after sharing your lady friend's cookies over coffee, we might—"

"No talking. No making table look better. No thinking. No call me darling. Just eat supper and go. Understand?"

Heaving a sigh, Ursula nodded.

"Take cookie box to hotel with you."

Ursula snickered. "Can you just imagine if I allowed myself to indulge in all that fat and sugar? My goodness, I'd look as lumpy as your lady friend, Danielle."

Mindful that Ursula was egging him on, Varik chose not to correct the mistaken name again. And he certainly wasn't going to comment on his ex-wife's figure or Delaney's. There were specific subjects any man with an ounce of intelligence knew should be off limits.

"I can tell you one thing," Ursula said after a few blessed minutes of silence, licking barbecue sauce from her fingers. "If you had gone through all this trouble to cook a wonderful, romantic dinner for me, I never would have stood you up. Your ill-mannered lady friend has no idea what she's missing."

His insides churning, Varik merely grunted in response. The last thing he felt like was making small talk with Ursula, especially with Delaney as the topic.

"Hmm..." Ursula mused a short while later, chewing and swallowing a forkful of potato before continuing. "I wonder what Darlene and her date are having for dinner." She shrugged. "Whatever it is, I'm sure it can't hold a candle to this exquisite meal you've prepared. They're probably eating some mediocre restaurant food by candlelight. You know, something like steak or lobster or—"

"Ursula." Usually a man in control of his emotions, Varik felt the raw heat of anger clawing up from his gut.

"Yes, darling?" She sipped from her wine glass. "Mmm, so good. What is this?" She lifted the bottle. "Riesling, just as I thought. The perfect accompaniment for ribs. Ready for a refill?"

Ignoring her question, Varik replied, "I do not care what Delaney is having for dinner. I do not want to discuss her with you. Just let me eat in peace." Too agitated to focus on his food, he could have been eating barbecued cardboard instead of ribs without knowing the difference.

"Oh how thoughtless of me." Conveying a look of sympathy, she reached across the table, covering his hand. "My poor wounded Varik, of course you don't want to hear about what's-her-name and the man she took off with. It must be terribly painful. What shall we talk about instead?"

"Nothing. Just finish your food and go."

"All right, I will. I can understand why you'd prefer to be alone," she said, her tone soft, full of concern. Shaking her head, she tsked.

"It's so easy to fall for the wrong sort of person when you're on the rebound. Believe me, I know. She clearly took advantage of your kind nature, Varik...you poor dear."

This time Varik kept his mouth shut, recognizing how close he was to roaring his displeasure and blurting a vile string of derogatory words, strong enough to strip the varnish off the furniture. He feared once he started it would be difficult to stop.

His gaze lifted, watching his ex-wife's lips opening and closing as she prattled on, doing her damnedest to assure Varik knew how terribly he'd been wronged. If he was a man of violence, he thought for the second time this evening, he could easily see himself strangling his verbose ex and burying her in the backyard.

The resulting image brought a smile to his face for the first time since he'd gotten out of the shower. He polished off the wine in his glass and poured himself another.

"There, see?" Ursula beamed a smile. "I can tell you're feeling better already. I told you I was good company."

Varik ignored her. Though she made several more attempts to engage him in conversation, he maintained his silence while luxuriating in a pleasing assortment of homicidal scenarios. Perhaps he was inclined to be a man of violence after all. The notion had his lip curling into a half-smile.

"There is one question I have," he said, curiosity getting the best of him toward the end of the meal.

"Yes?"

"Did you tell Delaney you were my ex-wife or," he swallowed hard, "my wife?"

"She thought I was your sister when she heard my last name," Ursula recounted with a chuckle. "Isn't that amusing?"

"And you told her...?"

Ursula gave a nonchalant shrug. "That I am your ex-wife, of course." Almost looking as if she were about to cry, she leaned toward him, folding her hands on the table and positioning her breasts to rest there. "I love you, darling. If only you'd let me prove it to you," she said, her earnest tone matching her facial expression.

"If you love me, you know nothing more important to me than truth and honesty."

"I know. Believe me, Varik, I am being entirely truthful when I say I love you and only you."

"And are you honest about everything else?"

He watched Ursula's fist clench until it was white-knuckled.

She licked her lips before asking, "What do you mean?"

"Everything you tell me about Delaney." With his gaze locked on hers, he watched his ex-wife closely for any gesture, any nuance that might give her away.

"Certainly. Please don't make me remind you that you've already seen the proof of my honesty with your own eyes. The woman and her lover were perfectly framed for all to see, right there in her window." Ursula gestured in the direction of Delaney's townhouse.

Varik's eyes narrowed as the unsavory image of Delaney and the other man embracing permeated his brain. While Ursula was untrustworthy, she was right about him seeing the proof of her words.

"What earthly reason would I have for lying? I don't know the woman from Adam." She drained the wine from her glass, pouring another.

"Because you are a woman of great..." He paused, tapping a finger on the table as he searched for the correct word in English. "Great jealousy," he finished. "You want Varik only for yourself. You want me to take you back. Yes?"

"Yes." Nodding, Ursula let out a breathy sigh. "I know I've done some terrible things, Varik, but deliberately trying to hurt you is not one of them. I regret causing you pain more than I can possibly say.

Believe me, I would never make up a spiteful lie, even if I thought it might help to win you back."

Grabbing his hand, she clasped it tight. "I love you and want you to be happy...even if it's not with me."

"So if I tell you I find woman who make my heart happy," he touched his chest, "you would give your blessing?"

"Well," Ursula chuckled, "no, I'd definitely be lying if I said I'd give you my blessing. But if you're asking if I'd step aside...if I'd be willing to give you up so you could live happily ever after with a good woman who loved you, then the answer is a resounding yes. I would make that sacrifice for you because I love you that much."

She seemed so sincere, as if she spoke from her heart. Varik wondered why he and Ursula had never bothered to talk this way before. As he recalled, most of their discussions had been frivolous, focusing on trivial matters like the pricey new shoes, purses or dresses she'd bought, or her newest hairstyle or manicure. He'd never realized she had this much depth as a person. Maybe Ursula really had changed.

"Let me to prove to you that I've changed and that I can make you happy," she said as if reading his thoughts.

"How have you changed?" He eyed her skeptically.

"Oh my God..." Her eyelids fluttered closed and she shook her head back and forth. "In so many ways, Varik." Opening her eyes, she smiled brightly. "If you want babies, we'll have babies. If you want a house in the country or in the mountains, we'll live like happy hermits. If you want me to learn to cook, I'll take classes on how to use the oven and the stove and all those pots, pans and utensils. I'll even learn to keep house. You can teach me how to use the vacuum." She laughed and Varik couldn't help joining in.

"Whatever it is you want, I'll do it. Whatever it takes to make you happy."

Lost in thought, Varik was silent for a long moment.

"I will give up my acting career," she announced. "I'm obligated to the studio for three more films but after that, I'm walking away from all of that. You have my word."

That was one thing Varik never expected to hear. He supposed it could be possible that his self-absorbed ex had matured enough to be ready to focus on the important things in life rather than fame, fortune, and a glamorous, flashy lifestyle.

And other men.

Again, as if she could read his mind, she said, "Being loyal and faithful to you is at the top of my list."

"I want to believe you, Ursula but..."

"Don't you think by now I've learned the importance of not lying to you?" Ursula's expression, tone of voice and body language gave Varik the impression that, maybe for the only time in her life, Ursula was telling him the truth.

"I've been such a fool." She bowed her head, looking contrite. "Concerned with silly, unimportant things...always focused on myself and my looks. I don't want to be that self-centered immature woman anymore, Varik. With you by my side I could develop into the woman you always hoped I'd be. Do you think there might still be a chance for us?" She held her thumb and forefinger an inch apart, giving him a beseeching look. "Just the whisper of a chance?"

Cognizant that he needed to protect his heart from the stomping it had received under Ursula's previous care, Varik gave plenty of thought before he responded. At least he knew fairly well what he had with Ursula. With Delaney, he *thought* he knew her but was profoundly mistaken. He'd been deluded once again by a pretty face and the pack of lies that came with it. He'd presented his heart to Delaney and she'd made mincemeat out of it.

"We have a history together," Ursula urged, her voice soft, sweet, nearly inaudible. "We know each other. Understand each other. I would devote my life to making up for the heartache I caused you in the past, Varik, if only you'd give me the opportunity."

Varik spent a long silent moment, looking off into the distance, images of Delaney seizing his thoughts. God how he had cherished the woman. Her spontaneous laughter was infectious, her spirit full of fire, her demeanor sweet, kind and generous.

That one very special evening they'd shared the day he landed on her doorstep was one he'd never forget. Delaney had captured his heart in a way Ursula never had...and never could. He had allowed Delaney to infiltrate his very soul until he believed they were destined for each other.

How could he have been so wrong?

Regardless of what the future held for him and Ursula, it was time for Varik to lock Delaney out of his life. From this moment forward, she would be relegated to the deepest, darkest recesses of his mind where she'd dwell as nothing more than a ghostly reminder of how he'd been foolish enough to give her his heart. His trust. His love.

Varik turned his attention to Ursula, noting her hopeful, expectant expression. There were times when she could be rather endearing.

"No promises but maybe we can try taking small steps," he suggested, willing to consider the possibility of renewing their relationship, even though he would never give her his love again, at least not in the way he had the first time. Regardless of how much she may have changed, Ursula would never have the opportunity to stomp on his heart again.

Wiping a tear from her eye, she clasped his hand and squeezed. "Thank you, my darling Varik, for believing in me. Maybe we can start by clearing the table and doing the dishes together." Smiling up at him from beneath her lashes she added, "You can teach me how."

~<>~

After everything that happened, it would have been nice to hold a warm, sexy woman in his arms while he slept but, as enticing as she was, Varik wisely sent Ursula on her way, promising he'd meet her for lunch after his English lesson with Tore.

It was difficult concentrating on his session with thoughts of Delaney insistently rising to the surface, regardless of how hard he tried to squelch them. Picking up on his uncommon inattentiveness, Tore asked him about it. After hearing what had transpired, Tore advised Varik to leave both deceitful women in his past, warning that Ursula wasn't to be trusted no matter how sweet and innocent she came across. She was, after all, an award-winning actress, he reminded Varik.

He knew his cousin was right. As Tore pointed out, a good woman would never proposition her husband's happily married cousin, especially when the man's beloved wife was dying. Varik strongly doubted there could be a future for him and Ursula. If she really had changed, he'd be able to tell over time. And he had plenty of patience. It was easy for her to gush out all those promises during their dinner, while doing her utmost to convince him they belonged together. The hard part for Ursula, Varik knew, was being able to keep up a front for any length of time if she was lying.

Lunch was uneventful, with Ursula maintaining her new, improved persona, jabbering away about all the happy, fun-filled things they'd do together once they started living together again. It was during lunch that she told Varik she'd left her diamond encrusted lighter at his townhouse. She must have tucked it under something because he would have spotted it otherwise. It seemed to be a well-planned excuse for returning to his place so she could finagle him into sleeping with her.

Since he'd already made up his mind that wasn't going to happen, Varik agreed to take her back to his house so she could retrieve her lighter, informing her she couldn't stay long because he had a performance of the Viking play that evening.

As they turned down the street Varik's eyes widened at the for sale sign in Delaney's front yard.

"She's moving," he said absently.

"Yes," Ursula said, "she mentioned it to me last night when she stopped by. Didn't I tell you?"

Stopping the car in the middle of the road, Varik turned to her. "No."

"She's moving in with her boyfriend."

Driving two houses down, Varik pulled into his garage, dazed and bewildered. Considering his past with Ursula, he couldn't help wondering if all women were two-faced or if he just had rotten luck.

The more Varik thought about it, something just didn't feel right.

In the kitchen, he turned to Ursula. "It seems you and Delaney did much talking together for two women who not really know each other."

With a blasé flip of her hand, Ursula said, "I'm sure it comes as no surprise to you that your friend has a penchant for chattering away." She made a clicking teeth motion with her fingers.

"But why she tell so many personal things to stranger?" It didn't make any sense to him that Delaney would so freely share her personal information with Ursula.

"Who knows? She just prattled on and on about all sorts of things, her dog, her ex, her job...probably because she was so excited about the return of her boyfriend. You've never seen her like that before?"

Varik recalled that when Delaney got nervous she did tend to jabber a lot. She'd even made fun of herself for doing it. "Sometimes," he admitted.

Clasping Varik by the shoulders, Ursula gave him yet another pitying look. "Women often feel comfortable talking to other women about such things as boyfriends and relationships." Her expression full of compassion, Ursula squeezed his shoulders. "I'm sorry you've been hurt again. It seems Delaney played my poor Varik for a fool...a sucker. Do you know what that means in English, darling, or should I explain it?"

"No need for explain. I understand perfectly." Varik hated that she was right. Hated he'd been so incredibly gullible. "Sucker is like what you do to me before."

Letting out a sigh, Ursula nodded, allowing her hands to drop to their sides. "Sadly, yes. I hate seeing another woman put you through what I did. My poor Varik."

He realized it was useless telling Ursula to stop all the annoying pity references. He'd already told her numerous times and it hadn't done any good. She was clearly intent on coddling him.

Ursula closed the distance between them. "Don't worry." She wrapped her hands around his neck, stroking the back of his hair, "I'll make you forget she ever existed. I know just what to do to take your mind off Delaney." Licking her lips, she rocked herself against him.

"I'm sure you do." Varik stepped out of her embrace before he forgot himself and gave in to her considerable charms. "But for now, it's time for you to find your lighter and be on your way."

Pouting, Ursula went to the living room, making sure to treat him to the jiggly sway of her backside as she walked. Retrieving the lighter from beneath a throw pillow, she said, "Well what do you know? It was right here on the loveseat all along."

Varik noted she'd made a beeline for the lighter. The quick discovery was interesting, seeing as how they hadn't sat on the loveseat at all the night before.

Chapter 14

~<>~

ABSENTLY FINGERING the heartwish ring, Delaney knew for certain if there had ever been any magic lurking in the stone, it was gone now. She'd tried removing it from her finger, even using butter to help it slip off, but it wouldn't budge. Although it had no magical powers, the ring would remain a fond memory of her grandma.

In the two weeks that passed since she put her house on the market, Delaney was still at a loss about what happened between her and Varik. While baffled, it's not like she was a complete idiot. She understood the charmer had purposely led her on, conveniently forgetting to mention he had a blonde bombshell actress wife with a bun in the oven.

But why go through all the trouble to court her the way he had? Why bother making her fall in love with him if he knew his wife was arriving soon? If he just wanted to have an affair, why do the whole platonic *let's wait two weeks* bit when he probably sensed Delaney would have agreed to jump into bed with him long before that?

Varik probably enjoyed playing mind games with women. She frowned at the thought. Sometimes there simply aren't any pat answers to puzzling questions. There's no logic, no reason, just the infuriatingly unsolvable puzzle. She'd have to accept that reality, do her best to put Varik out of her mind, and move on with her life.

Shaking her head to clear it, Delaney thought about her job. Margaret was thrilled to move up to the executive secretary position Delaney vacated. Delaney spent the last two weeks training her and she seemed to have no trouble learning any of the required tasks.

After a few showings, Margaret's husband expected Delaney's townhouse to sell quickly. The money from the sale, along with the earnings from her newly syndicated "Delaney's Diary" column, would help tide her over until she was making a steady income.

"It's almost six," Astrid noted. "The cab should be here soon." Lifting the drape to glance out the window, she said, "I'm so glad you've got nice weather this morning for your flight."

"Me too." For some inexplicable reason, Delaney's thoughts leapt to the first day she and Varik met, when she'd knocked the poor guy on his ass after *accidentally on purpose* shoving him. She couldn't help smiling as she pictured him sprawled out in the snow wearing nothing but his skimpy Viking costume.

If I knew then what I know now, I would have shoved him harder.

"Do you have everything?"

Looking down at her suitcases and back up at her mother, Delaney offered a wistful smile. "I have that haunting feeling that I've forgotten something but I think I've got it all."

"If you left anything behind, I'll send it to you."

Thursday whimpered.

Laughing, Delaney bent to cuddle her dog. "Aw, don't worry, Thursday, I would never leave my best buddy behind." Glancing up at her mom, she said, "I hope he does well on that long flight."

"He'll be fine." Astrid bent to pet her granddog. "You've been such a good boy these last two weeks, Thursday. I'm going to miss you." Smiling up at Delaney, she said, "He'll love romping around that big yard behind Bekka's house. It'll be fun taking him to the beach where you can both walk along the shore. The ocean's just a nice, short scenic walk from the house. You'll love it."

"I'm sure I will." Delaney nodded, loving the idea of walking barefoot in the sand, especially at sunset. Her mom was right, she'd love being so close to the water. "I think this change will be good for me, Mom. I only wish you'd agree to make the move with me now instead of waiting. There's plenty of room for the two of us."

"Your grandma's place is probably big enough to house the whole Malone family," Astrid confirmed with gentle laughter. "Mom always liked big, open spaces."

"All the more reason for you to move. You really don't have anything holding you here."

"Soon, honey. A packrat like me has a lot to do before she can just pick up and make a cross-country move. My mother's house may be big, but not big enough for all my precious junk."

Delaney's gaze roamed her mother's knickknack-lined living room and she couldn't help snickering. It was difficult finding an empty spot anywhere. "Okay, you have a point." Her mom had a propensity for collecting everything under the sun. It was a miracle there was enough space in Delaney's old bedroom for her to stay with all of Astrid's latest finds, like fancy perfume bottles with atomizers, ceramic salt and pepper shakers, and blue and white delftware.

While Astrid had tons of collected...*junque*...everything was neatly placed, organized, and even dusted regularly.

"Your sisters would understand. Laila, Reen and Kady have all inherited my packrat gene. Fortunately, your brothers haven't." Astrid chuckled.

That had Delaney laughing. "I can't begin to imagine Gard or Nevan stopping at a garage sale or a thrift shop—ever!"

"Maybe one day when they get married," Astrid mused, "their wives will drag them to a flea market or estate sale."

"Kicking and screaming," Delaney added. "Seriously, Mom, you need to come to Oregon. What will we all do without you there?"

"I'll be joining you before you know it, honey," Astrid promised, "after the tenth or so garage sale it'll take to get rid of all my stuff."

Delaney's eyebrow hiked. "*All* your stuff?"

As her gaze followed her daughter's, Astrid indulged in a sigh. "Well...except for the sentimental things." She smoothed her fingers over the grouping of glazed clay figures Delaney and her siblings had sculpted in grade school, nestled next to the wood carvings and metal jewelry they'd made in high school. Then there was the fat portfolio of every card and drawing any of her children had ever made for her. With six kids, that amounted to a lot of sentimental artsy-craftsy stuff. Delaney knew there was no way in hell her mother would ever part with any of those.

"And the valuable things." Astrid gestured to the glass-front cabinet holding her prized collection of first edition books. "And the—"

"Uh-huh." With a wink, she gave her mother a fierce hug. An unexpected sob escaped her throat. "Oh, Mom, I'm going to miss you so much." Leaving her mom behind was almost as tough as coming to terms with Varik's deception.

"No, no, no. Don't do that," Astrid said into her daughter's hair as she hugged her tight. "You'll have us both bawling nonstop." Holding Delaney at arm's length she studied her daughter. "Oh Delaney..." Astrid dragged her bottom lip through her teeth, "are you sure you're making the right decision? This is a major move. Your entire life is going to change."

"Absolutely, Mom." Delaney had asked herself the same question a dozen times and always came to the same conclusion. It was time to go, time to start fresh and move on with her life. When the universe kicks your butt, letting you know in no uncertain terms your life has been derailed, you listen. Then you head in a new direction and start the next leg of your life's journey.

"I need to leave. After the fiasco with Roger, and then Varik breaking my heart, I need to get away. New surroundings will help."

"You've never even visited Oregon. What if you don't like it there?"

"Then I'll come back." Shrugging, Delaney crafted a reassuring smile for her mom's benefit. "But I don't think that will happen. I feel like Glassfloat Bay is meant to be my home. I can so easily envision myself biking along quiet mountain roads and hiking along all the forested trails."

"Me too...me too, honey. And you know what I always say. Everything's going to be—"

"Hunky-dory," Delaney finished for her with a smile. It was her mom's favorite expression.

"Absolutely. You and your grandmother had such a close connection," Astrid told her, and Delaney nodded in agreement. "Mom told everyone in town all about you. When I visited she was always taking out her phone and showing friends your latest photos."

"Grandma was so sweet. I miss her so much. I know you do too, Mom." She gave her mother a quick side-hug.

Unshed tears glistened in Astrid's eyes. "Yes...but she's with my dad now, your grandpa, Jamie. And that makes me happy. They're together, watching over us."

"I believe that too," Delaney assured her mother. "I can't wait to see my sisters and brothers when I get to Glassfloat Bay," she said, deciding it was best to change the subject or they'd both be bawling. "It's been too long."

"They're *so* excited you're finally coming." Astrid took her daughter's hands, squeezing gently. "I think we'll both love the Pacific Northwest. There are more than enough turn of the century homes in those coastal towns to keep me in seventh heaven for years. I can just imagine going to all those garage and estate sales. First edition books, art deco jewelry, vintage magazines, one of a kind salt and pepper shakers..."

"Good! That's exactly what I want to hear. Promise you'll make plans to join me soon, okay?"

"I will." Astrid's eyes closed in a long blink. "But you have to remember it's a lot easier to pick up and relocate to another state when you're in your thirties than your fifties." She pulled her daughter into another hug, rubbing her back. "I'll be there before you know it, you'll see."

"I hope so." Delaney kissed her mother's cheek. "I really enjoyed spending the last two weeks with you here, Mom."

"It was just like old times." She nibbled on her bottom lip again.

"Now what's worrying you, Mom?"

"It's just...are you...I mean, are you okay about..."

"Varik?" Delaney indulged in a lengthy sigh. "As okay as I can be. I fell hard for him. I could have sworn he was the one, my soul mate, my destiny, you know? Everything seemed so right."

"I know, sweetie, I know..." Wrapping an arm around Delaney's shoulder, Astrid rubbed her daughter's arm. "Right after you leave I'll head to your townhouse to get things ready for the estate sale tomorrow. We've got ads online and in the paper so there should be plenty of shoppers. I'm betting you'll pull in a nice, tidy sum."

"Thanks. I hope so. I feel bad about sticking you with all this though."

"Don't be silly. I'm happy to do it. It makes me feel useful. Besides, I enjoy hosting an estate sale almost as much as I enjoy shopping at them."

Delaney knew her mom was being honest. Helping people was one of Astrid's top priorities, and helping her children ranked at the top of the list.

"Go ahead and price things however you think best. Keep whatever you want for yourself but," Delaney waved a warning finger, "try hard to get rid of most of it so the movers won't cost you a fortune. You might be better off just donating whatever doesn't sell."

"I know you're right, I'll—"

Their eyes opened wide at the sound of a car horn and Thursday barked. A quick peek out the window told them it was Delaney's ride.

"Oh no...already?" Astrid said, and Delaney could tell her mom was doing everything she could to avoid crying.

Fighting like hell to hold back her own tears, Delaney pulled her mom into one last hug before she left. "I love you, Mom. Now and always."

"Don't forget, sweetheart," Astrid whispered as they held each other close, "everything's going to be—"

"Hunky-dory," they said in unison.

A few minutes later, Delaney and Thursday were off.

As the cab driver headed for the airport, Delaney reminisced about her wondrous time with Varik. Although stunned by his deceit and the trail of lies that broke her heart, she had to admit he'd also provided her with some of the best, happiest, most satisfying moments of her life. She'd always be grateful to him for that.

She didn't think Varik was a bad guy necessarily, simply misguided and probably spoiled. He was a handsome, captivating man used to getting his own way...and used to women falling at his feet.

It wasn't the man's fault that the delusional Delaney had mistaken him for a male prostitute and dragged him into her house to have her naked way with him moments after he arrived at her door. Really, how could she blame him for making the most of the situation she'd inadvertently foisted upon him?

Even though their brief relationship had dived headlong into a bad soap opera finish, Delaney believed Varik really did find her attractive and desirable. She needed to believe he wasn't faking all that. And, God, how she'd needed that boost of self-confidence, and those memorable hours spent in his arms, and the wonderful talks they'd shared, and all the laughter they'd enjoyed. It was all one hundred percent heavenly.

Until she discovered she was an accidental adulteress.

The thought made her shudder.

After a year of hauling around a weighty cluster of resentment surrounding her heart because of Roger dumping her, Delaney knew how detrimental it was to feed anger and resentment. The only one it hurt was her.

This time she wouldn't make the same mistake. She'd let it all go...as soon as she allowed herself a good long cry, followed by a brief pity party. Steeping herself in negative thoughts would only make her bitter, sick and old before her time. This time she'd focus on the positive rather than the negative, centering on thankfulness for all the good things she'd experienced and the life lessons she'd learned.

The constructive resolution had her breathing a sigh of relief and acceptance.

Looking down at her hand, she fingered the heartwish ring. Thoughts of Grandma Bekka made her smile as Delaney clutched the ring to her heart.

She remembered what Bekka said in the letter...*Each owner of the ring may use it only once. Though your mind may be cluttered and uncertain, your heart will know the right wish to make when it's time. Always trust your heart, my dear.*

Her voice a soft murmur, for her ears only, Delaney spoke from her heart to her grandmother's. "You were right...my heart knows. It wouldn't feel true making a wish for another man in my life, Grandma, because I'll never let anyone into my heart again. Just as you promised, I found my handsome Viking, my glorious Varik the Bold. Our time together was sheer magic and I don't regret a moment of it. I'll love him till the day I die."

A lone tear coursed down Delaney's cheek.

"The wish I make now comes from the depths of my tattered heart...my wounded soul. It's a wish born of gratitude rather than pain, and it definitely feels right."

Although she swore she felt the metal band grow warm against her skin, Delaney still doubted the ring had any magical powers. But in the off chance it did, she closed her eyes and whispered her simple, sincere heartwish...

"May Varik and his family, and my mom and my sisters and brothers..." she sucked in a deep breath, "and, yes, even Roger, Karen and their baby, all be blessed with love, good health, and great happiness for the rest of their lives."

The taxi suddenly filled with bluish light. Clearly alarmed, the cab driver slammed on the brakes, propelling the equally startled and unprepared Delaney and Thursday forward in their seats until they tumbled to the cab's floor.

"What the hell was that?" the driver asked.

The glow, emanating from her ring, dimmed as quickly as it had appeared.

"I have no idea," Delaney claimed, getting back to her seat and brushing off her clothes.

But she knew. She *knew*. And so did Thursday, who, incredibly, had been silent through the entire event. Head cocked, he sat gazing skyward, placing one paw on Delaney's thigh.

Clasping Thursday's paw the same way she'd enclose a friend's hand, Delaney closed her eyes again, sending up a silent heartfelt *thank you* to Grandma Bekka.

~<>~

After two weeks of Ursula's clingy ways, Varik had reached his breaking point. He had to give her credit for trying, but though she'd struggled to maintain her façade, it had noticeably slipped soon after their talk. His ex-wife was back to her old habits of talking down to restaurant servers and salespeople, being overly possessive of Varik wherever they went, and turning the topic of conversation to Ursula's next facelift or newest jewelry find.

She foisted one limp excuse after another on him about why she had to make another few movies after her current obligations were over. It was clear the woman had no intention of leaving the industry or being the sort of relationship partner she'd promised him.

Thankfully, her two week holiday was at an end and she was heading to California this morning to start shooting her next film. He couldn't wait until she was on that plane and out of Illinois.

Avoiding her endless suggestions of intimacy became easier as the days passed. Varik found her far more annoying than appealing. Even his previously traitorous *mannlig kjonnsorgan* eventually behaved when his ex-wife ground herself against him, much to Ursula's surprise and disappointment.

Driving home after dropping her off at O'Hare airport, enjoying a renewed sense of freedom, Varik grinned. He'd forgotten how cloying Ursula could be, how demanding, anxious and insecure. The first thing he'd do when he got home was to open the windows and air out the stench of her French perfume. The stuff was so strong it overpowered the aroma of every dinner he'd cooked when she'd been there.

Thinking of those meals made him snicker. That first night she was so eager to help clear the table and do dishes together. It was the last time she'd show any interest in being helpful. Her excuses after that included the need to preserve her manicure, and to avoid dishwater hands for her upcoming film. When he suggested she learn to vacuum, she offered another battery of excuses.

When he brought up the subject of children, she told him at first that her biological clock had probably stopped and it was too late to consider pregnancy. When Varik suggested they meet with a fertility expert, Ursula grudgingly admitted she'd had a hysterectomy several years ago and hadn't told him.

She brought up adoption, an option Varik fully supported. Ursula said it would work as long as they had a staff large enough to watch the children because, Lord knew, with all her celebrity obligations she couldn't be expected to tend to their runny noses, dirty diapers, pouting, whining, and endless attention-getting. Ursula had actually shuddered as she went through her list of childhood annoyances. Her demeanor improved when she talked about sending the children off to boarding school as soon as they were old enough.

Same old Ursula, indeed.

Before getting out of the car at the airport, Ursula turned to Varik, a peculiar, forlorn expression across her perfect features. Taking one of his hands in hers, she clasped it tight. "I've lost you, haven't I, darling?"

The question caught Varik off guard. He'd treated Ursula well during the last two weeks but his heart simply wasn't in it. There was no magic, no thrill at the thought of spending time with her. There was none of the exhilaration he'd experienced with Delaney. He'd felt apathetic, lackadaisical. He'd wanted to believe she'd changed, but in the short time they'd spent together she'd left no doubt that wasn't the case.

Clearly, she had picked up on his disheartened vibe.

"I'm sorry, Ursula. Truly. But..." What else could he say? He wasn't cruel enough to say, *but you're just not Delaney*, even if it was true.

"But you've gone and lost your heart to someone else," Ursula said on a sigh.

"Not that it will do any good," Varik admitted.

"This Delaney...she was really that important to you?"

A flood of images whisked across his mind. He'd tried so hard to erase Delaney's face, her gestures, her voice, her fragrance, from his memory. But how can you erase a part of your soul?

"She was...but it doesn't matter now. That's a closed chapter in my life. I need to forget about women for a while. I haven't had much luck in that area." He gave in to soft laughter, though there wasn't much humorous about the situation.

"I gave it my best shot," Ursula told him. "I tried everything in my sexy bag of tricks, but nothing has worked. I can't ever remember spending so much time with a man without sleeping with him." She glanced at his crotch, giving a wistful laugh. "Even little Varik isn't interested anymore. I must have lost all my charisma."

"No, Ursula, it's not that. You're a beautiful, sexy, desirable woman. We...we're just not right for each other."

She studied his face for a long time, then smiled. "You're a good man, Varik. You deserve happiness with a good woman. One day I hope you will be able to forgive me." She appeared to be on the verge of tears.

"For what? I told you I've already forgiven you for what happened during our marriage."

Again, he saw that odd forlorn expression take hold. It was quite unlike Ursula's playacting or her dramatic pouting scenes. This look seemed to stem from deep within her heart.

"No, not that. I mean..." She closed her eyes in a long blink before patting his hand. "Just try to remember what I said when the time comes, and don't think too unkindly of me. *Jeg vil elske deg alltid, min kjaere Varik,*" she said as a single tear trickled down her cheek. *I will love you always, my darling Varik.*

After giving him a tender kiss on the cheek, she sucked in a deep breath, donned her bejeweled movie star sunglasses and exited the car.

Having no inkling as to what Ursula's cryptic words meant, it was crystal clear to Varik that, though he might be an academic genius, he was more like a village idiot when it came to women. From now on he'd spend his time burying his nose in books, preparing for the first course he'd be teaching for the fall term, instead of pondering the abundant complexities of women.

After turning down his street, Varik spotted a woman exiting a car and walking to Delaney's townhouse. When she unlocked the door and let herself in, he reasoned she must be the real estate agent. A quick glance at his watch told him Delaney, if she still lived there, had already left for work, so he decided to stop and talk to the woman.

Without Ursula's nose in his business, or her arm twisted through his as if they were conjoined, he could converse with the agent without any interruptions. It would be interesting to hear what she had to say about Delaney's abrupt move. There wasn't any harm in getting a little information. It certainly didn't mean he still had any interest in Delaney.

He rang the doorbell and the woman he'd seen answered a moment later.

"I didn't expect you so early," she said. "But that's okay, I've got everything ready to go. Come on," she waved him in, "I'll show you where everything is."

Varik followed the woman as she chatted, pointing out stacks of boxes here and there. It seemed clear by the state of the house that Delaney had already moved out.

"Sorry, I tried to keep everything in one room for you movers but the boxes were too heavy for me to move by myself."

"Ma'am, I'm not—" Varik began.

"Oh dear, you're not the only one they sent, I hope." The woman looked beyond him into the street. "Some of the boxes weigh a ton. In fact—"

"You misunderstand. I'm not one of the movers," Varik cut in while he had the chance.

The woman's puzzled, wide-eyed expression seemed vaguely familiar.

"Sorry, I didn't realize you were a real estate agent," she said. "I expect all the boxes to be gone within the next couple of hours so it's probably best not to bring your buyers through until then. But go ahead and have a look around. The owner has made a number of updates throughout."

"I'm not a real estate agent either," Varik explained. She gave him that doe in the headlights look again. "Actually, I'm—"

"You're not? Oh. You're here for the estate sale?" She sped on without waiting for Varik's response. "Sorry, that's not until tomorrow. Nothing's ready to purchase yet. I just started pricing items a little while ago." She started shooing him out. "The sale starts at eight a.m., you can come back then. You'll find lots of great stuff priced reasonably."

"I'm not here for the sale either, ma'am."

Her eyes grew impossibly wide. "Well then what are you doing in here?"

Varik smiled. "You invited me in."

"Ooh..." Frowning, the woman shuddered, rubbing her arms. "That's like Dracula. In the movies they say he can't come in unless you invite him and that's exactly what I did, isn't it?" She looked him up and down and smiled. "Of course, I sincerely doubt you're Dracula. You're not...are you?"

And that's the moment it hit Varik.

"No ma'am." He stifled a laugh. "I'm only a neighbor. You must be Delaney's mother," he guessed, noting the uncanny resemblance as well as the apparent family penchant for misunderstandings and nonsensical ramblings. Her features were similar to Delaney's but the attractive fifty-ish woman had short blonde hair instead of long black locks, and a few crinkles around her eyes and mouth.

"Yes, I'm Astrid Malone." The woman had the same radiant smile as her beautiful daughter.

"My first guess would have been that you're one of Delaney's sisters but she told me they've all moved from the area."

"As they say," the woman beamed a smile, "flattery will get you everywhere. And you are?"

Impressed by Astrid's youthful appearance, he couldn't help thinking how fortunate Delaney was to have those genes. He extended his hand, giving his best smile. "My name is Varik Jen—"

"Jenssen?" Astrid's voice boomed a full octave higher. As Varik gave an affirmative nod, she blanched, her hand flying to her throat while her wild-eyed expression told him she was either terrified or livid.

"Oh my God. I wasn't paying attention to the accent. Dracula doesn't have a Norwegian accent, but the man I invited into my daughter's home is worse than any vampire!" She staked him with a lethal glare, pointing to the door. "Get out!"

The abrupt change in her facial expression and the vehemence in her tone had him puzzled.

"But...Mrs. Malone, is something wrong? I think—"

"Out!" Her finger jabbed through the air. "How dare you show your lying, two-timing face here. Get out before I call the police and have you arrested for trespassing."

Hands raised in self-defense, Varik spoke slowly, calmly. "Mrs. Malone, please, I think you may have me confused with someone else. I'm your daughter's neighbor. I thought perhaps we could talk."

"Talk? Talk!" Her face was etched with outrage. "About what?" She poked him in the chest with an outstretched finger and he backed up. "How you broke my daughter's heart, you Viking snake in the grass?" She poked harder and he kept backing up, wondering if she'd had an iron finger implant. "That accent of yours...damn it, I should have known immediately."

"How I broke *her* heart?" Varik said incredulously. "Ha! That's a laugh."

"I don't see a damn," *poke*, "thing," *poke*, "funny about it." *Poke*. "You have a hell of a lot of nerve showing up here. Out!" Astrid shoved him this time.

Standing on the threshold, Varik tried once more to reason with the bent on violence woman. Once again lifting his hands in surrender, he said, "Mrs. Malone, listen, I—"

"*Komme seg ut!*" Astrid yelled *get out* in Norwegian. "There, maybe now you understand what I'm saying," she spat, giving a final shove strong enough to send Varik toppling backwards over the large ceramic planter on the doorstep and falling onto the snowy lawn.

He wasn't sure but he thought he bounced. He felt his eyes jiggle from the impact to the back of his head.

In an obvious instance of déjà vu, he remained there, spread-eagle and stunned for a moment, looking up at the woman, thinking mother and daughter had far too much in common. He eyed her cautiously, marveling at how an average-sized woman could so easily topple over two hundred pounds.

"Oh dear." Astrid clapped her cheeks. "I didn't mean to do that. Well, I did, but—" Gazing down at him, his back flat on the snow-covered grass, she almost looked remorseful. Almost.

"Are you all right?" Her hand reached out to help him and he took it, getting to a sitting position.

Thankful he was in good physical condition, he leapt to his feet. His ass and the back of his head hurt like the devil but he sure as hell wasn't about to admit it. "I'm fine."

"I'm glad. Now get out of here." She turned her back on him.

"You know, your daughter did the same thing to me the day we met." He chuckled as he brushed off his jeans.

"I'm sure you deserved it. Go away." She bent to adjust the large planter Varik had tripped over. "We have nothing to talk about." Back inside the house, she started closing the door. "You should go find your wife. Maybe your little blonde cuddle-bunny will kiss your sore behind and make it all better."

Evidently noting Varik's look of surprise, Astrid added, "Yes, that's right, Delaney and I know all about your sexy movie star wife." Her head bobbed up and down. "And the baby on the way." She nailed him with a gaze mimicking the same expression he'd received from Delaney the day they met.

"You, Mr. Jenssen, should be ashamed of yourself." She folded her arms across her chest, looking defiant. "Did you think you could just waltz back into my daughter's life? Her heart? Thank God in heaven my Delaney has more sense than to let you slither your way back into her good graces."

"Wait...wait..." He jammed his foot in the doorway, preventing her from closing the door. She banged it against his foot anyway. Hard. He should have known that was coming.

"Ow! Astrid, listen, you're not making any sense. First of all, Ursula is my *ex*-wife. Second, what baby?"

"Ha! Some father-to-be you are. And since when is she your *ex*-wife?"

"We divorced two years ago."

"Two years?" Astrid looked doubtful.

"Yes."

"That's not what she told my daughter."

"Ursula was lying. She does that a lot. Look, I didn't come here for a third-degree, Astrid, I—"

One of her eyebrows arched. "You may call me Mrs. Malone."

"Mrs. Malone," Varik corrected. "I just wanted to hear about your daughter's spur of the moment decision to sell her house after she decided to move in with her old boyfriend."

"What?" Astrid looked genuinely baffled. "What old boyfriend?"

"The one she left me for. The one she's been living with."

"Are you okay up in the head?" Astrid tapped three fingers against her temple, eyeing Varik as though he were some kid's failed science fair project.

"What are you talking about?" Varik asked.

"What are *you* talking about?" Astrid countered.

"Your daughter." Stepping fully inside, Varik closed the front door. "Can we sit for a moment and try to get this straightened out instead of providing entertainment for the neighbors?"

"Go ahead, sit." She pointed to the sofa while she remained standing, leaning against the closed door. "I hear the Norwegian accent but why aren't you speaking broken English? Were you lying to my daughter about that too?"

"No, I've been taking English lessons," Varik explained. "And I never lied to Delaney...about anything."

"Uh-huh, and in a few weeks you speak like a natural?" She rolled her eyes in disbelief. "Fast learner."

"Yes, I am." He figured this wasn't the right time to mention he was a genius. "Delaney knows all about that. Now if we could just—"

"Where is your ex-wife?"

"Ursula's on a plane, heading to Los Angeles. I just dropped her off at O'Hare."

Astrid's eyes closed in a long blink. "Dear God...please tell me she's on a nonstop flight."

"No, she's got a stopover in—"

"Oregon," Astrid muttered. "Flight 837."

Varik nearly did a double take. "How could you possibly know that?"

"I can't believe you put that movie star bimbo on a plane with my little girl."

He swore daggers shot out of her eyes as she growled at him. Thoroughly confused, he cocked his head. "What?"

"My poor baby. As if she hasn't already suffered enough heartache." She covered her face with her hands.

"Are you talking about Delaney?"

Astrid's arms flew into the air, slapping hard at her sides. "Who else would I be talking about?"

"She's on the same plane? You mean with her boyfriend?"

"What boyfriend?"

"The one she moved in with."

"The only male my daughter lives with is her dog."

"Where is Thor's Day?" Varik asked, having a devil of a time trying to make heads or tails out of the conversation.

"On his way to Oregon with Delaney. And your ex-wife, apparently."

The more they talked the more muddled things became.

"But why?"

"How am I supposed to know?" Astrid said. "You're the one who put her on the plane."

"No, I mean why is Delaney flying to Oregon?"

"Because of you. Because you turned my daughter's world upside down. There. Are you satisfied?" Astrid started to cry and Varik panicked.

"No, no, no. Please don't cry." Rising, he went to Astrid's side, guiding her to the sofa. "Sit down. Relax. I will make you a..." About to say *a drink*, he wondered what a distraught woman her age might want. "Some tea," he said instead, not wanting her to think he was an alcoholic on top of everything else. "We will talk. Everything is okay." He managed a smile.

"What I could use is a good stiff drink," Astrid said. "But the liquor is packed away with the tea and everything else." Giving him another appraisal, she added, "You really are quite charming."

"Thank you very much. You're quite lovely yourself. You and Delaney look very much alike."

She glared at Varik. "I wasn't giving you a compliment."

"Oh..." He stood leaning against the kitchen counter next to the living room, afraid to say anything else.

"Where did you get the screwy idea that my daughter is living with an old boyfriend?"

"From Ursula. She said Delaney told her all about it two weeks ago."

"And you believed her? You big dumb cluck." Astrid shook her head in disbelief.

"I saw Delaney with him myself, through the window. They were sitting right here," he patted the sofa cushion, "with their arms around each other."

"When?"

"The night she was going to come to my house for dinner."

"That's ridiculous. My daughter told me the only people she saw that night after talking to your...to Ursula, was her boss and her real estate agent. And I know damn well there's no funny business going on between Delaney and either of those married men."

"Or maybe she didn't tell you she had a lover," Varik said and Astrid gave him a look so incredulous it made him feel two feet high.

"I'm her mother," she said, clearly intending for that to be more than enough of an explanation as to his idiotic assumption. "What else did Ursula tell you?" she asked.

"That Delaney came to my house when I was in the shower to let me know she had to cancel our dinner date. You see, we were going to celebrate—" He stopped abruptly, remembering who he was talking to. "Never mind."

"Oh I know all about your seedy two week celebration plans, mister," Astrid said, and Varik's shoulders sagged. "What else did your ex say?"

"She told me she saw Delaney's lover waiting for her in the car. He was impatient for Delaney to finish so they could get to the hotel they were staying at for the night." Varik paused, trying to recall the other important specifics. "And, of course, there was the part about them being in love and Delaney selling the house so she could move in with him."

"Mmm-hmm. Did Ursula describe the car?"

Varik thought for a moment. "A blue Mustang. I saw it myself, parked right out front." He pointed out the window.

"That was Paul Richardson's car."

"Her lover?"

"Her happily married boss." Delaney's mother grumbled something Varik couldn't make out. "They were probably exchanging a goodbye hug after she gave him her two-week notice." Astrid gave him a pitying look. "You know what, Varik?"

"What?"

"You're definitely not the brightest crayon in the box."

He had no trouble deciphering the meaning of the saying. "Not as far as women are concerned," he readily admitted.

"You might be interested to know that your blonde, who said she was your pregnant wife, told my daughter you were in the shower and she was just about to join you. She told Delaney you were about to cancel the dinner date because it was unimportant to you now that your wife had returned from Norway."

Varik stood stone still, stunned at what he'd heard. After what seemed a small eternity, he spoke.

"Pregnant wife..." He huffed a humorless laugh. "I haven't slept with Ursula for more than two years. And if she's pregnant the baby is a medical miracle because she had a hysterectomy a few years ago." A moment later, he added, "And I showered alone."

"My daughter went to your house early, and alone, with a box of cookies. She'd spotted Ursula kissing you at the door and, naturally, she wanted to investigate. There never was any boyfriend. Your ex told Delaney that you had a habit of charming women into your bed and that she was sorry Delaney was one of many others to fall under your spell."

"No. No!" Gripping the edge of the kitchen's Formica counter he heard it crack under the pressure. Letting it go, he plowed his hands through his hair instead, pacing back and forth as he swore a blue streak in Norwegian. He knew Ursula wasn't to be trusted but he couldn't believe she could be so blatantly underhanded and conniving.

On top of his off color remarks, he threw in a few choice words about what he'd like to do to Ursula.

"Um...this would be a good time to tell you," Astrid said, "that, while Delaney doesn't speak Norwegian, I speak it fluently."

Mortified, Varik cringed, knowing his tirade would have made a sailor blush. "I apologize. I didn't realize. I just needed to vent."

"And regardless of how angry you may be with Ursula, I'd seriously recommend you think twice about tying an anchor around her neck, then rowing out to sea and dropping her in." Her lips curved into a half-smile.

Stepping back into the living room, Varik sat across from her in an armchair. "So...you understood all that?"

"Every word. You've got quite a colorful way with words, young man."

Shaking his head back and forth in disbelief, Varik said, "Lies. Everything my ex-wife said was a lie. I can't believe it. She had me convinced Delaney cared nothing for me...that all she cared about was her lover."

"Ursula sounds like a possessive, devious and very jealous woman."

"She is." Varik's head bobbed up and down in agreement. "She came here to the States to try to win me back. I understand now that she saw Delaney as a threat, a...how do you say it? A roadblock in her plan to get me to return to her."

"So you're telling me you never had any intention of calling off your...celebration date with my daughter?"

"Absolutely not. I fell in love with Delaney, Mrs. Malone. You can believe that or not. It was supposed to be our special evening. I'm not the world's most romantic guy but I'd worked hard to plan a very romantic night. I'd hoped it would be the beginning of our life together." Anguished, Varik growled, mindful not to resort to swearing again in Norwegian.

"Do you swear by all that's holy that you're telling me the truth?"

Searching the floor for answers that weren't there, he finally said, "The most important person in the world to me was my Grandpa Anders. He raised me, basically taught me everything I know. When he died a couple of years ago I lost not only the only parent I've ever known, but also my mentor and best friend."

Varik lifted his gaze, looking directly into Astrid's eyes. "On my grandfather's memory, Mrs. Malone, I swear to you that every word I've told you is the complete truth."

"Varik..."

He expelled the breath he didn't realize he'd been holding. "Yes?"

She offered a warm, genuine smile. "Call me Astrid."

~<>~

At forty-seven, Ursula Lovdahl's fame was declining. She'd played ingénues, sexy sirens and everything in between. Now she was being offered parts as the ingénue's mother, boozy barflies, or the no longer desirable wife the husband leaves for a younger woman. It was demoralizing to be thought of as a washed-up actress with nothing but a sea of character roles in her future. Maybe, if she was lucky, she might score an award-worthy dramatic role as a matriarch in another few years. She rolled her eyes at the bleak thought.

If all that weren't enough, she'd lost the only man she ever really loved. Well...as much as she could love any man. She wasn't really sure what real love felt like. In books and movies it meant a man and woman, the hero and heroine, who were selfless, who put each other before themselves, who would give up anything and anyone to strengthen their union. Ursula had never been that kind of woman. She'd been spoiled and pampered her entire life. She was too concerned with her career, her looks, her fame to be truly generous or unselfish.

Funny, it had never really bothered her until now. She'd had it easy, happily flitting through life on the foundation of her looks and sex appeal alone.

Varik, on the other hand, had been the perfect hero. The ideal man. Classic happily-ever-after husband material. She'd not only lost him, she'd single-handedly destroyed any chance he might have had of finding true love and lasting happiness with...what was her name? Delaney.

Maybe if Ursula hadn't been so self-involved she might have had a chance to build a quality life with Varik. Perhaps if she hadn't turned to her usual deceitful ways, telling lies some might perceive as unconscionable, things would have turned out differently.

The sad thing was Ursula honestly had no idea how to handle life's problems without resorting to trickery or deception. It's what had always worked for her.

The flight was nearly full, leaving little chance of Ursula securing a row to herself. It was the second time she wouldn't enjoy the luxury of flying first class. Apparently only the top rung contract stars rated that privilege. It seemed second raters on the fast track to cinema obscurity only deserved coach.

Upon locating her seat, Ursula was dismayed to find a young mother in the window seat, trying to pacify a cranky infant. A rambunctious little boy was squirming in the middle seat, clearly already bored and dissatisfied with his confined seating. "I want to get up! Why can't I get up? I want to get up!" the kid droned on.

Gingerly sliding into the aisle seat, Ursula did her utmost to avoid eye contact with the frazzled mother or her irritable children. Drawing a magazine from the seatback pouch in front of her, she gave it her full attention, hoping to dissuade any attempts at conversation. The absolute last thing she wanted on the long flight was to be chummy with a fatigued mother and her snot-nosed children.

Almost immediately, the boy began talking to her, touching her, asking her to play games with him, which she pointedly declined. Then the baby started bawling and the boy, who Ursula assumed must be the baby's brother, started whining for the baby to shut up, shut up, *shut up*! Without another moment's hesitation, Ursula pushed the call button to summon a flight attendant.

After explaining that she couldn't possibly remain seated with a pair of monster children, she demanded another seat assignment—at a good distance from any children. There were only two spots left open, a window seat with a pair of teenage girls beside her, and another seat where she'd be seated between two women. She took the second option.

Sitting stuck between two strangers for the first leg of her flight left much to be desired. Her shoulders slumped in resignation. At least they were adults. Once she got situated she noticed the old woman on the aisle babbled to herself and the woman in the window seat was turned toward the window, crying and sniveling quietly but steadily.

An hour into the flight and the sobbing still hadn't ceased. Ursula had no idea a woman could produce so much water. The hiccupping little sobs from one side and the incessant chatter from the other made it difficult for Ursula to catch up on her beauty sleep. Though she certainly wasn't the mothering type, she decided it was probably good karma to offer some concern.

"Are you all right?" she asked the crier.

"I was just about to ask the same thing," the old woman on the aisle said. Holding her knitting needles close to her chest, she leaned across Ursula and asked, "Everything okay, dearie?"

The crying woman lifted her face from the wad of tissues she held clumped in her hand, turning to her left. Both she and Ursula gasped.

"You!" they chorused.

"Who?" the old woman asked.

"What are you doing here?" Delaney asked Ursula.

"The same as you, I suspect," Ursula answered. "Going to California."

"I'm on my way to Oregon." Delaney had a defeated look in her eyes. "Honestly, of all the people on the planet why did it have to be you sitting next to me?" She cried harder.

"I could say the same thing," Ursula agreed, annoyed beyond reason to discover Varik's love interest was her seatmate for the long flight. She wondered for a moment if the mother with her monster children, or the two giggly teens might be better flight companions after all.

"Why are you going to Oregon?" Ursula asked.

"To-to start my life over. To get away from everyone and everything. To-to-to..." she collapsed into tears again. "Just leave me alone...please."

It was then that Ursula noticed the snapshot clutched in Delaney's free hand. Upon inspection she realized it was Varik dressed as a Viking. As usual, he looked scrumptious.

"You're crying over Varik?" Ursula asked. It was a silly question. Anyone with half a brain could see the brokenhearted woman was crying her eyes out over the man in the picture.

"You don't have anything to worry about," Delaney assured, dabbing her eyes and nose. "He's all yours. Yours and your..." as her gaze fell to Ursula's midsection, Delaney's soft cry became a distinct wail "...your baby's." She covered her face again, sobbing into the tissues.

"Oh hell..." Ursula winced. Granted, she'd been responsible for causing many a crying scene, but this was the first time she'd been wedged in a position where she had no choice but to experience the resulting aftermath of her unkind actions.

No doubt about it, Delaney was crushed. So much so that the lovesick woman was moving clear across the country to escape her pain as well as the man she loved.

And it was entirely Ursula's fault.

"You're having a baby?" the old woman asked Ursula. "Congratulations! When are you due?"

Ursula knew it was time to make amends, time to change her selfish ways, and it seemed the universe had conspired to dump an opportunity in her lap at this very moment. But, contrite as she may be, she only had enough patience to deal with one difficulty at a time.

"Mind your own business and go back to your knitting," she told the old woman, whose stunned expression was laughable. Since she imagined the new, kinder, gentler Ursula wouldn't laugh at the misfortune of others, she refrained from her natural instinct.

Turning her attention to her other seatmate, she took in a fortifying breath, placed her hand over Delaney's and said, "We have to talk."

Chapter 15

Glassfloat Bay, Oregon: The Next Morning

~< >~

"YOU HAVE BEKKA'S eyes," the woman behind the busy counter at Griffin's Café said as she poured Delaney's fourth cup of coffee. The hue of her striped apron and pink uniform matched her rosy cheeks. Annalise Griffin, the coffee shop's pretty owner, was about Delaney's age and the spitting image of Grandma Bekka's description. The bustling café with its 1950s décor was just as Delaney had envisioned it.

"Thanks, I've heard that before." Her eyelids fluttering closed in delight, Delaney murmured her satisfaction as she sipped from her cup. "Mmm...have I told you your coffee is fabulous?"

"Only a dozen times or so since you came in this morning." Annalise's rich laughter filled the area. "I'm glad you like it. Your grandma said you like your coffee good and strong. I use dark-roasted Sumatra Mandheling beans, they're rich and earthy, yet low in acidity. Here's something else you'll like." Annalise set a scone on a plate before Delaney. "This is Laila's newest recipe, date-nut with orange zest. It's a big hit already."

Delaney took a bite. "I can see why. It's delicious. I've missed all my sister's baking...although not all the weight I was putting on testing her recipes." She rolled her eyes.

Making a raspberry sound, Annalise patted her trim midsection. "Tell me about it. I keep gaining and losing the same fifteen pounds because of your too-creative sister. Which is why I was thrilled when she started making her lighter alternatives." She gestured to Delaney's scone.

"This?" Delaney held up the scone, studying the fragrant fruit and nut-studded baked good. She should have learned by now not to be surprised by Laila's incredible feats as a baker.

"Mmm-hmm. Amazing, huh?"

"It really is." Though she was tempted to sleep in after yesterday's long flight and the two-and-a-half-hour drive from Portland's airport to the Pacific Coast, there was no way Delaney was about to miss the activities she'd planned for her first full day in Oregon, including starting her day at her grandma's favorite hangout. She could easily see why Bekka was so fond of Annalise. With the woman's inviting personality, Delaney felt as if they already knew each other, which really put her at ease.

Charmed by the small coastal town, she appreciated the cordiality she'd been shown by the townspeople in the café. She'd spent the last hour happily listening to their personal accounts of Bekka and found it difficult not to get teary-eyed when they expressed their sympathy at her grandmother's recent passing.

The streets and buildings in the center of town were a quaint blend of old and new architecture. Many of Ocean Charm Boulevard's storefronts and owners were familiar to Delaney from her conversations with her grandma.

It was easy to picture herself buying coffee and a scone at Griffin's and taking a brisk morning walk down to the waterfront to watch the sea lions crowding the docks. What a perfect spot to pen her column.

Fatigued from her long flight and all those hours of pity-party-weeping, she allowed her wayward thoughts to wander until she pictured Varik taking Thursday's leash and walking alongside Delaney as she led them to the ideal seaside spot to savor the sunrise along with their coffee and scones. She'd work on her column while Varik threw sticks for Thursday to retrieve. They'd plan their day together, right up until dinner, dessert, and then—

"We're all excited to welcome Bekka's famous writer granddaughter to town."

Snapped out of her fruitless daydreaming, Delaney looked up to focus on the sprightly older woman speaking to her. A genuine smile lit the elderly woman's crinkled face as she patted Delaney's hand. "My sister and I never miss one of your columns."

Delaney felt a rush of delighted warmth in her cheeks, as well as gratitude for being whisked out of her pipedream. "Thank you, but I'm far from being famous. My column just went into syndication a short time ago. Do you read it in the Glassfloat Bay Register?" She'd heard the name of the local paper from her grandmother.

"No, not the paper. We found them on the machine."

That had Delaney stumped. "The machine?"

"Yeah, you know," the woman's fingers flitted as if typing, "the one that has the Google on the world wide web."

"Oh!" Though she clearly meant finding her blog online on the computer, Delaney wasn't about to be rude and correct her. "Well how nice. Thank you very much."

The old woman offered a nodding smile, said, "You bet, cookie. See you later," and tottled off.

"Don't be so modest." Annalise leaned close on the chrome-trimmed counter. "We all read your column and can tell you're headed for the big time. Once your name is a household word we'll be able to tell everyone we knew you when. By the way, it was nice of you not to correct her. Caroline likes to think she's quite savvy when it comes to technology." She winked as she pulled a folded sheet of paper from her apron pocket.

With a wave of the paper, she told Delaney, "If I don't write it down I forget it." Glancing at her notes she went on, "Caroline Crowe and her sister, Peggy, are making a batch of their marionberry cobbler this morning so make sure you stop by Crowe's Coastside Bakery before heading home. Caroline," she nodded in the direction the old woman had walked, "is the younger of the two sisters. Their cobbler gets snapped up fast but they're saving a nice big serving for you. The sisters are so sweet, and they're a real hoot. You'll love them almost as much as their cobbler."

"She was delightful. I'd guess she's close to my grandmother's age," Delaney whispered. "And she's still working in a bakery?"

"Yup. She's got to be in her late seventies at least. It must be that old-world work ethic. My grandparents were like that too. She and Peggy are there at the bakery every morning at four, believe it or not."

"Wow."

Annalise gave an agreeing nod. "This is Caroline's morning break time." She looked up at the wall clock with a wistful smile. "It's about the time your grandma would come in for her hot cocoa and scone each day." She leaned closer. "There are rumors the sisters might be selling the bakery soon."

"Ooh...it's always been Laila's dream to own a bakery," Delaney said.

"She's the first one I told." Annalise gave a bright smile. "But she said there's no way she could ever afford it." She gave Delaney her notes. "Here's the bakery's address. It's just a couple blocks down. I jotted a few other things for you too. There's always something going on in town."

"Great, thanks. I'll definitely be stopping by for cobbler. I haven't even been here a full day and I can already feel my waistline expanding." Delaney laughed.

"Well there's always TBT instead of the bakery," Annalise said with a teasing chuckle. "I'm sure you've heard about it from your sisters."

"Ah yes, Tuned by Turner...the weight loss company where Laila and Reen work. I just might need to sign up." Delaney puffed out her cheeks.

Cupping her hand at one side of her mouth, Annalise engaged in a conspirator's whisper. "Whatever you do, don't get sucked into buying their food. It's awful. We're talking nightmare worthy...even their baked goods and desserts."

"So I hear." Laila and Reen's descriptions of TBT's unpalatable food were enough to make Delaney shudder. "And yet, it's a popular, thriving business. Go figure."

"No competition," Annalise said with a shrug. She tapped the paper where she'd scrawled her notes. "Make sure to keep Saturday afternoon open. Miriam Schmidt's hosting a luncheon so everyone can meet you. You'll like her, she's quite a character." Looking amused, she elbowed Delaney. "She likes to think she's the town's unofficial mayor."

"I look forward to meeting her." Delaney enjoyed the small town vibe. Such a close-knit community where it seemed everyone knew each other was something foreign to her. But it was something Bekka loved.

"Just a heads up," Annalise continued, "she prefers to be called Mrs. Schmidt. She's in her sixties and prides herself in knowing every last bit of gossip about everyone in town...and probably the next couple of towns over too." She laughed. "She's a little pushy, maybe a little intimidating at first, but she means well and is a real sweetheart."

"You think I'll pass muster?" Delaney half-teased, excited but nervous about meeting everyone, knowing they'd all be checking her out. Being the center of attention always made her anxious.

Annalise made a raspberry sound. "You have nothing to worry about," she promised, brandishing a wide dismissive wave. "Everyone will love you. After all, you're Bekka's granddaughter. I doubt there's a soul who disliked Bekka."

Annalise's assurance was so matter of fact it helped take the edge off Delaney's nerves. Although being compared to her wonderfully gregarious tall-tale-telling grandmother didn't necessarily put Delaney's mind at ease. She only hoped she wouldn't disappoint Bekka's friends.

"Sounds like fun," Delaney said. "Will you be there too?"

"Are you kidding? I wouldn't leave you all alone to face the town's razor-sharp scrutiny."

Delaney's eye's bugged.

"I'm just teasing," Annalise assured. "I'll be there along with Laila and Reen—which reminds me, I talked to your mom on the phone a few days ago."

"You did?" Delaney wasn't really surprised. Astrid had made fast friends with a number of people in town when she was there visiting Bekka. She told Delaney that Annalise was especially kind and helpful when Bekka died, catering the food free of charge for the gathering at Bekka's house after the funeral.

"She called to tell me about something she felt was important."

"Oh..." Delaney squirmed in her seat. Knowing her overprotective mother, she'd probably filled Annalise in on the entire story of her poor daughter's broken heart. "So she told you about what happened with me and my Viking?"

"Your who?"

"Varik," Delaney clarified. "The man who—" She stopped abruptly, realizing Annalise looked genuinely surprised and a bit uncomfortable.

"Uh, no...Astrid wanted to describe something she thought you might want to pick up for your dessert tonight. Or maybe for your dinner. But, um..." She covered Delaney's hand, giving it a gentle squeeze. "If you ever need to talk, I'm a good listener. And nothing you tell me will ever go any further. In other words...you have my word Mrs. Schmidt will never know." Her mischievous smile made Delaney laugh.

It didn't take much more encouraging on Annalise's part. Delaney found herself feeling so relaxed with her that she ended up telling the near stranger everything that happened. Annalise was right, she was a great listener—the kind who just let Delaney vent without offering advice.

"I'm sorry I babbled on like that, taking up all your time. You should have stopped me." Delaney glanced up at the clock noticing it was close to lunchtime as a new wave of customers came into the cafe. "But I have to tell you, Annalise, it felt *so* good to talk to someone and get it all off my chest. Thanks for listening."

"Anytime, that's what friends are for. Under the circumstances, I probably would have done the same as you...hop on a plane and get as far away from the guy as possible." She made a flying plane gesture with her hand. "I will tell you one thing though. Never consider a door completely closed until you lock it yourself and throw away the key." In response to Delaney's obvious confusion, she added, "In other words, it's possible this may not be the end for you and your Viking."

"I appreciate the sentiment but..." Delaney shook her head from side to side, unwilling to keep bruising her fragile heart by getting caught up in an ongoing cycle of wishing or hoping. "It's over. I'm all the way out here starting the next phase of my life, and Varik is back in Chicago getting ready to teach for the fall term at the university there."

"Well, whatever's meant to be will be," Annalise said.

"I believe that." Delaney was fully prepared to move forward, putting all the heartache and difficult times behind her. "What about you? Anyone special in your life?"

"Oh boy. Got a few hours?" After an exaggerated roll of her eyes, Annalise laughed.

"As a matter of fact, I do." Delaney offered an inviting smile.

"Tell you what, we'll get together for lunch soon and you can listen to me spill my latest tale of romantic woe. Deal?"

"Absolutely. Now...about that dessert-for-dinner my mom called you about..." Delaney sat forward perching her chin on her hands.

"Ahh yes. You need to stop by Parasol Cove Ice Cream Parlor before you go home today. The address is in my note." Her eyes crinkled at the corners when she smiled. "They've created a new flavor in honor of your move here."

Delaney's eyes grew wide as she clapped her chest. "No...you don't mean..."

"Yup," Annalise confirmed. "Their homemade butter pecan ice cream with a caramel ribbon and fudge brownie chunks. They're calling it *Delaney's Scoop*. Get it? It's kind of a play on words, you know, with you being like a reporter and all."

"*Delaney's Scoop*...how clever. I love it! That settles it, Annalise. I'm definitely having ice cream for dinner on my first day in my new home town." She received a hearty smile and big thumbs up from her new friend.

"Perfect. *Live every day like it's your last*...that was Bekka's motto." Annalise came around to the front of the counter to give Delaney a hug. "Welcome to Glassfloat Bay, Delaney. I think you and I are going to be great friends."

Delaney had no doubt she was right.

Dear Diary: It looks like I made the right decision to pack up my life and move to Oregon. Things could have been so different if I hadn't so readily, and foolishly, believed the lying, scheming Ursula, but it's too late for regrets. What's done is done. Varik could have called or come over to explain...but he didn't. And I'm okay with that. It won't be anytime soon that I'll be forgetting my Viking and the sexy, romantic times we shared together, but I believe making the move, being close to my sisters and brothers, and meeting new friends like Annalise Griffin will turn out to be the best medicine for me.

Chapter 16

Two Months Later

~<>~

ONE OF THE FIRST things Delaney did to make the house feel like home was set up her aluminum Christmas tree, complete with ornaments and four-color rotating light wheel. Closing the door after a visit from her sisters and a few neighbors, her gaze fell to the pattern across the carpet that the afternoon sunlight hitting the shiny branches had created. It immediately brought a smile to her lips.

"If some women can become eccentric cat ladies, there's no reason why I can't be an eccentric Christmas tree lady," she told Thursday. Taking center stage on the glittery tree were the two ornaments Varik had given her, hanging right next to the similar Norwegian figurine ornaments that had belonged to her grandmother. She couldn't help but smile each time they glinted in the daylight, catching her gaze.

A short while later, Delaney was on the phone with her mom. "The more I get used to it, the more I like small town living," she said as she brought plates and coffee mugs to the kitchen sink.

She licked a couple of crumbs from her fingers as she spoke. "Laila, Reen, Annalise, and two other women just left. You'll be jealous when you hear what they brought me on this bright, sunny Saturday afternoon."

It didn't take much coaxing from her mom for Delaney to report, "A pan of fresh baked triple chocolate brownies, a basket of warm marionberry muffins, and a plump sour cream streusel coffeecake. And guess what? Nevan made one of his special Irish pork pies just for me." She listened as Astrid asked about her younger brother. "He's doing great. Nevan's Irish Pub is always packed...and, no, Mom, he doesn't have a girlfriend yet," Delaney chuckled, "but he's very popular with the ladies—of all ages."

"Is his pork pie with that scrumptious bazillion-calorie lard-crust-pastry wrapped around it as delicious as I remember?"

"I couldn't help sampling it as soon as everyone left earlier. Mmm, outrageously good," Delaney assured. "Nevan's customers are crazy about it."

"Uh-oh...between your sister's baking, your brother's pork pie, and all the delicious goodies from the townspeople, your waistline is in dire danger."

"I know!" Delaney laughed at her mom's perceptive words. "Thank God I found the pair of elastic waist jeans I packed because I'll need to wear those soon if I keep eating this way. This afternoon they even brought their own thermoses full of Griffin's good, strong coffee to share. The only thing missing was you to share it with, Mom."

It was a perfect lunch, with her sisters and the other women staying a couple hours sharing interesting tidbits about Glassfloat Bay and its inhabitants. During *The Roger Years*, with her standoffish ex preferring to socialize as little as possible, Delaney had missed the opportunity to cultivate many friendships. It was so nice to have her friendship status changing.

Opening her refrigerator, she stood staring at the contents, dumbfounded. It would take some creative placement to fit more food in there. Along with those stretchy jeans, she was going to need a bigger refrigerator and freezer.

She swooped her finger through chocolate buttercream frosting, depositing the dollop on her tongue before closing the fridge.

"Thursday just nudged me to go out," she told her mom. "I enjoy watching him prance around the big yard each time I let him outside." The fenced backyard was sizeable compared to the suburban Chicago townhouse's postage-stamp sized plot. Along with the house itself, the Malones had inherited all of Bekka's furniture and belongings. Everything felt familiar, which helped make Delaney feel at home.

"Speaking of the yard, did you know everyone around here calls this Bekka House?" Delaney asked.

"Yes, Annalise told me that started shortly after Bekka died. I think that's sweet. They really loved her."

"Well I love living here in Bekka House and I know you will too, Mom."

Remembering Grandma Bekka's descriptions of the house, accompanied by plenty of her photos, Delaney could almost walk the place blindfolded. Feeling this comfortable was exactly what she needed after the stress of the last year, and the last few months in particular.

"It's been fun examining Grandma's possessions." Delaney dusted the rim of a Norwegian beer tankard as she let Thursday back into the house. "I remember some of them from when I was little." The items Delaney brought with her, as well as the few crates that had arrived from her Chicago townhouse, mixed well with Bekka's furnishings and décor. It was an eclectic melding of contemporary and old world.

Perching on the arm of a plump-stuffed living room chair, Delaney mindlessly twirled her fingertip in the soft nap of the sherpa throw. At night when she closed her eyes, listening to the soothing chorus of ocean waves slapping against the shore in the distance, Delaney could swear she felt Bekka's presence. She liked to think her grandma had become her guardian angel, watching over her.

"Sometimes it's as though I can sense Grandma whispering in my ear," she confided. "At other times I could swear I hear the faint chirp of her laughter. Remember how infectious it was?" Astrid readily agreed. "I think Thursday's aware of it too. He'll stand, head bent, as if listening to someone or something. He never barks or gets rattled. He seems as comfortable and relaxed with the presence in the house as I am."

She also told her mom about the delicate ginger fragrance of Grandma Bekka's delicious *pepperkaker* that occasionally snagged Delaney's attention. She'd gone in search of the mysterious smell in vain when she first noticed it. Now she simply welcomed the inviting cookie aroma, accepting it as another comfy sign of her grandmother's presence.

"If visitors hadn't commented on the ginger fragrance, I might have thought I was going batty," she confessed. "The first time it happened with other people in the house, I fibbed, saying I'd baked a batch of cookies earlier. Of course, then I had to admit I ate them all by myself since I didn't have any to offer guests." Delaney and her mom shared a laugh. "After the repeat of this fragrant situation another few times, I figured they'd soon be whispering about Delaney Malone, the Glutton of Glassfloat Bay."

"While I haven't experienced the phenomena myself yet," Astrid said, "I believe it's real. Our deep affection for my mom, and her love for her family seems powerful enough to cross seemingly impassable barriers." Delaney agreed with that. "In fact...after I move to Oregon and have all six of my children together, I'll share a remarkable story about your grandmother with all of you."

That snagged Delaney's attention. "You can tell me now," she egged her mother on, "and I promise not to breathe a word to a single soul."

Astrid laughed. "Nope, sorry, honey, you'll have to wait. But I promise it will be worth it."

That only fueled Delaney's determination to learn more. "How about a hint? Just a teensy one?" Out of habit, she held her thumb and forefinger an inch apart even though Astrid couldn't see it.

"All right. But then no more of your infernal nagging," she teased. After a long pause, Astrid said, "It's about something very special and quite amazing that happened when I was there visiting my mom for the final time...and that's all I can say now—other than it was amazing."

"It sounds very mysterious. You have me completely intrigued. Mother?"

"Hmm?"

"You need to get your butt out here to Oregon a.s.a.p."

The full round sound of her mom's laughter rang out again. "I will. It won't be long. I promise."

Delaney looked forward to having her mom in Oregon. The only other Malones missing were Delaney's sister, Kady, who was backpacking across Europe, and her brother, Gard, who was on assignment as a glaciologist in Antarctica.

"I can't wait until we're all together again," Delaney said.

The first two months in her new home passed in the blink of an eye, with Delaney getting settled quickly. She remembered how fast Varik had organized his house after his move, something she never thought she could accomplish.

When her thoughts slid to Varik, as they often did, it made her wistful but less gloomy as the days passed. She was glad she'd had her eye-opening talk with Ursula on the flight. While furious to learn of the woman's ruse, Delaney was grateful to her for admitting what she'd done. It certainly couldn't have been easy for Ursula to make that confession.

Their odd heart to heart talk was the last thing Delaney expected when boarding the plane. Learning Varik and Ursula Lovdahl were divorced, hadn't slept together since, and that his ex-wife wasn't pregnant after all was jarring but positive news.

Their discussion left her pitying the actress. It was hard to conceive of a woman so desperate to hold onto a man that she'd stoop to spinning such a cruel, elaborate web of lies. Delaney wondered if the woman's expertise at playing unsavory, disturbed women on screen had filtered into her personal life.

She couldn't help the escaping sigh at the thought of the highly anticipated romantic rendezvous that never took place. She wondered how different her life would be today if she and Varik had kept that date.

"That was a sad sounding sigh. Are you okay, sweetie? I know it's hard about you and Varik..."

Her thoughts returning to the present and her conversation with her mom, Delaney smiled at Astrid's protective instincts. She'd probably be treating Delaney and the rest of her brood the same way thirty years from now.

"I'm fine, Mom, just a little tired."

At least she would forever have the delicious memory of being held in her Viking's strong arms, the sensation of skin on skin, the succulent feel of his lips on hers. Closing her eyes in a long blink, she luxuriated in the secret pleasure of her reminiscence.

"I've accepted that Varik and I simply weren't meant to be, Mom." Slipping into the overstuffed armchair to relax for a moment, she stared vacantly at the dog, patting his flanks. "But I made my heartwish and I know Varik will be happy—and that makes *me* happy." As she spoke, her ring grew warm and she spotted a faint, gentle glow.

Propping his head on her knee, Thursday gazed at her ring, then up at her...letting Delaney know he sympathized with her.

"I hoped that Varik and I could rekindle the extraordinary connection I thought we had, but it's obvious his feelings for me weren't as deep as mine for him. It's not like I could afford to pick up and move back to Illinois this soon anyway...but then...he didn't ask me to, did he?"

"No...I-I'm sorry, honey."

Once her plane landed in Glassfloat Bay two months ago, Delaney called her mom to let her know she'd arrived okay, and about the conversation she'd had with Ursula. It was after that call, hearing what her mother had to say about Varik, that Delaney put her romantic hopes and dreams to rest, finally accepting the reality of the situation.

Astrid told her Varik had stopped by, asking her to convey his regrets to Delaney about his ex-wife's interference. He wanted Delaney to know he was sorry things hadn't worked out for the two of them, and that he wished her well in her new life in Oregon.

So, that was that. Adios and goodbye. They were officially over. Done. Finito.

Hopefully she'd soon be able to keep from sighing every time she thought about his *so long, have a good life* wishes.

And there it was again. Another tuneful sigh.

Clearly it was going to take a while.

When Delaney heard her mom's next question, she laughed. "Do you know how many times you've asked me that same question since I moved here? Every time you call." She rolled her eyes. "No, I haven't met anyone I'm interested in yet. I keep telling you it's *way* too soon for me to even think about anything like that."

"Good, that's exactly what I want to hear," Astrid said, sounding pleased as she offered the same response as always. "You need to take time, plenty of time before getting involved with anyone again."

Rising from her chair, Delaney headed to the gallery of framed photos in the hallway, straightening the multi-image frame that held the shots of Varik in his Viking gear taken moments before they'd made love. Rather than living with the soul-deep ache of rejection the rest of her life, she'd at least have bittersweet memories of their time together and of what might have been.

Gazing at the other framed photographs on the wall, she gave a contended sigh. There were black and white photos of Delaney's mom and her late dad, Sean Malone, several of Grandma Bekka, a few of her paternal grandparents, and a single, precious snapshot of dear Bekka and her soldier husband, Jamie, who'd died in WWII.

Rounding out her photo collection was a series of shots featuring her best buddy, Thursday. Delaney had managed to capture a smile-making assortment of his best expressions, including those where she could swear the dog was laughing, as well as Thursday's big-eyed, guilt-inducing *feel sorry for me* face.

The photo gallery always lifted Delaney's spirits and made her smile.

While listening to her mom, she returned to the large family room. "I imagine Varik will be hugely successful as the university's new Scandinavian Studies professor," Delaney said, absently speaking her thoughts aloud while tracing her finger around the fireplace mantle. "Young women will be lining up around the corridors to sign up for Professor Jenssen's classes." Remembering his terribly broken English when they first met made her smile. The notion of all those coeds drooling over her Viking also triggered a smidgen of jealousy.

He wasn't *her* Viking anymore, she reminded herself.

She'd acted rashly, perhaps, in her haste to get as far away as possible from Varik and his supposedly pregnant wife, but there was no way she could cope with the idea of living only two doors away from the hunky Viking and his expectant movie star wife. Even though moving across the country meant she'd lost Varik forever, Delaney was still convinced it was the only decision she could have made under the circumstances.

She stroked Thursday's fur as they headed to the kitchen.

"I-I hope you're doing okay, Delaney. I hope you're happy. I promise you things will be getting better very soon."

"I'm sure you're right." Delaney gave a wistful smile. She knew her mother meant well but how in the world could she promise that? Mending a broken heart takes more than good wishes and an injection of positive thinking.

"I'm fine, Mom, really. Thursday and I will carve out a good life for ourselves here on the Oregon coast, right Thursday?" She massaged behind his ears and he gave her a tongue-lolling smile in return. "We'll grow old and gray together." There was no need to whine to her mother about her shattered heart or how long it would take to heal.

She was happy here. Monday she'd start her new job as a writer and Features Editor for the *Glassfloat Bay Register*. She was a writer fortunate enough to be living her dream.

"I'm so proud of you, Delaney. I brag to everyone I know about your new job at the newspaper," Astrid said as if she knew what Delaney was thinking. It must be one of those mother-daughter psychic connection things.

"Thanks. I worried about getting a job and never imagined I'd end up working fulltime doing what I love best." The paper's owner was one of the first people to visit after Delaney arrived. She told Delaney their longtime editor was retiring and they were looking for someone to bring the paper up to date by giving it an online presence. She'd read Delaney's blog and subscribed to her email newsletter and felt sure she'd be perfect for the job. Delaney readily agreed.

"I see it as another sign that my moving here was meant to be," Delaney told her mom, believing every word.

Dear Diary: I'm happy. I really am. Thursday and I will grow old together in our cozy house tucked away in Glassfloat Bay, content with our memories, our year-round Christmas tree, and collection of Bekka's glass float balls. One of the good things about not having a man in my life is that I can eat chocolate for breakfast, lunch and dinner, every day if I feel like it, and never worry about growing fat because there won't be anyone here to notice...

For fun and self-improvement, Delaney signed up for a knitting class at the String Me Along yarn shop where Bekka had taught. The shop's aging owner, Ruthie Brone, was a wonderfully patient instructor, and the first Black business owner in Glassfloat Bay. Delaney was also taking a Norwegian language course through the local college. It would help her to decipher her grandmother's letters and diary entries, many of which were written in Norwegian. There were two stacks of letters, tied with red grosgrain ribbon that she was eager to translate.

One of the things she'd learned in her Norwegian class was that Varik, being unable to speak English, was an anomaly among Norwegians. She remembered him telling her it was due to his Heidi-esque upbringing with his grandfather, and couldn't help wondering how far along Varik was now with his English.

"I've already got my office organized and equipped for working on my column," she told her mother. "The only thing I need now to make everything perfect is to hear when you're moving out here to join me."

"Soon. By the end of summer. Before you know it, though, you won't be missing me at all," Astrid promised. "You'll see..." Along with her singsong voice, it sounded like she was muffling soft laughter. "Trust me."

"Don't be silly," Delaney tsked, "of course I'll still miss—"

There was a knock at the door. Barking, Thursday ran around the kitchen, forcibly nosing Delaney's knee in case she didn't realize they had a visitor.

"There's somebody at the door, Mom, I'll have to let you go."

"Oooh, I wonder who it could be."

If Delaney didn't know better she'd swear her mom was giggling, which was impossible because Astrid wasn't a giggler.

"Probably one of the neighbors," Delaney said. "With more platters of fattening goodies." She welcomed the company. The more people she got to know, the better her features editing would be.

"Call me tomorrow, Delaney."

"But, Mom, we just spent forever talking on the—"

"Tomorrow," Astrid cut in. "Promise."

She enjoyed talking to her mom a couple times a week but they'd pretty much exhausted things to talk about during this afternoon's call. Maybe her mother was feeling especially lonely. "Sure, okay." Whoever was at the door was ringing the bell now. "Okay, gotta go. Love you, Mom."

She set her phone on the counter, grabbed a kitchen towel and wiped her hands to make sure there wasn't any telltale chocolate frosting residue decorating her fingers. Towel in hand, Delaney headed for the door with Thursday prancing at her heels.

"Be right there," she called out, checking her watch again. It was nearly five o'clock, which meant some kind soul was probably delivering another casserole for her dinner.

She opened the door and nearly fainted.

Chapter 17

~<>~

NOTHING COULD HAVE prepared Delaney for coming face to face with Varik. Seeing him standing there now was as shocking as the first time she'd opened her door to find a Viking across her threshold. Only this time he wore jeans and a dark, long-sleeved pullover.

Her eyes wide, Delaney gasped, clutching the blue plaid towel to her chest, sure her heart was about to burst from a surplus of happiness. She wondered for a moment if he was real or if her eyes were playing tricks on her.

Of all the warm, heartfelt, love-filled comments whooshing to the surface, the only words making it out of the stunned Delaney were, "You cut your hair and shaved off your mustache and beard."

A deep round of surprised male laughter rushed forth. "I'm happy to see you too," he teased.

"Varik...oh *Varik*!" Jumping up on him, she wrapped her arms around his neck, her legs around his waist, and she kissed him with all the fire and passion of a woman in love. She was immediately enveloped in his arms, exactly where she wanted to be...where she was *meant* to be.

Unquestionably thrilled about Varik's arrival, Thursday joined in the reunion, pouncing on them to join in the fun.

The force of Delaney's enthusiastic leap and her dog's zealous tackle caught the unprepared Viking off balance. He tripped over the ten-inch-high iron frog doorstop behind him and fell backwards onto the porch's wood floorboards, with Delaney on top of him and Thursday happily barking while galloping over and around them.

Varik's pained groan had her cringing. "Oh no, Varik, I'm so sorry," she said as soon as she'd caught her breath. It took him a moment longer to find enough air to speak.

"Between you and your mother," he croaked, lifting his head enough to look into her sorrowful eyes, "this is becoming a very bad habit."

As she scrambled to get up, he held her tight in place against those two hundred pounds of solid muscle she'd been dreaming about.

"My beautiful Delaney." His fingers smoothed down her face from temple to chin. "How I've missed you." He kissed her with such heat she felt the delicious burn clear down to her soul.

Eager to share in the attention, Thursday clambered over them, rolling around and licking both their faces. Their reunion had clearly made him one happy pooch.

"Thor's Day!" Varik patted the dog as best as he could being pinned beneath Delaney. "How's my best buddy?"

"I can't believe you're here in Oregon." Crying happy tears, Delaney planted a million little kisses all over Varik's face. Hearing his labored breathing, she blinked. "I hope you're okay. From the fall, I mean."

Wincing, he said, "I hope so too. At this rate I'm not sure I'll make it to forty."

"We should probably get up." Delaney hated leaving his embrace even for a moment, but was still rational enough to realize her Viking could have a broken back, sprained butt, and whopping concussion.

"Probably," Varik agreed as she rolled off him. Groaning briefly the way a stubborn man did when refusing to admit he was hurt, he quickly got to his feet, moved his joints, flexed his muscles and smiled. "Looks like I survived intact."

He picked up a large, weighty-looking hiker's backpack from the porch, along with his guitar, which he strapped over his back.

Gathering Delaney into his arms, he kissed the tip of her nose, then carried her and everything else across the threshold.

Resting her head against his chest, she sighed. "This is like a dream. I thought I'd never see you again."

"I thought so too for a while. But life couldn't be that cruel to us. Not when we're meant to be together."

When he put her down she gazed up at him, almost afraid to blink, afraid he might be a mirage disappearing at any moment. Overcome with emotion, she fought to keep from crying, laughing, and bombarding him with questions all at the same time.

After closing the door with his foot, Varik walked to the Christmas tree, depositing his backpack and Delaney on the floor before tapping the pair of ornaments he'd given her, watching them swing.

"You saved them."

"Of course I did." Her head tilted as she studied him.

Following her gaze, he patted the top of his head. "So, do I look like a professor now?"

"I'm not sure. I've never seen a professor look this handsome or sexy." She'd tried picturing him with shorter hair and without the facial hair and couldn't. His flowing mane of golden waves had been so wild and sexy. Now his hair was corporate length...and he looked astoundingly handsome.

"Good answer." He drew her into another kiss. After making a sweeping gaze of his surroundings, Varik said, "Bekka's house?" Delaney nodded. "It suits you perfectly."

"I think so too." She glanced around with fondness. Everywhere she looked she found something to remind her of her grandmother. "It feels like I was always meant to be here."

"I'm glad you feel that way. Moving so far couldn't have been an easy decision."

"It was, and it wasn't. It was kind of a snap decision." The first two weeks after she'd arrived Delaney was in a serious funk, missing Varik, missing her mom, and missing her job and the people she'd worked with. It was during that time she felt the most comforted by the spirit of her grandmother, as well as by Thursday's often comical antics.

His hands bracing Delaney's shoulders and holding her at a distance, Varik locked gazes with her. "I'm sorry. It was all my fault. After the stormy history Ursula and I shared, I should have known better when she told me those lies about you."

"I sat next to Ursula on the plane. She told me everything...which must have been really hard for her to do."

Nodding, Varik said, "I got a lengthy, apologetic email from her, telling me about your conversation. It's going to take a long time for me to be able to forgive her."

Smoothing her hand along his arm, Delaney smiled. "It's all over now." It was difficult seeing so much pain in his eyes. She looped her arm around his waist and leaned into him. "Let's forget it and move on from here."

She really had no idea what *moving on* might mean, since Varik had to return to Illinois to teach classes in a few months. The idea of uprooting herself now, after falling in love with Glassfloat Bay and its people, would be hard but she'd do it in a heartbeat if it meant being with Varik.

She realized he hadn't asked her to do that yet.

Maybe she was jumping to conclusions.

If Varik had a long distance relationship in mind, where they took turns traveling across the country for a rousing bout of lovemaking once or twice a year, she couldn't do it. It would be too painful each time they parted.

Delaney looked up into his eyes, opening her mouth, then closing it when she realized she was too afraid to ask him about their future. Taking him by the hand, she led him to the sofa. "Sit with me. We have so much to talk about."

"And...so much to do besides talk."

His words and the unmistakable look in his eyes made her heart skip.

"So..." she said after a few moments of silence, "how do a couple of brandy-laced coffees with a dollop of vanilla ice cream sound?"

"Interesting." He didn't look particularly convinced. "I can build a fire while you put those together."

"Sounds great. It's a little brisk and windy today." As Delaney bustled around the kitchen her thoughts raced. She still had no idea what he had in mind. "My mom gave me your message—that you wished me well and hoped I'd have a good life." It was easier talking to him about this when he was in the other room and she didn't have to look at his face.

"Did she?"

"Mmm-hmm. That made it sound like there was no chance of a future for us."

"It did, didn't it?" There was a distinct teasing quality to Varik's tone.

As she poured jiggers of brandy into their mugs, her thoughts whirled. Frankly, she didn't find anything humorous about his kiss-off message and couldn't imagine why he seemed to find her mention of it so amusing. Her eye twitched as she remembered the call she'd just finished with her mother and how odd and cagey Astrid had acted.

Finally, it dawned on her...

"Wait a minute...Varik Jenssen, are you telling me you and my mother were in cahoots with each other?" Her eyes flashed and she gasped aloud. "Does my mother know about you coming here today?"

Striding into the kitchen, Varik said, "I'm not sure what cahoots means but," he squinted one eye, "I think you've reached the right conclusion. Yes, Astrid knows."

Stirring the brandied coffee with more gusto than she'd intended, Delaney accused, "You two purposely wanted me to think I'd never see you again." She cleaned up the mess she'd made from the mixture sloshing as she stirred. "I can't believe it. Why would you do that?" The ice cream landed in each mug with a haphazard plop and she had to clean the counter all over again.

"Clever, hmm?" Varik looked quite pleased with himself. "I like your mother very much. We hit it off great. After she shoved me to the ground, I mean."

"How could my own mother do that?"

"Well in her defense, that's when she thought I'd broken your heart."

"No, not to you, to me." Delaney carried their mugs into the living room, placing them on the coffee table before sitting on the sofa. "I can't believe Mom would join forces with you to deceive me. There's no logical reason for her to—"

"Astrid wanted to be a part of something that would make you smile. Once she got to know and trust me we came up with a plan, a surprise, we thought would make you happy." Varik rose to his feet. "Ta-da!" He motioned to himself. "So, did it work?"

Taking in her big, handsome Varik the Bold from head to toe, Delaney couldn't help grinning. "Like a charm. But," she wagged a finger at him, "you and my mother have a lot of explaining to do, Mr. Bold."

Sipping his coffee as he hauled Delaney next to him on the sofa, Varik made a satisfied sound. "Do you have any idea how difficult it is being hard all the way from Illinois to Oregon while sitting next to a stranger on the plane?" Delaney followed Varik's gaze as it drifted to his tented crotch. "You're entirely to blame. Just thinking about getting you naked and picking up where we left off makes me—"

"That picking up where we left off part has me kind of confused." Delaney cleared her throat. "Varik, why are you here? I mean other than wanting to have sex with me."

His eyebrows bounced playfully. "Is there any better reason? You, me, hot sex tonight." Setting his mug down, he drew Delaney into his arms, kissing her until her toes curled.

Oh Lord, he was going to make her spell it out for him. She was going to come across needy. Clingy. Possessive. She'd have him hightailing it right back to the airport for the next plane to Illinois.

"I was thinking along the lines of something not quite so...transient." Her hand smoothed over his knee, ensuring he wasn't a figment of her imagination.

"Transient..." He frowned, clearly perplexed. "You're going to make me dig my Norwegian-English dictionary out of my backpack, aren't you?"

"It just dawned on me. Your English has improved phenomenally."

"Phenom..." he scratched his head, "yes, I definitely need to find that translation book."

Delaney smiled. "Phenomenally means remarkably and transient means something temporary. I was hoping for something a bit more...permanent," she managed, just above a whisper.

Varik's face blanched as soon as the words left Delaney's lips.

Thursday chose that instant to whimper and Delaney was tempted to utter a whimper of her own.

"I can't believe it." Varik dropped his head into his hands, groaning.

Aw hell. She crumpled inward. So all he wanted was a long distance romance after all.

"I apologize." Varik's big hands cupped her face. "I was going to tell you after I asked you about my haircut, but I got distracted."

"Tell me what?" She hated the way her voice sounded like a lost little girl's.

"I'm here to stay." He spread his arms wide. "I'm not going anywhere."

Her heart thudded against her chest. "But-but I don't understand. I thought you were starting at the university in the fall."

"I am!" His smile was a mile wide. "But not in Illinois. You're looking at the new Professor of Scandinavian Studies for Wisdom Harbor University." Rising from the sofa he engaged in a dramatic bow.

"Wisdom Harbor?" Every nerve in her body shot to attention. "You mean just two towns from here?"

"That's the one."

Leaping from her seat she grabbed Varik into a hug, practically squeezing the life out of him. "But how?" She reluctantly let him go so he could breathe enough to respond.

"My cousin, Tore. As Chair of the English Department, he has a network of connections all over the country. He put out some...what are they called? Feelings?"

Delaney giggled. "Feelers."

Varik nodded. "He found a couple of different options. One was at Rainspring Grove College, in Oregon's wine country, but that's more than an hour's drive from here."

Delaney cringed, imagining the traffic jams on Highway 101 during the tourist season, and in the rainy season with all the flooding. "That drive would be murder there and back."

"I told Tore I'd take it if there was nothing else. I'd travel to the ends of the earth and back if it meant being with you, Delaney."

"Ohhhh..." The sigh escaping her lips was probably the longest one on record. "That has to be the sweetest, most romantic thing I've ever heard." She clutched his hand, weaving their fingers together.

"A week later Tore got the news about WHU from one of his associates at Portland State University. Apparently the Wisdom Harbor area has a small but thriving Scandinavian community. After a significant number of inquiries from residents they recently updated their curriculum to include Scandinavian Studies and," he spread his arms wide again, "the rest is history."

They held each other for a long moment, rocking in each other's arms. At a loss for words, Delaney couldn't remember being happier.

"Astrid was in on everything. We didn't want to say anything until we were sure I'd secured the WHU position."

"But you two made me wait two months. *Two months*, Varik! That was cruel! You and my mother let me believe I'd never see you again. I spent all that time pining over you."

"Pining?" Varik's eyebrows knitted. "Like the trees? Ah...perhaps it is a reference to tree sap being like tears?"

"No!" Delaney laughed, then gave his arm a playful whap. "Don't make me laugh when I'm chastising you."

"Chastising..." Varik looked clueless. "I thought I was doing very well with my English until we started talking." He gave her a teasing look.

"It means scolding, and this isn't funny," Delaney clarified with a roll of her eyes. "Seriously, Varik, can you imagine how I felt after my mom delivered your *so long, have a great life* speech?" Delaney rubbed the sudden chill from her arms. "Just wait until I talk to my mom tomorrow. She's going to get an earful from me."

"I'm sorry, truly sorry, my love. I never meant to upset you. And your mother would sooner cut off her arm than hurt you, you know that, right?"

Delaney uttered a lengthy sigh of acceptance. "I do. And to think I just spent the last sixty days planning my old age with nothing but Thursday and buckets of chocolate to keep me company."

"I'll be right here with you and Thor's Day when we're old and gray, sharing those buckets of chocolate." He hooked a lock of Delaney's hair behind her ear and held her close, soothing her. "I only did it because I love you so much. Forgive me?"

How could she possibly be angry after hearing those words? And after he'd turned his world upside down just so he could be here with her?

"I love you too." Cuddling as close as possible, Delaney rested her head against his chest. "Of course I forgive you." She held him tight. "And I know you and my mom would never purposely try to hurt me."

"We were idiots."

"Please don't expect me to argue with you, Varik, because that's not going to happen." They laughed together. "But I love you both anyway. It's kind of weird...you don't sound like yourself anymore. I mean, you still have the Norwegian accent but now you speak nearly perfect English."

"I told you I learn fast."

"It's a little disconcerting."

"Disconcerting...aaand there's another word for me to look up." Offering an acquiescing smile, he closed his eyes in a long blink.

Delaney recalled how she'd doubted his implausible claim when he first told her he was an academic genius. "Would I be terrible if I said I miss your broken English?" She lifted one shoulder in a shrug. "You were hard to understand but it was kind of adorable."

"You mean I've lost my adorableness?" He slapped a hand against his chest in a mock-wounded gesture. "If it makes you feel better, I still get mixed up sometimes. Bigger words, contractions, slang."

"Nope, your adorability quotient hasn't changed," she assured him. "Nothing could ever diminish that. I just started taking a night course at your new place of employment, WHU, to learn Norwegian. We can help each other."

"I'll enjoy whispering Norwegian words of love in your ear when we're naked in bed together."

"Hmmm," she tapped her chin in thought, "I doubt I'll be learning any of those words in my class but I can't wait to hear you whisper them to me." Her eyes roved his perfect, muscled body and she frowned. "How come you're not wearing your Viking costume?"

"It's not exactly appropriate travel attire."

"Yeah but it's so sexy." She pouted. "I dream about you wearing that outfit." Her fingers tiptoed from his waist, up his abs, and to his sculpted pecs where they came to rest.

"So you've been obsessing about my body hmm?"

"Mmm-hmm." She felt the warmth of a blush tinge her cheeks and smiled through it. "Definitely."

"I feel like I'm being objectified," he teasingly accused.

"Just because I happen to enjoy gawking at you while you're wearing your Viking getup...as well as when you're out of it," elevating her chin, she cleared her throat, "doesn't mean I'm objectifying you."

"Oh I think it does." He folded his arms across his chest. "But that's okay. I know you can't help obsessing about my *mannlig kjonnsorgan*." He clutched his crotch, plainly enjoying Delaney's resulting blush as heat spread across her cheeks. "It just so happens I have the Viking costume in my backpack."

Scooting forward, Delaney felt her expression light up like her Christmas tree. "You brought it?"

Varik gave an affirmative nod. "If you're a good girl I may agree to put it on before we make wild, passionate love together."

Narrowing one eye, Delaney crossed her arms over her chest. "If I'm a good girl, hmm?"

"That's what I said."

After a long spell locking gazes, they collapsed into laughter.

"I almost forgot how much fun we have together." Delaney was beyond delighted to have this amazing man back in her life.

"Just one of the reasons we're perfect together." He patted the sofa cushion next to his thigh. "Sit close. I want to feel your warm, supple, womanly curves press against me as I tell you about my heartwish."

"You're objectifying me, aren't you?" Delaney accused.

"Definitely. Any objections?"

"Nope." Delaney snuggled close, enjoying their close proximity and the body warmth they generated.

He kissed the top of her head. "You know I dream about you too."

"Am I dressed like a Viking girl?" Batting her eyelashes, she fluffed her hair. "Wearing a horned Brunhilde helmet?" She wiggled her forefingers above her head.

"No, like a cartoon character." He laughed at her scrunched face reaction.

"You mean like Bugs Bunny?" Her expression was still twisted at his unexpected, unsexy revelation. "Gee, Varik, that's kind of funky."

"Snow White," he told her, combing his fingers through her dark hair. "You're like the cartoon come to life. Same raven-black hair, snowy skin, rosy cheeks, kissable lips." His finger outlined each feature as he spoke. "I had a mad crush on Snow White when I saw the movie as a boy."

"That's so much better than Bugs." Delaney smiled. "I always thought Prince Charming was hot." Her hand curved over his jaw and her finger smoothed across his lips. "But I think Vikings are hotter."

"So we're both turned on by fantasy characters. I guess that means we're made for each other." Varik gave her a sexy grin. "Oh, I almost forgot. I came across something in my grandfather's papers I'm sure you'll want to see." Reaching into his back pocket, Varik drew out a small journal, covered in well-worn brown leather.

"This looks really old," Delaney said, taking it gingerly as he handed it to her.

"Probably about two hundred years old. It's notes my grandfather's grandfather kept about the family." He flipped through the pages and smiled. "Here, this is what I want to show you." He tapped his finger on the faint pen scrawling.

Glancing down at it, Delaney laughed. "It's in Norwegian."

"Ah yes, I forgot." Resting his head against Delaney's he read aloud from the page. "Dinner at Viking Lodge this Sunday to commemorate our brave Viking ancestor, Varik the Bold, and all his many accomplishments." Raising his eyebrows, he glanced at Delaney and smiled. "If it hadn't been for Varik's single-handed bravery against the enemy," he read on, "our entire family may have ceased to exist."

"What!? You had a Viking relative named Varik the Bold? And he was a hero? Wow, that...that means you're the real deal, Varik."

"The real deal?" His expression skewed.

"A Viking. A real, honest to goodness Viking!"

Remembering the vision she'd seen in Grandma Bekka's eyes so long ago, Delaney had no doubt it was Varik Jenssen she'd envisioned. "You're my very own Varik the Bold. My grandma was right after all. Fairytales really do come true." The potency of their kiss punctuated her statement perfectly.

Chapter 18

~<>~

THURSDAY SNIFFED around Varik's backpack. "Whatever you have in there is making Thursday crazy."

"It's the makings for our long postponed celebration dinner date, just as we'd planned before my ex-wife threw a hammer into the job." He angled his head as Delaney's lips curved into a smile. "That's not right, is it?"

"I think you mean she threw a wrench into the works."

Varik swore an oath in Norwegian. "You see what you do to me? Just being in your presence has me backsliding with my English." He rummaged through his backpack and pulled out two packages wrapped in butcher paper. "Ribs for you and me," he placed the longer package on the coffee table, "and this," he waved the smaller package, "is the steak I promised my best buddy, Thor's Day."

At the sound of his name, Thursday dropped his rubber chew toy, gluing himself to Varik's side, sniffing the meat packages and licking his muzzle. Varik clapped the dog's flanks. Another reach into his bag provided a small bottle of beer and a bottle of sparkling wine. "Your promised beer," he nodded at the dog, "and our champagne," he held the bottle aloft, smiling at Delaney.

Cupping his hand at the side of his mouth, Varik whispered, "Don't worry, I'll water down his beer." His laughter filled the room.

"You didn't bring all this on the plane, did you?"

"No, it's from..." Varik drew a brown paper grocery bag from his backpack, turning the lettering toward him. "Glass Ball Market," he read aloud. "The grocer on Ocean Charm Boulevard. The butcher and his customers wanted to know if I was related to Bekka because of my accent. I told them I was here to see you."

"That's where I do my grocery shopping. By now I'll bet everyone in Glassfloat Bay knows you're here to see me. That's what happens in a small town."

"I know. I come from a small town, remember? We'll have to give them many reasons to talk about us." Varik winked before planting a kiss on her lips. "The ribs will take at least an hour so I'd better get them on now." He brought everything into the kitchen.

"I've got a refrigerator full of salads and side dishes from visitors welcoming me to town, I'll get some out." Delaney followed behind him.

"You," he turned, pointing at her, "just sit and relax. This is my treat. I'll go through what's in the refrigerator."

"Can't I do something to help?"

"Yes. You'll find another bottle in my backpack."

Delaney read the label on the bottle of clear liquid she drew out. "Aquavit. I've never had this."

"I wasn't sure I could find it here so I brought it on the plane with me. It's Norwegian liquor with caraway, fennel, anise, cardamom, and citrus peel."

Delaney wrinkled her nose. "It sounds like rye bread in a glass."

"It tastes better than it sounds," Varik assured. "Pour us a couple of small glasses to have while we're waiting for dinner. It's perfect for a toast."

"Oh?" Delaney's ear perked. "What are we toasting?"

"Too many questions." His teasing smile was just as charming as he was. Once he had the ribs and potatoes roasting, Varik rejoined Delaney in the living room.

Sitting next to her, he spread his fingers, displaying his ring with the heartwish stone. "I used this to make my heartwish. Grandpa Anders left it to me in his will with a letter of explanation, cautioning me to make the right wish because it only works once for each owner."

Varik tipped her chin up. "My heartwish was the most important thing I could think to wish for." His smile was warm and loving. "A wish that would bring the smile back to a deserving woman at a very sad time."

Tears sprang to Delaney's eyes. "Thursday," she whispered, throwing her arms around Varik's neck. "Oh, Varik, you used your special heartwish so I wouldn't lose my dog."

"I'm not sure I even realized yet that I was in love with you but when I saw you so heartbroken, I had no doubt whatsoever that the time was right." He clapped his chest. "My heart spoke to me then and I knew."

"You'll never know how much that means to me."

"I think I do." His kiss was sweet and gentle.

"I remember seeing the kitchen fill with blue light when you took Thursday in there to talk to him. So that's why."

"It was unsettling to say the least," Varik said.

"The same glow happened when I made my heartwish. The inside of the taxi illuminated, scaring the devil out of the poor cab driver." Delaney held her hand aloft, gazing at her ring.

"When was that?"

"On the way to the airport the day I flew here to Oregon. I wished for love and happiness always for you and your family, for my mom, sisters and brothers, and for Roger, Karen and their baby."

"Even though you thought I had lied to you? And after all Roger did to you?"

Delaney clasped his hand. "I realized there were many more positives than negatives from those experiences. If Roger hadn't left me, I never would have pulled you in off the street and jumped your bones."

"Best bone jumping of my life." Varik's smile reached his eyes.

"And even though I thought you and Ursula were married with a baby on the way, I was thankful for the magical time I'd spent with you, the Viking I'd waited for my entire life. It was important to me that my heartwish be one of love and gratitude."

"Sweet, loving and unselfish." Gazing at her as if he cherished her completely, Varik stroked the contours of Delaney's face with his thumb. "Is it any wonder why I can't imagine my life without you?"

He remained silent for a long moment as he studied the rings on their fingers. "Remember the day we met, when we realized our rings looked like opposite sides of the same stone?"

Delaney focused her gaze, comparing their rings. "As if Odin had broken the stone in two," she said. "Like the ancient legend." Tearing her gaze from the rings, she looked into Varik's eyes. "Do you think it could possibly be true?" With the magic that had come into her life today, Delaney could no longer deny the possibility.

"As far as I'm concerned, it's a pure case of Viking magic."

The instant Varik had spoken the words, an arc of electricity passed between the stones. The long blue curve of light was gone as quickly as it came.

"Please tell me you saw that," Delaney whispered.

Varik looked as dazed as she felt. "Any doubts I've ever had about the validity of the stones has just been put to rest." He slid from the sofa to the floor, getting down on one knee before her. Reaching into his pocket, he withdrew a ring box, opening it and presenting it to her, eliciting a stunned intake of breath from Delaney. A silver ring with an oval black onyx stone surrounded by tiny diamonds sat nestled inside.

One glance at the stunning ring told her Varik must have consulted her mother about the sort of ring Delaney might like because it was exactly what she would have described.

She clutched her chest, uncertain if she could take even one molecule more of bliss this day before disintegrating into a pool of unadulterated joy.

Taking the ring from the box, he held it at the tip of Delaney's ring finger, gazing up at her with a hopeful smile. "Delaney, my truest heartwish," he began, his striking blue eyes locked on hers. "Will you marry me?"

"Oh Varik..." She lingered for a moment, savoring his life-altering words. "Yes. Yes, of course I'll marry you." He slid the ring on her finger. It was a perfect fit. Happy tears blurred her vision as she gazed at her hand.

"When you made your heartwish," Varik told her, "unselfishly asking for happiness for me and my family, you were unknowingly making the wish for yourself because you, my lovely fiancée, will soon be my family." He wiped away the tears on her cheek with his thumb and they embraced.

Once their kiss ended, Varik held his glass of aquavit aloft. "And now you know why we're toasting."

"Best reason ever." Raising her glass, Delaney doubted her smile could grow any wider.

"To us," Varik said. "Viking magic has brought us together. May it forever keep our love strong as we enjoy a long and happy life together."

"And may the magic of our heartwish rings never fade," Delaney added as they clinked glasses. She licked the taste of the unusual liqueur from her lips. "What a day full of wonderful surprises. My mind is spinning."

"Much better than the unhappy surprises we had with Roger and Ursula." Holding the bottle over her glass, he asked, "Like the aquavit?"

Delaney cocked her head, deciding. "I think so. I can taste the caraway seeds. I'll have a little more." He poured before adding to his own glass. "I've thought of another perfect toast," she said. "To the end of unhappy surprises. As in, no more ex-husbands or wives showing up on our doorstep. Ever." She raised her glass and they clinked.

"I'll drink to that," Varik readily agreed.

The doorbell rang as they were about to sip, leaving them both wide-eyed with mouths agape.

"No..." they chorused.

"Varik..." Delaney clutched him. "You don't think...?"

"There's only one way to find out." Grim-faced, he headed to the door, yanking it open. "Ah, Mrs. Schmidt! How nice to see you again."

Breathing a sigh of relief, Delaney joined Varik at the front door to see the apple-cheeked woman bearing food gifts.

"Mrs. Schmidt and I met earlier today at the butcher counter," Varik told Delaney.

"When I learned you were having company, dear," Miriam Schmidt said to Delaney, "I thought I'd stop by with one of my apple strudels for you. Just baked it this morning." She craned her neck to peer inside while Delaney took the container the woman offered. It was covered by a colorful knitted cozy. "I know you're having ribs and you know how well apples pair with pork."

"How very thoughtful of you, Mrs. Schmidt. And what a nice job you did with this cozy." Turning to Varik, she explained, "Mrs. Schmidt and I are in the same knitting class. This will be perfect with coffee later," she told the woman, suspecting Mrs. Schmidt would be meeting with her cronies after leaving to make a detailed report.

"That's for you to keep, dear." The woman patted the cozy. "So, son, how long are you staying in Glassfloat Bay?"

Delaney thought it was adorable the way Mrs. Schmidt batted her eyelashes at Varik. She noticed a pink tinge to her cheeks too. Varik and Delaney exchanged amused smiles.

"Permanently." Wrapping his arm around Delaney's shoulder, Varik drew her close to his side, boasting a proud smile. "Delaney has just agreed to marry me...and you're the first to know, Mrs. Schmidt."

"Oh...oh!" She clapped her cheeks. "How wonderful!" Mrs. Schmidt's wide-eyed, enthusiastic expression told Delaney the woman was thrilled to get such a scoop. "Congratulations! I hope we'll be reading all about this in the Glassfloat Bay Register. We're all so excited to have you working for the paper."

In answer to Varik's quizzical look, Delaney said, "I haven't had a chance to tell you about my new job yet." She patted his arm. "I'll tell you later."

"She's our very own Erma Bombeck," Mrs. Schmidt said with a giggle. "Well, it's time for me to be off. I'm meeting the girls for cocoa at the café. They'll be so excited to hear your happy news. Come here you two." She gestured with her fingers, inviting them to bend down for a kiss. They both got a big, congratulatory smooch on the cheek.

Delaney and Varik breathed audible sighs of relief as they closed the door, then laughed as they spotted the red lip imprints stamped on each other's cheeks.

Sniffing the plate Delaney held, Varik grimaced. "All I can smell is her flowery perfume."

"She tends to have a heavy hand with it. I think she might have sprayed it on the cozy too. Whew!" Waving her hand, Delaney chuckled. "She's a good cook though. This will be perfect for dessert."

"No...better for a late night snack," Varik suggested. "I have something entirely different in mind for dessert." His devilish expression left no doubt as to his meaning.

Heading for the kitchen, Delaney felt like she was walking on air.

"I do have one more surprise," he said, following her. "This one is about your mother."

Stopping mid-step, Delaney shifted into concerned daughter mode. "Please tell me it's good news."

"No, I wouldn't call it good." When he paused Delaney's heart did too. "It's *excellent* news."

Delaney let out the breath she'd been holding while Varik took the dish of apple strudel from her hands and set it on the kitchen counter. He opened his mouth to speak, then scrunched his face, sniffing the air. "I smell *pepperkaker*." He gave Delaney an odd look. "Do you have cookies in the oven?"

The ginger cookie fragrance permeated the kitchen, mixing pleasantly with the aroma of roasting pork. "If I did they'd be burned to a crisp by now. No, it's...well...you see, Varik..." Sucking in a deep breath and letting it out with a whoosh, she figured he may as well hear the truth. "It's Grandma Bekka."

Varik's eyes bugged. "But I thought you said she—"

"She did. Pass on, I mean." Resting her hand on his arm, Delaney smiled. "It's Grandma Bekka's ghost."

"What?!" He looked at her like she'd lost her marbles.

"The house is haunted. Just a teensy bit." She gestured with her fingers. "It's a friendly ghost. Nothing to worry about. I think she's just trying to tell us that she's happy about our engagement."

"Friendly ghost. Like Casper in the cartoon?"

"No, silly." She offered a reassuring smile that didn't seem to work. "I like to think of her presence more like a guardian angel than a ghost." She wasn't at all surprised by Varik's skeptical expression. "You don't have to worry. She's never intrusive on private times if that's what you're concerned about."

"Delaney..." It was like the tone of teacher to child, a combination of caution and disappointment. He gave her that disbelieving look again.

"I know it sounds a little crazy but, trust me, it's true." She cleared her throat. "Um...you were about to tell me something about my mom?" Repositioning the apple strudel at a far end of the kitchen to dispel some of the perfume, which didn't blend well with either the pork or the cookie fragrances, she smiled up at him, doing her best to look innocent...and sane.

With one eyebrow hiked high, he studied her for a long moment, shaking his head. "We'll get back to this ghost business later," he said, folding his arms across his chest. Delaney happily nodded.

"Anyway, the day I took Astrid shopping with me for your ring, we stopped for lunch at a little French bistro near the university. Earlier I'd asked Tore to meet me there for lunch, without mentioning your mom would be joining us. Ready for this?"

Delaney couldn't imagine where this was leading. "What? What!"

"Sparks flew when they met, Delaney. Sparks!"

"My mom and Tore?" Delaney's jaw dropped. "No...really?"

Varik nodded. "I had a feeling they'd hit it off. You should have seen the two of them together. They were jabbering away," he made the motion with his fingers, "as if they'd known each other for years. After a few minutes they didn't even know I was still at the table...so I finally left." He laughed. "Since that lunch meeting they've been inseparable."

Stunned, Delaney sat speechless for a moment. "Mom never said a thing to me," she said finally. "How could she not tell me something so important?"

"Astrid didn't want you to know she and I had become friendly. It might have made you suspicious and spoiled our secret. We wanted my arrival to be a complete surprise. She told me it was killing her not to tell you about her and Tore."

"I can imagine. The three of you all schemed together. You little devils!" She tried for an angry expression but couldn't pull it off. "So the man I'm going to marry is not only a genius, he's a matchmaker too."

Blowing on his fingernails, Varik polished them against his sweater. "Apparently so."

Framing his face with her hands, she kissed him. "Thank you so much for thinking of bringing my mom and Tore together."

"Tore's like a brother to me. This makes me just as happy for him as you are for your mother. He's making a trip to Oslo over the summer to facilitate a graduate class at the university and has asked your mom to go with him."

"Wow..."

"They'll stay at the cabin in Lillehammer that Bekka left to your family. At the end of summer they're both moving here to Glassfloat Bay. Tore's already lined up a teaching position at the university for himself."

Delaney was floored. Her smile felt so wide she feared her face might crack. "That means my heartwish for my mom came true too." Crossing her hands over her chest, she hugged herself. "Oh Varik, I've wanted so much for my mom to find someone to love again. I worried it would never happen."

"She's a good woman, and Tore's a good man." He pulled a small envelope from his jeans pocket, opening it and drawing something out. "These will make you smile." He handed her four photos. "Astrid had me take these with her camera."

Delaney chuckled. "Mom's never without her Kodak." She studied the photos of her mom and a handsome man, looking for all the world like they were a couple of teens on a fun date. "So that's Tore? I had no idea your cousin was so handsome. And look at my mom laughing. She looks so young! I can't remember the last time she's looked that happy." Close to erupting into tears of joy, Delaney didn't know if she was happier for herself or for her mom.

"Love is ageless," Varik acknowledged.

When the reality of the situation hit her, Delaney's approaching tears transformed into laughter. "So my mother is flitting off to Norway to shack up with a guy she just met two months ago, huh? Just wait until I get Mom on the phone tomorrow."

"She'll be so happy she can finally talk to you about it."

Contemplative, Delaney twisted her heartwish ring. "You believe in the magic of our rings, right?"

"Do you even have to ask, especially after what we witnessed together?"

"Interesting." She trailed her fingers along the inside seam of his jeans.

"I can almost see the little gears inside your head turning." He twisted a finger at her temple. "What does *interesting* mean?"

"Well," her shrug was casual, "I was just thinking that a man who believes in magic should have no trouble believing in friendly ghosts." She chanced a glance up at him and caught his knowing smile.

"I figured you were going there. If you claim Bekka's ghost is here then I believe you." He kissed the tip of her nose.

Her thoughts still wandering, Delaney nibbled her bottom lip. "Varik, you've made me the happiest woman on earth but..."

"But?" His expression took on a scowl. "I don't like the sound of that..."

Delaney took him by the hand, leading him to the oversized chair, and she sat on the ottoman. She worried her news would be a major disappointment. She remembered her mother telling her how disappointed Varik said he was when Ursula had a hysterectomy and kept it from him.

"What is it, Delaney?" He leaned forward, rubbing her back. "What's made you look so sad?"

"You want children, right?"

Varik pulled her from the ottoman onto his lap, enveloping her in his arms. "You're worried I don't want them? I love children. I want as many as you'd like to have, starting with a little girl as beautiful as her mama." He planted a kiss on her cheek. "I can't wait to be a papa to our babies. And then a grandpa so I can start smoking Grandpa Anders' pipe."

Her eyes brimmed with tears as her heart broke all over again. She'd never be able to give the man she loved one of the most important things he wanted.

"What's wrong?" He brushed the tears from her cheek with his fingers. "Why are you sad on such a happy day?"

"I'm not able to have children." She looked down at her lap, not wanting to see the disappointment in Varik's eyes.

"I'm sorry. I didn't realize." He brought her hand to his lips, kissing it, then lifted her chin so he could look into her eyes. "It's all right, Delaney. You'll always be my love, whether we have children or not."

"You always know the right thing to say, whether your English is broken or perfect." Delaney caressed his face.

"Why can't you have children?"

"I had my tubes tied," she said on a regretful sigh. "I foolishly listened to Roger who convinced me children were a bother and would stall his career. He said the responsibility would be like an anchor around his neck for the rest of his life."

"But Karen..." Varik's hands formed a generous sphere over his flat belly.

"I know...what can I say?" She gave a resigned shrug. "I guess Karen is more persuasive that I was."

A frown marring his handsome features, he said, "What kind of man insists that his wife have surgery, then turns around and gets another woman pregnant?"

"A man like Roger. It's not all his fault. I could have said no." She remembered how naïve and trusting she'd been. "The doctor was his close friend and colleague. They convinced me getting my tubes tied was the wisest decision. Condoms could tear and the pill's side effects were dangerous. At the time, I thought Roger and I would be married forever."

She felt her chin tremble and willed herself not to cry. "It was devastating. I'd always wanted to have children. A little girl. I'd call her Rebekka, after my grandmother." A single tear rolled down her cheek. "Little Becky..."

Pulling Delaney close, he hugged her so tight he nearly robbed her of breath. "My poor Delaney. I'm sorry this happened." He rocked her silently.

Delaney absently traced the outline of the engagement ring on her finger. "You should be with a woman who can give you children, Varik."

Holding her at arm's length, his expression was incredulous. "How can you even think such a thing? I love you." He kissed her soundly, then looked off into the distance for a moment, ire coloring his gaze. "That selfish bastard. If Roger was here I swear I'd make sure with one swift punch that he'd never father another child."

"Oh no, please don't say that." Delaney's hand flew to his arm. "It's over now, Varik. It's in the past and, while I don't want to see Roger again, I've forgiven him in my heart."

One of Varik's eyebrows arrowed high. "In our relationship," he gestured between them, "it will be your job to be the kind, sympathetic one. I will never forgive what Roger did to you. And," his finger poked the air, "I will never forgive what my ex-wife did to tear us apart."

Delaney opened her mouth and Varik moved his finger to rest over her lips. "I know what you're going to say. I don't want to hear about how I should feel sorry for Ursula or forgive her. Package closed."

"Case closed." Delaney smiled.

"Right." Varik gave a resolute nod. "All of it—closed." He gave her a sideways glance. "We can always adopt. What do you think?"

His encouraging smile warmed her heart. "I'd like that very much."

He gave her a hungry look. "*Forventning*."

Delaney slanted her head. "For what?"

"*Forventning*. In English the word is *anticipation*. In any language the definition means how I feel about getting you naked."

"Mmm...nice segue." The sensation of liquid warmth flowing through her caught Delaney's attention.

He looked as puzzled as she was a moment ago. "Seg...?"

"Smooth transition from one topic to the next," Delaney clarified. "I'm awfully glad you brought your Viking costume." She snaked her hand beneath his sweater, exploring his chest.

"I brought it along in case you refused my proposal." Varik gave her a knowing look.

Delaney lifted an eyebrow in question.

"I knew once I slipped into those reindeer hides you wouldn't be able to resist me. Just like that," he snapped his fingers, "your hands would be all over my *mannlig kjonnsorgan*." His gaze fell to his crotch.

She burst out laughing at his unexpected answer. "And the helmet." Her fingers walked up from his chest to the top of his head. "You definitely have to wear the helmet," she informed him.

"I hope you have your Mrs. Julenissen outfit," he whispered against her mouth. "I want to watch the bottom make that slow glide down your legs again."

"Sorry. That went straight into the trash. It wasn't even good enough to donate." Delaney laughed, remembering the ancient crumbling elastic. "Luckily I do have one of Grandma Bekka's billowy, floor length flannel nightgowns though. I hope it turns you on."

"We'll leave that for another night...when we're old and gray and eating our buckets of chocolate." Varik positioned Delaney back on the ottoman and got up to get his seemingly bottomless backpack. He pulled out a shirt-sized box, handing it to Delaney. "This is for tonight."

She opened the box to find a sexy red teddy. "Varik...it's gorgeous. So pretty and feminine."

"I love you in red," he said, drawing her tight to his chest. "And out of it too."

Chapter 19

~<>~

"I HOPE THURSDAY doesn't decide to make this a threesome," Delaney mused, carrying her tomato-red nightie into the bathroom to change after they'd enjoyed the fabulous celebration dinner Varik had prepared.

"Don't worry, I had a talk with him. In Norwegian. Thor's Day won't be bothering us." He set two stemmed glasses of champagne on the nightstand.

"You amaze me," Delaney called, peeking from behind the bathroom door. "In more ways than one."

"If you want to see amazing, just wait until you come out here and I get my hands on you."

"I'm hurrying," she promised, practically pulsating with expectation. Checking herself in the mirror, she fluffed her hair and practiced seductive poses. "Did you light the candles on my dresser? And light the lavender incense?"

"Done. There's soft music playing in the background, and I turned down the bedding. All I need to make me one very happy Viking is my beautiful Snow White here in my arms."

"Snow White and the Viking...who knew we were so kinky?" Delaney laughed. "Speaking of Viking, don't forget to put on your outfit...and the helmet."

"Yes ma'am."

She could hear Varik chuckling while muttering something in Norwegian. "I can hear you laughing at me, you know. Just wait until I become fluent in Norwegian. Then you won't be able to talk about me behind my back."

Opening the bathroom door, Delaney stepped into the bedroom. There stood Varik the Bold, in full Viking costume, Brunhilde helmet in hand. Tingles of excitement rocked through her as she caught the way her sexy fiancé ate her up with his eyes.

"Delaney, you look just like a..." He frowned, cocking his head.

"Yes?" Maybe she wasn't the silky teddy type and he was disappointed. She shifted her stance, doing her best to look alluring. "Please don't say cartoon."

"No..." Lifting his finger, Varik thought for a moment, then broke into a grin. "A sex puppy."

Delaney's impromptu burst of laughter ruined the sexy come hither pose she'd practiced.

Varik looked baffled.

"It's sex kitten." She undulated toward him, the way she imagined a sensuous sex kitten might. The moment she reached him her hands were on his chest, slipping beneath the reindeer hides, exploring his flesh, squeezing his biceps.

Happiness beamed from her every pore as she stood there eyeing the man she loved...the man she thought she'd lost forever. "I swear, Varik, I'm so happy I could burst." She imagined her words would become a self-fulfilling prophecy once they got their hands on each other.

Varik bent to nibble her earlobe, before trailing a sultry path of kisses to her mouth, tugging on her bottom lip with his teeth. She savored the glide of his fingers as they slid over the teddy, tracing her curves.

"I want to eat you up," he whispered, removing her teddy with agonizing slowness. "You're like a tempting smorgasbord, full of one delicious lick and nibble after the other." He took his time tasting her from her throat to her belly, making her sigh with delight.

His kiss spoke of lust, hunger and desire as he carried her to the bed. He placed her in the center and straddled her, looking down at Delaney as if she were a Viking's prized treasure, earned in fierce, hard-won combat.

Every nerve ending in her body quivered with anticipation. "Please don't make me wait another moment." Delaney traced her fingers along his hard body, starting at his square jaw, loitering on his pecs and working down to his groin where his *mannlig kjonnsorgan* bloomed mightily.

"Delaney." Her name rumbled up from his chest, emerging as a near growl as he lifted her hips, claiming her, making her his forever.

As her eyelids drifted closed, she sensed the force of all-encompassing love between them. They were undeniably destined for one another. Soul mates in the truest sense. She opened her eyes, watching his primal expression, determined to savor every moment.

Part of her feared it was all a magnificent, mystical dream and Varik would disappear when she awoke.

"Don't disappear..." she whispered.

"Never." Whispering her name, he fisted her hair and leaned close. "Varik the Bold will always be with you. Forever." The soul-reaching power of his kiss told Delaney he meant every word.

They moved in tandem like they'd been precision engineered for each other in some heavenly factory. The first time they'd had sex together was incredible, but this time there was something almost otherworldly about their union.

The glint of the heartwish ring on his finger caught her eye. She glanced at hers as well. No one would ever believe the story behind their magical rings. No one would believe...

Caught in a whirlwind of pleasure, she was about to shatter.

"Mighty Odin!" Varik roared, clutching Delaney as if she was his lifeline, dragging her like a ragdoll hard against him, and kissing her with more passion than she could have dreamed possible. That kiss seemed to hold the secret of the ages as she succumbed to it.

Collapsing in a depleted heap, they lay silently, tangled together for what could have been minutes or hours. As long as she was in her Viking's arms, time had no meaning.

Delaney noticed his Brunhilde helmet had fallen off at some point during their lovemaking. Sexy as the fearsome helmet was, she decided her Viking didn't need the extra trappings. He was plenty sexy just on his own.

It was a while before the power of speech returned but when it did, the first words out of their mouths came at the same instant.

"I love you," they chorused.

Bent over Delaney's supremely satisfied body, Varik leaned close for a kiss as they basked together in afterglow. The heartwish ring on his finger clinked against the one Delaney wore.

With a near blinding spark of blue light, the rings disappeared from their fingers.

Bolting upright, they sat gaping at each other, breathless with astonishment.

"Oh my God...what just happened?" Delaney felt her heart skip as she examined her naked finger and Varik's, as if perhaps the rings were still there but had become invisible. "Where did our rings go?"

"I don't know. This can't be happening." The same incomprehension Delaney felt was evident in Varik's dumbfounded expression. He inspected his hand and Delaney's. They patted the mattress, looked under pillows and hunted beneath the sheets searching for the absent rings.

"Ow!" Looking aghast, Varik's hand flew to the back of his upper arm. "Why did you pinch me?"

"I was checking to see if we're dreaming." It sounded totally illogical, ridiculous, as soon as the words left her mouth.

"Then you should have pinched yourself instead." Rubbing the reddening spot on his arm, he looked at her like she was crazy and this time Delaney thought he might be right.

"Sorry." She offered an apologetic shrug. "Ouch!" Her hand smoothed along the sore spot on her backside where Varik pinched her. "Varik!"

"Well now we know I'm not dreaming," he told her. "And it seems you're not either. So what's going on? This is insane." He got to his hands and knees on the floor, searching for the rings.

"Try under the bed," Delaney suggested.

"I did. Nothing there but dust rabbits."

"Bunnies," Delaney corrected. "Varik..." She cradled her belly. "I-I feel something."

He was back at her side in a flash, cradling her against him. "You're going to be ill?"

"No...something I can't explain."

The pair erupted in another gasp as they spied a bright golden glow shining through the spaces around and beneath the closed bedroom door.

Varik grabbed Delaney close as she clutched onto him for dear life. Glancing at the clock on her nightstand, she noted it was twelve.

"It's midnight. The bewitching hour."

"Don't be silly," Varik said, "there's no such thing as—"

A thunderous noise boomed from somewhere in the house, jolting them both.

Outside the bedroom Thursday started barking his head off.

"*Hellig dritt!*" Varik said the same instant Delaney cried, "Holy shit!"

"I have a feeling we just said the same thing," she surmised.

"We did," Varik confirmed, his jaw clenching.

"What in the world *is* that?" Delaney covered her ears. "Varik, what's happening?"

"It sounds like a *blaedhorn*, a Viking blasting horn." He was obviously just as stunned as Delaney. "I think it's coming from the living room."

"Oh my God, it's ghosts. Viking ghosts! I told you the house was haunted."

"Delaney..."

"Maybe they're in there doing some sort of traditional Viking midnight welcome to the neighborhood ritual," Delaney said. "Or maybe Grandma Bekka told all her deceased Viking buddies we're engaged and this is their idea of an engagement party."

As his gaze shifted from the bedroom door to her, Varik's expression was beyond incredulous. "Delaney, this is no time for foolishness." No doubt about it, he thought she'd lost it—her sanity, not the ring.

The horn's blaring finally subsided. Releasing her, he leapt from the bed and shrugged into his jeans while she grabbed his sweater, yanking it over her head.

"Stay here," he instructed, waving her back. "I'll see what's happening." He crept ahead, peeking in her closet."

"What are you looking for?"

"A baseball bat."

"Why would I have a baseball bat in my closet?"

"For protection," Varik said matter-of-factly as he grabbed the alarm clock from her nightstand and yanked the cord from the wall.

Delaney frowned. "What are you doing?"

"It's the only thing in here heavy enough to use as a weapon." His gaze fell on her dresser top. "Wait, one of those perfume bottles is probably heavier."

Delaney gasped aloud. "My grandma's antique perfume bottles? Break those and you'll be getting a fast ticket to Valhalla, mister."

Ignoring Varik's warning to stay put, she clung to his back like a shadow, searching the room for something she could use as a weapon. She grabbed the pair of crochet hooks sitting next to her perfume bottles.

Pushing her back, Varik said, "There are intruders out there, Delaney, this could be dangerous. Get under the bed and hide."

"No way." Delaney seized the waistband of his jeans and held tight. "I just found you, Varik. If there's an alien spaceship out there and it sucks you in, I want to go with you."

Pausing, he turned to her, slanting a befuddled look. "Spaceship? Seriously, Delaney?"

Fisting the crochet hooks tight, she said, "Well it's either that or Roger just drove his Lexus, with headlights blazing, into the living room."

Varik's expression screwed. "I'd rather be hijacked to Mars."

"This is no time for jokes," Delaney chastised, foolishly chuckling in the face of possible death.

Varik looked at her hand, a smile curling a corner of his lips. "And you're planning to knit the Martian a sweater?"

"Yeah, right after you clock the Martian on his big green noggin with my alarm clock." She waved her crochet hooks and retorted, "I can do plenty of damage with these if it becomes necessary."

"Right." He had the nerve to snicker at her.

"You know, I liked you better when you couldn't speak English."

Varik turned and reached for his champagne glass, taking a big slug.

"A little liquid courage sounds good." Delaney followed suit.

Opening the door, they tiptoed out. Varik stopped in his tracks, sniffing the air.

"Do you smell that?"

Delaney sniffed. "It smells like pipe tobacco. Just like your—" Her eyes bugged. "Whoa...it seems Grandma Bekka's not our only ghost." She and Varik exchanged awed looks.

The bright light began to fade as they crept around the corner and down the hall into the living room. Thursday was at the far corner of the room next to the Christmas tree, barking at the ceiling.

Varik and Delaney watched two white feathers float down from the ceiling just above the spot where Thursday stood.

"A bird must have gotten in here somehow," Delaney said. "Maybe through the chimney."

Varik shook his head. "Bird's don't make light. Besides, I closed the fireplace flue before we went to bed."

"Look," Delaney said, her eyes widening as she scanned the mantle and the coffee table. "Somebody lit all the candles. This is creepy. Why would robbers light candles? Or why would ghosts need candlelight to see their way around? Or why would—"

"Shhh..." Varik instructed. "This is not the time for jabbering."

Tiptoeing, they padded cautiously toward Thursday who was quieting now. As soon as he spotted Varik and Delaney, he came to their side, brushing against Varik's leg as Varik patted his flanks.

"It's okay Thor's Day. Good dog."

Before the last glimmer of light died away, a spot at the center of the aluminum tree glowed with warm golden radiance.

"Do you see that?" Delaney wondered if she was entrenched in some bizarre dream. This time she pinched herself instead of Varik.

"Yes, I see it." Close enough to the tree now to touch it, Varik bent to examine the glowing spot. An instant later, he stood ramrod straight, doing a classic double take as he prattled something in Norwegian.

Eyeing the spot Varik examined, Delaney did a double take of her own.

Jaws dropping in astonishment, they gazed at the tree and then at each other.

There in the center of the glow, on the tip of a tree branch, both heartwish rings swung together, as if they'd just been tapped. The pair of Norwegian ornaments Varik had given Delaney now flanked the branch, the man suspended on one side of the rings and the woman on the other.

A folded note card rested on the silver branch just above the dangling rings. The moment Varik removed the card from its resting spot, handing it to Delaney, the glow faded.

Delaney immediately recognized her grandmother's flowery script. "This is Bekka's handwriting," she said, astounded.

"You've made your heartwishes," she read aloud by candlelight, her voice wavering. "And have found your true loves. As promised, the stones have worked their magic. It has been more than a thousand years since the twin heartwish rings, each with one half of the same stone, have found each other. Their reuniting has amplified the potency of each ring. It is not necessary for the rings to be kept together for their magic to work, nor do they need to be kept within the same family. The only requirement is that the rings' owners be pure of heart."

Her own heart overflowing with love, Delaney paused to smile at Varik.

"You will each learn the identity of your ring's next recipient when the time is right," she read on. "It may be a family member, a friend or, perhaps, even a stranger. Your hearts will know when to pass your rings on to the right person. Until then, the rings will remain affixed to your fingers."

The instant Delaney read those words, the rings disappeared from the tree and were positioned back on the ring fingers of their right hands. Holding their hands aloft, Varik and Delaney clasped hands, threading their fingers together.

"This can't be happening," Varik muttered. Glancing at the card Delaney held, he frowned. "How can you read that? It's all in Norwegian. You haven't learned that much already, have you?"

"No it's not. What are you talking about?" She waved the card beneath his nose. "It's in English."

Varik's eyebrows knitted as he took another look. "Every word I see is Norwegian. And it's in my grandfather's handwriting."

Astonished, she said, "Wow...I guess this is more Viking magic."

"Read the rest," Varik urged.

"Now and forever more," Delaney read, her hands trembling, "the magic will live in your hearts. Congratulations, dear deserving children, on your upcoming nuptials as well as—"

Staggered, Delaney gasped. "Oh my God..." Her fingers flew to her lips while she cradled her belly with the other hand. Thursday brushed his muzzle against Delaney's belly, then sat in place, lifting one paw and resting it there as he looked up at her.

"Delaney? Are you all right?"

Unable to speak, she replied with tears as well as an affirmative nod. She gave the card to Varik to finish reading.

"...as well as the baby girl growing in Delaney's womb," Varik finished reading the sentence aloud. "Delaney!" His grin stretched as he held her gaze.

Thursday punctuated Varik's words with a soft bark.

"He knows." Delaney smiled so wide her jaws ached. "Thursday knows."

Swallowing hard, Varik looked from the card to Delaney and back. "There's more." He took in a deep breath and continued to read. "Your hearts have spoken the name you've both chosen for your child, Rebekka Anders Jenssen." He turned to Delaney. "That's exactly what I was thinking," he said, his voice full of wonderment.

"Me too," Delaney agreed, taking the card again. "From the great halls of Valhalla," she read, "with all our love, Grandma Bekka and Grandpa Anders."

"A baby! Oh Varik, isn't it wonderful?"

"Our little Becky." Varik looked up from the heavenly card in his hand, a joyous smile taking hold. "You were right, my love. It wasn't a bird, or men from Mars, or even a ghost." He gathered the pair of white feathers from the floor, brushing one across her cheek. "It was angels. Our very own guardian angels from Valhalla."

"Angels," Delaney repeated, taking the feather Varik handed to her. "I knew it. I felt it in here." Shedding gentle tears, she clasped the feather to her heart.

"I don't understand it...but I don't think you can explain a miracle." Varik's eyes glistened with tears. "You just accept it and give thanks." Placing both hands on Delaney's belly, cuddling the area, he gazed at her in wonder.

"Back in the bedroom I knew something special had happened," Delaney insisted. "I felt it deep inside." Throwing her arms around Varik's neck, she cried the happiest tears she'd ever shed. "A baby, Varik! We're having a baby girl! I'm so happy I could belt out a chorus of "In the Hall of the Mountain King," in Norwegian!"

"First the gift of finding my true love, and then the miraculous gift of childbirth where it seemed an impossibility." Varik leaned close, giving her a sweet kiss. "It's like we're in the midst of a dream. We're not, are we, Delaney?" He gave her a soft pinch after pinching himself. "I thought I'd save you the trouble this time." His laughter was warm and tender.

"As long as we inhabit the dream together and never wake up, my darling Viking, I don't care," she said as the adoring father of her baby enfolded her in a loving embrace. "All I know, Varik, is that we are so very blessed."

As they parted, Delaney looked at the card she held. "We need to save this so we can show our daughter one day. It's proof of our Viking magic."

Nodding, Varik held the other side of the card. "When she reads it I wonder if she'll see it in English or Norwegian." He gave a clueless shrug. "I still see it in Norwegian, in Grandpa Anders's hand."

"We'll just have to wait to see what happens." As they folded the card together, creasing it down the center, the card glowed bright in their hands, then disappeared in a flurry of sparkly sprinkles.

Varik nodded with understanding. "The magic was meant for our eyes only..." He looked into his fiancée's eyes. "Just for this very special moment. *Jeg elsker deg*," he whispered in her ear. "I love you," he repeated in English. "My darling heartwish."

"*Jeg elsker deg*," Delaney harmonized. "I cherish you, my darling Varik the Bold. I always have and I always will." Placing her hand on his chest, she added, "We may not have the card but we'll always carry the proof of this magical night deep in our hearts."

Lifting Delaney into his arms, he carried her back to the bedroom, the candles extinguishing themselves one by one as they passed by.

The kiss they shared was so full of love, joy, promise and gratitude that Delaney was certain Varik felt the effects clear down to his soul, just as she had.

~<>~

Dear Diary: It finally happened. It was on the night Varik and I were reunited and he proposed; the same night our mystical, magical miracle happened. For the first time, my treasured, recurrent dream finally reached its perfect, sigh-worthy conclusion:

~ ~ ~

"Is it you?" I asked. "My Viking? My Varik the Bold?" Fire danced in his eyes as his lips drew close and he whispered...

"How I adore you, my sweet, beautiful bride to be. Your kind heart, warm humor, and loving, generous spirit all combine to make you a woman of great worth. And, oh, how I cherish the babe that grows inside you. I am indeed a fortunate man. I will love and protect you both until the day I die...and far beyond that. *Jeg elsker deg*, my darling Delaney...now and forever."

~ ~ ~

There, you see? Enchantment, fairytales, miracles, ghosts, angels...honestly, Dear Diary, how can I ever again doubt their existence? Or the very real magic of happily-ever-afters...

Until next time,

Delaney Malone Jenssen

~<>~

Turn the page for a sneak peek of **THE GENIE'S HEARTWISH**, book 2 in the Heartwishes series, featuring Delaney's sister, Laila, who unearths a 5,000 year old genie at an estate sale!

ABOUT THE GENIE'S HEARTWISH

~<>~

In the musty basement of a historic mansion, thrift sale enthusiast Laila Malone rummages through estate sale castoffs and laughingly wonders if the ancient bottle she's just unearthed might be worth a fortune.

Uncorking it, she gasps as an imposing, saber-wielding genie whooshes out in a vapor. With sun-bronzed muscles, long dark hair and hypnotic eyes, he's devastatingly handsome, the epitome of her fantasies. And he claims he's here to give her pleasure? Well hell, if she has to lose her mind, this is exactly the hallucination she wants.

Five thousand years ago, Sumerian warrior Zakkar Tymon gallantly protected the virtue of a love struck virgin priestess, dooming him to an eternity of servitude to women. Reduced to being a slave to women's impulses, the bold, brave hero now exists solely to give women pleasure, act upon their every urge, and grant them three wishes before being sucked back into the cold, dark, empty abyss of the bottle.

Zak's newest possessor, Laila, is an opinionated female who spouts gibberish, speaks into a handheld box, instantly cooks food in a magic contrivance, and wears male garb rather than flowing dresses more befitting a woman. Her considerable potential stirs Zak's desire to grant the wide-eyed beauty all the pleasure she deserves.

Heartwishes, Book 2: Stubborn warrior hero with heart of gold, selfless devoted heroine, abundant humor, adorable dog, heartrending choices, snarky powerful goddess, fantasy, and a magnificent magical noble wish. This guaranteed HEA romcom can be read as a standalone but is better appreciated when read in order.

~<>~

NOTE: While I usually include only one chapter for an excerpt at the end of my books, I've made an special exception here because I really wanted to introduce you to the amazing hero of The Genie's Heartwish, and he doesn't appear until Chapter 3. After meeting sisters Laila and Maureen Malone in the first two chapters, you'll meet the extraordinary genie, Zak, in the third chapter. Just wait until you find out how this astonishing ancient warrior ended up in the bottle Laila finds 5,000 years later!

Turn the page to read Chapters 1 through 3 of The Genie's Heartwish...

The Genie's Heartwish: Chapter 1

Glassfloat Bay, Oregon: present day

~<>~

"EMPATHY AND SYMPATHY, people. That's key," Bunny Turner stated with conviction, rapping her pointer against the image on the screen. "If we want to keep clients coming back, we must convince them we know what they're going through." Her gaze roamed the crowd. The picture of sincerity, she tapped her fingers on her chest in the area where her heart would be—if she had one. "Let them know we've been there too. That we feel their pain."

Laila Malone knew what was coming next. Working for Tuned by Turner the last few years, she'd been through enough of her boss's corporate training seminars to be able to repeat the rarely varying sermon word for word.

And how do we make clients believe we've been tubby and can relate with their problems if it's not true? Laila silently mouthed along as Bunny spoke, resisting the temptation to roll her eyes and groan.

"With creative embellishment!" the room of weight loss counselors replied.

Nodding, Bunny offered a calculated smile. "While TBT offers a proven weight loss program incorporating diet, counseling and exercise along with our nutritious line of packaged foods, those aren't the things that keep our satisfied clients coming back each week, is it?"

"No," the counselors dutifully chorused.

"It's you." Bunny's voice a reverent whisper while her benevolent smile bordered on heartfelt tears. "Without you dedicated counselors, Tuned by Turner would be just another diet program." Bunny's brown-eyed gaze swept the room of ninety men and women who had traveled to TBT's corporate hub in the small coastal town. "Let me hear it. What are we, people?"

"We're number one!" Hoots, hollers and clapping ensued as the troops rallied. Punching her fist high into the air, Bunny boasted a proud grin.

"At Tuned by Turner we turn tubbies into triumphs!" Bunny crowed.

While most overweight women don't like being called fat, Laila seriously doubted they found *tubby* any more endearing. With a surreptitious gaze around the room, she noted only a handful of the counselors were bigger than a size four.

She'd often heard her lean coworkers, most of whom had never been overweight by more than five pounds, openly ridiculing overweight clients behind their backs.

An eighty pound weight loss veteran, Laila had a strong sense of compassion for TBT's clients. She didn't need *creative embellishment* to understand what it was like to be the fattest woman in the room, to catch people snickering behind her back, to be heartbroken when a glimpse in the mirror revealed a reflection looking nothing like her imagined self.

She'd also learned losing weight wasn't necessarily a panacea. Shifting one's internal self-perception wasn't easy. Sometimes she'd catch her reflection in a store window, momentarily wondering who the slender, attractive blue-eyed brunette was staring back at her. Her default thinking still had her picturing herself as...tubby.

Still waiting for the profusion of changes guaranteed to come with weight loss, Laila felt cheated. The diet industry promised her life would transform after reaching her goal. Men were supposed to fall at her feet, dumbstruck by her leaner visage.

Although finding good men was challenging, Laila knew they were out there. Her fiancé, Tim McKevitt, had been a salt of the earth sort of guy. He lost his life three years ago, falling into an icy crevasse in Antarctica.

"Take me for example."

Bunny's commanding voice snapped Laila back to the present as the chic owner of TBT gestured to her pink-suited, model-thin frame.

"I convince clients that I can personally relate to diet and deprivation. They know I once battled a heartbreaking weight problem." She paused before adding, "It's true. I used to be nearly obese." Bunny validated her statement by puffing out her cheeks and positioning her arms to indicate a substantial belly. With a sensitive sniffle, she shuddered as she smoothed her TBT-pink fingernails along her beige-blonde hair, tucking a nonexistent stray lock into the bun at her nape.

"I ate my way all the way up to a size six back in college." A practiced speaker, Bunny allowed for a pregnant pause, slowly nodding as her gaze swept the room. "It took me more than a semester of living on coffee, lettuce, cigarettes, and sticking my fingers down my throat to get back into my size zeros."

Formerly a luxury car saleswoman, Bunny Turner had built a financial empire on her reputation as a fat guru. Disillusioned, Laila discovered early on that Bunny was cold, calculating and devoid of compassion. Especially when it came to TBT clients, people who'd struggled with the pain and complexities of living as a fat person in a thin world.

"Get ready," Laila's sister Maureen whispered near her ear. "Here comes the glorified bullshit."

Laila bit the inside of her cheek to keep from laughing at Reen's knowing remark. Her cute, sassy blonde sister was one of the only other people over the age of thirty in the room, and one of the only who'd lost a significant amount of weight.

Reen's fiancé had also died. Robert Brechler was an English professor. He and Reen purchased a house together, a fixer-upper, to move in after their wedding. They were happily making wedding plans until Bob fell off the roof while repairing the shingles. He and Tim died within weeks of each other.

Laila and Reen supported each other through their weight loss journeys, and the loss of their loves.

Emotional eating had the sisters packing on pounds due to stress, grief, and loneliness, along with poor eating habits. After losing weight, Laila and Reen applied for employment at Tuned by Turner, idealistic in their shared mission of helping people shed excess weight and live healthier, happier lives.

"Of course," Bunny continued, "it wouldn't be prudent for me to expound on how I actually lost the weight. I allow clients to believe I accomplished it by following TBT methods. It's essentially a helpful LWL. *Little white lie*," she clarified, hanging invisible quotes over the words with her fingers.

"That LWL doesn't hurt anyone because TBT is the best weight loss solution out there. Since we care, *really and truly care*," her expression was infused with soap opera dramatics, "about their health and wellbeing, we understand how LWLs can help clients achieve their goals. Right, counselors?"

The room exploded with shouts of "Right!" and booming applause while Laila and Reen slunk low in their chairs, exchanging dubious looks.

As the session closed, Bunny held aloft a navy blue canvas bag embroidered with the company's pink logo. "I'm giving each of you a TBT tote containing our ten newest foods. They're dynamite, people. Fabulous fat-burning gems."

Setting the bag on the table behind her, she drew out each *gem*, describing them in such a way that would make anyone unfamiliar with TBT's line of foods salivate. Those already familiar with the company's barely palatable edibles knew better.

Arms wide, in a universal embrace, Bunny told them, "During lunch you'll sample our tofu-based salad dressings, shelf-stable Saucy Chicken Cakes, and...are you ready?" Bunny looked as if she were about to announce she'd be serving gooey hot fudge sundaes. "Our brand new Berry-Lime Tapioca Tofu Pudding Cups!"

Again, rousing applause, while Laila and Reen engaged in inadvertent shudders.

"Our poor clients," Laila muttered beneath her breath.

"Your main focus this quarter, counselors, is to push TBT foods. Sell, sell, sell, people! Remember, our main revenue comes from our exclusive line of foods. And the more money TBT makes, the more money you make!"

"Sell, sell, sell, huh?" Reen whispered to Laila. "Heck, I can't even give those foods away they taste so bad."

"Makes you wonder who they use as taste testers," Laila whispered back.

With a confirming nod, Reen murmured, "My mind is screaming *Dutch baby!* Let's grab one at Griffin's Café after we get out of here."

Laila gave her sister a sideways glance. If she didn't watch herself, under Reen's dastardly influence she'd start packing on the pounds again. "I'll split one with you."

"Bacon too? Seriously, what's a puffy pancake without bacon?" Reen gave a wicked conspirator's wink. "We deserve it. We've been soooo good. Um...unless you'd rather stick around and dig into tapioca tofu pudding cups instead."

Just the name was enough to make Laila wince. "Bacon it is. Just a strip. And only if we walk afterward."

"Deal."

At the end of the seminar, Laila and Reen claimed their embroidered totes packed full of inedible edibles before surreptitiously heading for the exit. They almost made it before Bunny's piercing voice seized them.

"Uh-oh..." Laila recalled the last time they'd tried to sneak out of a meeting only to have Bunny hook them into being on a panel to sample the newest foodstuffs. Laila had no appetite the rest of the day after ingesting all that gloppy, chemical-laden stuff that tried to pass for real food.

"Oh please God, please, please, please don't let her make us stay for lunch again," Reen muttered, crossing the fingers on both hands and closing her eyes.

In lieu of an invitation to dine on TBT *goodies*, Bunny handed each of them a sealed letter. After brief innocuous small talk, she turned on her stiletto heel, wiggling her miniscule butt as she headed for the unappetizing lunch spread.

"Let's get the hell out of here while we can." Reen snagged Laila's uniform jacket, hauling her to the door.

~<>~

"I haven't seen you two in here in weeks," Annalise Griffin, owner of the retro-themed café said, handing menus to Laila and Reen. "Great to see you back."

"Thanks, Annalise. It's been too long since we've treated ourselves to one of your Dutch baby pancakes," Reen said.

"How've you been doing?" Laila asked.

"Good. Crazy busy—and you won't hear me complaining about that." She grinned. "Lots of tourists lately. I need to add a couple more servers. My sister, Sabrina, is moving back home from Pennsylvania." Annalise's expression twisted. "She just filed for divorce and said she'll need a job so that'll work out great."

"Sorry about the divorce," Laila said. "I'm glad we'll finally get a chance to meet her though. She was already gone when we moved here from Chicago."

"You'll love her. She's a doll and so is my adorable little nephew, Harry."

"How's Hud doing," Reen asked, dropping her gaze to the tabletop and drawing invisible circles with her finger. "Is he around?"

"Nope. Hudson doesn't take time to eat." Annalise tsked. "I think my brother's even busier than I am. The guy never stops working. He and his crew are renovating the old library. You can imagine what a job that is. Hey, I've made some changes around here too. What do you think?"

"I was just checking it out. I love what you've done," Laila gestured across the room. "The corner area with the loveseat, coffee table and cushy-looking chairs looks so cozy and inviting."

"It's a big thumbs up from me," Reen agreed, making the sign.

"Thanks. I'm getting a lot of positive feedback from the customers. I got the furniture at the Maythorne Manor estate sale up on the hill. It's been going on the past few days. Have you two gone yet?"

"No." Laila gave a little bounce of excitement. "I had no idea."

"Thanks a lot, Annalise," Reen said with mock annoyance. "Now she's going to drag me all the way up to Beauregard Hill just so we can go to that sale."

Annalise laughed. "It's worth it, Reen. Aside from furniture, they're selling most everything else too. You're still knitting and crocheting, right?"

Laila laughed at that. Before Reen could answer, she said, "Are you kidding? The two things Reen will never give up are knitting and chocolate."

"I saw lots of yarn when I was there," Annalise told Reen. "Skeins in all different colors." Her eyebrows jiggled playfully.

Reen's eyes went wide. "Really?"

"You did agree to a walk," Laila reminded her sister, nailing her with her best guilt-producing look. "Can you think of a better way to burn off the bazillion calorie lunch we're about to order? Plus you know you can't ignore the lure of yarn."

Folding her arms across her chest, Reen sat back in her seat and grumbled. "I suppose."

Returning her attention to Annalise, Laila asked, "Did you spot any baking-related stuff, or ceramic salt and pepper shakers?" While she'd been trying to cut back on her packrat tendencies, she had a passion for collecting kitchen antiques.

"Yes and yes." Annalise smiled.

"Great. We'll be there all afternoon," Reen mumbled.

"Yarn," Laila reminded her.

"Have you heard anything lately from Delaney, or your mom and stepdad?" Annalise polished the gray marbleized 50s era chrome-trimmed Formica table as she spoke. She was one of the first people their sister, Delaney, met when she moved to Glassfloat Bay from Chicago.

"Delaney and Varik are due back from their honeymoon cruise anytime now, and Mom and Tore are still enjoying themselves at their cabin in Norway," Laila said.

"Last time I talked to Mom," Reen added, "she said they'd be back in another month or so."

"I've got to tell you, a vacation sounds good just about now." Annalise flashed a bright smile. "So you're here for Dutch babies? I've also got a killer pecan pie fresh baked this morning."

"Oh my God, Annalise," placing her hands over her ears, Reen laughed, "don't tell us that. We're just going to split the pancake."

"No need. I've got special kid-portion pans that make half-sized Dutch babies. I'll make one for each of you, along with plenty of fresh lemon wedges, lots of butter and powdered sugar."

"And a side of bacon for us to split," Reen added.

Laila groaned. "I think I gained five pounds just listening to that description."

"Oh puhleez. Look at you two." Stepping back, Annalise studied them. "You're practically skinny."

Laila nearly choked on her sip of water. "We need to come in here more often. I forgot what a great BS-er you are, Annalise."

"I'm not kidding. You look great. Sooo...eating that TBT diet food must be the secret? Or, um," she leaned down, elbowing Laila, "maybe it's staying away from their godawful food that did the trick."

Laila and Reen shared knowing smiles.

"Let's just say Reen and I do our best to follow TBT's guidelines," Laila replied diplomatically.

The 30-something café owner bent toward them, cupping her hand at the side of her mouth. "Tried their food myself once."

"You were on their program?" Reen said.

"Nope. I just had to give it a try after hearing from some of my customers how awful it was. I figured they must be exaggerating because nothing could taste *that* bad." She made an exaggerated eye roll. "I was wrong. You should talk to their management team, Laila. Strike a deal to have them include your amazing reduced calorie scones in their food line. They fly out of here each time you bring in a batch."

"That's what I keep telling her," Reen said, rapping the tabletop with her fingers.

"Thanks...but I highly doubt Bunny would be interested."

After jotting down their order, Annalise was off.

"See, I told you we look good," Reen said. "Even if we have gained a few pounds each, those threatening letters we got from corporate are ridiculous."

"Do not," Laila raised a cautionary finger, "mention those contemptible letters until after we leave. I'm already feeling guilty ordering a Dutch baby and bacon. If I'm going to eat it I want to enjoy it."

"Not a word." Reen made a locking motion over her lips. "Pecan pie."

"What?" Laila shot her a disbelieving look.

"Sorry," Reen shrugged, "that just sort of slipped out."

"Well don't let it slip out again because we are absolutely not having any pecan pie. Honestly, Maureen, you're such a bad influence!"

"We both know Annalise is right about TBT's food," Reen said as they waited for their order. "Just the thought of eating it makes me..." An involuntary shudder finished her sentence better than any words. "If TBT sold your healthy baked goods, Laila, the clients would be thrilled. Why not talk to Bunny about contracting you to provide your scones, muffins, and cookies?"

"Bunny?" Laila gave Reen a deliberate look. "That would mean she'd have to pay me something, Reen, and we're talking about—"

"Tightwad Turner." Reen sighed. "Say no more. Besides, she'd hate giving you the credit when the compliments started rolling in."

"Right. She's not our biggest fan," Laila reminded her. "Plus I'd be making the food out of my own kitchen and I doubt insurance would cover that. A business insurance policy would cost a small fortune."

"Well we heard that the Crowe sisters are planning to close their bakery and retire to Barcelona. Maybe you could buy—"

"Reen..." Laila closed her eyes in a long blink. "Caroline and Peggy Crowe are close to eighty. They've been talking about selling the bakery for the last ten years. I doubt they have any intention of retiring, much less moving all the way to Spain."

"Yeah, I guess," Reen agreed. "I wouldn't be surprised if they're still there baking when they're ninety."

"There's no way I could afford to buy Crowe's Coastside Bakery or any other bake shop, anyway. I can barely make ends meet as it is. Although..." she gazed off into the distance as a familiar daydream took hold, "I'd give anything to own that beautiful historic building with all its Victorian charm. It's in a prime location too, right on Ocean Charm Boulevard."

Once they were served, she salivated while spreading butter and squeezing lemon wedges all over her pancake. Reen was ahead of her, already spooning powdered sugar over her eggy pancake.

"An approved Tuned by Turner meal, I see," a familiar voice said, dripping with so much sarcasm Laila feared it would plop onto their Dutch babies.

Nothing good ever came from run-ins with Saffron Devington, their ice queen cousin. A glance at the woman's conservative navy skirted suit told her Saffron must be working. With her rich nutmeg-brown hair and deep blue eyes, the stunning woman always seemed to look like a mortician. The daughter of their late father's sister, Colleen Malone Devington, Saffron was a real estate agent.

"Stuff it, Saffy," Reen said, not bothering to look up at their cousin.

"These are kid-sized portions," Laila offered, hoping it made their calorific indulgence sound more acceptable while, at the same time, being angry at herself for feeling the need to make any explanations about what she ate.

"So, five thousand calories instead of ten thousand, hmm?" Folding her arms across her chest, Saffron sneered. "Keep this up and you'll be TBT clients instead of counselors." She poked her finger in Reen's direction. "And stop calling me Saffy. You know I hate that."

Reen looked up now. "Sorry, Saffy. Wanna bite?" She waved one of the thick strips of crisped bacon beneath her cousin's nose.

"You think you're so funny, don't you, Maureen?" Resting her hands on the edge of their table, Saffron leaned down. "I wonder what my good friend Bunny Turner would say if she knew her counselors were seen eating one of these artery cloggers at the local greasy spoon."

"What I want to know, Saf," Reen glared at her cousin, "is what you're doing eating lunch at a place so obviously beneath you."

With a quick look around, Saffron spoke discreetly. "Needless to say, it's my buyers' choice, not mine." Spotting a man and woman entering the diner, she straightened, turned on her heel and headed for the couple, greeting them with her syrupy saleswoman shtick.

"Saffy's just as much of a stick in the mud now as she was when she was ten," Laila noted before sinking her teeth into her first forkful of pancake and humming her delight.

"I guess that's what happens when you grow up in a rich, pretentious family," Reen said. "Weird how she and Lorraine, are so much alike and their brother, Red, is so opposite."

"Hard to believe Lorraine is even worse than Saffron," Laila said. "Poor Red. He's such a sweetheart. I can't even imagine having those two as my big sisters."

The troublemaking Saffron aside, their Dutch baby lunch was delicious. Laila made sure to leave a bite of the pancake on her plate along with an inch of bacon, just to prove to herself she could. Although the bacon called to her while she and Reen chatted, Laila remained unflinchingly strong.

Until...

Along with their check, Annalise brought a slim slice of pecan pie with two forks—on the house. "I don't want to sabotage your diets," she explained, "so I just brought a sliver for you to sample. Enjoy!"

"We're doomed." Reen stared at the nut-crusted slice.

"Talk about sugar overload... Laila eyed the tempting sweet. "Aw what the hell." She picked up her dessert fork, digging in to half the slice and enjoying every last calorific morsel.

Heading out of the restaurant, she confessed to Reen, "Our discussion about opening a bakery, as well as all the sugar we just ingested," she laughed, "got me thinking."

"Good."

"Picture it, Reen." She spread her hands through the air, willing her sister to see what Laila envisioned. "My own bake shop brimming with healthier versions of decadent treats...muffins, scones, cakes, cookies and breads for people counting calories, as well as those who are vegan or paleo, gluten-free, sugar-free, and for diabetics too. I could help people by making weight loss pleasant instead of a drudge."

"You could help people like..." Reen's expression twisted, "poor obese Bunny."

"A whopping size six." Laila groaned. "Can you believe her?"

"Last time I checked, I think one of my thighs was a size six." Glancing down, Reen smacked her leg.

They window shopped as they walked, with Laila tugging Reen away from the gloriously tempting windows of Crowe's Coastside Bakery. The aroma wafting from the bakery as a customer opened the door to enter was an absolute killer. It cemented them in place, mesmerized.

"Oh my God, Laila, look." Reen pointed at the sign in the window. "It's their final day of business. I can't believe it. I never thought they'd actually retire."

Sucking in a deep breath, Laila was stunned. "It's for sale. The bakery, all the equipment, and the whole building, including their fully furnished apartment. Wow..." She took a few steps back to take in the large storefront and the building in general. "Remember that time the Crowe sisters invited us to afternoon tea in their apartment upstairs?"

"Yeah, and we had to cancel because Bunny called one of her *critically important*," Reen made double air quotes, "impromptu meetings. Wish we could have seen it. I've heard their place is really impressive. I wonder how much they're asking."

"It's got to be a few million at least because of the location, all the kitchen equipment, the furnished apartment, and the historic importance of the building."

The door opened again and they were entranced by the fragrant marriage of butter, sugar and flour transformed into heavenly morsels. A minute longer and Laila knew she and Reen would be magically sucked inside.

"We have *got* to get out of here." She broke into a jog, distancing herself from the bakery, unsure if her increased pulse was due to excitement about the bakery, aggravation about the letters Bunny gave them, or the brisk jog. They'd opened their TBT letters as soon as they left the meeting, jaws dropping as they scanned the warning communiqués. Laila wanted to burn hers and mail the ashes to Bunny.

"What a bunch of crap." Laila slowed her pace as they walked up a tree-lined side street. "You and I have more satisfied clients than any other counselors."

"Because they know we've been there too."

"They relate to us better than someone who's never been bigger than a size two," Laila said. "I remember when I was at my biggest, dreaming about being slim again. That cute red dress I kept hanging at the front of my closet as a goal reminder was a size twelve."

"Mine was a fourteen." Reen's hazel eyes narrowed. "A twelve or fourteen to our fat-phobic coworkers is heifer size."

"The average TBT client doesn't care about being a size zero, she just wants to get down to whatever magic number makes her feel good about herself. Corporate wants us to..." Laila cocked her head. "What was it they said?"

Reen dug the letter out of her purse. "*Streamline your body in accordance with the lean, healthy TBT image.*" She huffed a humorless laugh as she jammed the offending missive back in her bag and resumed walking. "They want me to lose twenty-five pounds in the next six weeks. Hah! Ain't gonna happen." She stopped. "Ooh look, String Me Along is having a sale."

Laila tugged her sister away from the yarn shop's colorful window. "Nope, uh-uh. If we stop we'll be there all day and I'll have to find a crowbar to pry you out. Come on, we need to get to that estate sale before all the good stuff is gone." They started walking again.

"Okay, you're right," Reen admitted, picking up speed. "We'll have that butter-soaked Dutch baby burned off by the time we get back to my car."

"By walking just a couple of miles? In your dreams. To burn off the number of calories we consumed at lunch it would take—"

Reen clapped her hands over her ears. "La-la-la-la. I'm not listening. Don't burst my joyful little exercise bubble, no matter how unrealistic it may be. After all, walking a couple of miles is better than just sitting on my ass, isn't it?"

"Absolutely." Laila draped her arm over Reen's shoulder as they trudged along the sidewalk. "Corporate says I need to drop thirty pounds in six weeks." Laila fumed again at the idea. "It's not only absurd, it's unhealthy. Neither of us is meant to be rail thin."

"Exactly. And that's why God created pecan pie," Reen noted and they laughed together. "I wish we'd crossed those stupid no-more-than-five-percent-weight-gain clauses out of our employment contracts before we signed on with TBT."

Stopping in place, Laila stood bracing a fist against her hip, the burn of anger simmering through her veins. "Explain how the hell my measly seven pound weight gain somehow translates into TBT telling me I have to lose thirty."

"The same way my six translates to twenty-five. Jerks."

Growling, Laila started walking again.

"If you had your own bakery we'd make a fortune. I say *we* because you'd hire me and I'd help you build a scone empire so wildly successful, and with food so superior to TBT's, it would put them out of business." Reen snapped her fingers. "Just like that."

"Of course I'd hire you but I wouldn't want to put anyone out of business. Lots of money would be great but that's not why—"

"Yeah, yeah, I know," Reen cut her off with a flippant wave. "I've seen those big blue idealistic eyes of yours looking off into the distance with grandiose thoughts of selflessly helping thousands of unhappy people often enough to know your intentions are pure."

"Jeez." Laila scrunched her nose. "You make me sound like a sappy televangelist or phony infomercial actress."

"Ooh, infomercials. We'd *have* to do those."

Laila barked a laugh. "Can you imagine us trying to get through a script without cracking up? All it would take is one look at each other and—"

"Laila, if you don't start giving your bake shop idea positive energy and visualizing your success, it won't happen. Before we lost weight, you would have sworn that us walking, mostly uphill, and neither of us keeling over, would be impossible. But see? Nothing's impossible if you want it enough. Our dream came true because we *made* it come true. Now that's positive!"

"True," Laila agreed, "but losing weight isn't the same as making a fortune from thin air. I can chant and visualize until I'm blue in the face but it won't change the fact that I'll never have enough money to start my own business, much less buy Peggy and Caroline Crowe's bakery."

"All I'm saying is a positive attitude never hurts."

"Okay, I'm positive I need a fairy godmother, or a genie who can grant me three wishes." Laila grabbed Reen's sleeve and pointed to a sign for the estate sale at the corner.

Reen gazed up. Way up. "Good grief that walk's gonna be murder. It's times like this that I really miss Chicago's flat landscape." She gave Laila a purposeful look. "Plus that address is just a few doors away from Aunt Colleen and Uncle Walter's place." She shuddered. "I don't want to run into them or Lorraine at the sale."

Laila let out a pop of incredulous laughter. "Come on, Reen, do you honestly think any of the Devingtons would be caught dead shopping at an estate sale?"

Once she thought about what she said, Reen laughed too.

"Just think," Laila went on in her quest to convince her sister, "they might have dozens of skeins of yarn tucked away in the back of a closet. Rare yarn that's not available anywhere anymore," Laila encouraged, knowing just how to push the avid knitter's buttons. "Plus we'd burn off more calories than we ate."

With another glance at the top of Beauregard Hill, Reen uttered a dramatic growl. "Dammit, Laila, you know searching for yarn is second only to being a foodie on my list of vices." She looped her arm through Laila's. "Let's go."

Once they reached the address they stood on the sidewalk, out of breath and gaping in awe at the enormous Victorian mansion. The whimsical fretwork, gingerbread shingles, balustrades, spindles, turrets, and fanciful ornamentation was incredible to see up close.

"This place is huge." Laila stood mesmerized as her gaze washed over the impressive manor.

"And really old," Reen noted as they raced up the long concrete walk and stone steps.

A current of anticipation coursed through Laila's veins. There was something deliciously appealing about digging through people's castoffs and discovering fabulous goodies.

She couldn't help the rush of excitement that whispered, *Maybe this time you'll find a rare, priceless trinket that will change your life forever.*

The Genie's Heartwish: Chapter 2

~<>~

IT WAS NEARLY a whole house sale, the estate sale's organizers explained as they handed out flyers and shopping bags. The kind of sale Laila and Reen loved most. While Reen might claim not to be as addicted to rummaging through other people's castoffs as Laila, Laila knew better. They could scrounge around the attic, closets, basement, garage and many of the rooms in between, giddy as they hunkered down on hands and knees, checking dark, cobwebbed nooks and crannies for treasures.

A brief paragraph about the house's history stated it had remained within the same family since it was built for Abigail Maythorne in 1859. The last owner, Franklin Maythorne, a retired attorney, had died. There were three known heirs, brothers, who were great-grandnephews of the original owner. Proceeds of the estate sale were going to the Abigail Maythorne Foundation.

After rifling through the kitchen, finding a few items to add to their shopping bags, they headed for the basement, carefully navigating the narrow, rickety wood steps that led to a dim, cavernous area, piled floor to ceiling with all manner of stuff.

Only a few others surveyed the dank basement. Apparently not many were eager to dig through the layers of dust, cobwebs, and whatever it was that reeked of mildew.

"Laila!" Reen practically screeched after an audible intake of breath. "Look!"

Taken by surprise, Laila turned to spot her sister looking like a dog who'd discovered a cattle boneyard, excitedly waving her hand toward a row of shelves piled high with skeins of yarn and all sorts of sewing goods.

"There, you see? What did I tell you?" Laila said, highly amused at her sister's unbridled enthusiasm. "Stick with me, kid and you'll go places." While Laila searched the basement's perimeter, Reen was busy filling bags with her needlework finds.

Ten minutes later, Reen was at her sister's side. "You were right, Laila. There's all kinds of stuff here that you can't find in stores anymore. I really hit the jackpot." With a supremely elated expression, she presented her bounty for Laila's inspection.

"Wow, Maureen, look at all you found!" She bent to examine the contents of one bag only to bolt upright with a horrified expression. "Oh, Reen, sweetie, you can't buy that old yarn."

"What?" Reen's eyes were bugged. "Yes I can. Why not?"

Laila winced, waving her hand over the bag Reen held out to her. "Did you get a whiff of that strong odor? It's mildew."

"No." Reen sniffed the bag. When her head popped back up it looked like she was about to cry. "No! That's so unfair. Maybe I can salvage some of it. Maybe it's not all moldy." She and Laila went through everything together and were able to save about a third of what Reen had collected.

They continued making their way around the basement, making several good finds and being forced to put some of them, like vintage books and magazines, back because of the mildew. Laila was fortunate to find a couple of century-old cookbooks that had escaped getting moldy.

"Ooh, these are nice, Laila." Reen rummaged through deep wood shelves holding vintage salt and pepper shakers. She cooed over a delft blue set of ceramic wooden shoe-shaped shakers. "You still collect salt and pepper shakers, right?"

"No. I sold most of them at my last garage sale." Intrigued with the vast assortment, Laila searched through them.

"Then how come you're still here looking instead of going off in search of something else?" Reen snickered.

"Oh...well I..." She laughed to herself. "Don't judge, Maureen. You never know when I might find the world's rarest salt and pepper shakers that would look perfect on a shelf in my cozy future bake shop. How's *that* for positive thinking?" She beamed a grin at her sister before getting down on her hands and knees to examine the lower shelves.

"You're preaching to the choir." Reen hunkered down next to Laila so she could dig through a bin of vinyl record albums on the floor.

Laila scooted a few feet to the right, coughing at the cloud of dust her movement created. "My uniform pants are going to look like I crawled through the mud." Her laughter stirred up more dust. "Which would probably be an improvement."

"A perfect excuse to burn them, and the godawful jacket that goes along with them."

Laila glanced at her hideous TBT uniform. "They make us look twenty pounds heavier."

"We look like cotton candy hawkers at a carnival." Reen barked a laugh. "Can you picture Saffron or Lorraine wearing this getup?"

"Ha!" The ludicrous thought tickled Laila. "Our fashion-conscious cousins wouldn't be caught dead in it."

The jackets for female counselors were peppermint pink with dime-sized navy polka dots. A sleeveless pink knit top and navy slacks or a skirt completed the ensemble. Male counselors wore navy jackets with pink polka dots over pink oxford shirts topping navy trousers.

"What on earth was Bunny thinking when she chose these ugly uniforms?"

"She claims they're distinctive," Laila said. "And unforgettable."

"She's spot on about that, especially here in Glassfloat Bay where getting dressed up means wearing your good jeans. If we were still living in Chicago we'd be laughed out of the city."

"You can say that again." Laila leaned forward, tucking her head under the deep shelf above and bracing her hand on the bottom shelf so she could get a better look. Without any warning, the rotted wood gave way. Her hand plunged through the soft, splintered surface while her cheek fell hard against the wood.

A strangled whoop and holler followed.

"Jeez! Laila, what happened?"

"The shelf's damp and mildewed. It must be rotten."

"Are you okay?" Reen stuck her head under the shelf. "Whew, it stinks down here. You'd better be careful you don't get mildew lung poisoning from breathing that in."

"Mildew lung..." Laila's eyes bugged. "Is that a thing?"

"I dunno. I guess you'll find out."

"Thanks, sis, that's a big help."

"You're welcome. Can you get your hand out?"

"I think so, but..."

"Yeah...? But what?" After a long moment of silence, Reen piped up again. "But what!?" she asked with more vehemence. "But you're stuck? But you're hand's resting on a dead rat? But your fingers got snapped off in a mousetrap? But you're passing out from flesh-eating toxic mold poisoning? For heaven's sake, *what*!?"

"Oh my God, Reen, you sound just like Mom." Laila laughed. "Stop using your mom voice on me, it's not helping. There's something under here and I'm trying to grab it."

"Something as in treasure something or as in huge nest of spiders something?"

"Like I'd be trying to grab a nest of spiders. It's hard. It feels like stone or marble."

"A gargantuan petrified spider!"

"Stop with the spider talk, you're creeping me out!" Laila was quiet a moment longer as her fingers stretched for the object.

"Holy mackerel, I knew it!" Gasping, Reen raised her head so fast it hit the shelf above her, rattling the ceramic salt and pepper shakers overhead.

"Knew what? Watch it, Maureen, or you'll have this old thing crashing down on us."

"You've found the world's most prized salt and pepper shaker set, hidden away by the house's owner before he died because of its enormous value."

"Don't make me laugh when I'm stuck down here on all fours with my face plastered against a moldy shelf." She snaked her hand in deeper, trying to get a good grasp. "It's too far to the right. I can't get a good grip. And it's heavy." The challenge spurred her on. By this time Laila didn't care what the hell it was under there, she *had* to have it.

"Laila."

"Maybe if we try to punch out more of the shelf I can get to it." Laila pounded on the rotted wood with her other hand to no avail. Apparently she'd found the only vulnerable spot.

"Laila."

"Come on, Reen, help me pound on it."

"Laila!"

"What? *What!*" she growled, frustration tingeing her voice.

Reen removed a set of ceramic cat salt and pepper shakers from the bottom shelf, setting them on the concrete floor before erupting with laughter.

"I'm scrounging around in this spider-infested hole struggling to unearth a possibly costly treasure to secure our financial future and you're laughing?"

Reen reached in the back of the shelf, looping two fingers in the small circular hole at the center and easily lifting the removable shelf, exposing the floor beneath.

"Oh," Laila said sheepishly. Withdrawing her hand from the rotted wood, she cringed as she brushed cobwebs and bug carcasses from her skin and hair. Returning her attention to the area beneath where the shelf sat a moment before, she zeroed in on the item she'd been trying to reach. The stone box was about the size of two thick paperback books stacked together.

"It looks really old," Laila noted.

"Maybe it's filled with rare gold coins." Reen watched as Laila grasped the box with both hands, carefully drawing it out of the grubby cavity. "Or diamonds."

"Look at the strange writing on the metal strips around the box." Laila blew a thick layer of dust from its surface. "Maybe it's an antiquity."

"It probably says made in Taiwan," Reen joked.

Laila fiddled with the latch. "I think it's stuck," she said an instant before the latch popped open on its own. Cradling the heavy box in her lap, Laila lifted the cover and gasped at the sight of the multi-colored glass bottle nestled in layers of what looked like silk.

"It's beautiful." Laila gingerly fingered the exquisite glasswork. "It looks like it's made of thousands of strands of glass. I've never seen anything like it."

"Neither have I," Reen agreed. "Maybe it's an antique perfume bottle. Whatever's inside is probably so old it smells like ass."

Laila laughed at that. With the stench of mildew from the timeworn basement assaulting her senses, she wouldn't be at all surprised if the contents smelled atrocious. "I'll wait until I get it home to examine it more closely."

"Good idea." Trailing her finger through the dust, Reen shuddered. "That way you can set it on something other than a basement floor crawling with ancient crud."

"Maybe we've finally found a real treasure." Laila couldn't help a shiver of excitement at the thought. Noticing a wave of bargain hunters descending the staircase, she closed the box, latching it and placing it in her bag.

"We've seen everything down here," she said to Reen. "C'mon, let's go back upstairs."

Twenty minutes later, as they were about to leave the last upstairs bedroom, Laila paused. It was as if something in the room called to her. Instinct led her to a Victorian writing desk where she spotted a faded photo.

"Find something else?" Reen asked as Laila fingered the photograph. "Ooh, damn, he was a hunk."

"What a gorgeous man," Laila breathed, gazing at the sepia image of a tall man with nearly shoulder-length dark hair, dressed in Victorian garb and standing behind an elderly woman seated at the same writing desk Laila now stood at.

"Look at those dark, piercing eyes. Like he's looking at me through the centuries. And that broad chest..." Laila felt a twinge of longing as she studied the striking man.

Reen seemed nearly as mesmerized by the photo as Laila. "With that longer hair maybe he was a Native American from one of the Oregon tribes."

Scrutinizing the photo, Laila said, "I think he looks more Mediterranean."

"Yeah, maybe Greek." Reen took the picture, turning it to the back. "Abigail Maythorne and unknown gentleman, 1859," she read aloud. "She's the original owner of the house."

"Interesting." Laila traced her finger over the man's arm to where his hand rested on Abigail's shoulder.

"He looks solemn and stern, while Abigail looks exceedingly pleased about something," Reen noted. "I think Miss Abby had herself a boy toy."

Laila took the photo back from Reen. "Imagine what he must have looked like shirtless."

"Or pants-less," Reen offered.

They exchanged a giggle belying their years as Laila stuffed the unframed photograph into her bag of treasures. "I have to have him."

Glancing up again to catch Reen's perceptive smirk, she smiled. "Okay so he's been dead for more than a hundred years. So what? I have an imagination, don't I?"

"And a vibrator too, I presume." Reen nudged Laila in the ribs as they headed for the checkout table.

The Genie's Heartwish: Chapter 3

Sumer—Third Millennium BC

~<>~

IT WAS THE GENTLE hum of a woman's chant that stirred Zakkar Tymon from the oppressive fog of shadowed darkness. Calling upon his warrior's strength, he fought to rouse himself from the dream, the commanding trance that had imprisoned his awareness. His head was thick and heavy as he tried to shift position. The weight of his eyelids hindered him from opening them to scrutinize his surroundings.

How long had it been since he'd been trapped between worlds, drifting amid the living and the shades? The last thing Zakkar remembered was defending the mud-brick walls of the Sumerian cities against the siege of Sargon of Akkad's army. On the bloody banks of the Euphrates he ordered his men into phalanx formation, shouting the battle cry to protect and defend at all costs as he led them forward.

Wielding his great penetrating axe with its narrow blade and strong socket, Zakkar had just pierced the bronze plate armor of yet another Akkadian soldier when...

He struggled to remember what occurred next. There was the ever-present metallic tang of blood is his nostrils. Hacked bodies stacked all around him. The anguished cries and groans of dying men roaring in his ears...and then...

And then there came the pain. The searing sharpness of a sword slashing his back, his ribs, his shoulder.

By gods, he, the great Zakkar Tymon, had been felled!

Agonized by the realization, Zakkar once again found himself focusing on the soothing sounds of the woman's song.

Nay, there were no women on the battlefield to offer the comfort of a sweet melody or the tender warmth of a soft breast. It could only be—Zakkar's body tensed as the unsavory prospect of his own death assailed him. The alluring voice tempting him back from the abode of the dead no doubt belonged to Ereshkigal, goddess of the underworld.

Owing to his rank and reputation as the bravest, noblest and fiercest warrior throughout all of Mesopotamia, the dark queen had come personally to escort him through the seven gates of *Kurnugi*, the land of no return.

"O my mighty, magnificent Zakkar," the woman's voice said, interrupting his introspection. He felt the cool, bracing touch of a damp cloth dabbed against his face. "Under your fearsome radiance, your terrible glare and storm, the Akkadians turned their steps away from you and your men in mute dread."

"Ereshkigal?" he managed to speak, his voice sounding dry and raspy to his ears. "Is it you, come for me?"

"You awaken!" the woman said. "At last."

On her sharp intake of breath Zakkar's eyelids parted. His unsteady gaze was met by a softly lit room and an abundance of voluminous veils hanging around him. It was then that Zakkar understood he was flat on his back on a padded platform, a bed far softer than those to which he was accustomed.

"The gods be praised. Fear not, Zakkar, for it is only I, Sabit the priestess, who calls you back from the brink of the underworld."

He listened to her words, which only brought more questions to mind. Her voice and her countenance were familiar, but he could not remember from where or when. "Do I know you? Why am I here?"

Shushing him and forcing him to remain still as he struggled to sit up, Sabit hummed the same haunting melody Zakkar heard earlier. "You have been in my care for near half a lunar cycle." Her small hands roamed his thighs as she removed the large fur covering him. "We have come to know each other quite well as you lurched back and forth over the threshold of the living and the dead."

With considerable effort, Zakkar pulled himself up far enough to brace himself on his elbows. A glance left, right and ahead brought a series of food, beer and wine-laden altars into focus as well as precious gold, lapis, ornate mosaics, harps, pottery and decorated clay tablets. These sumptuous accouterments were found only in the dwellings of royalty, abodes of the upper class or in *ziggurats*, the towering temples to the gods.

His brow furrowed in confusion. "I am in a ziggurat?"

"The tallest in the city," Sabit answered proudly. "Because of your rank and extraordinary service to Sumer and the gods, Ibi-Utu deemed you should remain here for the duration of your mending." She smoothed her soft, cool hands over his body from the top of his head to his feet.

"Ibi-Utu?"

"He is *patesi* of this temple," Sabit explained, her fingers traversing the path of dark hair from his chest, down his belly to beneath the flax cloth covering his *gis*.

As she spoke, Zakkar remembered Ibi-Utu. Named for the sun god, Utu, he was the powerful and revered high priest.

"Do you remember what happened to you?" Sabit asked.

Zakkar glanced at his body and the new set of jagged marks zigzagging across his flesh, adding to the extensive assortment of previous battle scars. "I was felled from behind," he surmised.

"Yes, you were sorely wounded in battle. Most feared you were doomed to be whisked away to the nether regions in the arms of Ereshkigal but I saved you from that fate, Zakkar, my beloved." She combed her fingers through his hair and kissed his forehead.

She was a pretty young thing, if somewhat plain, boyish and certainly too young for his tastes. She wore the traditional gown baring one shoulder, which appeared bony. His gaze fell upon her breasts. Far less than a handful, they stood firm against the softly draping cloth of her garment. As Zakkar lifted his gaze he noticed her staring at him as if she wanted to devour him lick by lick.

If he wasn't feeling so vague at the moment he would have chuckled. He was used to women seducing him. His reputation as a skilled lover perhaps even exceeded his celebrated standing as a great leader and warrior. His rumored heritage as half god only added to his apparent appeal.

"My thoughts are hazy, Sabit." Zakkar tried to regain his senses. "You call me your beloved, and yet I don't recall the two of us ever..." He arched an eyebrow in question.

"Nay, you have not yet moored in my new moon crescent, Zakkar, but I wish nothing more than for you to take my chaste *sal-munuz* and make it yours forever. I have fallen in love with you."

Zakkar's thoughts reeled. This bold, lovestruck wisp of a woman, this seemingly naïve virgin priestess loved him? Wanted him to bed her? He felt his *gis* stir at the thought. Not because she was particularly alluring, but simply because she was there, available and evidently more than willing.

Moreover, it seemed to Zakkar it had been a near eternity since he'd...how had Sabit phrased it? Ah yes, since he'd *moored himself in a new moon crescent.* He clamped down on his tongue to keep from laughing at the lustful girl and her romantic, poetic terms.

"You said you were a priestess, Sabit?" he asked gently.

"Yes." She breathed a melodious sigh. "I am priestess of Nanna, the Moon God of Ur. He is my betrothed. Symbolically, of course," she added quickly. She locked her gaze on Zakkar's *gis* swelling beneath the cloth covering his groin, a look of anticipatory bliss across her features. "Now that you are awake and well, Zakkar, we can join."

To Zakkar's amazement, the young woman tore the bed covering from his body and straddled him. By gods, she was preparing to mount him!

"Sabit!" He tried holding her in place. It was then that he felt how much of his strength had yet to be restored, for he was near as weak as a lamb. "Sabit," he said more softly this time, "you must know it is against our laws for you to bed a mortal man once you are betrothed to a deity."

"But once I take my sacred oath I shall never have my hungry *sal-munuz* soothed. I must experience a proper bedding at least once in my life. And who better to do it than the brave warrior whose wounds I have tended—the man I have come to love?"

"You could be beheaded if it became known you seduced a man, Sabit." Little by little, memories of her benevolent and loving ministrations flooded his thoughts. She'd chanted to him, spoke incantations, fed him, dressed his wounds with herbs and poultices as he lay immobile, battling his way back from the clutches of eternal darkness.

"You have been good to me, Sabit. Kind, sweet and caring. You are far too lovely to lose your pretty head." Zakkar stroked her arm, patting it with brotherly affection.

"Oh, Zakkar, must I resort to tearful pleading, lamenting and wailing before you will agree to bed me?"

Zakkar groaned as his *gis* strained at her provocative words.

"I long to feel your mighty essence inside me," she continued. "Your powerful arms around me as, enraptured, we take wing to the stars together." Sabit leaned forward, clutching his biceps with one hand while resting a finger on his bottom lip and tugging down with the other. She smoothed the tip of her finger over his teeth, giving him a wistful smile.

"With your legendary strength, a tooth can even crush flint. Crush me, Zakkar. Pierce me. Let me bear your babe."

"My babe?" a startled Zakkar said.

Sabit's eyes grew wide. "How could the gods be angry if a priestess bedded one of their own?" she reasoned. "Are the stories not true that you have a mortal mother and were fathered by Enlil, the great god of air and storms?"

Zakkar closed his eyes for a moment, gathering his thoughts. Women oft sang praises and composed poems about his supposed, yet unconfirmed, half god heritage and striking masculine beauty. They seemed to favor his long locks of dark-as-raven-wing hair, his firm jaw and bark-brown eyes. It was both a blessing and a curse to be so favored.

Sabit's eyes were still wide when he opened his eyes again. Her cheeks pink with expectancy.

"My mother has said it is so," he told her, "but—"

Before Zakkar could stop her, Sabit drew up her skirts and sank fully onto his engorged *gis*, yelling out in pain as the membrane in her virgin channel tore.

The sweet feel of her chaste tightness wholly clasping his *gis* was overshadowed not only by the shock of what Sabit had done but by the sound of rapid footsteps approaching the chamber in answer to her anguished cry. Gathering every measure of his strength, Zakkar switched their positions, fast withdrawing himself from her depths as he now kneeled astride her.

"Zakkar Tymon!" Ibi-Utu's thunderous voice rang out as he raced to the bed, eyeing in horror the lightly bloodied bit of cloth between Sabit's thighs. Soon three other priests had sped into the chamber, all staring with revulsion at the incriminating scene. "Is this how you repay me and my priestess for our healing care? What say you, man?"

"Nay, Ibi-Utu," Sabit cried. "It is not as you suspect. Zakkar is innocent. I am the one who—"

"Silence," Zakkar roared, interrupting the death sentence the foolish, callow girl was about to draw upon her head. He had led a good, mostly honorable life, had led many brave Sumerian men into battle in honor of their king and the mighty gods. While his heart spoke of breathing his last as a white-haired old man, blessed with a good wife and many grandchildren at his knee, as a warrior Zakkar never really expected he'd live that long.

Perhaps he was meant to die in this last, fierce battle against Sargon's army. Sweet, idealistic Sabit had given him life. It was only fair that he reciprocate. Having butchered many a warrior for Sumer, Death was his constant companion. But he couldn't imagine living with the knowledge that this young, naïve girl he'd unintentionally sullied had met a fearsome death simply because she was enamored of him. Nay, Sabit did not deserve to have her life cut short on his account.

"Do not try to protect me, Sabit," Zakkar soothed, gazing down into her terrified eyes. "I alone am responsible, Ibi-Utu. I-I awoke with a start from my long sleep between worlds and, in my clouded mind, somehow mistook the innocent young priestess for one of my consorts."

Ibi-Utu's gaze again fell upon the blood-spotted cloth. "You have ruined Sabit for her betrothed. Nanna, the Moon God of Ur demands his wives be virgins. She is no good to him now, nor to this sacred temple. Both of you must die."

Sabit gasped, a strangled cry escaping her lips as her hands flew to her throat.

"It is not Sabit's blood," Zakkar lied, unobtrusively digging his thumbnail into one of the still fresh scars at his side and slicing along the tender ridge. Once he felt the warm trickle of liquid he continued, "It is mine. You see?"

Rising from the bed and gesturing to his side, he held his bloody fingers out and away from his ribs. "The wound still oozes blood. You arrived just as I was about to thrust into her but her cry of terror brought me to my senses before I could enter her channel. Sabit is still pure."

"Is this true, Sabit?"

The petrified girl looked up at Zakkar, who did his best to give her a reassuring nod and smile. He saw the pain in her eyes, the deep sorrow, the longing, fear and dread. She turned her head to face the priest. "I-yes," she said, collapsing into tears. "Zakkar speaks the truth."

"Make peace with the gods, Zakkar. Your beheading will take place first thing in the morning." Ibi-Utu spun on his heel to leave.

"Patesi, spare his life, please!" Sabit cried out. "You must know it was not Zakkar in his right mind who came upon me in such a crazed manner. He was fevered and under the influence of the potent healing tonics we have forced him to swallow." Rising to her knees, gesturing with one hand outstretched to Zakkar and the other to Ibi-Utu, she pleaded to the high priest, "You know this man. You know his reputation. He has fought and won many wars for our people, our king, the gods, has he not?"

Arms crossed over his chest, Ibi-Utu remained in place, silent while digesting Sabit's beseeching words.

"Stories of queens, maidens and wives falling to Zakkar's feet, offering themselves unto him abound, Ibi-Utu, do they not?"

The priest frowned at Zakkar. "They do. But that does not mean he has the right—"

"It is clear," Sabit forged on, "the mighty warrior Zakkar Tymon can have his pick of the fairest and most succulent women of any land. Look upon me, Ibi-Utu." She swept a hand from her head downward as tears coursed down her face.

"Do you really believe a man of Zakkar's uncompromised beauty would have any reason to glance twice at a plain, unappealing girl like me when the temple and streets abound with dazzling, full-breasted, fair of face women only too willing to bed him at the mere crook of his finger?"

Until that moment, Zakkar had forgotten he still had a heart buried deep within his chest, but he was reminded of the fact now because he felt sure it clenched as he listened to Sabit's harsh depiction of herself.

It seemed as if a small eternity passed as the priest stood silently, gazing from Sabit to Zakkar and back again.

Finally, he spoke. "What you say is true, Sabit. I have followed Zakkar's exploits since he was a boy just entering Sumer's army and never was there a time when I did not believe him to act with honor. His past actions, however, do not excuse his present. The gods are clear on that. Our laws state directly that Zakkar must pay with his head for the intended ruin of a virgin priestess. Unless..."

Ibi-Utu's frown etched deeper still while Zakkar's heart pounded out a hasty beat as he awaited his fate at the hands of the pious high priest.

"Unless?" Sabit asked, a glimmer of hope lighting her eyes.

"Imprisonment," Ibi-Utu finally muttered. "For the rest of his days."

Both Zakkar and Sabit gasped. "By gods, I would rather die," Zakkar spat. Folding his arms over his chest he stood tall, bracing his still-weakened body against a pillar as he elevated his chin in a proud manner. "Just lop off my head and be done with it so I may accompany Ereshkigal to the underworld. I am ready to die."

"Nay, Zakkar, do not speak that way!" Sabit implored. "What about the incantation of service to womankind, patesi?" she suggested. "It is more deserving than death. More humane than watching a valiant warrior rot away in chains."

After an infinite amount of time, Ibi-Utu nodded. "A fair solution. It shall be so." He stepped to one of the altars, selecting a clay tablet inscribed in cuneiform.

"Nay!" Zakkar said, not even understanding what an incantation of service to womankind was. He had learned long ago to be wary of the spells, rituals and incantations of those in devout service to the ferocious and mighty gods.

"Do you have an appropriate vessel, Sabit?" the priest said, ignoring Zakkar's protest.

Sabit scanned the chamber, pointing to a small stone box secured with metal strappings atop one of the altars. "There, patesi. Inside there is a bottle of the finest spun glass brought as an offering by one of the city's wealthiest matrons. It was meant to hold perfumed oil or for use as a tear vase, but is still empty and should be a perfect vessel."

Ibi-Utu gestured to one of the lesser priests who immediately brought the box forward, opening the latch for Ibi-Utu's scrutiny.

"Yes, this will do," he agreed. "It has significant weight, appears strong and sufficiently protected to survive at least one lifetime." He looked at the altars already set with lambs for sacrifice, lard and roast meat, as well as dates, fine meal, dried fruit and a confection of honey and butter. Nodding to Sabit, he stated, "We can proceed. The goddess will be pleased."

Zakkar's mind whirled. How he wished he had both his strength and his full senses to help him comprehend what was happening. Stories from his childhood of men imprisoned in jars and bottles, trapped in the abomination of perpetual servitude, slowly surfaced. Surely this is not what the patesi had in mind?

As the high priest and his subordinates examined the clay tablet bearing the incantation, Sabit rose to stand at Zakkar's side.

"Fear not, brave and honorable one," she whispered. "I shall discern a way to free you from your servitude soon. I shall never forget that I owe you my life as well as my eternal gratitude, dearest Zakkar." With that she crossed the room to join Ibi-Utu, who held his right hand aloft and began to read aloud from the tablet.

"O great Inanna, Queen of Heaven, goddess of love and war, I summon you. I am Ibi-Utu, he who withdraws the first fruits from the temple. He who has received divine powers from the most elevated dais. You are the great lady of the gods. Your terror is fearsome as it weighs on the land. No man anticipates your commands. The heavens fold themselves in your presence like a mourning garment. You are she who hastens like a north wind storm into the midst of the people. You are she who hears prayer and pleading."

He looked to Sabit and nodded. She took the tablet from him and continued.

Zakkar released the pillar when he felt the room shake. He tried to take a step forward but was frozen in place.

Drawing upon his warrior's courage, he steeled himself for whatever may come, for he would not cry out in fear. Never! Zakkar Tymon feared nothing and no one! Even to the gods and demons who toyed with the lives of mortals, he feared not. Given that he no longer had the power of speech, Zakkar repeated those words inside his head, fortifying himself as the incantation continued.

"Great Inanna, I, Sabit, priestess of Nanna, the Moon God of Ur, summon you to intern Zakkar Tanojin Lugalbanda Tymon, mighty warrior who has fought many battles in your name, into this sacred vessel." She motioned to the open box containing the bottle, which Ibi-Utu held aloft, bowing as he did so. "So that Zakkar Tymon may obliterate his transgressions to womankind by serving them for all eternity."

Eternity. The thought of ceaseless captivity rose in Zakkar's throat like the bitter tang of bile. Sabit's words seemed to drone on forever as she delineated Zakkar's verdict of indentured servitude.

"The language of his possessor will Zakkar Tymon speak and understand," Ibi-Utu added, as the lesser priests chanted in the background while lighting fragrant incense.

"The matter of pleasing his female possessors and satisfying their every urge shall be Zakkar's sacred duty," Sabit read.

"Within the period of six lunar cycles," Ibi-Utu, said, "will Zakkar grant his possessor three wishes."

As the priests chanted and Sabit and Ibi-Utu spoke the endless words of the incantation, Zakkar became aware of a pervading heaviness seeping into his being. Servitude to women. By gods, Zakkar, the great and mighty warrior, the sought after lover of queens and women of the greatest beauty and wealth would be reduced to no more than a slave to women's peculiar impulses, which, he knew, could shift with the mere blink of an eye.

Zakkar would have shuddered at the thought had he not still been frozen in place like a great pillar of salt. Truly, it was a foul fate worse than death to which he was being condemned. He only hoped Sabit would be true to her word and quickly discern a method for his liberation.

"O make it be, great and wondrous Inanna! Let it be so!" Ibi-Utu nearly roared as he pulled the stopper from the bottle, elevating the container high above his head.

The ethereal visage of a woman, as beautiful as she was fearsome, suddenly loomed over the proceedings.

The last thing Zakkar remembered seeing before feeling his body curl and contort into naught but a vaporous substance that voyaged through the air of the temple chamber and into the bottle, was the tortured expression of repentance mixed with gratitude on Sabit's tear-stained face.

~<>~

And So, Dear Reader,

You've finished reading The Viking's Heartwish, a Daisy Dexter Dobbs book that (*fingers crossed and hopeful sigh*) you were sorry to see end. Meanwhile I, author DDD, am gleefully clacking away at my keyboard, writing yet another sensational, utterly phenomenal (*please don't burst my bubble*) book. I'd like to conclude our time together with a heartfelt THANK YOU for choosing to read this book, the 1st in my Heartwishes series.

I loved writing Delaney and Varik's love story, with all the mix-ups and misunderstandings. Each scene with Thursday kept me smiling, and giving Roger his comeuppance was pure joy. The original version of this book didn't include heartwish rings or any paranormal elements. Early in my career I'd been cautioned by agents and editors not to include any magical features in my romantic comedies because it wasn't standard and readers wouldn't like it.

Since I've always loved a touch of magic combined with humor, I believed others might feel the same way, so I turned down a publishing contract, deciding instead to become an indie author, then happily added the rings, angels, ghosts, and a Norse god to this first book in the series, as well as the rest of the Heartwishes books (if you're a paranormal fan, books 2 (Genie), 3 (Firefighter), and 5 (Nymph) are especially full of magical elements!). I'm glad I followed my heart, and I hope you are too!

With the Heartwishes series, I've strived to create the sort of caring, and supportive relationships with family and friends I wish I'd had growing up. You'll get to know the whole close-knit, loving Malone clan in the rest of the books. Hopefully you'll fall in love with them just as I did. One of the best perks of being a writer is creating fictional worlds, populating them with a large cast of characters, then living in that world, fraternizing with them all, for hours on end as I tell their stories.

~<>~

If you enjoyed The Viking's Heartwish I'd be delighted if you left a positive review or rating on the site where you purchased it. (Not that I check daily for new reviews. Or ever Google myself. Or do anything else indicating I'm an insecure creative person craving validation. Nope, nothing like that.) Your review can be long, short, or just a star rating. Reviews help other readers find my books, and keep my stories from getting lost in a site's complicated algorithms. Plus, it gives me encouragement to keep on writing!

Speaking of other readers, you can help them find this book by recommending it to your friends, neighbors, relatives, coworkers, your dentist, doctor, mail carrier, all the strangers you meet in the grocery store, at the mall, the neighborhood pub, your favorite coffee shop, and, of course, everyone you know online. (I'm ready with additional suggestions if needed.)

Thanks again! Wishing you love, laughter, romance and happy reading!

—*Daisy Dexter Dobbs*

~<>~

DAISY DEXTER DOBBS BOOK LIST

SERIES
Heartwishes

Small town Contemporary Romance / Romantic Comedy (mild to medium spice level)

Family legend says the magical heartwish ring was given to the matriarch of a Viking king by Odin, the most powerful of Norse gods. It must be held against the heart when making a sincere heartwish and will remain on the finger until it's time to pass it on. Though the mind may be cluttered and uncertain, the heart knows the right wish to make. Always trust your heart.

(Can be read as standalones but better appreciated when read in order so you can get to know all the characters and fall in love with the Malones!)

The Viking's Heartwish (Book 1: Delaney and Varik)
The Genie's Heartwish (Book 2: Laila and Zak)
The Firefighter's Heartwish (Book 3: Gard and Sabrina)
The Knitter's Heartwish (Book 4: Reen and Drake)
The Nymph's Heartwish (Book 5: Nevan and Aladee)
The Psychic's Heartwish (Book 6: Kady and Rylan)
The Daughter's Heartwish (Book 7: Bekka and Jamie – coming soon)
And at least 2 more Heartwishes titles are planned

~<>~

The Drakos Brothers
(releasing summer of 2024)
Small town Contemporary Romance / Romantic Comedy (scorching-hot spice level)

Bold, opinionated Greek men, the Drakos brothers star in this hot, hot, HOT laugh out loud romantic comedy series featuring lots of hunky, delicious Greek men and the women who capture their alpha male hearts. (Can be read as standalones but better appreciated when read in order so you can get to know all the characters.)

Trained by the Greek (Book 1: Jordan and Riley)
Vexed by the Greek (Book 2: Dino and Sophie)
Bossed by the Greek (Book 3: Sebastian and Ardine)
Conned by the Greek (Book 4: Benedict and Angel)
(additional stories for more brothers coming)

~<>~

STANDALONES
Don't Even Think About It (Mindy and Archer)
Laugh-out-loud Romantic Comedy (scorching-hot spice level)
Avowed chocoholic Mindy handles her upside-down life with as much grace and aplomb as possible—by attempting chocolatcide. This steamy, spicy, laugh-out-loud, award-winning romantic comedy novel is brimming with love, snappy banter, sexy inventive scenes that sizzle, and numerous naughty words.

~<>~

MORE SERIES AND STANDALONES
COMING SOON FROM DAISY
Daisy has written close to 100 novels and numerous novellas and short stories over the last few decades. She certainly can't have novels full of pay phones, answering machines, landlines, no email, or the internet, or social media now, can she? Nope, nope, nope. Of course not. So now that she has the rights back to all of her books and stories from her previous publishers, she's been hard at work rewriting and updating her books for release as an indie author.

Revisiting umpteen stories featuring gorgeous, handsome, oh-so-sexy hunks is a tough job, but somebody's gotta do it. So here's a sneak peek at just some of the dozens of titles Daisy's been maniacally, um, I mean, *diligently*, working on (check her website and newsletter for updates!).

(NOTE: many of these are working titles and may change upon publication.)

~<>~

Visit DaisyDexterDobbs.com for a full, up-to-date listing of Daisy's books. Sign up for Daisy's newsletter and mailing list to get notifications for new book releases, contests, and more.

~<>~

---

1. https://www.daisydexterdobbs.com

About the Author

A born storyteller, Daisy Dexter Dobbs started writing stories at five, satisfying her inner ham by reading them aloud, using a toilet plunger as a microphone. Today, Daisy creates written voyages of the imagination, infused with love, laugh-out-loud comedy, friendships, family and guaranteed happy endings. Some of her books include paranormal and fantasy elements. And some books are scorching HOT on the spice scale.

Having worked at more than 40 different jobs provides Daisy with a ridiculous amount of questionable experience to draw on for her characters. She's been: a ghostwriter for politicians; a library art director; a weight loss counselor; mayor's executive secretary; a Realtor; travel agent; editor; and a butcher's meat wrapper, quitting after she spotted a big eyeball coming toward her on the conveyor.

A Chicago native, Daisy and her husband, now live in the Pacific Northwest. Happily, Daisy no longer feels the need to use a bathroom plunger as a microphone when entertaining.

You can find Daisy here:
Facebook: DaisyDexterDobbs
Instagram: DaisyDexterDobbs
TikTok: @daisydexterdobbs
Amazon: Daisy Dexter Dobbs
Goodreads: daisydexterdobbs
BookBub: Daisy-Dexter-Dobbs
Twitter/X: DaisyDDobbs
Threads: @DaisyDexterDobbs
Pinterest: DaisyDDobbs
Email: DaisyDexterDobbs@gmail.com
Read more at www.DaisyDexterDobbs.com.